Karen
THE RESURRECTION MYSTERY
The Detective Lavender Mysteries

THE RESURRECTION MYSTERY
© Karen Charlton 2024

www.karencharlton.com

Visit Karen Charlton's website to learn more about her historical novels and sign up for her occasional newsletter for the latest news about her writing, competitions and events.

www.karencharlton.com

Published by Famelton Publishing
Cover design and illustration by Lisa Horton

Chapter One

The wealthy and esteemed surgeon Sir Richard Allison considered himself a smart man of fashion. If you'd dared to ask him – and few dared – whether he was more famous for the skill with which he wielded his lancet on his rich and titled patients or for the exquisite cut and tailoring of his Savile Row coats, his sharp eyes would have narrowed. He'd lower his chin to give you a better view of his thick mop of greying curls, styled in the 'Brutus' fashion favoured by Beau Brummel, then snap: 'I'm famous for *both.*'

But innocent curiosity like this came at a price. Sir Richard would then declare you a saphead who asked stupid questions. As every one of his nervous medical students knew, Sir Richard Allison didn't suffer fools gladly.

However, despite his vanity, even Sir Richard wasn't foolish enough to wear his best burgundy coat, his silver damask waistcoat or a pristine white silk cravat while undertaking a full day of human dissection on rotting cadavers at his place of work, Guy's Hospital for the Incurables. Those clothes were hung, along with a sweet-smelling nosegay of dried flowers, in the cupboard squashed into the corner of his cluttered office.

And his clothes needed this care.

Despite the open window, an unpleasant stench pervaded his office. It emanated from a sickening row of human organs, harvested for further investigation during that morning's dissections and now sitting in trays of blood on a side table.

Undeterred by the malodorous atmosphere, Sir Richard took off his soiled gloves and apron and the paper cuffs that protected his sleeves, and enjoyed a plate of lamb chops at his desk.

He had another half an hour before this afternoon's demonstration. Picking up the latest edition of *The Times*, he skimmed through the pages.

Across the office, his emaciated junior doctor, Kingsley, who was swamped in his cheap second-hand coat, was less immune to the smell of rotting organs. He lit his clay pipe and inhaled the nutty aroma of the billowing tobacco smoke.

Sir Richard frowned. 'You know I don't like tobacco smoke, Kingsley. It's a weak doctor who needs to mask the stench of human decay. Put it out.'

'Sorry, sir. Sorry.' The younger man grabbed a pestle from one of the shelves on the bookcases lining the room, tipped the contents of his pipe into a mortar, and extinguished the burning tobacco.

'Ridiculous,' Sir Richard said.

Kingsley blinked his tired eyes. 'I'm sorry, sir? What's ridiculous?'

'They've printed another story about Lavender! Good grief! This newspaper is in love with the damned man!'

Kingsley chose his next words carefully. Despite Sir Richard's irritation, Kingsley knew his superior and the famous officer from Bow Street often worked together on murder cases. Their relationship was frequently strained, but Kingsley had seen enough of them together to know it was underlain with respect. 'What's the detective done now, sir?'

'Only dashed like a fiend down the Thames in a boat in hot pursuit of a cut-throat called Hodge. Apparently, he leapt from his own vessel on to the other boat and launched himself into a dramatic struggle with the villain on the heaving deck, which nearly tossed both men into the river.'

Kingsley hid his smile. 'You can never trust what you read in the newspapers, sir.'

Sir Richard threw down the paper in disgust. 'That's the second time this week *The Times* has seen fit to give us a fawning account of Lavender's heroics. I'm beginning to wonder why I pay for this drivel. I might as well read one of my wife's Gothic horror novellas.' He turned sharply towards his assistant. 'So, what do you have lined up for me this afternoon? Not more women who died in childbirth, I hope?'

Kingsley puffed out his chest with pride. 'I think you'll enjoy this afternoon's session, sir. I have something special for you.'

The surgeon eyed him with suspicion; he rarely welcomed acts of initiative from his subordinates.

'I've acquired two male cadavers. One died in his sixties, probably from malnutrition or consumption...'

Sir Richard groaned. 'Not again.'

'...and the second is a strong and healthy young man in his twenties, with no obvious cause of death or sign of disease.'

'He's dead, Kingsley. That hardly makes him strong and healthy. Where did you get this fine specimen from?'

'The usual place,' Kingsley said vaguely. 'I thought these corpses would make an excellent contrast – and the mystery of the young man's death will give you ample opportunity to demonstrate the correct procedure for an *autopsia cadaverum*.'

He was about to add '...and show the other students how you assist Detective Lavender in his murder inquiries...' but he thought better of it at the last minute.

Sir Richard rose to his feet. 'Very well. Let's get it over and done with. Lady Allison and I are dining with Lord Trevelyan tonight, so this young specimen of yours had better give up his secrets quickly.'

Situated next to the hospital morgue, the blood-splattered dissecting rooms were cold, tiled and poorly lit by two grimy windows placed high in the walls. The remote location of these rooms and their high windows ensured privacy for the surgeons, away from the prying eyes of the public, who, despite their love of public hangings, often recoiled at the thought of surgeons butchering the dead criminals afterwards.

Half a dozen excited medical students clutching textbooks of anatomy were already awaiting Sir Richard's arrival. A porter leaned idly against the wall with his mop and bucket, prepared for the next flood of body fluids to wash across the floor. He hadn't bothered to fetch clean water since the morning's session, Sir Richard noted. His bucket was still half full of bloodied water.

Sir Richard beckoned to one of the students to push over his trolley of tools, and sorted through them. He pulled out a large selection of vicious-looking knives, saws, drills and hooks.

A buzz of anticipation went around the room when Kingsley wheeled in the dead young man on a trolley.

Sir Richard glanced up, and his eyes glittered at the sight of the well-toned, muscular body of the youth. The same age as most of the medical students, the corpse had a thick head of wavy blond hair, a clear complexion unmarked by disease, and looked like he'd never missed a meal in his life.

The flesh on the man's fingers and palms was smooth and uncalloused. Sir Richard paused with a slight twinge of unease. This was no working man with a manual trade. Legally, the only cadavers they were permitted to work with were the bodies of hanged criminals, who normally came from the lower orders. And this corpse bore none of the marks of strangulation from the hangman's noose.

But Sir Richard wasn't a man to look a gift horse in the mouth and indecisiveness wasn't a trait he tolerated in anyone, especially himself.

'Fetch two more lamps,' he said. 'This fine specimen deserves the closest scrutiny.'

Kingsley bristled with pride. Two students hurried to fetch and light the oil lamps.

Sir Richard chose his lancet and, like a sculptor in his studio, he raised his arm with the tool of his trade poised over his next work of art. His acolytes gathered around, and the porter readied himself with his mop.

But the pose was part of the theatricality of his teaching. He lowered his arm and stepped back. 'Before I begin the *autopsia cadaverum*, give me your theories about the cause of death. I need to hear a hypothesis, gentlemen.'

The students fell silent, then moved forward to prod, poke and turn over the cadaver. Every inch of skin and orifice was carefully examined with magnifying glasses. One student forced open the mouth to check the airways were clear and there was no sign of blisters caused by poison. Another picked up the hands to check there were no defensive wounds or anything suspicious caught behind the neatly clipped nails.

'There's no sign of an accident or violence being visited upon the corpse,' concluded one student.

'Nor any sign of livor mortis,' another added.

This observation sent another flicker of unease through the surgeon. 'How long has he been dead, Kingsley?'

'At least two days, sir. He's lain in our morgue for one of them.'

The students eventually settled on heart failure or apoplexy as the cause of death, although most agreed he was very young for either of those.

Sir Richard nodded. 'But it happens. A thorough examination of the internal organs will prove decisive in the case of heart failure or apoplexy. And as we know, heart failure can be congenital.'

'What about opium poisoning?' one suggested. 'Perhaps an overdose?'

The others frowned. Poisoning – even an overdose of opium – was notoriously difficult to prove.

'That's enough discussion,' Sir Richard said. He raised his lancet above the corpse and prepared to make the first incision.

At the end of the slab, one of the doctors suddenly squeaked loudly. It put Sir Richard off his stroke. He lowered his blade and glared at the offender.

The young man's eyes were round with horror, his face drained of blood. 'I saw his eyelid twitch.'

'What?'

Everyone turned to examine the face of the man on the slab. Nothing moved. The corpse remained still and lifeless, as if in a deep sleep.

'Are you absolutely certain he's dead, Kingsley?' one of the young doctors quipped. 'You did check for a pulse, didn't you?'

The others burst out laughing.

'Of course I did!'

'Did you listen for a heartbeat with your stethoscope?' someone else asked. His tone was mocking. Everyone knew Kingsley was too poor to afford one of these new-fangled pieces of equipment. There was more laughter.

Blushing with embarrassment, Kingsley ignored the question. 'This is nonsense,' Kingsley snapped. 'You're seeing things in the poor light.'

Inclined to agree with him, Sir Richard raised his lancet once more.

'It might be escaping gas,' another student volunteered. 'That causes twitching.'

'Not at this stage of decomposition,' Kingsley insisted.

Distracted by the discussion, Sir Richard paused, frowning.

'I hope it's gas,' stammered another student, 'because he's just clenched his fist.' His eyes were fixed in horror on the man's hand, which dangled the other side of the table.

'Oh, for God's sake,' barked the surgeon. 'Somebody pass me a stethoscope.'

But it was too late.

The cadaver's vivid blue eyes flew open and fixed on the blade hovering over his naked chest. He let out a hideous scream and threw himself off the slab, knocking down two doctors and the trolley of equipment in the process. The lethal knives, saws and hooks clattered to the flagstone floor and the startled porter dropped his mop and knocked over his bucket.

Sir Richard hastily stepped out of the way of the swirling wave of bloodied water.

'Murderers!' screamed the terrified corpse.

The students already on the floor attempted to restrain him. The others rushed to their assistance.

The resurrected cadaver fought them off valiantly with several deft blows to their noses and chins. 'You murdering bastards! I'll have you thrashed for this!'

Sir Richard's heart sank. That was a cultured, accent-less voice with the clear, clipped vowels of the upper class.

He turned to one of his horrified students. still hovering at the end of the slab.

'Send for Detective Lavender – now!'

Chapter Two

Clutching a copy of *The Times* and accompanied by his loyal constable, Ned Woods, Stephen Lavender strode up the wooden staircase of Bow Street to Magistrate Read's office. Except – as he remembered with a twinge of fury and frustration – it wasn't James Read's office anymore. Lavender's handsome, fine-boned face was dark with anger.

His irascible – but much trusted – friend and employer had recently retired from civic duty and been replaced by the elderly, but demanding, Sir Nathaniel Conant from Marlborough Street Magistrates' Court. A change that the principal officers, clerks and horse patrol men at Bow Street still struggled to accept.

Lavender didn't knock, or wait to gain permission to enter, when he reached the door. He threw it open and stormed across the creaking oak floorboards towards the magistrate's desk.

Sir Nathaniel was a tiny man of sixty-nine with pure white hair that contrasted dramatically with his thick black eyebrows. He glanced up with irritation. 'Lavender! And Constable Woods!' he said mildly. 'This is a pleasant surprise – I was just about to send for you both!'

Lavender frowned. He still didn't know how to gauge this man. He sensed sarcasm, but wasn't sure. Conant spoke quietly, had an annoying habit of ending many sentences with 'et cetera, et cetera' and looked like an innocent lamb with those white curls. But he had a reputation for ruthlessness in court and had been nicknamed 'the whispering assassin' by several defendants.

Two clerks, sitting behind huge piles of documents at desks on the far side of the room, cast curious glances at the officers.

Another change, Lavender thought sadly.

Magistrate Read never allowed clerks to work in his office, which gave him privacy with his officers: something Lavender appreciated. Read always had the time to listen while Lavender explained the intricacies of his latest case.

But the chairs where he'd sat talking to Read had also vanished; everyone now had to stand before the magistrate's desk. Conant didn't welcome discussion and debate. You entered his office to receive your orders and left quickly. Judging by the vast expanse of scratched mahogany visible on Conant's desk, the man delegated everything that came his way to his overworked clerks.

Lavender and Conant hadn't got off to a good start, and had been circling around each other warily for the last three weeks. During their initial meeting, Conant had questioned Ned's role by Lavender's side and suggested he should return to the horse patrol immediately. 'You have an excellent record, Lavender. You don't need an assistant.'

'My record would be far poorer without Woods' help,' Lavender retorted. 'He's played a huge part in every case I've solved.'

'I want him to return to the horse patrol.'

'He can't. Constable Woods received a serious injury to his shoulder some years ago and is unable to spend a full day in the saddle without considerable discomfort.'

'If he's unable to do the job he's paid for, then perhaps he needs to retire from service?'

Lavender didn't like the avaricious gleam that had leapt into Conant's eyes behind his spectacles. 'Constable Woods was injured in the line of duty, while trying to apprehend the man behind the murder of Prime Minister Spencer Perceval. Bow Street doesn't discard its valiant officers after such acts of bravery. We look after our own.'

Conant tutted and shook his fluffy head. 'But this is a most irregular arrangement! Magistrate Read appears to have had a rather lax approach to our remit from the Home Department. The principal officers are expected to work alone et cetera et cetera.'

'Magistrate Read recognised that Woods and I are a good team. Our results show it.'

'No one disputes your results, Lavender. But Magistrate Read is no longer in charge.'

'The reputation of Bow Street has always benefited from this arrangement,' Lavender persisted. 'Woods is a great detective. He's as thorough and conscientious as any of your other principal officers.'

'Why didn't Magistrate Read promote him?'

'Because Ned didn't ask.'

'Does he lack ambition?'

Lavender's eyes narrowed. He didn't take kindly to criticism – implied or otherwise – of the man he regarded as his closest friend. He tried to stay calm. Money, and balancing Bow Street's financial accounts, appeared to be Conant's priority – and this was probably his weakness, too. 'Quite frankly, I think Magistrate Read made a point of avoiding the conversation. In the interests of economy, he preferred to keep Ned on the lower patrol man's salary.'

Sir Nathaniel tutted. 'Most irregular.' He dismissed Lavender with a vague promise to think more about this situation later.

But the interview had unnerved Lavender. He was worried about Ned's position.

This wasn't, however, going to stop him complaining today.

He slapped his copy of *The Times* down on Conant's desk. 'Have you read this drivel, sir?' he asked.

Unfazed by Lavender's anger, the corners of Conant's soft mouth twitched. 'Ah. You're referring to the article about yourself, I assume? Yes, it's excellent publicity for our office.'

'But it's utter rubbish, sir! I was never on a boat on the Thames – and neither was that cove Hodge. We waited for him in an alley beside the Black Bull tavern at Smithfield Market. I aimed my pistol at his heart the moment he emerged from the tavern and Woods clapped him in irons. It was over in seconds.'

'It were, sir,' Ned confirmed. 'That cut-throat barely had chance to draw his blade.'

'This arrest was made after weeks of painstaking questioning of Hodge's known contacts and long dreary hours of surveillance,' Lavender continued. 'It was proper police work – meticulous but boring. There was no dramatic chase down the river!'

15

Lavender stabbed the offending newspaper with an angry finger. 'And it's the second time this week *The Times* has published a load of tripe about me.'

Beneath his black court gown, Conant's thin shoulders shrugged. 'Yes, reporters often have a vivid imagination and a tendency to exaggerate et cetera et cetera.'

'Well, I want to know *how* this keeps happening. How the devil do they know so much about my work here? Who's reporting to the reporters?'

The magistrate's black eyebrows rose in mild surprise. 'You *want*...?'

'Yes, I do *want*. And I also *want The Times* to print a retraction. I'm a detective, for heaven's sake. My role is to uncover the truth. The last thing I need is for my work to be turned into fiction by a newspaper reporter!'

Conant smiled, and reached into a drawer in his desk for a buff-coloured cardboard file. From it he drew out a single sheet of paper, headed with the words *Stephen Lavender*. Lavender was good at reading upside down. It was a list of his most recent cases with their outcomes.

'I can see how irksome this must be for you,' Conant soothed. 'However, it does have benefits for Bow Street overall.'

'Benefits?'

'Wealthy clients, Lavender. *The Times* is read by nearly every educated and wealthy man in the country – and this is the clientele we need to cultivate for our enhancement. The stipend given to us by the government barely covers the cost of the horse patrol.'

Conant ran his finger down the list on the paper. 'You already have an excellent reputation with the nobility. They're comfortable with your presence in their homes, let you question their servants et cetera et cetera.'

'Woods is better than I at questioning the servants.'

Conant ignored him. 'Among other cases, you solved the mystery of a burglary for Sir Nathaniel Ogle; retrieved the Countess of Skelton's stolen diamond necklace and caught a pickpocket who'd robbed the Duke of Clarence's mistress, the actress Dorothy Jordan, et cetera et cetera. I rest my case.'

Lavender frowned. 'I don't pander towards the ton. I'm interested in justice for all, and I have my integrity. I treat every case the same, whether it's a Long Acre shopkeeper who's been robbed – or a countess. In fact, it's not so long ago I arrested Lady Tyndall for the murder of her lover.'

Conant hastily shut the folder. 'Yes, yes. That was an unfortunate aberration. I'd prefer it if you don't mention this case in public in case you deter any aristocratic clients.'

'John Townsend is already the favourite of the Prince Regent,' Woods suggested.

Conant waved a dismissive hand at this mention of Bow Street's oldest and most eccentric officer, who had a strange taste in hats. 'It amuses Prinny to keep Townsend trotting after him like a pet dog – and the rest of the nobility know it.'

Well, he's right about that, Lavender thought.

'But it's you they turn to when things go wrong,' Conant continued. '*The Times* already calls you the 'chief of constables', and although you don't appreciate their reports about you, the ton are fascinated by your exploits, Lavender. They trust you.

'In fact,' he continued, 'I've just received a request for help from the Earl of Beverley. He's returned to town after a stay on his country estates to find his house on Russell Square has been robbed.'

He picked up a sheet of expensive cream paper with a gilt crest and handed it across to Lavender. 'The details are in there. Normally such an esteemed gentleman would set up his own inquiries, but he asked for you by name, which leads me to suspect he's read about you in *The Times* this week. He asks you to call on him immediately.'

Lavender took the paper but barely glanced at it. 'Am I to understand you don't intend to ask *The Times* for a retraction, or plan to investigate how they seem to know so much about my cases?'

'Of course I'll deal with it. The editor of *The Times* is a member of my club. The next time I see him, I'll have a word with him about your concerns et cetera et cetera.'

'And that's all?'

Conant's voice dropped to a whisper. A steely whisper. 'That should be sufficient, Lavender. Now I'll bid you goodbye – the Earl of Beverley awaits your presence.'

Frustrated by this summary dismissal, Lavender turned and moved towards the door. Instinctively, Woods followed him.

'One moment, Constable Woods – I've another job for you.'

Lavender and Woods stopped in shock.

Conant held out a creased and dog-eared sheaf of papers. 'There's been a rash of defamatory posters appearing all over London. This is a nasty and libellous habit; respectable traders and bankers have been targeted. I want it stopped. People with grievances need reminding of the law.'

'Woods works with me,' Lavender snapped.

'Not on this occasion.'

The temperature in the room plummeted as the two men glowered at each other. The jaw of one of the clerks dropped open.

Woods glanced between Lavender and Conant, then laughed.

He stepped forward and took the scruffy sheaf of papers from the magistrate. 'I'll set to it straight away, sir, and have these scurrilous coves clapped in irons and under the boards in Newgate before nightfall. Or at least, before they can stir their glue pots and slap up another piece of poison.'

'There's two posters in that bundle,' Conant said. 'One attacks a local landowner for cutting short his tenants' leases; the other poster is an attack on a banker called Alfred Gotobed for usurious rates of interest. I know Gotobed. He's a decent man and also a member of my club. The final sheet is an advertisement from *The Times* that insults a printer for overcharging him. All these complaints are anonymous.'

'Well, *The Times* will tell us who placed the advertisement.'

'Not necessarily,' Conant warned. 'They're stubborn about protecting their sources. Their founder even went to prison rather than divulge a name.'

Woods tapped the side of his broad nose and winked. 'There's ways and means, sir.'

'Yes, you'll need cunning and guile to track down those responsible for this vile calumny. I need you to visit those who have been vilified and offer Bow Street's help. Once they've agreed to pay us, find out who their enemies are – or if they've received any threats et cetera et cetera. There's been a proliferation of this behaviour of late, and the only way to stop it is to make an example of someone in the courts.'

'Have I been advanced to principal officer now, sir?' Woods asked. 'Only as I sees it, these folks might not take this investigation seriously if it's a member of the horse patrol who turns up to do the detectin'.'

Conant frowned. 'No, this is not a promotion, Woods. But go home and change out of your patrol uniform. Once you're dressed like Lavender, there's no reason why anyone shouldn't take you seriously if you tell them you work for Bow Street Magistrates' Court.'

'Yes, sir.' Woods' smirk broadened. He was still grinning when he and Lavender left the building and strode across the cobbled yard towards the stables. Beside him, Lavender was silent and seething.

'That chitty-faced magistrate is testin' me, ain't he?'

'Yes. I'm sorry, Ned. You've nothing to prove to anyone.'

19

'You ain't got nothin' to be sorry about, sir – or to worry about. Unless you think I'm not good enough for this job?'

'Of course you're good enough! I just don't want it to be this way. Things were simpler – more comfortable – when James Read was in office and we worked together.'

Woods' grin widened. 'Are yer worried *you* won't be able to cope on yer own?'

The corners of Lavender's mouth twitched. 'Naturally. I shall be a helpless, gibbering wreck without you by my side during this investigation, Constable.'

Woods reached out and gave him a patronising pat. 'You'll be all right, lad. I've taught you well.'

Lavender relaxed. Ned never failed to lift his spirits.

A groom waited with their saddled horses. 'There's been a message for you, Detective. It's from Sir Richard Allison. He says for you to call on him sharpish. There's been a problem at Guy's Hospital.'

'Gawd's teeth!' Woods exclaimed as he swung himself up into the saddle with the agility of a man half his age. 'What's that wheedling old sawbones done now? Cut the wrong leg off one of his patients?'

Lavender managed another wry grin. The antipathy between Woods and Sir Richard was legendary; the two men could barely stand in the same room in silence without clashing.

The groom added hastily, 'Sir Richard's note said you're to go alone, Detective – without Constable Woods. It's a private matter.'

Woods burst out laughing. 'Heaven and hell! It *must* be bad if I ain't wanted.'

Lavender mounted his horse and gathered up the reins in his gloved hands.

'Don't forget it's our Rachel's birthday today. Betsy's made a cake and invited you and Doña Magdalena to come for a slice and a cup of tea,' Woods said as they rode across the cobbled yard.

'Don't worry, I'll see you tonight.' *Is this how it will be from now on?* Lavender wondered sadly. *Just a few snatched hours together with Woods every week?*

Woods distracted him from his misery. 'Who will you see first: the Earl or the Sawbones?'

'Sir Richard. I know you dislike him, Ned. But he's been a huge help to both of us over the years. Thanks to his skill, you still have your arm. Loyalty matters.'

Woods' brown eyes twinkled. 'If you say so, sir, although I think the magistrate expects you to hot-foot it round to Beverley House.'

'Conant can be damned.'

'And what'll you do about that ruddy newspaper?'

'I'll attend to it. I'll track down the informer and deal with the editor myself. He's in for a shock – not a cosy chat in a gentlemen's club. In fact, hand over that scurrilous advertisement, Ned. I'll enquire about that at the same time I visit the editor. You get yourself off home early and enjoy your daughter's birthday.'

Woods' eyes twinkled as he passed across the newspaper clipping. 'If you're still after the name of the informer, that's three mysteries you've got to solve on yer own.' He lowered his voice and added in a whisper, 'You'd better holler for help if you need it, sir.'

'Thank you, Constable.' Lavender smiled, and urged his horse forward. Once they were through the arched entrance of the stable yard and out of earshot of the grooms, Woods reined in and jerked his thumb over his shoulder in the direction of the magistrate's office. 'Have you thought it might be him who's tittle-tattlin' to his chum at *The Times*?'

The hairs on the back of Lavender's neck bristled. He hadn't suspected Conant. But now Ned mentioned it…

'He seems to like it when they write about you,' Ned added.

Lavender nodded, frowning. 'Thanks, Ned. I'll think about that.'

They turned and rode off in opposite directions – and Lavender's guts churned with misery when Ned disappeared from sight.

Chapter Three

Guy's Hospital for the Incurables was an impressive, classically styled structure consisting of three imposing wings built around a cobbled courtyard. Elaborately carved ionic pillars supported the huge triangular stonework frieze above the entrance. The weak April sunlight glinted off the great arched windows of the ground floor, giving it a cheerful demeanour.

Inside, however, the hospital was grim. As the place of last resort for the desperately ill and the dying of London, the hallway was crammed full of injured and sick men, women and children waiting to see one of the doctors who gave their services for free. Some patients were bent double with pain; many wailed, groaned and cried out.

Lavender braced himself as the sickly, sweaty miasma of disease and camphor assaulted his nostrils. Blocking out the terrified screams of a woman in the final stages of a tortured labour, he side-stepped a pool of vomit on the tiled floor and hurried to Sir Richard's office. Here, to his surprise, Lavender was admitted immediately.

The office smelled just as bad as the rest of the hospital, thanks to the trays of bloody organs on a shelf, but at least once the door closed they were able to shut out the screaming.

One of the surgeon's students, Kingsley, was slumped in a chair at the back of the room. A few years ago, Kingsley had assisted Sir Richard with an autopsy on a long-dead corpse Lavender had exhumed from a graveyard in Chelmsford. Lavender nodded in polite recognition, but the young man didn't acknowledge or return the gesture; he looked wretched.

Sir Richard, who was a short man with a loud voice, rose to his feet and leaned across his desk to shake Lavender's hand. 'Lavender! Good to see you! Thank you for coming so quickly.'

The surgeon's colour was heightened, Lavender noted, and there was a nervous flicker in his pale-grey eyes.

Intrigued by this unusual and ebullient welcome, Lavender sat down in the chair opposite the desk and pulled out his notebook. 'What's the matter, Sir Richard?'

'Well, I won't prevaricate,' Sir Richard said as he sat down. 'I – we – Kingsley and I – have an unusual problem. It requires a discreet and sensitive investigation. I know you're the man for the job.' He jabbed an irritable finger in Kingsley's direction. 'That nick-ninny brought me a live man to dissect. I nearly killed him.'

Lavender blinked and fought down the explosive laugh gurgling in his throat.

'Obviously, I'm blameless in this situation,' Sir Richard continued. 'I rely on my subordinates to bring me corpses. I don't ask how they've acquired them – or who they are. And I expect them to be dead.'

'There was no pulse!' Kingsley wailed. 'I checked – *twice.*'

Sir Richard ignored him. 'It is my job to demonstrate the correct procedure for an *autopsia cadaverum.* That's what the hospital trustees expect of me. Nothing more, nothing less.'

'There was no pulse!' Kingsley moaned again. 'He'd lain for days in our morgue.'

'Of course there was a damned pulse, man! How else did he recover and leap off the slab? Do you think this is a resurrection? God's work? An act of divine intervention?'

Lavender swallowed hard to strangle the laugh and held up his hand to silence the doctors. He couldn't wait to tell Woods about this. Ned had missed a treat. 'Sir Richard – did you insert your knife...?'

'No, I didn't. And it's a lancet, Lavender – not a bloody butcher's knife. Fortunately, I didn't touch him! In fact, I had my doubts and I'd just asked for a stethoscope to check for a heartbeat.'

'Then there's no harm done? You've given the man a nasty scare but he's unharmed?'

'Well, he was dehydrated and weak from lack of nourishment when we put him in a hackney carriage and sent him home—'

'And hysterical,' Kingsley interrupted. 'With a touch of hypothermia, perhaps? He'd lain naked in the morgue for nearly two days.'

'But apart from that, he's in no worse state than when he first arrived at Guy's Hospital,' Sir Richard said cheerfully.

Both the doctors fell silent and stared at Lavender expectantly.

'But?' he prompted. 'What is the problem? What's the *but*?'

Sir Richard's next words came out in a rush. 'His name is Baron Poppleton. He lives on Bedford Street in Bloomsbury. He's threatened to expose me as an incompetent, charge Kingsley with kidnap, and sue us both for grievous distress. Word of this debacle has already reached the ears of the hospital's trustees.'

'There's calls for an inquiry,' Kingsley added.

Lavender's eyes widened and the corners of his mouth twitched again. 'Ah, I see your problem.' He wasn't sure that causing grievous distress was a crime under British law, but kidnapping certainly was. He turned to Kingsley. 'How on earth did Baron Poppleton end up in your morgue? I thought you were only allowed to work on the bodies of hanged criminals.'

Kingsley's distress swamped his features once more. He broke eye contact with Lavender and worked his mouth soundlessly. Another strained silence filled the room.

'This cork-brain found one of the Cross Bones body snatchers on the back doorstep of the morgue,' Sir Richard said. 'He had the baron's body with him. In an act of unprecedented stupidity, which he thought was initiative, Kingsley decided it looked a promising specimen and paid him five shillings for the corpse.'

'A body snatcher?' Lavender's mirth subsided. Sir Richard may be dismissive about the situation, but this farce had just taken an unpleasant twist.

Cross Bones cemetery – also known as the paupers' graveyard – was a medieval burial ground situated in one of the most impoverished and lawless parts of London. The cemetery held the remains of tens of thousands of people. The poor who lived south of the river still used it for burials, and at night it was haunted by body snatchers. The fiends were also known as *resurrection men*.

'Who was this body snatcher? Have you worked with him before?'

'Of course he hasn't,' Sir Richard said quickly. *Too quickly.* 'Our corpses always come from legitimate sources.'

'I didn't ask his name,' Kingsley murmured. 'But he'd brought a young boy with him to help carry the body. A lad of about seven or eight – I got the impression it was his son.'

Lavender grimaced. The thought of a child involved in this ghoulish work was even more disturbing.

'He wore an expensive – and clean – pair of tight-fitting pantaloons. Light coloured.'

'Nankeen?'

'Probably. I suspect he'd just stripped them off the baron. The "corpse" was delivered in his undergarments, which I noted later were of good quality. There was no sign of a shirt, waistcoat or coat.'

Lavender nodded and made a note. Body snatchers often stole the clothing of the corpses they unearthed to sell or use themselves.

'So how did you know he'd dug up the corpse from Cross Bones cemetery?'

Kingsley squirmed. 'I didn't know for sure. I just assumed it.'

'Stop lying, Kingsley,' Lavender snapped. 'You've done business with him before, haven't you?'

Kingsley bowed his head of shaggy greasy hair and looked at the floorboards.

Lavender sighed. 'And when he brought you this fine specimen, did you question him further? Did you ask where he'd found the baron?'

Neither of the surgeons replied.

Lavender fought back his disgust and wondered how these intelligent and educated men, whose mission in life was to help people, could justify the part they played in one of the vilest and most distressing crimes known to mankind.

Sometimes the grieving relatives of the dead buried at Cross Bones felt compelled to sleep beside the graves of their loved ones to try to deter the body snatchers. If men like Kingsley and Sir Richard didn't fuel the demand for body parts for their anatomy classes, those poor folks might sleep easier in their beds.

'Can you describe him?'

Kingsley nodded. 'He was in his late forties. Ugly-looking chap with curly grey hair. Shabbily dressed, of course – apart from the trousers – and filthy.'

Like half the male population of Southwark. 'Did he have any distinguishing marks?'

Kingsley's eyes brightened. 'Yes, he suffered from acute dermatitis. I noticed bullous, and pustular eruptions on his forehead and neck and the palms of his hands.'

'Bullous, you say?' Sir Richard leaned forward. 'Were the blisters weeping?'

'Yes, I noticed fissuring on his fingertips.'

'Did his son have the same condition?'

'Is this significant?' Lavender interrupted sharply. 'Will diagnosing the man's skin condition help us find him?'

The two doctors sat back in their chairs, subdued.

'I assume you *do* want me to find him. That's why you've called me here, isn't it?'

Sir Richard picked up a quill from his desk and twirled it. 'Actually, Lavender, we want more from you than that. We need you to find evidence to redeem us.'

Lavender laughed. 'Redeem you? Kingsley's been consorting with body snatchers, and you nearly carved up a healthy man. If there's anything left of the pair of you by the time Baron Poppleton has dragged you both through the law courts, the hospital trustees will trample on the rest.'

27

'Thank you for reminding us of our unfortunate position, Detective.' The surgeon's voice was icy.

Lavender checked himself. 'Look, I'm not a miracle worker, Sir Richard, and I'm not sure what you mean by redemption. Normally those things are only provided by the Almighty.'

Sir Richard recovered his good humour, smiled, and tapped the newspaper on his desk. 'Oh, but you *are* a miracle worker, Detective. I've read about your exploits in *The Times*. We need some of your magic here.'

Lavender opened his mouth to protest, but Sir Richard hadn't finished. 'Let me explain, Lavender. We've a mystery on our hands. Never in my illustrious career have I seen – or heard of – a case like this.'

Lavender fell silent. The word *mystery* had got his attention.

'It is impossible for a man – any man – to lie in a death-like state for so long, barely breathing and with no discernible pulse.'

Lavender frowned. 'What do you mean?'

The surgeon's eyes gleamed with excitement. 'It's poison, Lavender. Baron Poppleton was poisoned. A heinous crime has been committed here. Was it the murderer's plan all along to bring me the body to dissect? If he'd slept for another half an hour, there would have been nothing left to identify him!'

Lavender grimaced at the thought, but he still wasn't convinced. 'Could it have been a medical condition that rendered him inert?'

'Absolutely not. No such condition exists.'

'But what kind of poison would leave a man unconscious for days?'

Sir Richard smiled. He knew he'd reeled Lavender in. 'That's what I want *you* to discover – and I'm prepared to pay you handsomely to solve this mystery. I don't know the name or nature of this vile substance – but I *want* to know what it is. There are thousands of poisonous substances in this world, Detective. The Roman naturalist Pliny the Elder described over seven hundred of them in his *Naturalis Historia*, and many more have been discovered since.'

28

'Then there's every chance he's imbibed a naturally occurring poison. Did the baron explain how he fell unconscious?'

'He was too busy threatening to thrash us,' Kingsley said.

'Did he complain about being poisoned?'

'No, but—'

'Sir Richard, you've no evidence a crime has been committed and someone attempted to murder Baron Poppleton.'

The surgeon dismissed his scepticism with a wave of his hand. 'As you know, Lavender, I'm rarely wrong. Once he calms down, the baron will realise there's been an attempt on his life – and he'll be delighted you're on the case. You must interview him, find out the sequence of events before he lost consciousness and discover what he'd ingested and who gave it to him. Once you have a suspect, you can search them and their homes for this mysterious poison and bring me news of it.'

Lavender spluttered. 'It's not that easy, Sir Richard. And apart from arsenic, cyanide and digitalis, I know nothing about poison.'

'Kingsley and I will assist you. We'll work together on this.'

Lavender scrutinised Sir Richard for signs of insanity, and felt hopelessly out of his depth. 'This substance sounds like something the priest gave to Juliet in *Romeo and Juliet*.'

Sir Richard dismissed this notion with a vigorous shake of his head that threatened to dislodge his carefully sculpted pile of grey curls. 'Medical scholars have pondered the same question for centuries. No such poison existed in Shakespeare's time. The bard invented it. In fact, if I hadn't seen Baron Poppleton rise from the dead with my own eyes, I wouldn't believe it existed now. But it obviously does. I want to know where this new threat comes from and what it is.'

'Look, I don't want to try to tell you your business, Sir Richard, but shouldn't you and Kingsley be preparing your defence? It sounds like you'll have to answer a lot of awkward questions.'

The surgeon narrowed his eyes and looked at Lavender as though he was an idiot. 'Please expand your mind, Lavender! The results of your inquiry will be our defence! There is nothing the medical world loves more than a new discovery! Somewhere out there is a terrifying but unknown poison that gives the victim the appearance of death. We will wow the establishment once we announce its discovery! And this unpleasantness will disappear.'

He waved his hand lightly in the air to show how easy it was to dismiss charges of kidnapping and aiding and abetting body snatchers, along with the wrath of the hospital trustees. 'In such an event, Kingsley may even keep his job,' he added as an afterthought.

Lavender fell silent. Was Sir Richard fooling himself – or was there a genuine mystery at the heart of this sordid and farcical affair?

He licked his pencil. 'Right, start from the beginning, Kingsley. Tell me exactly how you managed to procure a living, breathing baron for dissection.'

Chapter Four

The white cap perched on Betsy Woods' mop of grey curls quivered with indignation when she bent down and stirred the simmering pot over the fireplace. The delicious aroma of rosemary and lamb made Woods' stomach rumble. He leaned from side to side to try to catch a glimpse of the bubbling stew, but Betsy's ample rear blocked his view. 'So, you're to work as a principal officer for nothin' – and get the pleasure of ruinin' your own clothes at the same time?'

Woods dumped the blue coat and scarlet waistcoat that gave the horse patrol their nickname of *redbreasts* on the kitchen table. 'It seems that way.' He reached for his old brown coat and pulled it over his broad shoulders. 'It won't be for long, sweetheart.'

'That new magistrate is a weasel. I don't trust him. And don't think you're leavin' that coat in my kitchen,' Betsy added, without turning around.

After twenty-two years of marriage, Ned had become accustomed to the fact that his feisty little wife had eyes in the back of her head. He beckoned to their six-year-old daughter, Tabitha, who was sitting at a corner of the table with her slate, studying her letters. 'Be a good girl, Treacle, and take these upstairs.' The child left the room.

Betsy straightened up, still brandishing her ladle, and turned to face him. 'When you say it won't be long, do you mean it won't be long 'til they send you back on duty with the horse patrol – or before you get this advancement? Because I tell you this, Ned Woods, if you go back in the saddle all day, with your shoulder injury, it will be the end of you.' The soft skin of her lined face was more flushed than usual.

He gave her his best smile. 'Now don't you worry your pretty head about these things, Sweetheart – there's plenty of life in these old bones yet. I'm not ready to be put out to grass.'

Betsy raised a disbelieving eyebrow. 'I hope so, Ned – because our savin's won't last for long with two young daughters to keep – and the money the boys give me barely covers their food.'

31

'Have faith, woman! I've always provided for this family and always will!'

'What does Stephen think? Magdalena told me last week he's still grievin' for his father.'

Woods nodded sadly. He and Betsy had been friends with John and Alice Lavender since Lavender was a child. 'Aye, he's taken John's death badly. He weren't pleased with this contrary arrangement any more than I were. I think he were worried he wouldn't be able to cope without me.'

Betsy rolled her eyes. 'So how hard is this case that the weasel has set you?'

Woods snorted with derision. 'It ain't nothin' I can't handle.'

Betsy eyed him thoughtfully for a moment, then said: 'Well, make sure you're not late tonight for Rachel's birthday. I've already had to stop our Eddie killin' our Dan once today.'

Woods frowned. 'What happened?'

He and Betsy adored their two strapping sons, but they were a handful – and had been ever since Betsy gave birth to the pair of them less than a year apart. Big, broad and muscular like their father, they'd been inseparable and cheeky rogues in their youth. But they'd become more distant lately, and bad arguments between the brothers were common.

'After you'd left for work, Eddie brought Rachel a posy of flowers for her birthday.'

'That were kind of him,' Woods said cautiously.

Betsy shook her grey head. 'They was white lilies, like the ones used at funerals. Rachel slapped Eddie over the head with 'em and screamed at him for bringin' her "death-flowers" that was "only fit for stiffs".'

Woods didn't know whether to laugh or cry. Or which of his two children he needed to remonstrate with first: Eddie, for being so daft or Rachel for her unladylike language. 'What on earth possessed the saphead to give her lilies?'

'It were Dan. He'd told Eddie they was her favourite – and the cork-brain believed him.'

Woods scowled. 'That were mean of him.'

'Dan thought it were a great jest and burst out laughin' – but our Eddie were so upset at the trick, he nearly flattened him. They broke a plate in the fight. I'll tell you straight, Ned: I'm too old to deal with this now.'

Woods held out his arms to give her a comforting hug. For once, she didn't resist. Her white mob cap barely came up to his chin when she nestled into his broad chest. 'I'll have a word with all of 'em when I get home. The lads can pay for the plate out of their wages. Let's hope they've put their differences aside by tonight.'

Betsy made a disparaging noise into his chest that suggested his hope was probably too optimistic.

'Now, how about a plate of that tasty stew before I go back to work, Mrs Woods?'

Betsy wriggled free and smacked him on the hand with her ladle. 'Away with you, you great lummox! It ain't ready yet – and ye've only just had your breakfast!'

'That were hours ago!' Woods protested.

'And that slice of meat and potato pie I wrapped up for you?'

Woods winked. 'My hoss ate it.'

Betsy raised her ladle again and Woods beat a hasty retreat to the back yard, where his horse waited for him. He rubbed his sore hand as he mounted, and reminded himself not to tease Betsy when she was armed with kitchen utensils. That never worked out well. But Betsy was laughing when she chased him out; the bruise was worth the knowledge he'd made her smile again.

But when he crossed the Thames on the Southwark Bridge, his thoughts shifted back to Betsy's complaints about Eddie and Dan. The problem, as Woods saw it, was Dan's new job: it was driving a wedge between his lads.

Seventeen-year-old Eddie worked as a stable hand at Bow Street and hoped to follow his father into the horse patrol, which – according to Betsy – was how things ought to be. *Like father, like son*, she'd said.

Woods had hardly known his own father. But Betsy had said it was usual for boys to follow in their father's footsteps, and she was rarely wrong about such matters.

But when Dan left school, he'd laughed at his parents' suggestion that he, too, got a job at Bow Street. He announced he was destined for greater things. He got himself a job as a junior clerk in a shipping office.

Woods knew Dan was the cleverer of his two sons. The boy always found book learning easy and wrote his letters in a neat hand, whereas poor clumsy Eddie was forever snapping both the chalk *and* the slate when he was a nipper. But he'd never thought Dan had an inkling to become a quill driver, and had been hurt by the lad's comment. *Greater things than the horse patrol? Was that possible?*

He still felt a pang of disappointment every time Dan left the house for his new job or chatted about the new set of chums he'd made at his office. His big brother was abandoned. On the evenings he was free, Dan dashed out to meet these new friends. Eddie was grumpy, and missed Dan's company.

Betsy tried to soothe their ruffled feathers. 'Our Dan don't like gettin' his hands dirty,' she explained. 'He'd have been hopeless workin' with hosses.' Well, that was a nonsense – Dan came home every night with his hands blackened from ink. But there was a nugget of truth about the hosses.

But Woods had to give the lad his due. Dan was generous with his wages – especially the amount he gave Betsy for his keep – and he seemed keen enough about this work; he often stayed late at the office to help them out when they were busy.

As he approached the smart offices of the Davies Estate, Woods turned his mind back to the job and glanced again at the grubby dog-eared poster he clutched in his large hand.

According to the anonymous author, the company was owned by Sir Bernard Davies, Bart., whom the pamphleteer described as an *agent of Satan prone to barbaric, unchristian acts of greed, who conspires at the inns of Chancery with lawyers, huddled like cawing rooks, to cancel leases and deprive decent men, women and children of their beloved homes...*

Woods was looking forward to meeting the horned baronet, and speculated on the nature of his *unchristian acts*. But he was in for a disappointment. Sir Bernard wasn't at the offices, and he found himself ushered into the office of the estate manager instead.

Mr Edwin, a full-bodied fella clad in a tight emerald-green coat, and with a voluminous neckcloth swathed in intricate folds beneath his many chins, regarded the pamphlet Woods handed him with distaste. His scowl didn't improve his appearance. His flabby face was dominated by the inflamed red nose of a gout sufferer. 'Did you say these scurrilous libels have been circulating freely in the district?'

Woods nodded.

'I'd no idea about this. Sir Bernard would be most upset. He's a decent man, raised to the baronetcy only last year by the Prince Regent. He owns a lot of property in the city and is fair with his tenants.'

'It came to the attention of Magistrate Conant at Bow Street.'

'Yes, Nathaniel is a good man.'

Woods hesitated for one second at this surprising use of Conant's Christian name, then said, 'The magistrate would like to know if you want to hire us to track down the cove who's issuin' these slanders.' He held out a piece of paper that outlined Bow Street's terms of remuneration.

Davies reread the pamphlet. 'It's a libel, Officer Woods – not slander.'

Woods was crestfallen for a moment at his mistake, but brightened the next second when Edwin nodded and reached for the offered paper. 'I act for Sir Bernard. I'm sure he'd like this calumny stopped.'

'I'll need a list of your tenants with a grievance about their lease,' Woods said.

Edwin raised an eyebrow but didn't look up as he signed the agreement. 'That may take a while to compile, Officer. There's quite a few. It doesn't matter how much we do for our tenants; some of them will always complain. Only this morning, in this very office, I had a bad-tempered discussion with three tenants about the cost of rebuilding their homes after a street fire. But I'll have a full list of those with a grievance about their leases drawn up for you by tomorrow.'

Woods' next stop was at the Holborn Printing Shop, set back from the high street in a busy courtyard. Small delivery boys dashed out of the building with large brown-paper parcels beneath their arms. Men unloaded huge bales of fresh paper from a horse-drawn wagon on to wooden barrows. Woods caught a whiff of the sweet, nutty odour of the paper when he walked past.

The dark interior of the Jacobean building was well lit with lamps, but the almond smell of the paper was now drowned out by the unpleasant sulphuric tang of ink and body odour. The large room behind the wooden counter was full of clanging printing presses, operated by men in ink-stained aprons. Other men sat at desks, pushing and snapping the type into the metal frames. Above their heads, dozens of wet pamphlets were hung over strings, drying out like Betsy's laundry in the back yard.

Harrison was a huge, scowling, bad-tempered man whose rolled-up shirt sleeves strained over the bulging muscles of his upper arms. He was hollering at one of his workers as Woods approached and turned on him with a growl. His breath reeked of ale.

Woods explained who he was and his business, and gave the man the advertisement from *The Times*.

Harrison growled again, screwed up the advertisement and tossed it into a corner of the room. 'Yer, I've seen it. The bloody saphead. I'll not forget this nonsense when he comes crawlin' back here, wantin' another one of his damned pamphlets printin'.'

'Do you know the cove who placed this advert?' Woods asked sharply.

'Aye, I reckon I do. It'll be that fool Garbutt. Richard Garbutt is his full name. I've done a lot of work fer him over the years. He's a litigious sort of man – allus fallin' out with someone and takin' them to court. We had a tussle over the price of the last job I did for him. This'll be his revenge.'

Woods shoved the other two pamphlets in his possession towards the printer. 'Were that last job you mentioned these scurrilous posters about Sir Bernard Davies and a banker called Alfred Gotobed?'

Harrison glanced at the posters, grunted, and nodded. 'Aye. But there ain't no law against printin' things. It's the writin' of 'em that's libel. We just copy what the customers want us to print.'

'Of course you do. I never said *you*'d broken the law.' Despite his bad temper, Harrison was proving helpful; Woods didn't want to get the man's back up.

'Garbutt is a saphead,' Harrison said, mirroring Woods' own thoughts.

'You might not get many customers now Garbutt has blackened your name in *The Times*.'

Harrison laughed: an ugly, deep belly kind of laugh that was more threatening than his scowl. He pointed towards the busy print room. 'Does it look like I ain't got no customers, officer?'

Woods had to agree that business at the print shop appeared to be booming.

'Tell your guvnor I thank him for his offer,' Harrison continued, 'but I ain't prepared to pay for no writ to be brought against Garbutt. I'll deal wi' him in my own way,' he added menacingly.

Woods raised a bushy grey eyebrow at the implied threat, but ignored it. 'Where does this cove live?'

'On Soho Square. Or at least he did,' Harrison added. 'He were tossed into Newgate a few years ago after fallin' out wi' some parliamentarian he claimed had robbed him.'

Again, Woods raised a surprised eyebrow. Offending small traders like Harrison was one thing – but taking on a member of the ruling class in a British court was a risky business.

'I heard he's lost all his money. He might have moved.'

'You've been very helpful,' Woods said, and took his leave.

Woods mounted his horse and turned it in the direction of Gotobed's bank, distracted by his thoughts – but smiling.

He couldn't believe his luck! The same man responsible for all three libels? Why, he'd have the cove below the hatches before nightfall!

Chapter Five

Lavender's journey to the Russell Square mansion of the Earl of Beverley took him over London Bridge. As usual, the traffic was slow and the bridge congested. Pedestrians spilled over from the pavements on to the narrow road, making it even more difficult for a rider on horseback to weave in and out between the cumbersome carriages and delivery wagons.

He reined in behind a shabby hackney carriage and took a moment to admire the great dome of St Paul's Cathedral that dominated the skyline ahead, glittering in the weak April sunshine. It towered over the roofs and chimneys of the thousands of buildings packed tightly along the curved bank of the Thames. From his elevated position on horseback, he also saw the multitude of little rowing boats criss-crossing the river like water skaters, and the tall ships lying at anchor.

He pulled out his pocket watch and made a decision about his route.

Baron Poppleton, Sir Richard Allison's unfortunate victim, lived a few streets from the Russell Square mansion of the Earl of Beverley, but the offices of *The Times* newspaper were en route. He decided to deal with his niggling personal problem first.

Unlike the rest of the London newspapers, which had gravitated towards Fleet Street, the founder of *The Times,* John Walter, had set up his business in the aptly named Printing House Square in the building formerly used by the printers of King Charles II.

The newspaper had acquired a reputation for quality reporting and had prospered – but there had been lapses in journalistic integrity. If Lavender remembered correctly, Walter had served two stints in gaol for libel and had passed ownership of the business to his son of the same name. The editor was a man called Stoddard.

The Times wasn't above pandering to the salacious taste of its readership, either. It often reported vicious attacks and murders in the capital in grisly and bloody detail. As Conant said, they also had a reputation for protecting their sources.

We'll see about that, Lavender thought as he spurred his horse forward in a gap in the traffic.

There was nothing left of the original Carolean building on Printing House Square but there were one or two gnarled oak trees behind railings that might have stemmed from that era. The newish, bland and towering newspaper offices dominated three sides of the square. A delivery yard made up the fourth.

As Lavender dismounted and tied the reins to the railing, he was hailed by a lanky man with long, greasy hair and a pockmarked face. A former spy for the Home Department, Vincent Dowling was a reporter with *The Day* and an old acquaintance.

Dowling strode across the cobbles, shook Lavender's hand and smiled warmly. The two men had worked together in the past, especially during those horrific weeks around the time of the assassination of the Prime Minister, Spencer Perceval.

'You're a long way from Fleet Street,' Lavender said.

'I've jumped ship.' Dowling jerked his ink-stained thumb in the direction of *The Times* building. 'I left *The Day* last year and joined this crew. And you're a long way from Bow Street, Lavender. I understand it's all change for you, too. I heard James Read has retired, and Conant from Marlborough Street Magistrates' Court replaced him.'

'Yes, that's right.'

'So why are you here? Come to arrest someone, have you? That'll shock 'em,' he added, laughing. 'You're quite the darlin' of our news writers this week.'

'Yes, I've noticed,' Lavender said drily. 'I hope you're not behind these exaggerated accounts of my work, Dowling?'

'No, it's not me, guv. I'm a court reporter these days. I spend most days in the Old Bailey.'

'Do you know who is behind these ridiculous articles about me?'

Dowling shook his head. 'I can't help you with that.'

Can't? Or won't? Lavender thought with a flash of irritation.

'Are you here to complain?' Dowling asked.

'Yes.' The two men fell into step towards the entrance. Lavender knew he wouldn't shake Dowling off until he'd answered the reporter's questions. 'I want to see your editor, and I also need information about someone who placed an advertisement.'

'You're out of luck today, I'm afraid. Stoddard has driven out to Berkshire to see the owner, John Walter.'

Lavender stopped in his tracks, deflated. He didn't like the delay. He wanted this nonsense stopped today. God only knows what rubbish would be printed about him in tomorrow's edition.

'What's this advertisement you're so curious about?' Dowling asked.

Lavender handed it over. The left side of the reporter's mouth curled cynically as he read. The movement emphasised the disfigurement of his skin caused by the smallpox; the scarring was worse down that side of his face. 'Ooh, someone's been a naughty boy. That's a clear case of libel.'

'I need the name of the customer who placed the advertisement, and his address.'

Dowling hesitated. 'We don't reveal our sources, Lavender. The desk clerks won't give you this information.'

'That's not a source. It's a passing member of the public who's paid you money to place an advert. Come on, Dowling!' he pleaded irritably. 'Help me out here.'

'All right. You stay here with your horse and I'll get it for you. It'll be quicker if I deal with it anyway.'

Lavender only had to wait for a few minutes before Dowling returned with a slip of paper bearing the name *Richard Garbutt* and an address on Soho Square.

Lavender took it gratefully and thanked him.

'Did your Conant ask you to track down this libeller?'

41

'Yes,' Lavender replied wearily. His mind was still on the problem of the absent editor. 'There's been a spate of libellous posters and adverts. Conant wants it stopped.'

'Actually, there's an interesting coincidence at play here,' Dowling said. 'That fellow Garbutt and your magistrate have a chequered history. Garbutt is taking your Conant to court for assault and questioning his authority.'

'What?'

'Garbutt's quite a character. An obsessive litigious fool who will never back down. He's always in the courts suing someone and doing daft things like this.' He held up the advertisement. 'A few years ago, he placarded Lord Ellenborough. He claimed the peer had cheated him out of ten thousand pounds.'

Lavender's eyes widened. 'The Lord Chief Justice?'

'Yes. Ellenborough had him arrested for libel – and it was your magistrate who took the warrant to his house. Garbutt resisted arrest and was injured in the process. But that didn't stop the court tossing him into gaol. He came out of Newgate last year and served a writ against Conant for the injuries he suffered during his arrest.'

'That is quite a coincidence,' Lavender said slowly. *Dear God, was this investigation Conant's personal revenge against the man?*

'Garbutt also claims magistrates don't have the right to arrest decent citizens.'

'He's questioned the British legal system?' Lavender was almost speechless with shock.

Dowling's eyes never left Lavender's face and he smiled wryly. 'Every newspaper in the city is looking forward to this case. It's not often a civilian takes on the lawmakers.'

Lavender frowned. This press interest wasn't good news for Bow Street.

'Mind you,' Dowling continued, 'if you arrest Garbutt over this libel against a printer, Garbutt may find himself back in Newgate and be forced to drop his case against your magistrate. That would be rather convenient for Conant, don't you think?'

Lavender thought fast. Dowling was right. To the public it would look like Conant was using his position to stop a man who was out to damage his integrity. He needed to put Dowling off the scent while he worked out how he and Ned would handle this situation. 'Magistrate Conant had no idea that the man behind this advert was Garbutt.'

'Really?' Dowling laughed. 'Garbutt's case against your magistrate will probably come to nothing anyway. After two years in Newgate, the man is close to bankruptcy. He's also placed advertisements in *The Times*, begging for financial support from the public.'

Lavender thanked Dowling and took his leave. Of course, this could be an unfortunate coincidence. But if Conant knew Garbutt was behind the advertisement, then he was using his authority at Bow Street for his own ends.

And Ned was caught up in the middle of these political machinations.

His own problem suddenly faded into insignificance.

Lavender decided to call on Baron Poppleton on Bedford Street before his appointment with the earl. He was curious to see the man who had risen from the dead.

Does resurrection leave lasting side effects? he wondered, as he mounted the shallow steps of the house and rang the doorbell.

A bewigged footman in a faded uniform answered the door – and promptly tried to shut it in Lavender's face. 'Tradesmen go round the back!'

Sighing, Lavender shoved his booted foot in the gap to stop the door closing. He hated it when this happened. 'I'm not a tradesman. I'm Detective Stephen Lavender from Bow Street and I need to see your master.'

The flunky hesitated with the door halfway open. 'There ain't no master here. This is the home of Lady Barlborough, a widow.'

Lavender gritted his teeth. 'I'm looking for Baron Poppleton. I was told he resides here.'

'Ah, my lady's nephew. Yes, he's here – but he's indisposed and not taking any callers.'

Lavender fished out a card from his coat pocket and held it out. 'I'm sure he'll want to see me. And I know why he's indisposed. Be a good fellow and take this up to him, will you? Tell him I'm here to help.'

The servant hesitated before grudgingly letting him inside the dark and dingy oak-panelled hallway. He pointed to the door of a small receiving room on the left and told Lavender to wait in there.

This antechamber was as dismal as the main hallway, full of heavy, uncomfortable Jacobean furniture and – like the hallway – in desperate need of redecoration. The paint was peeling from the sash window frame, the ceiling was yellow with decades of tobacco smoke, and above the dark wood panelling, the wallpaper was also falling down. Lady Barlborough clearly didn't do much entertaining.

Lavender knew there was a strong chance Poppleton would still refuse to see him today and he didn't blame him. The poor fellow probably needed a good night's sleep to get over the shock of finding Sir Richard leering down at him with a lancet in his hand.

Bored with waiting, he moved towards the door, opened it quietly and peered out.

Across the hallway were two more rooms, both with partially opened doors. In one he caught sight of the corner of a dark oak dining table and an uncomfortable stiff-backed chair, but his limited view of the front room suggested it was a more cheerful and well-lit drawing room. He heard the quiet murmur of female voices and the chink of teacups.

Lavender settled down to a bit of spying. He was curious to know more about this family. If Sir Richard was right and Poppleton had been poisoned, then everyone in this household was a suspect.

Suddenly, the front door opened and a stylish and attractive young woman in a lilac silk gown and dark green velvet spencer jacket entered the hallway, followed by her maid. Beneath her green velvet bonnet, a mass of smooth white-blonde ringlets framed the young lady's pretty oval face.

Both women carried parcels, which they deposited on the hall table before divesting themselves of their outer garments, gloves and hats.

'Lottie! Thank goodness you're home. I thought I heard the front door open.'

A large matron with frizzy grey hair and a large nose stood in the doorway of the drawing room. Behind her hovered a younger, plain-featured woman with soft brown hair but the same dominant nose. Both were dressed in the matte black bombazine gowns of mourning, and both wore spectacles. The lenses in the younger woman's spectacles were so thick her plain brown eyes were grotesquely enlarged in her face, like those of a young heifer.

Lottie, the young woman in lilac silk, continued to peel off her gloves and barely glanced up. 'Aunt Penelope – what a surprise! And Cousin Diana, too.'

The older woman crossed the cracked tiles on the floor towards her niece. 'We came as soon as we heard about your poor brother! What a terrible experience Humphrey's had! You must have been worried silly about him these past few days.'

The blonde goddess twitched her delicately arched eyebrows at this outpouring of emotion and turned to pat her hair down in the ugly mirror above the side table. 'I'm not sure who your spies are in this household, Aunt Penelope, but yes, I was baffled when Humphrey disappeared. Fortunately, there's no harm done – the doctor says he'll make a full recovery in a few days. He got himself into a silly scrape through drinking too much, that's all.'

The elderly woman ignored the insult. 'But who's nursing him?'

'Why, Aunt Barlborough's maid, Effy, of course.'

'What on earth happened?'

'I've no idea. As yet, Humphrey hasn't said.'

'We want to see him.'

'He's sleeping.'

'And where have you been?'

Lavender watched a flicker of irritation pass across Lottie's reflection in the glass. 'I had some errands to run. Have the servants brought you tea? Shall we return to the drawing room?'

'We've called to see poor Humphrey,' the aunt persisted. 'I must confess, Lottie, I'm surprised you've left him alone with my sister's nursemaid after such a traumatic experience!'

'Like I said, he's sleeping. Let's not bother him now.' The young woman tried to shepherd her reluctant aunt and cousin into the drawing room, but they stubbornly refused to move.

'I want to see my sister,' the older woman demanded. 'I've no doubt that she's also greatly distressed by this turn of events.'

The blonde goddess sighed wearily. 'As you well know, Aunt Penelope, Lady Barlborough only sees people when she invites them. I've had no word that she wants to see you.'

'But this is preposterous!' the matron snapped. 'Such a decree was never in place until you and Humphrey arrived and poisoned her mind against those of us who've cared for her for years!'

Lottie shrugged. 'That's unfair, Aunt Penelope.'

'But why?' wailed the matron. 'Why won't my sister see me anymore?'

Anger flashed across the young woman's face. She pointed a finger towards her silent cousin. 'Perhaps Diana should have kept her hands off Aunt Verity's silver.'

'That's vile calumny! Calumny!' shouted the older woman. 'Diana didn't steal anything!' Her daughter merely blinked behind her spectacles, her face impassive and expressionless.

The heavy tread of the footman coming down the wooden stairs disrupted the altercation between aunt and niece. Both women drew back from the confrontation.

'What do you want, Feathers?' snapped Lottie.

'I've a message for the Bow Street runner in the anteroom, ma'am.'

Lavender stepped back from the door into the shadows.

'What message? What Bow Street runner?' Lottie demanded in alarm.

'He's come about Sir Humphrey's stolen clothing and wishes to speak to him. But Sir Humphrey says not.'

Lavender stepped out into the hallway, ignoring the shocked expressions of Lottie and her aunt. The girl, Diana, showed no reaction.

'Sir Humphrey thanks you for your consideration, sir,' the lackey informed him. 'But he says not to worry about the pantaloons and coat; he's plenty of others.'

'Pantaloons?' Lavender snapped. 'I'm not here about a pair of stolen pantaloons, man. Go back and tell the baron I wish to speak to him on a different matter. A matter of some urgency.'

'He's gone back to sleep, sir.' The footman remained rooted to the spot.

Lavender bowed to Lottie Poppleton and bit back his frustration. Perhaps he might have more luck with her. 'I'm Detective Stephen Lavender from Bow Street, ma'am. I presume I've the honour of addressing the Honourable Miss Poppleton?'

'Lavender! Oh, my goodness! I've read about your exploits in *The Times,* Detective.' She pointed to the other two women. This is my aunt, Mrs Farrow, and my cousin, Miss Diana Farrow.'

Lavender bowed again.

'Well, if Lavender is on the case, Humphrey will soon retrieve his stolen clothes,' her aunt commented acidly.

'Alas, ladies, I'm not here to recover the items stolen from Sir Humphrey. I want to find out how Sir Humphrey ended up at Guy's Hospital. I need to speak to him urgently.'

'That's something we *all* want to know, young man,' said Mrs Farrow. 'Has he said anything about what happened, Lottie?'

Miss Poppleton's silky ringlets swung backwards and forwards over her shoulders when she shook her head. 'No. He raged for a bit about that surgeon, Sir Richard, but he's so exhausted he fell asleep the moment he'd eaten a bowl of broth.'

'You should have pressed him further, Lottie.'

'The doctor said to let him rest. Perhaps you can return tomorrow, Detective?' Her blue eyes looked up at him beseechingly.

He had one last chance to get around these gatekeepers who wouldn't give him access to Humphrey Poppleton. 'I wonder if I might have a word with Lady Barlborough? I understand this is *her* house.'

Again, the ringlets swung – and this time more vigorously. 'I'm afraid my aunt – that is, my *other* aunt, Lady Barlborough – is an invalid, sir. She's also a recluse. She sees no one. Ever.'

Lavender accepted defeat. Bowed again and left.

But when he crossed the road, he sensed he was being watched. He swung around just in time to see the lace curtain fall at one of the upstairs windows of the house. Before it fell, he'd caught a glimpse of the shadowy figure of a woman.

A curious servant perhaps? The nursemaid, Effy?

Or perhaps the mysterious Lady Barlborough?

Chapter Six

The bank of Messrs Knightley and Gotobed was situated on the busy thoroughfare known as the High Street in Southwark. Woods lived in Southwark and walked this street often, but he'd never noticed the bank before. But perhaps that wasn't surprising. It was a respectable brown-brick, square-windowed building, with a plain wooden sign above the door, that was overshadowed by its neighbours: a raucous tavern known throughout London for its ribald shows and erotic dancers, and a theatrical supplier with a glittering range of bejewelled velvet costumes in the window.

The bank's clientele were a mixed bunch. Burly tradesmen clutching their day's takings followed red-coated soldiers through the door. An elderly couple dressed entirely in black, with a small dog on a leash, stepped aside at the entrance to let out a pretty blonde gal in a purple dress, accompanied by her maid.

Woods followed a couple of gaily dressed actresses into the cool and gloomy interior. The gals were giggling together, their reticules clutched in their white-gloved hands. Woods shrugged. He'd never thought about it before but even Drury Lane actresses needed somewhere to keep their savings, he supposed. Personally, he'd no idea whether he had any money in a bank or not. He just handed it over to Betsy for safekeeping every week and it disappeared.

Woods didn't have to wait long for an audience with Mr Alfred Gotobed.

The banker's office was a luxurious room with a thick Turkish carpet across the floor and walls lined with gleaming teak panels and a matching teak desk. A neat row of crystal inkwells glittered on the inlaid leather surface. Even the door handles gleamed.

The banker, Alfred Gotobed, was short and skinny, with round spectacles perched on the bridge of his narrow nose and thin brown hair swept over his balding pate in narrow strands. His sharp eyes were almost colourless, and deep set in his expressionless face.

But his manners were impeccable. He rose to greet Woods when he entered the office and shook his hand. A cup of tea was offered, which Woods politely declined.

This man dresses well, Woods noted. The cut of Gotobed's black coat, which was shot through with a silver thread, was immaculate and the elaborate fold of his snowy white cravat was held tight with a diamond pin. His only other adornment was a thick band of high-quality gold studded with tiny diamonds, worn on the middle finger of his left hand.

Woods handed Gotobed the defamatory pamphlet and the banker laughed aloud when he read it. 'I'm an *anti-Christ and a usurer worse than Shylock himself*, am I,' he said. '*A defaulter of promises and the ruination of decent and trusting men*.' His voice was soft and silky and had a persuasive quality, but despite the clipped vowels of his educated accent, there was a twang of the East End docks lurking in the background.

'I'm afraid there's been dozens of those placarded around the city,' Woods said.

'What a shame I've missed them,' the banker said drily. 'I travel to work in my own carriage every day. It drops me at the door of this office and picks me up again every night.'

Woods nodded. 'That's what the last gentleman said. He'd not seen the scurrilous posters aimed at him neither.'

'The last gentleman?'

'Aye, an estate manager. This cove has also had a go at him. Magistrate Conant wants this libellous lark stopped and the villain put under the hatches.'

'Ah, the good magistrate of Bow Street.' The banker's neat manicured nails drummed on the desk. The diamonds in his ring flashed in the sunlight streaming through the high window.

'He's sent me to ask you if you want to employ us officers from Bow Street to investigate these libels.'

The corners of Gotobed's thin mouth twitched with amusement. 'He's sent you out touting for business?'

'I guess so.'

The banker smiled, and pushed the dog-eared leaflet back across the desk towards Woods. 'Please thank Sir Nathaniel for his concern, but I won't take him up on his kind offer.'

Woods was startled. 'These are serious allegations, sir. The rumour and scandal of usury can ruin a bank.'

'Only if it's true,' Gotobed said calmly.

'It might be bad for business.'

The banker's smile broadened. 'Does it look like my bank is suffering, Detective?'

'Well, no, sir...'

'You have to understand something, officer. Most bankers face these allegations every week – especially if we're forced to put pressure on a customer over a late loan repayment or threaten them with the bailiffs or the debtors' goal.'

The hairs on the back of Woods' neck prickled with the casual and compassionless tone of the banker's voice.

'Unfortunately, many of our customers are under the illusion we're their friends or – worse still – that we operate out of charity,' Gotobed continued, 'which I'm sure you'll agree is rather childish?'

'Yes, sir.'

'I'm afraid such nonsense is part and parcel of the job of loaning money.'

Woods nodded and picked up his hat, ready to leave. He was disappointed but he understood Gotobed's reasoning. 'Thank you for your time, sir. Oh, by the way,' he added casually, 'is a cove called Richard Garbutt one of your customers?'

Gotobed shrugged. 'We have hundreds of customers, Detective.'

'Would it be possible for one of your clerks to check?'

The banker's voice hardened. 'What would be the point, officer? Even if this Garbutt chap *is* one of our customers and he *is* the libeller whom you seek, I'm not prepared to bring an action against him.'

Woods nodded, sighed, and left.

Outside, the shopkeepers were closing their shutters and wheeling their trays of produce inside. The street was emptying of customers, and it was time for everyone to go home for their suppers. Woods knew he needed to hurry tonight to get back home for Rachel's birthday. But he was thirsty, and he decided that a quick flagon of ale was needed.

He avoided the gaudy flesh-pit with its lewd shows next door and nipped into the more sedate tavern opposite Messrs Knightley and Gotobed. The only table available was in front of the casement window with its leaded panes, which gave him a good view of the bank.

The barmaid filled Woods' tankard with ale from her jug and while he drank, he glanced out of the window at the bank and pondered his case.

There was nothing else he could do today to link Richard Garbutt to these scurrilous libels. Hopefully, Lavender would unearth Garbutt's name at the newspaper office. At this point he'd have enough to ask for an arrest warrant from Magistrate Conant.

Woods took another drink and watched Alfred Gotobed and his staff come out of the bank. The banker locked the door and walked a few yards to his carriage.

Woods nearly choked on his ale when she saw the coachman standing by the banker's horses.

It was Ulrich Monmouth, a notorious horse thief whom he and Lavender had caught ten years ago. The cove was a violent thug and had been sent on a seven-year ticket to Botany Bay for his crimes. Monmouth had had a mild dose of polio as a child and walked with a marked limp.

Woods leaned forward and peered through the dusty glass to make sure. He watched the coachman close the door behind Mr Gotobed, limp back to the front of the carriage and clamber up to the driver's seat. There was no doubt about it. The man's face was in shadow beneath his hat, his neck swathed with scarves. But it was the same lurching gait, the same fella.

Monmouth shook the reins and the horses lurched forward, picked up speed and trotted out of sight. *You always knew your horseflesh and handled the traces well, Ulrich,* Woods thought.

He sat back to ponder this latest discovery. Monmouth had every right to return to England from New South Wales after his seven-year ticket had expired. All convicts on a limited sentence were given that choice, although most of them couldn't afford the passage back to Britain. But why the devil was a rogue like him employed by a respectable banker?

Was Mr Gotobed one of those enlightened gentlemen of a charitable nature who took pity on ex-convicts? Woods dismissed this notion as addle-pated nonsense when he remembered Gotobed's impassive, compassionless face when he talked of bailiffs and the debtors' gaol.

Nor was it likely that Monmouth had had some form of Damascene conversion while sweltering in the heat of the Australian outback. Twenty years of experience of the criminal underbelly of this writhing city had taught Woods that coves like him didn't change their evil ways.

Downing the last of his ale, Woods left the tavern and looked for an alleyway that might lead to the back of the bank.

The back alley that ran behind the bank was strewn with foul-smelling rubbish and stank of rat urine. The smell emanating from the latrines at the back of the tavern didn't help either.

Woods soon located the rear of Gotobed's bank and found himself a shadowy corner to settle down and wait.

The back windows of the bank were obscured with drapes, but the light had begun to fade and through a chink in the curtains Woods saw the glimmer of a candle. Someone was still inside.

A few moments later, two rough-looking coves strode down the alleyway from the opposite end. *Customers heading for the tavern?*

As they drew nearer, Woods turned to face the wall, opened the fall flap of his trousers and pretended to urinate.

One of the men gave him a scowl but neither faltered in their stride. They paused at the door of the bank and knocked softly. Three soft knocks. A pause. Then two more, followed by another pause and a final three.

The door opened and they slid inside. Woods strained to see who had let them in, but he only succeeded in getting a crick in his neck.

Curious, he thought as he buttoned up his trousers. *What's happening here?*

This was the kind of mystery Lavender would love.

Chapter Seven

Lord Beverley's town house in Russell Square was an opulent and sprawling mansion. As the butler led Lavender up a marble staircase to meet his latest client, Lavender raked his memory for information about the earl.

He remembered that Beverley was a respected member of both the House of Lords and London society, with a reputation for compassion and treating his employees fairly. No hint of scandal had ever attached itself to his name and oddly, for an aristocrat, he was rumoured to be madly in love with his wife.

The south-facing drawing room was flooded with light from four tall windows, which led out on to the wrought-iron balcony that ran the full length of the first floor of the house. The room was tastefully furnished with a selection of cream and yellow striped silk chairs and sofas, which blended with the lemon silk wallpaper.

Three elaborate crystal chandeliers hung from the ornamental plaster ceiling roses. They caught the natural light and sent a dizzying pattern of flickering diamonds dancing across the walls.

Lord Beverley, a handsome, athletic man in his mid-forties, wore gleaming boots, nankeen breeches and a beautifully cut coat of dark-blue satin. He was pacing on the Turkish rug in front of the fireplace when the butler announced Lavender. His anguished face flooded with relief and he stepped forward with his hand outstretched. 'Lavender! Thank God you're available to help! I don't mind telling you, Detective – but this is a damnable mess!'

Lavender pulled out his notebook. 'I know you've had a robbery, Your Lordship – but don't worry, I'll handle this case with discretion.'

The earl nodded. 'Of course.'

'What happened? And can you give me a description of the stolen items?'

Beverley strode back to the fireside, threw himself down in a chair and pointed at the miserable dark-haired young man in his mid-twenties who sat opposite. His resemblance to the earl was striking: this was his son, Viscount Cottingham.

'My saphead of a son invited a load of rogues into the house – while his mother and I were on our estate in the country – and they robbed my strongbox! They took his mother's diamond necklace and earrings, and a pearl and diamond brooch. They were heirlooms, Lavender – precious heirlooms! They'd been in my wife's family for generations.'

Cottingham looked like he wanted the ground to open and swallow him.

Lavender cleared his throat and raised his pencil. 'Can you describe the jewellery in more detail?'

Beverley pointed to a magnificent gilt-framed portrait hanging over the intricately carved white marble fireplace. 'My wife's wearing them in this painting. My steward will give you the exact number of stones, their weight and shape et cetera – and details about the brooch.'

A lovely young woman with natural, unpowdered raven curls and a soft, loving smile stared back at Lavender from the portrait of the countess. It had been painted in her youth but despite her tender years, intelligence and compassion shone in those dark-brown eyes.

Around her neck, above the lace edging the low curved neckline of her rose silk gown, she wore a beautiful and tasteful cascade of diamonds set in gold. Matching earrings dangled from her tiny ears.

'Very beautiful,' Lavender said. 'I'm sure their loss has left the countess distressed. Perhaps the Viscount can tell me what happened?'

Beverley sat back and glared at his son. 'Yes. Frank, tell the detective how you let your dubious friends steal your mother's precious jewels.'

The wretched young man sat straighter. Dressed in the height of fashion, he had the pale complexion and dark rings beneath his eyes of a youth who burned the candle at both ends.

Lavender suspected he knew his type. Educated at Eton and Cambridge, the viscount probably now spent his time cutting a dash around London's high society with the other young bucks. His nights would be spent at the balls given by Lady Jersey and the Prince Regent or at the faro tables, where he would run up eye-watering debts. His afternoons would find him fencing, exercising his thoroughbred horse on Rotten Row in Hyde Park or visiting his tailor.

'I invited a few friends back here for supper after the theatre one night.'

'Which theatre?'

'The Sans Pareil.'

'When was this?'

'Last Friday.'

'There were actresses among them,' Lord Beverley interrupted. 'At least four. Our butler was scandalised.'

'During the evening, one of the women asked me about this portrait of my mother and the diamond necklace.' The young man paused and swallowed hard.

'Go on,' the earl badgered, his anger barely concealed. 'Tell the detective what you did next.'

'I was in my cups,' Cottingham explained. 'I wasn't thinking straight – and she was persuasive. I thought there was no harm in it. I showed her the real necklace in the strongbox.'

'Where is the strongbox?' Lavender asked.

'In my bedchamber,' Beverley said. 'It's only accessible if you have the key.'

'Where's the key kept?'

'In a drawer in my library.'

'Who is privy to this information?'

'Myself, our butler and my steward – and this young fool.'

Lavender turned back to the viscount. 'Did this woman watch you while you retrieved the key?'

The young man lowered his head in shame. 'She was with me, so I suppose she must have done. Anyway, I took out the necklace, the earrings and the brooch and let her wear them for a bit.'

'For a bit!' shouted the earl. 'According to the staff, the damned jilt paraded around the house in your mother's jewellery for the rest of the evening!'

'She was very persuasive,' Cottingham wailed.

'I bet she was! And no doubt she was grateful and rewarded your kindness in the usual manner of a harlot!'

The viscount blushed to the roots of his dark foppish fringe and declined to comment.

Beverley turned to Lavender. 'This young fool was so drunk he forgot about the jewels. It was down to Ingleby, our butler, to retrieve the diamonds from the jilt and replace them in the strongbox.'

'The jewels were returned to the strongbox?' Lavender asked, surprised. 'What happened next?'

The lad glanced down and shook his head. 'I can't remember. I passed out fully clothed on my bed.'

'And he wasn't the only one. Ingleby told me his friends and three of the actresses stayed here all night – some of the men and women were in the same room. Our parlour maids were scandalised when they went to make up the bedroom fires in the morning.'

Father and son fell into a hostile silence and Lavender paused to lick his pencil and let some of the emotion subside. His sympathies were divided. They lay mostly with the earl, but the youth looked so wretched. His mind flicked to his own family. He sincerely hoped none of his own children would ever abuse their home in this way and cause him and Magdalena such grief.

He turned to the viscount. 'You suspect someone – probably this actress – sneaked back into your father's library during the night, found the key, opened the strongbox and took the jewels?'

Cottingham nodded. 'That's the only explanation I have.'

'When did you discover they were gone?'

'He didn't,' snapped Beverley. 'My wife and I returned from the country yesterday. Last night I had cause to open my strongbox and discovered the theft of the necklace and the pearl and diamond brooch that was also in there. For some reason, they didn't take the earrings.'

'The thief might have been disturbed,' Lavender suggested.

'It's so hard to believe she did it!' Cottingham interrupted. 'She was so warm and pleasant the next morning.'

'Professional conmen – and conwomen – are often brazen,' Lavender said quietly.

The earl frowned. 'Do you think it was planned, Lavender? I'd assumed the woman was just an opportunistic thief.'

'Maybe. But either way, she probably had an accomplice who watched her back while she did the robbery. One of her fellow actresses, perhaps. I doubt it was the work of a single woman; they usually work in pairs.'

Cottingham put his head in his hands and groaned.

The earl reached across to a pile of papers lying on a rosewood side table. 'My steward has already questioned the servants, Lavender. Here's a note of everything they can remember about the actresses, which is a damned sight more than my drunken son can remember. The woman you need to arrest is a thin blonde, with pale skin, probably in her mid-twenties. We think she goes by the name of Louise.'

'She never said Louise. She just introduced herself as Lou,' the young man added. 'She calls herself Lou.'

Lavender sighed. 'And you'd never met her before Friday night? Was she on stage at the play you watched?'

'No. I don't recall her being part of the cast. There's always a lot of women hanging around the stage door. I was already bushed by then...' His voice trailed away. Then his face lit up and he added, 'I think Jonty knows her. I'm sure he introduced her to us.'

'Jonty?' Lavender asked.

'Lord Jonothan Furnish, one of my friends.'

Lavender asked for a description of the other women, but the viscount couldn't remember much, only that two of them were brunettes and one was blonde. Lavender closed his notebook, took the sheaf of papers from the earl and said, 'I trust if I need clarification you won't object if I question your servants further, Your Lordship?'

'Absolutely not – feel free to question them if you want. But while we're on the subject of my servants, Lavender, I've discounted the possibility that any of my staff are involved. They've all been here for years; I can vouch for them.'

Lavender nodded. 'Are you prepared to offer a reward for the return of the jewels?'

'Yes. I've agreed an amount with my steward. The details are on the last sheet I've given you. We've already contacted *The Times* to place an advert.'

Lavender glanced through the papers in his hand. It was unlikely the thief would read that newspaper. But he would circulate the news of the theft and the reward through his network of pawn shops and jewellers. 'There's no information about your male friends in this account, Viscount.'

'Eh?'

'The young men you also invited back to the house.'

'They're chaps I knew from Cambridge. Friends.'

'I still need their names. I may need to talk to them.'

'Surely you don't think my son's friends had anything to do with this?' the earl asked irritably. 'These boys have been in and out of our homes for years, without any trouble – until now.'

'No, but they may remember something significant.'

'Oh, very well. Tell him, Frank.'

'There were three of them: Jonty – that's Lord Jonothan Furnish; Harry Lawson—'

'*Sir* Harry Lawson,' his father interrupted.

'I'll need their addresses,' Lavender pointed out. The details were supplied for the first two men, and he wrote them down.

'And the last one was Poppers.'

'Poppers?' his father asked, frowning.

'Yes, Humphrey Poppleton. I knew him at Eton. I've met up with him again recently.'

'Is this the same Baron Humphrey Poppleton who lives around the corner on Bedford Street with Lady Barlborough?' Lavender asked. He knew it was a silly question. There would only be one man with a name as daft as that in London.

'Yes. You should remember him, Father. I stayed with him at his family estate in Cambridgeshire once.'

The earl was still frowning. 'Didn't his father lose everything he owned in a series of bad investments and pull the boy out of university?'

'Yes, but his old man died soon after. Poppers is the baron now. He's back in the chinks too. His elderly aunt, Lady Barlborough, is a wealthy woman and he's her heir.'

'Can you remember anything about the other three women?' Lavender asked.

The viscount shook his head. 'I'm afraid not... but the others spent more time with them. They'll know more about them.'

The earl rolled his eyes to the ornate ceiling.

Lavender closed his notebook. 'Right, I'll start this investigation immediately.'

The earl rang the bell pull beside the fireplace to summon his butler to show the detective out. 'Report back to us regularly, won't you, Lavender?'

'Yes, my lord.'

Outside, the daylight was fading. The street smelt of a thousand suppers cooking over coal fires, and there was a chill in the air.

Lavender frowned as he remounted his horse. Baron Poppleton, the suspected victim of poisoning, was also present when the Beverley jewels were stolen?

Meanwhile, Magistrate Conant had set Woods to arrest a man who was causing him personal trouble.

Lavender didn't like coincidences at the best of times – and uncovering two in one day was a nasty surprise.

Chapter Eight

The kitchen at Woods' house was crowded with relatives and Rachel's young friends when Stephen, Magdalena and their two children arrived.

The twelve-year-old birthday girl sat at the head of the long wooden table with her little sister and her girlfriends, opening gifts. Betsy and her own sister, Ginny, were busy around the hearth making cups of tea for the guests. Meanwhile, Woods and his two strapping sons hovered on the edges of the room, casting hungry glances at the large iced birthday cake in the centre of the table.

Lavender greeted Betsy and Ginny with a kiss, then found refuge at his constable's side in the corner of the kitchen.

The arrival of Magdalena and the children caused a lively distraction from the present-opening. All the young girls rushed to look at the sleeping babe, and a place was found for Magdalena at the table. Meanwhile, two-year-old Alice Lavender was scooped up by the excited little girls and whisked back towards the presents. Sofía, always a confident toddler, climbed up on to Rachel's knee and reached out towards the parcels.

The Lavenders' gift was a beautiful cobalt-blue fringed shawl, which Magdalena had embroidered with flowers in the Spanish fashion. Stephen had wondered if it was too grown-up and feminine for the athletic young Rachel. Woods' elder daughter played cricket better than her older brothers and shared her father's love of horses. But Rachel ripped off the wrapping paper, squealed with delight, and ran the silky fringe through her fingers.

'How were your day, sir?' Woods asked, as he handed him a tankard of ale.

'Frustrating and worrying.'

'Mine too. I thought I were gettin' somewhere – but there's been an odd development.'

Betsy – who had better hearing than a bat – paused mid-flow with the teapot. 'Don't you two start talkin' about work until after the cake!'

Lavender held up his hands in mock alarm. 'I wouldn't dare, Betsy!'

The oil lamps were dimmed, and a hush fell on the room as the candles were lit with a taper. Everyone gave three cheers for Rachel, while she blew with her eyes closed and made a wish.

Lavender smiled when his little Alice pursed her rosebud mouth and blew bubbles, trying to imitate Rachel's actions.

The cake was cut, enough plates were found, and the slices handed out. It vanished down the throats of the youngsters within seconds. The minute Betsy mentioned a second helping, she was mobbed.

'Betsy dearest,' Woods called over the clamour, 'sir and I will get out of your way for a bit.'

As the two men edged their way around the outside of the room towards the door, Rachel leapt from her chair and gave Lavender a hug. 'Thank you so much for that lovely shawl, Uncle Stephen. The other girls are jealous!'

He hugged her back and smiled.

'—and I'm so sorry about your pa. I loved Uncle John.' Lavender hastily blinked back his tears as Rachel darted back to her seat.

Woods led Lavender towards the front parlour, where Betsy had lit a fire in the hearth. It had been a mild month, but the evenings were still chilly. Dan had already escaped from the chaos and was enjoying his birthday cake in a chair by the window. A book lay open beside him.

He's a good-looking lad, Lavender decided. Like all of Ned's children, Dan had inherited a thick head of curly brown hair from his mother. But unlike Eddie, who was just a younger version of his round-faced, broad-nosed father, Dan's features were more chiselled. He had his mother's sharp cheekbones, a longer, thinner nose, and thick black eyelashes framed his intelligent brown eyes.

'Are you not goin' out tonight, son?' Woods asked.

Dan shook his head, 'Ma told me and Eddie to stay at home for Rachel's birthday. I've come in here for a bit of peace!'

Woods nodded in approval, sat down in one of the large threadbare chairs by the fire and stirred the coals with the poker. 'Aye, it's been a busy night. By the way, sir,' he said to Lavender, 'your ma called in earlier with a present for Rachel.'

'How was she?'

'Strugglin' to walk. But your sister Elizabeth helped her.'

Lavender felt his chest heave with another surge of emotion as he sank down into the chair opposite Ned. He wasn't usually this shattered so early. Magdalena had told him the grief over his father was behind his tiredness; apparently, grief was exhausting.

'We're trying to persuade my mother and Elizabeth to move in with us,' Lavender told him. 'Unlike the rest of my siblings, we've plenty of room.'

'Let me guess,' Woods said, 'she's stubbornly refusin' to come?'

Lavender nodded. Woods had worked in the horse patrol with his father and knew both his parents well. 'I don't know what the problem is – she gets on well with Magdalena and adores our children. She's in constant pain and I'm sure she'd be more comfortable with us.'

'She's a proud independent woman, is your ma. She'll come round to your way of thinkin' soon.'

'I hope so. Tell me what happened today, Ned.'

Ned sat back and gave Lavender a thorough report about his investigation into the libellous advertisement and posters written by the saphead Richard Garbutt.

Lavender relaxed, nodded and smiled. 'Vincent Dowling gave me the proof you need that Garbutt was behind the advertisement in *The Times*. But what sort of idiot uses a printer to damn and defame other people – then turns on his printer?'

'I did think it were a bit like cuttin' yer nose off to spite your face.'

Lavender handed across the sheet of paper Dowling had given him. 'You've solved the case, Ned. Magistrate Conant will be impressed. You can ask him for an arrest warrant for Garbutt tomorrow morning. Well done.'

'Thank you, sir. It were easy like – especially with the same villain responsible for all the libels.'

'But...' Lavender said slowly.

'But?'

'Just a word of warning, Ned...' Lavender told him about Garbutt's litigious nature and his connection with Magistrate Conant.

Woods' eyes widened in surprise. 'Do you think that weasel magistrate were usin' me to get even with the man?'

'Possibly. Play your cards close to your chest tomorrow. Just tell Conant what you've found out and don't let him know that you're aware of his connection with the man. Let's see how this plays out. If Conant arrests his rival, he needs to play this by the book.'

Woods nodded thoughtfully. 'I've heard about men like Garbutt. 'Tis said they spend all their time in the courts of chancery suin' other folks until it becomes a habit – like them opium addicts.'

'Oh, it can become an obsession, all right – and if they're clever enough, it's a good way to earn money without doing any work. But one slip and they're up to their neck in debt to the lawyers.'

Woods snorted. 'It sounds like Garbutt's luck ran out when he took on the Lord Chief Justice a few years back. I'll do as you suggest. But what do you think about this banker and Ulrich Monmouth?'

Lavender shrugged. 'Men like Monmouth and those other coves you saw have their uses. There's still too much highway robbery in this country – especially in the provinces – and bankers often need to transport large money chests around the country from one branch to another – or to and from wealthy clients.'

Woods shuffled uncomfortably. 'Aye, that makes sense, but my old bones and my old nose are tellin' me there's more to it. What happened with that cocksure sawbones?'

Lavender told him about Sir Richard's disastrous attempt to carve up a living baron – and Woods nearly fell off his chair laughing. He clutched his sides, and great tears of mirth rolled down his fat cheeks.

Over by the window, young Dan was in hysterics, too.

Woods' great guffaws of laughter brought the rest of the children running in from the kitchen. Rachel was annoyed when the two men wouldn't tell them what was so funny. 'Our Dan knows!' she protested. 'Why won't you tell me?'

Woods couldn't reply. He just waved a hand helplessly in the air.

Smiling, Betsy gathered up the youngsters and herded them back into the kitchen. 'Ten more minutes,' she warned the men, 'then I expect you back in the kitchen – you've got guests, Ned Woods.'

Still chuckling, Woods wiped the last tears from his eyes. 'Gawd's teeth! That's the best tale I've heard in a long time. How did you keep your face straight?'

'With a lot of difficulty.'

'No wonder that wheedlin' sawbones didn't want me there to hear about this!'

'Yes, it would have been hard to get the facts with you rolling on the floor, clutching your sides,' Lavender said drily.

'Will he get the push?'

'I don't know. There will be some scandal attached to his name if this goes public and his wealthy patients may not be so pleased to see him anymore – especially those in the peerage. '

'Aye,' Woods chuckled. 'They'll be worried he might go for a duke next.'

'But he seems to think that if we can track down the poisoner and find this mysterious poison, he'll be a hero in the medical profession.'

'You've got to let me help,' Woods said. 'I don't care what that wheedlin' surgeon says – this is the best mystery to come your way for years.'

'It's Conant I'm more concerned about than Sir Richard, Ned. He's the one who seems determined to keep us apart. Sir Richard's just embarrassed because he knows you'll tease him about this for years.'

Woods winked. 'And that's why I need to be involved. Come on, sir – let me help! Neither the sawbones nor the weasel need to know what we're up to, do they?'

'What do you suggest?'

'I'll hunt down that poxy trouser-filchin' body snatcher tonight. Cross Bones cemetery is close by – and I know a couple of the local watchmen.' He waved the paper Lavender had given him earlier. 'I already owe you a favour.'

'Are you sure?' Lavender asked. He was too weary to argue.

'Of course I am! We'll have this mystery wrapped up in no time.'

Woods had to visit three of Southwark's night watchmen before he got a clue about the possible identity of the resurrection man he sought. The watchmen were swathed up to their eyeballs with scarves and huddled around their braziers. All of them agreed body snatching was one of the most despicable crimes in the capital and that taking a nipper out on such a grisly mission was vile.

But the description given to Lavender by Doctor Kingsley wasn't much help because there were a lot of ugly men in their late forties with a bad skin disease in Southwark. Woods had to endure a lot of ribald discussion about whether or not the corny-faced cove had the French disease, and questions about whether or not the scoundrel still had a nose.

But it was mentioning the young lad who'd accompanied the body snatcher that finally got him his clue.

The third watchman Woods approached, an elderly whiskered fellow called Adams, coughed a lot in the smoky charcoal fumes rising from his brazier. He nodded sadly beneath his wide-brimmed hat when Woods explained what he wanted. 'Aye, I know the family. They live in an 'ovel down Water Lane Backs. I think they's called Yardley. You never see them out in the day.'

Woods thanked him and strode off in the direction of the notorious slum known as Water Lane Backs, where whole families lived and died in squalor in damp-ridden cellars. He stroked the loaded pistol in the pocket of his old brown coat and thanked heaven he wasn't in his uniform. The coves down here would think nothing of slitting the gizzard of a law man.

He eventually found the Yardley home: a single room in a crumbling tenement with rags at the window. A thin and terrified woman opened the door a crack and Woods recoiled at the stench wafting out of the hovel. She told him that her Bill was out and no, *I ain't no notion where 'e be*. But her sullen eyes gave away her lie when they glanced over her shoulder as if he was checking she was delivering the message right. Then she slammed the door in his face.

Smiling, Woods moved down the street and slid into the shadows of a shuttered building on the other side to watch. The walls above him bulged out with age and dripped with slime. There were no lamps down Water Lane Backs. But there was a good moon riding high over the chimneys and plenty of stars to lighten the night.

Half an hour later, a stooped, scrawny man and a thin child came out of the hovel and slunk down the street in the direction of the river. Woods slipped silently into their wake.

The expensive fabric of the cove's ridiculous light-coloured trousers glowed in the moonlight and reassured him he'd found his mark. *Nankeen*, sir had called it. Some fancy foreign stuff from Chinese China.

The baron's pantaloons had been tailored to show off his slim and muscular legs, but they hung like bags on the stick-thin frame of the resurrection man. They also seemed to cause him some irritation; every few hundred yards, Yardley reached down to scratch his legs as if in acute discomfort. In fact, the fella seemed to be unwell. Woods had to dive down a dark side alley at one point when Yardley abruptly stopped and cast up his accounts.

Woods gave them a minute or two to resume their journey and then slid back out on to the street, side-stepping the vomit. There was no sign of father and son, but he knew they were headed for the paupers' graveyard.

Thanks to its grisly history, most people avoided Cross Bones cemetery at night, but Woods wasn't a superstitious man. His biggest concern was the rusty and creaking iron gate at the entrance, which he feared would give him away. But his quarry had left it open, and he entered noiselessly.

Bordered on three sides by the towering unlit and ugly buildings that threw black silhouettes on to the starry sky, and on the fourth by the stinking river, the graveyard was a grim patch of misery, scattered with a few overgrown shrubs and stunted trees and criss-crossed with weed-infested paths. Ominous unmarked mounds of earth – said to contain the bones of thousands who'd died from the plague, or the cholera epidemics – rose beside him, interspersed with tight rows of crumbling headstones.

There were no ornate tombstones or mausoleums at Cross Bones and the unhealthy miasma that rose from the river mingled with the stench of death and decay.

It was eerily quiet. Only the mournful hooting of a small owl and the creaking timbers of the ships moored on the river assailed Woods' ears as he moved cautiously forward. The raucous laughter and occasional shout of a drunk spilling out of a tavern seemed distant and part of another world. The laughter and footsteps of the living didn't belong here.

Woods turned a corner and saw the boy in the distance. He stood nervously beside the raised earth of a newly dug grave, leaning on the handle of a spade. A pickaxe lay at his feet.

The coves must hide them tools somewhere in the graveyard, Woods realised. Carrying them around the streets of Southwark at night would attract too much attention.

He slipped beneath the straggly branches of a fir tree, pressed himself against the trunk to disguise his shape and pulled out his pistol. He intended to catch the pair in the act and use the weapon to stop and arrest them both.

His eyes picked out the mournful shape of a posy of flowers laid on the grave by a grieving relative. Revulsion and anger flooded through him.

Suddenly, the body snatcher emerged from a bush, buttoning up those nankeen pantaloons. 'What the 'ell are you waitin' for? Get diggin'!'

'I weren't sure it were the right one...' the lad stammered.

'It is. You'll have to do most of the work. The devil's scourged my guts. My blind cheeks are burnin'.'

Woods grimaced. Something told him Baron Poppleton wouldn't want those duds back.

The lad lifted his spade and slammed it down into the soft earth.

Suddenly, there were thunderous footsteps on the gravel path behind Woods. A searing pain shot through his head as someone coshed him from behind.

He fell forward, only just managing to twist his head in time and save his nose before his face smashed into the path. The gravel bit into his cheeks like dog teeth. Dazed, and half blinded by the blood streaming into his eyes, he braced himself for further blows.

But his assailants – there were two of them – leapt over his prostrate body and continued to race towards the body snatchers.

He managed to raise his throbbing head a fraction and watched the Yardleys shriek, throw down their tools and pelt off towards the riverbank with the two dark-coated thugs in pursuit.

Peace returned to the graveyard.

A breeze whispered through the branches of the fir tree, and the owl hooted nervously...

Woods slipped into unconsciousness.

Chapter Nine

'Absolutely not!' Magistrate Conant's face flushed bright red. 'No. We will *not* take on Sir Richard's case. This office should be aligning *with* the peerage – not working with those who try to carve them up!'

Lavender bit back his anger. Conant's reaction was disgusting. Magistrate Read wouldn't have hesitated to help their medical colleague. *Did the man understand nothing about loyalty?*

'In fact, Lavender, this is a clear dereliction of your duty,' the magistrate continued. 'You should have arrested this Kingsley fellow for consorting with body snatchers and kidnapping the baron!'

'I had no evidence for such an arrest.'

Conant slammed down his quill, snapping the nib in the process. 'You've just told me the man admitted to you the truth of how he procured the baron's body for dissection et cetera et cetera!'

'Those are words he would have vehemently denied the minute we dragged him into a courtroom. I had no witnesses to back me up and Sir Richard would have supported Kingsley.'

'Then Sir Richard Allison is an even bigger rogue than I first thought!' the magistrate snapped. 'This is an outrageous situation! And my brother, the Reverend Conant, is one of the trustees at Guy's Hospital – this is a clear conflict of interests for us!'

For you, maybe. Good God! Did Conant have cronies everywhere?

'You were quite wrong to assure Sir Richard we would work for him on this ridiculous quest to find an imaginary poisoner,' Conant continued. 'In fact, you've approached this case from the wrong direction – you should have asked the baron if he wanted us to arrest those sinful doctors!'

Lavender gritted his teeth. 'I was unable to get an interview with the baron and Sir Richard has been of invaluable help to Bow Street over the past ten years. There's not a surgeon in London with his brilliance. No one else can read and understand the final moments of a murdered corpse like he can. We may not like his methods – but no one else gets such results.

'And more often than not,' he added, 'he assists us without payment. He likes the challenge – as I do.'

This made Conant think twice. He broke eye contact with his detective and picked up his broken quill.

'Your loyalty is admirable, Lavender – but misplaced. And I've loyalties of my own to consider. No doubt my brother will have to investigate this disgusting matter. No, our path is clear. Send a message to Sir Richard that you cannot take on this ridiculous quest, and continue to investigate the robbery at Beverley House et cetera et cetera.'

Lavender bit back the sharp retort that leapt to his lips – and decided to deal with the matter in his own way. If he had to investigate Sir Richard's mystery in his own time, then so be it. This was the best mystery to come his way for a year.

Conant pushed a copy of *The Times* across the desk towards him. 'I see the earl has already placed a reward for the recovery of the stolen jewels. That should bring forward some information soon.'

Lavender rolled his eyes and ignored the newspaper. 'I doubt those particular thieves and their cronies read *The Times,* but I'll spread the word about the reward to our usual sources.'

Conant waved his hand in the direction of the clerks at the far end of the room and pointed at their chief clerk. 'It's already done, Lavender. Mr Grey has already drafted out the information and dispatched it to every jeweller and pawn shop in London.'

'Oh, well in that case I'll continue my inquiries into the woman we believe was behind the robbery.' Lavender hesitated for a second, his eyes fixed on the clerks.

Was one of them the newspaper's spy?

Oswald Grey, Bow Street's chief clerk, was a tall pallid man with pale humourless eyes and a preference for drab clothes. Lavender had worked with him for years and, despite his dour nature, he would trust Grey with his life, his money *and* his family. The other, younger, man was new to the job and unknown to Lavender – as was Conant.

'It's such a shame the young viscount was victimised by these thieves,' he said. 'He's a military man, you know, and was a major in Lord Wellington's army during the Peninsular Wars.'

Conant looked up from his desk in surprise at this abrupt change in topic. 'I didn't know that.'

'Yes, the poor fellow was badly injured at the Battle of Salamanca – he lost part of his left leg and still suffers.' None of it was true, of course, but if someone in this room was passing information to *The Times,* they'd pounce on that kind of detail.

'The bottom half of his left leg is a wooden stump, which causes him to walk with an awkward gait. His fellow officers in the 95th Regiment have nicknamed him *Bandy-legged Beverley.*'

For one horrible second, Lavender thought he might have gone too far. But Conant merely blinked behind his spectacles. His beetle-black eyebrows didn't twitch. 'I would never have guessed you were so compassionate about our clients, Lavender. I'd heard you were a bit of a cold fish.'

Lavender just smiled and turned towards the door. 'It's Constable Woods' humanising influence.'

'By the way, if you see Constable Woods, tell him I'm not happy.'

Lavender stopped abruptly in his tracks. 'Why? What's the matter? I saw Ned last night and I understood his investigation had gone well.'

'In that case, you know more than me. His wife sent word that Woods was set upon by footpads last night. He's injured and unable to work.'

'Good God!'

75

'Yes, this is an embarrassment,' Conant said primly. 'Our officers are supposed to protect the public from attacks like this, not succumb to them. Let's hope news of this doesn't reach the ears of those newspaper reporters! I shall dock him a day's pay for this tardiness.'

Lavender clenched his fists, shoved them into his coat pockets and turned away before he exploded. But Conant hadn't finished with him yet. 'I dealt with your problem last night, Lavender.'

'What problem?'

'As promised, I saw my associate, John Stoddard, the editor of *The Times*, at our club. He'll print a retraction and an apology before the end of the week.'

'Stoddard was in London yesterday? I thought he'd driven out to Berkshire to see the owner?'

'No, he had meetings in London all day. You can thank me later. Now get about your business, Lavender, and find that jewel thief.'

Not before I've seen Ned, Lavender thought grimly.

Lavender let himself into Woods' house through the back yard and door. Ned was sitting at the kitchen table with a bandage wrapped around his head, wolfing down a bowl of leftover stew with a spoon.

Meanwhile, Betsy was at the sink, hurling dirty crockery into a bowl of water and scrubbing it with a fury that threatened to remove its pattern. 'He should still be in bed!' she yelled. 'For God's sake, talk some sense into him, Stephen!'

Lavender sank into the chair next to Ned and gasped in horror. One side of Ned's face was hideously inflamed, scraped raw in places and pitted with sores. It contrasted starkly with the exhausted pallor on the other side. 'Good God, Ned, what happened? You look like the devil ran over your face with horse nails in his boots.'

Woods grunted. 'I bashed my phizog on the damned path when I fell. It ain't as bad as it looks.' He touched his cheek tenderly, feeling at a back tooth. 'I've loosened one of me ivories, though – and lost my hat.'

'Who were they? What did they want?'

'They were after that body snatcher – Yardley. Disturbed him in this business, they did. I'd followed him and his lad to Cross Bones and were just about to arrest the pair of 'em when these thugs came out of nowhere. I were in the way, so they gave me a tap when they ran past.'

'A tap!' Betsy snapped. 'You should have seen the state of him when he were brought home, Stephen! He were out cold for hours until he were found at dawn by some seaman who were on his way to visit his ma's grave.'

'It were a warmish night,' Woods said. 'I fancied a nap.'

Betsy snorted and hurled a gravy jug into her bowl. 'You've also torn your coat.'

'Did you get a look at them?' Lavender asked.

Woods shook his head then grimaced with the pain. 'I'll find the buggers though – and give 'em as good as they gave me.'

'What about Yardley and his son?'

'The last thing I saw were them runnin' for their lives.'

'Don't you think you should go back to bed, Ned?'

'That's what I've been tellin' him for the past hour,' Betsy grumbled.

A grim expression of determination settled on Woods' damaged face. 'No. I'll finish the job. Betsy sent word to Conant that I ain't well, so I've got the rest of the day to find the Yardleys and those coves who chased them.'

'Damn Sir Richard's ruddy case!' Lavender said. 'You ought to put yourself first, Ned.'

'I'm doin' that, sir,' Woods replied firmly. 'No bugger knocks my ivories loose and makes me lose my hat. This case has just got personal.'

Chapter Ten

Nothing Lavender or Betsy said could persuade Woods to go back to bed. Lavender had no choice but to leave him and resume his own inquiries into the earl's stolen jewellery.

The last thing he needed in his present black mood was to spend a frustrating morning waiting beneath a crystal chandelier in an elegant drawing room for an aristocratic young buck to get out of bed. But members of the ton rarely rose before noon and their servants were reluctant to wake them, even though Lavender insisted it was a matter of extreme urgency.

His first visit was to the home of Sir Harry Lawson, where the thick Turkish carpet muffled the sound from the household and the street outside, and the incessant ticking of the ormolu clock on the mantelpiece irritated him beyond measure. He sat down wearily on a chintz-covered sofa and pulled out the copy of *The Times* handed to him by Conant.

The advert placed by the earl's steward about the reward for news of the stolen jewellery was informative and concise, but Lavender's attention was distracted by a dramatic piece on the next page:

PEER SAVED FROM BEING BURIED ALIVE!

The perils of excessive alcohol consumption were highlighted yesterday when young Baron P fell down in the street and, believed dead, with no discernible pulse, was brought by the kindness of a stranger to Guy's Hospital. The eminent surgeon Sir Richard Allison called for his stethoscope, a new invention of French doctor René Laënnec, and discovered a faint heartbeat. A short while later, the young man awoke and was dispatched safely back to his home and the loving bosom of his family. This paper can only assume the relief of his loved ones that the peer had risen from the dead before he was interred! And the skill and calm foresight of the surgeon must also be noted.

Lavender chuckled. He'd no doubt that the quill of Sir Richard Allison was behind this article. Would the other young doctors back up these lies? *Of course they would.*

The door opened and the bleary-eyed and unshaven Sir Harry Lawson was ushered into the room by the butler. The young man had dressed hastily and wore a crumpled white shirt, buttoned up incorrectly, a stained pair of breeches and only one slipper. Calling for coffee from the servant, he threw himself down into the seat opposite Lavender, smelling faintly of stale alcohol.

Sir Harry was shocked to hear about the robbery at Beverley House and the news seemed to jolt him awake. But when Lavender questioned him in more detail about Friday night, his eyes glazed over. He remembered very little and confessed to being in his cups for most of the evening. 'It was a belter of a night – such a shame it ended this way!'

Could he describe the actresses who'd accompanied them back from the theatre?

'No. Yes. Wait a minute – one was a plump miss with a bit of a scar on her lip. But I'm blowed if I can remember her name.' He scratched his head of unbrushed thick brown hair. 'It might have been Annie.'

Lavender kept his face expressionless and made a note. 'And the thin blonde actress called "Lou", whom the viscount thinks may have opened the strongbox and stolen the jewels? Do you remember her?'

Yes, Sir Harry vaguely remembered the woman swanning around the house in the countess's sparklers, but he was too busy drinking with Poppers to pay much attention.

'Do you and these other gentlemen often go out together at night?'

'Of course! We're the best of pals! Known each other since Eton and Cambridge.'

'Which college did you attend at Cambridge?'

'Magdalene. Why?'

'I was just curious. I studied law there for a brief while myself – but that would have been well before your time.'

'I should say so, Lavender!' Sir Harry exclaimed. 'What are you, sir, fifty?'

Lavender, who despite the greying hair around his temples was only thirty-six, decided to ignore that comment and move on. 'What about last Saturday night, the ninth? The day after your trip to the theatre and this robbery at Beverley House – were you with the others that night?'

Sir Harry looked surprised and screwed up his eyes and his forehead as he tried to remember. 'Yes, but no. Sort of. We intended to meet up to go to a dog fight – a rough affair in Southwark.' He grimaced at the memory. 'It was a mistake. But only Jonty and Cottingham were there. Poppers never arrived. The place was a hellhole with poor ale, so we left and came back to our club in Mayfair.'

So that was why the baron was south of river on the night the body snatcher brought him to Guy's Hospital.

'I say, there's no trouble with that damned dog fight, is there? If the fight was unlicensed, we didn't know about it.'

'No, I only asked because your friend Baron Poppleton had an adventure of his own on Saturday night.'

'What sort of an adventure?'

Lavender pushed his copy of *The Times* towards him. 'You can read about it in there. But before you do, can you tell me how you met these actresses? The ones you took back to Beverley House.'

'Yes, we met at the theatre after the show. We went to the stage door to pay our respects to Miss Divine, the star actress—'

Lavender's ears pricked up at the mention of April Divine. He'd helped the actress out a few years ago after the kidnapping and bizarre death of her twin sister.

'—but before we gained access, the gals turned up and we decided to go out for supper with them instead. It's damned hard to get to see Miss Divine these days – she's so popular, and the Marquess of Kirby pulls rank.'

Lavender's eyebrows twitched. He'd already heard rumours that the recently widowed marquess was besotted with April. The high society tattle sheets were rife with gossip about a possible match and undecided how to react. Actresses were rarely welcomed in their drawing rooms. But April was the daughter of the late and impoverished Baron Clare and because of her birth, she had as much right to enter high society as her marquess.

'Who introduced these women to you?'

Sir Harry frowned and scratched his head again. 'I believe they were friends of Jonty's.'

Lord Jonothan Furnish, otherwise known as 'Jonty', was also dishevelled and confused when he staggered into the anteroom at his family mansion to be interviewed by Lavender. A nervous young man with dark circles beneath his eyes and a dark floppy fringe, he was alarmed by the presence of a senior Bow Street officer in the house. He became defensive when Lavender mentioned the actresses.

'I'm betrothed to be married. It's a good match and she's a sweet young woman. I took myself off to bed on my own that night – I had nothing to do with those harlots! I say, you promise you won't tell the pater about this, will you? There'll be one hell of a fuss if he finds out.'

'The Earl of Beverley has already placed a reward notice in *The Times*,' Lavender warned him. 'The theft will soon become common knowledge. The best you can do is co-operate with me as much as you can.'

'Of course, of course!'

Lord Furnish proved a far better witness than Sir Harry. He remembered the thin blonde actress called Lou. 'She was the ringleader,' he said. 'Two of the others were brunettes and the plump one had the scar from a harelip operation. I think the fourth was a cute red-headed jilt called Caro – Poppers soon had her by his side. But she left long before the others – before we went to bed.'

Lavender nodded and made a note. This was better evidence. And it tallied with the butler's account that only three of the actresses had stayed at Beverley House overnight.

'So, I guess you were left with the second brunette,' Lavender said drily. 'What was her name?'

'Mary,' the lad said sheepishly. 'But I'm damned if I can remember much more about her. I didn't want female company that night and hardly paid her any attention.'

'What else can you tell me about the women?'

'They seemed easy in each other's company – as if they knew each other well. Oh, and one of them called the brunette with the harelip *Annie Southerby*. She'd slid on to Harry's knee and spilled his claret. "You naughty girl, Annie Southerby!" one of the other gals teased.'

'So how did you meet these women?' Lavender asked. 'Who introduced you to them?'

Jonty thought for a while then shook his head. 'Damned if I can remember, Lavender – I was foxed. But I think it was Poppers.'

Chapter Eleven

The squalid nature of Water Lane Backs didn't improve with the daylight. The overhanging upper casements of the smoke-blackened and dilapidated buildings blocked out most of the weak sunlight. It gave the narrow thoroughfare an oppressive sense of gloom. The gutters spilled over with garbage and filth. Barefoot children crouched beside them looking for playthings, while two emaciated dogs scrapped with each other for morsels.

Before Woods had left home, Betsy had given him a spoon of the laudanum she'd saved from when he'd been shot in the shoulder. 'If yer determined to go, you'd better take this – you stubborn cork-brained fool. Only one spoon, mind you.'

Delighted, Woods thanked her – then surreptitiously pocketed the rest of the bottle while her back was turned.

The opium was working. Woods smiled and touched his hat politely as he passed a young mother sitting on a doorstep nursing a wailing baby swaddled in rags. He side-stepped a gang of suspicious youths greasing the walls of the street with their backs, and strode confidently towards the body snatcher's home. He felt light-headed rather than sore-headed.

Yardley's woman shrieked when she opened the door and saw his bruised and bloodied face and bandaged head. 'I told you last night 'e ain't 'ere!' she yelled.

'Aye, well, you lied to me last night – so mindin' yer pardon, I'll tek a look for myself.'

She tried to slam the door in his face.

But Woods was ready for her this time. He shoved his meaty foot into the gap, took hold of the warped, flimsy door and forced it back. It creaked and the wood began to splinter. He knew if she didn't let go soon it would snap off its hinges or crumble in his hands.

But she put up a good fight. 'What do yer want?' she screeched.

Woods hesitated for a second. This wasn't the time to mention that he was a police officer or that he knew her husband was a body snatcher. A brilliant idea flashed through his old noggin. 'I don't mean you and yer little nippers no harm, missus. I need to talk to you. I know somethin' to yer advantage.'

The woman relinquished her hold on the door and ran back into the room towards her small, undernourished and terrified children. They gathered around her skirts in alarm.

The stinking room, with its crumbling plaster walls and mould, was cluttered with mattresses and filthy bedding. Two battered chairs and a trunk were the only other furniture, besides a few cooking utensils. A meagre fire flickered in the hearth. It filled the room with a lot of smoke and very little heat. A line of damp laundry ran over his head. Unless Yardley and his skinny lad had squeezed themselves up the soot-blackened chimney, they weren't there.

'Like I said, missus, I don't mean you no harm. I came last night and again today because I've been asked to give you some good news.'

'S'cuse me if I don't ask you to sit down,' she hissed.

Woods shrugged. He wouldn't have sat down anyway. God alone knew what was crawling through those chairs.

Woods tried a different tack to put her at ease. He smiled down at the three filthy little faces staring up at him. All the children were drowning in oversized cast-off clothes, barely better than rags. 'What a lovely family you have, missus.'

'Well, what's this good news yer 'ave fer us?'

'I've come from a man named Baron Poppleton. The other night your man Yardley did him a huge service. He found the baron unconscious in the street and took him to Guy's Hospital for help. There, the baron made strong recovery. He wants me to thank Yardley and reward him.'

Woods paused and grinned at her in his friendliest manner, unaware that with the bloodied scraping and swelling it added to its grotesque appearance, rather than enhanced his looks.

The woman stared at him in disbelief – and mute horror.

'That were kind of pa,' said one of the little girls, 'it were kind of 'im to help that fella.'

'Aye, it were, Treacle.' Woods nodded at the filthy-faced child. 'And good deeds like that need to be rewarded, don't you think?'

'Well, give us the chinks.' The woman held out her hand.

Woods jangled the coins in his coat pocket; he knew the sound would tantalise her. 'I would do – but I've been told to give the reward to Mr Yardley *himself* – along with the baron's thanks. Do you know when he'll be back?'

'No.'

'Da and our Georgie didn't come 'ome last night,' the girl said. Her mother scowled and told her to be quiet.

A sense of foreboding washed over Woods. If those thugs had caught up with Yardley and his son last night and done them harm, this family would starve. Yes, Yardley's trade was despicable, but these little nippers were innocents. 'Are you worried about them?' he asked gently.

She nodded her head. 'Bert ain't been well. 'Is guts have bin bad...' Her voice trailed away.

Sighing, Woods reached into his pocket for a shilling and tossed it across to the girl. 'Catch this, Treacle!'

The surprised child dropped the coin and all three children fell to the floor to grab it.

'I'll leave this on account,' he said as he turned to leave. 'I'll come back later to see if Yardley has returned.'

Woods headed out of the slums and, conscious of a burning thirst, strode towards a quiet and respectable tavern for a pint of ale and a slice of meat and potato pie. His head was throbbing again, so he took another swig from the bottle of laudanum.

It was good stuff, this opium. Within minutes he felt better and decided to carry on. There was no point in losing a day's pay when you felt this good. In fact, when a fellow drinker at the tavern struck up a popular jaunty song on his fiddle, Woods bellowed out the words in his rich, melodious bass voice.

The landlord and the other customers were delighted with his rendition, and soon a crowd had gathered. 'Yer one of them runners from Bow Street, ain't you?' the chap asked.

Woods nodded as he set down some coins on the table.

'Oh, don't leave!' the landlord begged. 'Give us another song!' He turned to the rest of his customers. 'Who'd like to 'ear another ditty from the singing policeman?'

The customers cheered at the notion, but Woods smiled, shook his head and moved towards the door. 'I've me duty to perform.'

His next stop was back at the estate office of Sir Bernard Davies, Bart., where he was ushered into the office of the corpulent Mr Edwin. Today, the manager wore a coat of vivid sapphire blue with a matching waistcoat strained over his great belly and the shiniest silver buttons Woods had ever seen.

In fact, he could barely look at the man because of the gleam coming from those damned buttons. It was an odd thing but they scorched his eyes.

Edwin's fat fingers pushed three sheets of paper across the desk towards him. 'I've done what you asked, officer, and made up a list of our tenants who hold a grudge against us.'

Woods' bushy grey eyebrows rose in surprise at the length of the list, and he let out an involuntary whistle. The names covered three sheets of paper. At least, he thought they did. His eyes weren't focusing properly, and he couldn't read any of them.

Edwin frowned. 'Is something wrong, officer? Why are you squinting?'

'You said Sir Bernard were a decent landlord,' Woods complained. 'I weren't expectin' there to be so many folks with a grievance against him!'

Edwin's plump lips tightened with disapproval. 'I've also included a list of those tenants who are in arrears and have been threatened with eviction and the bailiffs.'

Woods nodded sagely and put the list down on his lap. 'Ah, that explains it – an excellent thought, Mr Edwin. 'Tis most unjust when folks don't pay what they owe. Tell Sir Bernard he has my sympathy. Now, tell me the truth, is there a man named Garbutt on this list?'

Edwin's surprise was genuine. 'Yes! At the top of the list of debtors on page three. He owes the estate hundreds for the rent of his house on Soho Square.'

Woods banged the desk with his fist in delight, making the lids of the inkwells rattle. 'Then we have him, sir! Once more this heinous rogue shall stand in the dock and face British justice.'

'Was it Garbutt who wrote that scurrilous pamphlet about Sir Bernard?'

'Indeed it was, sir. I found other evidence incriminatin' the cove yesterday. He's a most litigious gentleman, allus fallin' out with someone or other and draggin' 'em through the chancery court. He even took on the government, you know?'

'Good grief!'

'He has reduced great and honest men to tears with his libellous lies. Sir Bernard has my condolences. We'll have him under the hatches before sundown,' Woods promised, completely forgetting, in his drug-induced euphoria, that he needed a warrant from Conant first.

Edwin was swept up in Woods' enthusiasm; his eyes gleamed. 'This is most impressive, sir! But you'd better move quickly for the arrest, officer. I sent the bailiffs around to his house today.'

'You've sent round the shoulder-clappers?'

'Yes, and if we don't get some payment on account soon, I plan to evict him next week.'

Woods stood up to leave – and staggered slightly.

'Oh, just one thing, officer,' Edwin called out as Woods reached the door. 'Just remember that in the agreement we signed, this estate doesn't have to pay Bow Street unless there's a conviction.'

'Don't you worry your head about that, sir. You've got the best principal officer in London on the case. I'll arrest him now.'

Woods held back his giggle until he was outside in the street. *That last bit weren't true, of course. Everyone in London knows* Lavender *is the best.*

But it felt good to say it.

As Woods approached Soho Square, he struggled to put one foot in front of the other and wished he'd flagged down a hackney carriage. Betsy's dire warnings about his injury flashed through his head and dampened his good mood. And his euphoric bubble was further deflated when he turned into Soho Square and suddenly remembered he was supposed to get an arrest warrant *before* he approached Garbutt.

But it was the strange scene being enacted at the entrance to Garbutt's home that brought him back down to earth.

Two women were engaged in an argument with a couple of rough-looking men on the doorstep. A crowd of tradesmen, pedestrians and nursemaids with perambulators had gathered to watch the commotion.

Curious, Woods moved closer and leaned against the railings at the back of the crowd.

The two men, one tall, one short – but both ugly-looking brutes – had fists like hams. They were the bailiffs Edwin had sent. They were trying to gain entry to the house to take goods in lieu of some of the outstanding rent.

The women were both thin, angular, dowdily dressed and in their early thirties. They were mounting a spirited defence of the property. Listening to their firm but gentle voices, Woods had the impression they'd done this before.

'No, I've told you – you can't come in,' said one of the women. The soft skin of her face was lined with strain and her hair was prematurely silvered with grey streaks. 'Our father is out – and we don't know when he'll return.'

The short bailiff leered and waved a piece of paper in her face. 'Now listen 'ere, you 'atchet-faced tabby! We don't need to see Garbutt. This gives us the right to enter and take what's owed!'

'Absolutely not,' she replied. 'No one enters unless Papa is here.'

'You should tell your client,' her sister added, 'that payment will soon be forthcoming. One of Papa's cases is up in the court of chancery next week and we expect a favourable judgement. Please ask your client to be patient.'

''E's already waited three months for payment!' the tall bailiff snarled, red-faced with anger.

'Then a little longer won't hurt him.'

'Move – you damned mopsey! Or *I'll* shift your skinny arse!'

Woods growled: a deep throaty growl that made a nursemaid in the crowd turn round in alarm and clutch her small child tighter.

Woods knew this wasn't his business, but he wasn't prepared to stand by idly and watch these bum-bailiffs manhandle the gals.

The shorter man moved forward but fell back in surprise when one of the women suddenly produced a broom from behind her back.

Whether she planned to beat the bailiff over the head with it or jam it across the doorway in a feeble attempt to bar his way, Woods neither knew nor cared. He stepped forward. 'Enough! Stop this now!'

'Who the devil might you be?' snarled one of the bailiffs. His breath reeked of onions.

'Detective Ned Woods from Bow Street Magistrates' Court.'

A ripple of surprise went around the gathered crowd and the man in front of him scowled 'A runner, eh?'

'Aye, I were just passin' and I saw you threaten this gal. You need to stand down and come back when their da is here. Your business is with him – not these gals.'

'*Stand down!*' the bailiff laughed. 'Have you seen the state of yoursen, fella? You gonna mek us, are you? It looks like some cove 'as already done for you!'

Woods' voice dropped to his deepest and most menacing growl. 'Aye, but you should have seen the state of the other fella when I left him.'

There was something in the gleam in Woods' glaring eyes that made the man step back.

'Now look 'ere, Detective!' the other bailiff blustered. 'We 'ave every right—'

'And I've every right to clap you in irons for disturbin' the peace and threatening young gals! What's it goin' to be?' He pulled out a pair of handcuffs from his pocket.

Swearing, the two thugs turned and strode away.

'Oh, Detective! Thank you so much for your intervention!' Miss Garbutt was shaking with relief. Her younger sister looked close to tears. 'I'm not sure we could have held them off for much longer.'

Woods lowered his voice, one eye still on the retreating bailiffs. 'They might come back, Treacle, when they think I've gone. Don't answer the door until your da gets back. When are you expectin' him?'

The younger woman broke down sobbing. Her sister put a comforting arm around her. 'Would you step inside a moment, please, Detective? I need to speak to you,' she said.

Frowning, Woods hesitated. He'd done his bit to help the gals but if Garbutt wasn't there, then his business here was done. Besides which, he felt rather queasy and had a yearning for his bed.

'Please?'

Sighing, he wiped away the rivers of sweat on his brow and followed the two women into the house and a sparsely furnished drawing room.

One glance at the interior of this once elegant house told Woods the bailiffs would have been sorely disappointed if they'd gained access. The place was falling down and, by the look of things, anything of value had already been sold. There was no carpet in the room and only a few sticks of cheap furniture.

The faded silk wallpaper was peeling away from the wall and there'd obviously been a bad leak at some point, which had brought down much of the ornate plasterwork off the ceiling and left a large patch of black mould. No attempt had been made to repair the damage. Some rectangular sections of the wallpaper weren't as faded as the rest, indicating the walls were once covered with fine oil paintings that the Garbutts had now sold or pawned.

There were a couple of uncomfortable-looking chairs in front of the fireplace. Without waiting to be asked, Woods sank down in one of them. His legs were in danger of collapsing under him.

'I'm Miss Emily Garbutt,' the older sibling said. 'This is my sister, Jane.'

The younger woman made a valiant effort to stop crying, pulled out a handkerchief and wiped her eyes.

'Go to the dining room, Jane, and get a brandy to steady your nerves,' Emily said. 'I'll tell the detective what's happened.'

The younger woman nodded and left the room.

'What's the matter?' Woods asked.

'We don't know where our father is. He went out last night – about half past eight – and hasn't come home.'

Woods took in a sharp breath. *Has Garbutt learned of his impending arrest? Has he done a runner?* No, this was a crazy notion. He'd only decided thirty minutes ago to arrest the man.

Why am I having crazy thoughts?

'Is this normal? Has Mr Garbutt stayed out before?'

'No! Father always comes home for his supper. And he's a most caring man – a doting father. If he's going to be late, he always lets us know.'

'Could he be stayin' with friends?"

A look of intense sadness travelled across the woman's face. 'My father doesn't have any friends, Detective. A few years ago, he was convicted of libel and sent to Newgate.' She waved her hand and pointed to their shabby, dilapidated surroundings. 'We're nearly penniless, and all his friends have deserted him.' Then her eyes lit up and she added, 'But he has a case in the court of chancery next week and hopes for a favourable judgement.'

Woods rolled his eyes. Obviously, Garbutt had fed false hopes to his trusting daughters. Court cases in chancery often dragged on for years. 'Where did he go last night?'

She shook her head sadly. 'I'm afraid I don't know. He said he would be out for an hour on some business. He often visits his lawyer or his printer in the early evening. But he hasn't come back. Please try to find him for us, Detective.'

Woods hesitated. He was employed to arrest the damned man – not do his family a service. Besides which, he was desperate to find a hackney carriage and get his aching old bones back home. But he felt the distress of these two gentle and vulnerable women and a worrying thought niggled in his aching head: a man with as many enemies as Garbutt might be the victim of foul play.

He nodded and staggered to his feet. 'We'll have to give it another night, I'm afraid, Miss Garbutt – to make sure your da is definitely missin'. If he ain't returned home by tomorrow mornin', send word to Detective Woods at Bow Street.'

Chapter Twelve

As Lavender strode towards Bedford Street to interview Baron Poppleton about the Beverley House jewellery theft, he hoped the young man had recovered from his ordeal at Guy's Hospital – because he had no intention of being turned away for a second time.

To Lavender's relief, he was granted an audience with Poppleton almost immediately. Unlike his pals, the baron was already up and dressed, and sitting in the gloomy library at the rear of the ground floor. He wore a lawn shirt beneath a blue silk waistcoat that matched the colour of his cornflower-blue eyes.

The windows were partially obscured by thick brown drapes. Towering oak bookcases lined three of the walls; they and the shelves of dusty old tomes made the room claustrophobic. But the broad smile on the handsome young man's face lifted some of the oppressive atmosphere.

He left his desk and strode, smiling, across the carpet to shake Lavender's hand, 'Ah, Detective, two visits in two days. This is excellent service for the sake of a lost pair of pantaloons.' He indicated for Lavender to sit down in the old leather chair opposite the desk. Like the rest of old Lady Barlborough's furniture, it belonged to a distant century.

'I'm not here about your pantaloons – and I wasn't here about them yesterday. I've sought an audience for two entirely different matters. However, if you've a fondness for the garment, I can inform you it's in the possession of the man who took you to Guy's Hospital. But both this man and your pantaloons are currently evading capture.'

Poppleton threw back his blond head and laughed. He tapped the copy of *The Times* lying on his desk. 'I assume this is the same kind gentleman who saved my life by seeking medical help for me when I was unconscious?'

'It is the same man, yes.'

'Then I think I'll stop grieving for my pantaloons and let this good Samaritan have them. His need is obviously greater than mine.'

'I'm delighted to see you looking so well after your recent ordeal, Sir Humphrey – and in such a positive frame of mind.'

'But why are you here, Detective?'

'There are two matters I wish to discuss. Firstly, while you were perusing *The Times* this morning, did you happen to see a reward notice placed by the Earl of Beverley for some stolen jewels?'

'Yes. That's a rum deal. I like Frank's mother and feel for her loss – I know those baubles had sentimental value for her. How did it happen?'

'The robbery took place last Friday evening – when you, Sir Harry Lawson and Lord Furnish went back to Beverley House with a party of actresses.'

'Good grief!' Distress – or was it alarm? – flashed across the baron's face.

'The earl has employed my services to get to the bottom of this theft.' He told Poppleton what he knew about the theft of the jewels by the actresses.

'Dear God! Poor Frank! No doubt his pater is furious – he'll stop his allowance and clip his wings for a while. Probably stop paying for his club membership too, I shouldn't wonder.'

'The earl knows I planned to speak to you. I've already spoken to Lord Jonothan Furnish and Sir Harry. They've been very helpful and given me a rough description of the four actresses, but I hoped you may be able to provide more information.'

Poppleton shook his head and sat back in his chair. 'I'll be blessed if I can, Lavender! Sorry, but I was foxed that night. As my sister has pointed out many times, I drink far too much. I can't remember a blessed thing after we arrived back at Beverley House!'

'Well, let's try, shall we?' Lavender went through the events of the evening, but the baron had little to add to the information the others had already given him.

'What about the red-headed actress?' he asked in frustration. 'I understand you spent more time with her than the others.'

'Ah, yes. Young Caro. Well, I remember dandling her on my knee a while,' the young man said, laughing, 'but she was the first to leave. I was disappointed about that. She had a mop of tight red ringlets.'

'Was her name an abbreviation of Caroline?' Lavender asked.

Poppleton just shrugged.

'What else do you remember about her?'

'Not a lot, I'm afraid, Lavender – but yes, wait a minute, I *do* remember something. She had a big nose. Too large for her face. I don't think she'll ever land a leading role at the theatre with a conk like that. In fact' – he grimaced in mock horror – 'I may have blurted out something along those lines.' He slapped his forehead in frustration. 'Damn me! That's probably why the jilt ran off! I'm not always tactful when I'm in my cups.'

'How did you meet these women? Who invited them to join you and your friends?'

''Er… I think it was Cottingham. Look, I'm sorry I can't be more helpful. Lottie's always telling me I'm a hopeless case when I've had a drink – or three. But I do understand the seriousness of this situation. I'm accustomed to responsibility.' He waved his hand over the scattered papers on the desk. 'Unlike my friends, who are still hovering in the shadows of their capable fathers, I'm an orphan with an estate to manage.'

Lavender frowned, confused. 'I thought you'd sold your estate in Cambridgeshire?'

The young man shook his head. 'I didn't mean Netheredge, the Poppleton estate. That *was* sold. What I meant is I manage the affairs of my aunt, Lady Barlborough. She's an invalid and is happy to let me deal with her affairs.'

'She's most fortunate to have your assistance.'

'Well, to be honest, Lavender, she demands her pound of flesh. But it's the least I can do after her kindness towards Lottie and me. We didn't know Aunt Barlborough when we were growing up – there'd been a rift between her and my mother. But after my father's death – when we were destitute – the old lady opened her doors and welcomed us into her home.'

'How long have you lived with Lady Barlborough?'

'About a year.'

Lavender was impressed by the young man's candour. His straightforward honesty made the next part of his interview easier. 'Were you drunk again the following night, when you were found unconscious and taken to Guy's Hospital?'

The baron sighed. 'I think I must have been! I can't remember much about it.' He tapped the newspaper in front of him. 'It seems that someone thinks I was bushed. I take it you've read his article, Lavender? Did Sir Richard write it?'

'I think he did. I understand you were angry with him yesterday when you woke up at Guy's Hospital.'

The young man's face flashed with anger. 'Wouldn't you be? He was leering down at me like a demon with a blade poised over my chest!'

Then he laughed and waved a dismissive hand in the air. 'I was a bit upset at the time and *might* have imagined that. I've calmed down now. There's no harm done. My sister and aunt were a bit put out when I didn't come home for two nights. But I'm still in one piece – and in fact, I'm a bit mortified about the fuss I've caused.'

Lavender sat back, relieved by this unexpected turn of events. 'Then you don't intend to pursue Sir Richard in the courts?'

Poppleton shook his head. 'No doubt my friends will rib me for years about my resurrection and I'll be known as the peer who came back from the dead. But there's no point in stoking the flames of gossip, is there, Lavender?'

Sir Richard would be pleased with this news, Lavender realised. *But will he still want me to investigate the mystery now he isn't threatened?* Before the thought had even entered his mind, Lavender knew the answer. The surgeon smelled a mystery and the man was as obsessive as himself about solving them.

Sighing, he picked up his pencil again. 'What *do* you remember about Saturday night?'

Poppleton frowned and ran his fingers through his thick head of wavy blond hair. 'I dined with my sister and left for Southwark to meet Jonty, Cottingham and Harry at a dog fight. It was a pleasant evening, so I decided to walk.'

Lavender raised an eyebrow. 'That part of town can be rough and dangerous.'

The baron's grin returned. 'I can look after myself, Lavender. I box and I fence. In fact, yes, I remember now – I wanted to sober up a bit before I met the others. That's why I walked.'

'What happened next?'

'Well, that's the rub of it… I don't know. I cast up my accounts at the edge of the bridge and I seemed to lose my way. I found myself in a short street I didn't recognise. It had broken cobbles and a foul stink. Water dripped down the walls.'

He was disorientated, Lavender thought. *Maybe Sir Richard was right? This sounded like poison.*

'I was exhausted and wanted to vomit again. There was an old bench next to a church graveyard. My legs were about to give way, so I sat down for a bit.' He broke off, shrugged and threw up his hands in a gesture of helplessness. 'The next thing I knew, I woke up and saw Sir Richard and his blade.'

'How much did you drink with your meal?'

'Well, I'll have to ask Feathers, our footman. But I remember it was a decent claret and I had several glasses. My aunt keeps a good cellar. Lottie hardly touches the stuff. I suppose I might have mopped up a full bottle.'

'Who else dined with you and what did you eat?'

Confusion flicked across Poppleton's face. 'Just my sister. We had lamb, I think. Aunt Barlborough eats alone in her room.'

'Did you all eat the lamb and were either of the two ladies ill that night?'

Poppleton frowned. 'No. I don't think so. What is this about, Lavender?'

'I saw Sir Richard yesterday and he's worried you might have been poisoned. He wants me to investigate the case – for your own safety.'

'Strewth, Lavender! That's ridiculous!' He grabbed the newspaper and waved it in Lavender's face. 'He authorised *The Times* to tell the world it was the demon drink that was at fault!'

'He did that to give the poisoner a false sense of security. To let him – or her – think they'd got away with it, while I tracked them down.' None of this was true, of course. Sir Richard had published that account to save his own skin. But this was the best explanation Lavender could come up with on the spur of the moment.

'I appreciate this is confusing,' he continued. 'But I've worked with Sir Richard for years. He's a brilliant physician. The fact you were unconscious for so long is unnatural *and* worrying. He's convinced you imbibed some form of rare poison.'

Poppleton stared at him, angry and dumbfounded in his disbelief.

'For your own sake – and for that of your family – you need to think carefully about everything you ate or drank on Saturday – and try to remember anything unusual that you found. Did you touch an unusual plant, for example? The natural world is full of poisons – many haven't even been identified yet.'

'Stop!' The baron held up his hand in alarm. 'Stop this *now*. This is nonsense! Yes, I'm baffled about why I was out for the count for so long – but no one tried to poison me! I was drunk and passed out, for God's sake!'

'Not according to Sir Richard Allison.'

'This can't be happening!'

Lavender fell silent for a moment. Poppleton's face was twisted with shock as he struggled to digest this unwelcome information. 'I'm sorry to be the bearer of such alarming news, Sir Humphrey,' he resumed. 'I understand if you may want some time to think about it. I can always come back later.'

'*Think* about it? No, damn it, Lavender! I don't want to think about it! I want to *forget* it! I can't believe you and this surgeon have cooked up such a ridiculous tale between yourselves!'

Lavender leaned forward. 'Sir Humphrey, do you have any enemies? Anyone who might want you dead?'

He expected the baron to explode in a torrent of denials and abuse, but the young man paused with his mouth open instead. Emotion flashed across those cornflower-blue eyes – and this time Lavender knew it was fear.

There was a knock on the door and a tall, stooped female servant entered. Her thin dark hair was shot through with silver, her complexion sallow. But the most distracting part of her appearance was her large nose and the huge hairy wart on it.

Poppleton grinned. 'Ah, the beauteous Effy. Do you not think my aunt's nurse is one of the most divine women you've ever seen, Lavender?'

Lavender stiffened with embarrassment. Is this what Poppleton did when he was upset? Take out his anger on the servants? 'I'm sure Miss Effy is a competent nurse.'

The woman ignored Lavender and lowered her eyes to hide her reaction to the baron's cruel sarcasm. 'Please excuse the interruption, sir – but Lady Barlborough wishes to speak with you.' Her voice was flat, unemotional.

Poppleton recovered rapidly. 'Thank you, Effy. I'll come now.'

The woman nodded and left the room.

Lavender stood up to leave. 'Once you've had time to think this through, please get in touch.'

'All I want from you right now, Lavender, is for you to get the hell out of my home.'

Lavender ignored his rudeness. 'Be careful, Sir Humphrey – and keep an eye out for trouble and anything unusual. If this poisoning was a malicious attempt on your life – then the poisoner might try again. In that case, your aunt and your sister are also at risk.'

Chapter Thirteen

There was already a crowd of young bucks lounging around the stage door of the Sans Pareil Theatre when Lavender arrived. Most clutched posies of hot-house blooms that they hoped to deliver to the actresses. A burly porter, resplendent in the green and gold livery of the theatre, guarded the door and denied everyone entrance. 'Miss Divine is busy. She's in tonight's performance. She's not seein' no one today,' he told Lavender.

'Aye, you can wait your turn!' one the young bucks said.

Lavender pulled out his tipstaff, his badge of office, and held it aloft. 'I'm Detective Stephen Lavender from Bow Street – an old friend of Miss Divine's and her family. She'll see me.'

'Well, make sure you arrest the marquess while yer in there,' one of the young men quipped, 'and give us a better chance with the lady!' The others laughed and agreed with him.

The porter led Lavender through the dark maze of narrow passages towards the actress's dressing room. The Sans Pareil was famed for its spacious auditorium, with its plush red seats and its glittering chandeliers. But there was no gilt or glamour backstage. It smelled of fresh sawdust, tallow candles, greasepaint and body odour. At one point they had to turn sideways to squeeze past two scenery flats leaning against the grubby wall of the corridor.

However, April's dressing room was both opulent and comfortable – as befitting the private domain of the theatre's leading lady. It smelled of expensive perfume. Apart from the rails of brightly coloured costumes, there were two plush armchairs and a Chinese screen draped with shawls, and at least three large mirrors reflected the light from the small windows high in the wall.

When Lavender arrived, April was at the cluttered dressing table, applying stage make-up to her pretty oval face. She wore a plain cotton housecoat over her garish stage costume to protect it from her paints and powders. Her raven hair tumbled over her shoulders.

She put down her brushes, rose gracefully and held out her elegant hand. 'Lavender! How wonderful to see you again! But I do hope you haven't come to arrest me – I'm due on stage in thirty minutes!'

The first time Lavender saw April, she was strained and saddened by the kidnapping and death of her twin sister. In the interim years, she had bloomed. The young woman before him was at the peak of her career and the height of her beauty.

He bowed over her hand. 'It's a pleasure to see you again, Miss Clare – sorry, Miss Divine—'

'Oh, do call me April, Lavender.'

'You look well. I understand your career is flourishing. Your stepmother, Lady Caroline, keeps Magdalena and me informed of your continued success!'

'And I understand *you* now have a baby son! Congratulations! How delighted you all must be.'

'Yes, we're overjoyed with Baby Jack – tired, but overjoyed. He's a wonderful blessing.'

She laughed. 'Gosh, yes! Babies are *quite* exhausting!' Have you come to see tonight's performance?'

'I'm afraid not. I'm here on a work matter. But when Magdalena is fully recovered, we'll come again and watch you perform.'

Satisfied with his response, April sat back down on her stool and picked up her hairbrush. 'Now, what's amiss, Lavender? I do hope you haven't come to tell me my stepmother has caused an international scandal in Lisbon?'

Lavender smiled. 'No, as far as Magdalena and I know from her letters, Lady Caroline is enjoying herself decorously in Portugal.'

'I suppose there's a first time for everything!' April quipped, laughing. 'Mind you, I imagine Captain Sawyer knows how to handle her – although sometimes I think he's just as outrageous.'

Lavender's smile broadened. He and Magdalena had been quite surprised when they'd first met their friend's latest beau. Sawyer was a bushy-whiskered one-legged naval captain with a booming voice and jovial personality. Twice widowed, Lady Caroline was notorious in London circles for her choice of youthful consorts – but not this time. Captain Sawyer was older than her – and at least thirty years older than her last two consorts.

As if following his thoughts, April asked, 'Have you any idea what attracted her to him? I asked her once if the attraction was anything to do with the fact they both have damaged legs. I observed they limp and hop along at the same slow pace. I wondered if that was convivial?'

Lavender laughed. 'How did she respond?'

'She slapped me with her fan and told me I was a cheeky girl.'

'I think she finds him funny,' Lavender suggested kindly. 'He makes her laugh.'

April began to brush her long glossy hair. 'Now, what is this business you wish to discuss with me?'

'Did you hear about the robbery at the Earl of Beverley's house last Friday?'

April shook her head and Lavender explained what had happened.

'There's a connection with this theatre. Beverley's son, the Viscount Cottingham and his friends, met the four actresses here, at the stage door. I hope you might help me identify them.' He passed on the vague descriptions of the women given to him by the four young men.

April frowned, her hairbrush idle in her hands. 'This won't enhance the reputation of the Sans Pareil if it becomes common knowledge. And that's unfair – because none of those women are part of this acting company.'

Lavender's heart sank. 'Are you sure?'

'Absolutely. There were only four actresses on stage last Friday: myself, our Italian actress, Miss Helena Bologna, and the O'Keefe sisters. I happen to know Helena went off for a tryst with her latest lover that night and the O'Keefe girls went to supper with Miss Jane Scott, our proprietor.'

Lavender nodded. He didn't know these sisters but had met Helena Bologna and her sultry beauty didn't match the descriptions he'd been given by the young men. Besides which, she was too well known in London and the young peers would have recognised her. 'What about the other women in your company?'

She shook her head. 'Those descriptions don't fit. Did any of these foolish young men know these women before they latched on to them and took them home?'

Lavender sighed. 'I don't think so. They all think one of the others knew them and introduced them to the group. They were drunk.'

April turned back to her mirror and raised her hairbrush. 'This is a wild thought, Lavender. But it's quite common to find a gaggle of Covent Garden nuns loitering around the stage door, trying to attract the attention of the men who wait there.'

'Common prostitutes?' Lavender grimaced at the thought.

'The whores know these foolish men are rich, drunk and desperate for female company.'

'I find it hard to believe Cottingham and the others would be so undiscerning.'

April shrugged. 'According to my friend the Marquess of Kirby, the Earl of Beverley's had a lot of trouble with his son. The boy likes running with a common crowd.'

Lavender frowned and remembered the seedy dog-racing event the young men had attended in Southwark. Did they enjoy wallowing in the dirty and dangerous underbelly of the capital? And was cavorting with whores part of their degeneration?

April saw his scowl in the mirror and laughed. 'Some of these jilts can be quite clever,' she added. 'Their pimps make sure they dress well – sometimes smart costumes are hired for the evening. And of course, some of them have been actresses in the past but are now struggling to get employment in the theatre. Sadly, many untalented young women from the theatre fall into prostitution.'

Lavender rose to leave. 'You've been very helpful, April, and I know you're busy. But please can you ask around among your fellow actors? If you hear anything else about this group of women, please contact me – either at home or at Bow Street.'

'One last thing, Lavender, before you go.' She held up a Grecian-styled black wig that had lain on the dressing table among the pots of cream and rouge, discarded stage jewellery and an assortment of fans. 'All actresses are skilled at disguising themselves, with false hair pieces, greasepaint and patches. Some pad out their cheeks with orange peel. They know how to change the shape of their features with artifice.'

'Thank you, I'll bear that in mind.' He hesitated by the door. 'And this "friend" of yours – the marquess. Does he treat you well?'

Her face dissolved into the most natural and radiant smile. 'Very well. He is *very* attentive. In fact, he'll be in the audience tonight – again.'

'Take care of yourself, April.'

Her smile broadened. 'You've no need to be so protective, Lavender. This is my world – and I understand how it works. I've taken good care of myself for years.'

He smiled, recognising the truth in that. Bowing, he took his leave. 'I wish you all the best, April.'

But when he walked out into the chilly March air of the street, his frown returned. His case was no further forward. In fact, it had just become devilishly more complicated. It crossed his mind that the theft of the Beverley jewellery wasn't a random, opportunistic event.

He had a horrible suspicion the young peers had been deliberately targeted by a professional gang of thieves.

Lavender called in to see Woods before he went home for supper but only managed to get a few words with Betsy.

Red-faced with anger, she slapped a loaf of bread on the board and attacked it with her bread knife in a way that made Lavender wince. Her four children were sitting quietly at the kitchen table; they knew better than to speak or move when their diminutive mother was in one of her moods.

She told him Ned had come home in a hackney a few hours before and had taken himself back to his bed. 'He stole my bottle of laudanum, Stephen! And the muttonhead drank nearly all of it!'

'Oh dear.'

'He's been wandering around like a drunkard, singing in public.'

'Oh... well, Ned has a wonderful bass singing voice. They'll have enjoyed it.'

'He's told most of London he's the best detective in town!'

Lavender smiled. 'Possibly... he'll be fine in the morning, Betsy. Ned has a strong constitution.'

'It won't do, Stephen. If this comes to the ears of Magistrate Conant, there'll be trouble. Ned knows that weasel has set him a test.'

'If Conant gets to hear about it, Ned can just deny it,' he soothed.

But Betsy wasn't in the mood to listen. 'And what was it all for, I ask you? He didn't find that body snatcher – or that Garbutt fella either. He's made a cake of himself for nothing!'

Before Stephen could reply, there was a sharp knock at the back door. Betsy made to wipe her hands on her apron, but Lavender shook his head. 'I'll answer it.'

It was an elderly whiskered fellow, swathed in a thick coat and scarves and carrying the staff of a night watchman. 'Is Constable Woods 'ere? I'm Adams. I've news for 'im about the fella 'e were lookin' for.'

'He's busy at the minute, but can I help? I'm Detective Stephen Lavender. We work together.'

The old man nodded, coughed and wiped his nose with the back of his dirty sleeve. 'Aye, I reckon so. Tell 'im I've found Yardley dead on the river mud beneath one of the jetties.'

Lavender gasped. 'And the boy? His son. Is the boy all right?'

The old man coughed again and shook his grizzled head. ''E's missin'. I've seen Yardley's missus. She said they went out together last night and the lad ain't come 'ome.'

'Was it murder?'

The watchman shrugged his shoulders beneath his heavy coat. 'Can't tell 'ow he died. They've tekken 'im to the local morgue.'

Lavender pulled out his notebook and pencil and began to write. 'In that case, the body needs taking to Sir Richard Allison at Guy's Hospital – along with this note.' He signed the paper, ripped it out and handed it across. 'This is authorisation to have the corpse moved to Guy's.'

'Seems like a lot of fuss fer the likes of 'im,' the old man said as he shoved the note into the inside breast pocket of his coat. 'Oh, and there's summat else.'

'What?'

'The bastards 'ave stolen 'is breeches.'

Chapter Fourteen

Wednesday 13th April, 1814

Extract from *The Times*

FEMALE GANG ROB EARL

Further to yesterday's announcement of a reward for information pertaining to the recovery of the jewellery stolen from the London home of the Earl of Beverley, this correspondent now understands the thieves in question are female actresses who inveigled their way into Beverley House with the express intention of stealing this jewellery.

These pernicious women are said to include an ivory-skinned redhead known as Caro; a waif-like blonde called Lou and two brunettes, known as Mary and Annie.

But the thieves beware! – For Lavender is on the case!

Readers are reminded that the stolen items include a diamond necklace and earrings – and a pearl and diamond brooch. Any information about their whereabouts – or the whereabouts of these women – should be given to Detective Lavender at Bow Street Magistrates' Court.

Buy tomorrow's edition for a crime update!

'Dear God! They're at it again!' Lavender slapped the newspaper down on the magistrate's desk with such force, Conant jumped.

'*Where* is this information coming from? Who's the bloody spy in our midst?'

Woods stood behind him, in a fresh head bandage, grinning from ear to ear. He was far better this morning and bright-eyed with amusement. They'd met at the entrance and come up to Conant's office together. He liked watching Lavender harangue their employer.

Conant hastily grabbed a stack of papers that Lavender's violence threatened to send slithering to the floor. 'Calm yourself, Detective! No doubt this information has come from the household of the Earl of Beverley.'

'I doubt that – he claims his servants are loyal. The earl will be furious. This article makes him look a fool. No man would admit to the world his house was invaded by a gaggle of thieving women.'

'Well, perhaps the viscount talked inappropriately?'

'That's unlikely, considering he was so drunk at the time of the robbery he could barely remember his own name – never the mind the names of three of the four women. And how does this *correspondent* know those young peers were deliberately targeted? I only came to that conclusion myself last night.'

'It's probably a lucky guess,' Conant said.

'You think it were a sting?' Woods asked.

Lavender nodded.

'Come now, Lavender,' Conant continued. 'At least the writer held back from a description of the terrible war wounds sustained by the young hero of Salamanca, Viscount Cottingham.'

This checked Lavender's anger for a second. Conant's voice was calm, and his demeanour betrayed nothing. Did he suspect that Lavender had made up that story? Either way, it was obviously not Conant who sent that story to the newspaper – nor the two clerks who'd been in his office yesterday. No reporter would have missed the chance to mention that Cottingham was a badly injured war hero. His first ruse to trap the informant at Bow Street had failed.

'How's the case progressing?' Conant asked.

'Not well,' Lavender admitted. 'I've run out of leads and don't know where to turn next. The women have disappeared without a trace and those young bucks have been next to useless at providing clues.'

'Ah, hence your frustration this morning.'

'I'm frustrated because I thought your friend, the editor of *The Times*, had agreed to stop this obsessive interest in my work. Or did you misunderstand him when he made you that promise?'

A flush of annoyance crept up the soft skin of Conant's neck above the line of his cravat. 'The only promise Stoddard made was an apology would be issued forthwith for the inaccuracies in their previous article. He's been as good as his word: the retraction is in today's paper.'

'Yes, I saw it,' Lavender snapped. 'It's a tiny box hidden away among the shipping news. It's hardly noticeable.'

Woods grinned. 'Aye, but it's in the right place for a tall tale about a boat chase along the Thames.'

'Stoddard never promised to stop reporting your cases,' Conant said. 'But he did assure me his reporters would be encouraged to be more factual and accurate in future.'

Lavender opened his mouth to retort – but Woods was the first to speak. 'What I don't understand about your case, sir, is if this robbery were a sting – and planned from the outset – how did them gals know about those sparklers in the strongbox?'

Lavender and Conant looked at him in surprise. Distracted, Lavender's brain shifted gear as he examined his case from this new angle. 'What makes you think they knew about them, Ned?'

'Don't most of the nobs store their sparklers in bank vaults and just fetch 'em out when they need 'em?'

Conant nodded. 'I believe that's the usual procedure, yes.'

Woods nodded wisely. 'In that case, I think them gals had an informer on the inside. Someone told them about the portrait – and the strongbox. All these jades had to do was use them cork-brained lads to get them entry into the house.'

'Thanks, Ned. That's helpful. I'll go back to Beverley House, talk to the earl and viscount again – and question the servants.'

'Yes, well done, Woods,' Conant said. 'That was good thinking. In the meantime, how is your own case progressing? Your absence yesterday was most unfortunate. It must have delayed your investigation.'

'Oh, I've already cracked the case, sir. It's solved.'

'You have?'

'Yes, all I need from you now is an arrest warrant. And I weren't sick yesterday. I tracked down this villain.'

'You weren't? But Mrs Woods sent us a note claiming you were laid up with your injuries.'

'Mrs Woods is gentry mort, sir – she's a heavenly angel sent down to walk with us mere mortals. It were the best day of me life when we was yoked together – but she tends to fuss too much.'

Lavender hid his grin at this rather glowing account of Betsy.

Conant nodded wisely. 'Ah, I see. Mrs Woods sounds a caring woman indeed. But you were at work yesterday after all?'

'That I were—'

Conant made a note. 'Very well, I'll reinstate your pay. What have you discovered?'

'I did what you asked and spoke to all three of the victims of those libels. Mr Edwin, the estate manager who acts for Sir Bernard Davies, Bart. is prepared to pay us for our services in bringin' this cove to justice.' He paused to place the completed contract, signed by Edwin, in front of Conant.

The magistrate picked it up eagerly. 'That's good work, Woods.'

'I also found out who placed that damnin' advertisement in *The Times*.'

'I suppose the newspaper was reluctant to reveal their sources?'

Woods smiled and tapped his nose mysteriously. 'I've my own sources, sir.'

Lavender hid another smile.

'It turns out it were the same cove behind all three cases of libel,' Woods continued. 'He'd used the printer, Harrison, to publish spurious lies on the posters about Sir Bernard Davies and the banker Alfred Gotobed – then, when Harrison put up his prices, he turned on the printer and used the advert in *The Times* to defame him.'

Conant burst out laughing. 'What an idiot! And what is the name of this aggrieved fool?'

Carefully, Woods placed the information Lavender had extracted from Vincent Dowling on the desk. 'It's Richard Garbutt from Soho Square.'

Both officers held their breath and watched the magistrate's reaction.

Conant turned pale and spluttered when he recognised the name of his nemesis. But his next words weren't what they were expecting. 'Alas, Constable, it seems your efforts to track down this libeller and gain remuneration for our services at Bow Street have been in vain.'

Woods frowned. 'How so, sir?'

'Richard Garbutt was found dead two nights ago by a member of the public in a dank alleyway off Holborn High Street.'

'Gawd's teeth!'

'He was murdered. His throat was cut. Constable Barnaby was the first officer on the scene and brought the body back to our morgue. He identified Garbutt last night and has already informed his daughters of their loss.' He reached out for the contract signed by Mr Edwin and tore it in half. 'With no trial and conviction for libel, there'll be no payment.'

'Aye, but there will be a trial and conviction for *murder* instead. I'll start straight away.'

Conant held up his hand to stop him leaving. 'Er, Constable – I haven't given you the case.'

Lavender watched Woods' face fall, then snapped, 'Why not?'

Conant laughed. 'Oh, come on, gentlemen! Murder is the remit of the principal officers – not a member of the horse patrol!'

'I thought I'd already explained to you—' Lavender said, but Conant interrupted him.

'Yes, yes, I know what you're going to say: Woods is the most *experienced* constable at Bow Street et cetera et cetera.'

'I've already got three suspects in my sight,' Woods protested. He gave Conant a funny look. 'Possibly four. And as I see it, I've got a head start on every other officer in this place.'

'He's right,' Lavender said. 'Ned's quite capable of tracking down this murderer.'

'You don't understand, Lavender,' Conant snapped. 'I knew Garbutt *personally*. There was some antagonism between us.'

'Aye, we've heard,' Woods growled.

'This murder will have to be investigated in line with procedure et cetera et cetera,' the magistrate continued. 'If not, any subsequent court case might be destroyed – and the conviction quashed – especially if the defence lawyer thinks I tried to cut corners. I need to follow the Home Department guidelines. No. A member of the horse patrol investigating this murder simply won't do.'

They were interrupted by a knock on the door. One of the junior clerks entered and gave Conant a note. Lavender and Woods stood in stiff, angry and resentful silence while he tore it open, read its contents and gave a frustrated sigh.

'It seems this matter has just been taken out of my hands. Tell me, Woods. How do you know Miss Emily Garbutt?'

'I called around there yesterday for a friendly chat with her about her da.'

'A *friendly* chat?' Conant spluttered. 'You do realise, don't you, constable, that Bow Street officers are supposed to be feared across the country?'

'Ah, well, that's my *experience* helpin' me out there, sir. Sometimes with the nervous ones you get more out of them with a few soft words.'

Conant's lips tightened in disapproval. 'Miss Garbutt requests our help in solving the murder of her father – and asks for *Detective Woods* to be in charge. Well done, Woods. You've got your first murder case.'

Woods couldn't stop grinning when they left Conant's office. He strode down the scuffed wooden staircase as if he was ten foot tall instead of six. 'Betsy'll be impressed. I might even get steak and kiddley puddin' for supper. She's married to a detective now.'

Lavender smiled. 'I'm pleased for you, Ned – although I have to point out Conant didn't mention anything about increasing your wages or providing you with a tipstaff.'

Woods waved a dismissive hand in the air. 'That'll come.'

'Where will you begin?'

'I'll have a chat with the daughters and get a full list of everyone this fella has wronged over the last few years and pay them a visit to find out if they've got one of them alibi things.'

'That might take a while,' Lavender said thoughtfully. 'I suspect Garbutt upset more people than just Harrison, Gotobed and Sir Bernard.'

Woods' jaw tightened. 'I'll lay a wager it's one of them three, especially that bad-tempered printer – you should see the size of his fists. And Gotobed ain't no gentleman either, what with the company he keeps. That thug Ulrich Monmouth might have had a hand in this. It'll be good to send him back to Botany Bay.'

'Arrange for Garbutt's body to be sent to Sir Richard for an autopsy,' Lavender suggested. 'He might be able to give you a more precise time of death – then you can question your suspects about their movements at that time.'

'Aye, I will.'

'And if it turns out he was murdered two nights ago, you can cross Conant off your list of suspects. He dined with the editor of *The Times* two nights ago at their club, trying – and failing – to exact promise from him to leave me alone.'

Woods' eyes twinkled. 'Shame that. I'd have enjoyed questionin' Conant.'

'By the way, your body snatcher has turned up – dead.'

'Aye, Betsy said. What happened?'

'No one could determine the cause of death. I arranged for the body to be taken to Guy's Hospital. I'm going to see Sir Richard now.'

'I'll come with you.'

'What about your own murder case?'

Woods shrugged and gently tapped his cheek and the loose tooth inside it. 'Like I said, this Yardley case is personal.'

They'd reached the crowded hallway, which, as usual, was full of officers and a miserable line of manacled prisoners, waiting to go to the cells. The prisoners were the ragtag and scum of Covent Garden and St Giles: staggering drunks, foul-mouthed harlots and sly-eyed pickpockets.

But a few decent members of the public also hovered in the hallway. One of them, a stooped bespectacled middle-aged man with silver hair parted in the middle, stepped out in front of them. 'Detective Lavender? May I have a word, please? It's about the stolen jewellery from Beverley House.'

Lavender eyed him shrewdly. The promise of a reward for information brought all sorts of avaricious snitching rascals out of the woodwork. Their information often led to a lot of wasted time. But this man seemed honest enough, even though he was blinking nervously behind his spectacles.

Lavender led him to a quiet side office and asked him to take a seat. There was no chair for Woods, who leaned against the dirty wall.

'How can I help you?'

'Well, I hope, sir, that I can help you. My name's Benson – Joseph Benson,' he told them. 'I'm employed at the Attlee Exhibition of Historical Artefacts. I saw today's article in *The Times* about the women who robbed the Earl of Beverley. It reminded me of a similar and distressing situation we had a few months ago at the exhibition. Especially with the woman called *Caro*.'

Lavender's ears pricked up. 'What is the Attlee Exhibition?'

'It's a private collection of extremely rare and valuable artefacts collected by the last Lord Attlee – and his father and brother – during their travels around the Middle and Far East. Our exhibits range from the Old Babylonian period of Mesopotamia to the Twelfth Dynasty of Ancient Egypt and the second century of the Roman Empire.'

Lavender nodded. Last century, the Grand Tour was fashionable among the ton, who systematically looted the treasures of the countries they visited. The dominance of Napoleon Bonaparte and the French had curtailed this practice recently, and it had instead become quite the fashion to open public exhibitions to show off their collections.

'When Lord Attlee died,' Benson continued, 'Lady Attlee decided to make them public to a select audience of ladies and gentlemen. She purchased premises in Mayfair, and I was employed – along with others – to catalogue and display the items.'

'What happened?'

'A young couple claiming to be Lord and Lady Hatton wrote for an appointment to view the treasures. It was winter and already dark when they arrived. They were young and absolutely charming – especially the woman. During the tour of the Egyptian room, Lady Hatton – who was with child – took ill. She asked me to open a window for some air and requested a chair.'

'Did you leave them alone in the room?' Lavender asked.

'No. But the lady was in such distress, I was distracted. I thought she was about to give birth there and then! Eventually, her pains ceased, and they left in their carriage. I locked up. The next morning, I discovered one of the most exquisite broad collars in our collection had been stolen.' He fiddled self-consciously with his spectacles. 'I'm afraid my eyesight isn't very good – especially at dusk.'

'Let me guess,' Woods said drily. 'While you were distracted with this gal – her fella snatched the sparklers and tossed them out of the open window to an accomplice below.'

Benson nodded. He looked embarrassed and miserable. 'Yes, I believe that's what happened. We made some enquiries – but it turns out the *real* Lord and Lady Hatton were in Southampton at the time of the robbery – and Lady Hatton is not with child. The thieves impersonated them, and her pregnancy was faked.'

'Why didn't you report the theft to Bow Street?' Lavender asked.

119

'I suggested it, but although Lady Attlee was very distressed, she said she didn't want policemen involved. But our own inquiries came to nothing – and I was just grateful I was allowed to keep my job.'

Lavender pulled out his notebook and pencil. 'Describe to me this collar.'

'It's nearly four thousand years old and called a wesekh. It's solid gold, very large and decorated with carnelian, turquoise and dangling golden beads. The shoulder clasps are in the shape of an eagle's head, which has large rubies for eyes.'

Woods gave a low whistle.

'It's priceless,' Benson added. 'And extremely rare.'

And therefore difficult to sell in its present form, Lavender thought.

'And where does the actress called *Caro* come into this tale?' Woods asked.

Benson sat up straighter. 'That's the coincidence, you see. At one stage, when the thieves were whispering together around one of the glass cases, I'm sure I overheard him call her *Caro*. I didn't think much of it at the time; I assumed it was her Christian name. But when I read *The Times* article this morning, I was reminded of the incident at our museum.'

'Are you sure?' Lavender asked.

Benson's tone grew more confident. 'Absolutely. My eyesight may be weak, Detective, but I've the hearing of a bat to compensate for it.'

Lavender picked up his pencil again. 'Can you describe these thieves, please?'

'I'm afraid I didn't pay him much attention; I just remember him being young and fair. The woman rather dominated the limelight. I say,' he added suddenly, 'do you think there's any chance you can retrieve our stolen wesekh? Lady Attlee would be so pleased.'

Lavender shook his head. 'Probably not, after all this time – an item like that won't be sold as it is. It's too recognisable. The jewels will be prised out of it and sold, and the gold will be melted down into an ingot.'

Benson winced. 'That's sacrilege – a tragedy.'

'What else can you remember about this redheaded thief called Caro?' Lavender asked.

Benson suddenly looked worried. 'Ah, but that's the confusion, Detective – the other thing I wanted to tell you about. I think *The Times* have made a mistake. The thief called *Caro* who came to our exhibition was fair-haired.'

'What?'

'Yes. She was distinctive. She had a mop of tight blonde sausage-like curls peeking out from beneath her blue velvet bonnet. And she had a very big nose to match her large personality.'

Chapter Fifteen

'There might be something' in this newspaper business,' Woods said as they approached the entrance of Guy's Hospital.

'What?'

Lavender, who'd been pondering this latest confusing development in his case, snapped back to attention.

'It strikes me, sir, that although you railed against that article, it's brought forward new information. Maybe these newspapers have their uses?'

'Information that confused the case even more!' Lavender exclaimed. 'Is this woman *Caro* a redhead or a blonde?'

'You'll work out this tangle soon,' Woods replied confidently. 'There can't be more than one posh jilt called Caro swannin' around London robbin' the wealthy and titled. It strikes me Benson is the most reliable witness. Those young tosspots were so foxed, I doubt they'll remember their own grandmothers when they're in their cups. It don't surprise me they got the women mixed up.'

Lavender scowled. 'If you think I'll ever be prepared to co-operate with those lying journalists at *The Times*, you're mistaken, my friend. Hell would have to freeze over first.' He leapt down off his horse on to the cobbles, tied the reins to a post, and without waiting for his constable strode sulkily up the steps towards the entrance.

Woods chuckled and followed him.

They found Sir Richard in his office with Kingsley. Both men were poring over a large pile of battered leather-bound medical books.

'Ah! My dear friend, Detective Lavender – and his loyal constable!' Sir Richard enthused. 'Take a seat – take a seat!'

Lavender sat down in a chair opposite the large desk, but Woods narrowed his eyes at this unexpected welcome, crossed his arms defiantly and leaned back against the door. 'It's Detective Woods now,' he said. 'I've had an advancement.'

'Well congratulations, my dear chap! Congratulations! But good grief, Woods! What on earth happened to your head?'

'I weren't the only one interested in that dead body snatcher. It seems like they got to him after they'd clobbered me.'

'Not necessarily.'

Lavender frowned. 'What do you mean? I asked for Yardley's body to be sent to you for examination. Was it done?'

'Yes – I've completed the autopsy. But before we discuss Yardley, tell me how goes Bow Street's inquiries into my mystery and your search for the unknown poison? As you can see, Kingsley and I are busy with our own research.'

He pointed to the great volumes on his desk one by one. 'We have it all here: Culpeper's *Complete Herbal*; a first edition of the famous *London Pharmacopoeia,* published in 1618, and Kingsley is wading through Gerard's *Herball*, which lists some interesting new plants from the North Americas. We will investigate the East Indies tomorrow. There's so many new species of flora and fauna arriving in England every week it's hard to keep up.'

'It seems to me that's like lookin' for a needle in a haystack,' Woods said.

Sir Richard sighed. 'My thoughts exactly, Detective Woods. But we'll persevere.'

'I'm afraid our investigation into Poppleton isn't going well,' Lavender said. 'For a start, Magistrate Conant has refused to take on this case because his brother is on your hospital board of trustees, who – the last I heard – are investigating you and Kingsley for misconduct.'

Sir Richard waved his hand dismissively. 'That's sorted out now, Lavender. Baron Poppleton decided not to press charges and after the trustees read the article in *The Times* yesterday, they let the matter drop. Even Kingsley is allowed to keep his job. If you were behind that article, Lavender, we owe you thanks.'

'*Me?*' Lavender exclaimed. 'I didn't write it. I'd never heard of Dr René Laënnec and his stethoscope until yesterday.'

'You didn't?'

'No. I thought you'd written it and sent it to *The Times.*'

Sir Richard laughed and waved his hand again. 'Oh well, it was probably one of my more enterprising students – or possibly a grateful patient at the newspaper offices. London is *full* of my grateful patients.'

Lavender decided to deal with that puzzling turn of events later. 'Despite Magistrate Conant's reluctance to take on your case, Woods and I have decided to help you out.'

'We'll need payin', mind,' Woods interjected.

'Of course, of course. I admire and welcome your rebellious spirit in the face of an oppressive management. Not that I would have expected anything less from you, Woods. Belligerence and truculence should be your middle names.'

'Belly what?'

Sir Richard ignored his scowl. 'Now, what have you learned from Baron Poppleton?'

'He doesn't want the matter investigating.' Lavender told him about his interview with Poppleton the previous day.

But even this news didn't deter the enthusiasm of Sir Richard. He drummed his fingers on the desk thoughtfully. 'So, the baron ate lamb and was disorientated.'

'But no one else in the household was affected by either the food or the claret.'

'In that case, he must have imbibed the poison in a different form... it was nothing to do with his evening meal.'

'Look, Sir Richard, I don't know how we can investigate this mystery if the baron won't co-operate with us.'

'Nonsense, Lavender. Do what you do best. Investigate the man from the periphery. Talk to his friends and family discreetly, build up a picture of his life. Somebody wants him dead – find out who it is, and they'll lead you to the poison.'

'You seem very sure about that,' Woods commented.

'Oh, I am. I am – there's a skilled poisoner on the loose in London and they've got our young friend Poppleton in their sights.' He rose from his seat. 'I know this because of what I found on that wretch Yardley. Come!'

He led them down the stairs and the corridors to the cold and dimly lit room he used for dissecting corpses. Lavender wrinkled his nose at the ferrous tang of blood and both officers side-stepped the splatter of body fluids on the floor.

The emaciated and naked body of Yardley lay on a bloody slab, staring at the ceiling through lifeless eyes. On a metal trolley at the side of the room stood a rat cage containing a large dead rodent, its face contorted in a grimace of pain, with dried froth at its lips.

Kingsley fetched over two lanterns and the men stared at the corpse. The resurrection man's face looked more peaceful in death than he deserved to be, Lavender decided, and there was definitely no sign of violence. Yes, the dead man had a good collection of scars, and a suspicious lump on his upper right arm suggested a historic break that had healed badly, but the cause of the death was a mystery.

The only unusual things about the corpse were the blistering sores, boils and lesions all over his body. His legs were in a particularly bad state; they looked like he had scratched himself raw. The inflamed skin was cracked and encrusted with dried blood.

'That's a nasty case of the "enduring itch",' Woods said.

'Indeed,' Sir Richard agreed. 'The Greek physician Aetius of Amida came up with the word *eczema*, which means "to boil out". That's a good description of the process that killed him.'

'Gawd's teeth! He died from an itch?'

'No, Woods, I suspect his trousers or breeches were poisoned.'

'His kickseys?'

'Yes, probably with aconitine.' Sir Richard pointed to the dead rat in the cage. 'I took a swab from these pustules on his legs and fed them to that creature on some meat. It died an hour later, writhing in agony.'

Woods took a step back from the corpse on the slab.

Lavender frowned. 'The pantaloons were poisoned with wolfsbane? I thought the skin was an effective barrier that protected us from harmful substances.'

126

'Usually, yes. The fatty layer of the skin prevents substances from being absorbed. However, this man's legs were blistered and bleeding because of his severe eczema. No doubt the poison entered his bloodstream through the lesions. *Wolfsbane*, as you so quaintly call it, is well known as one of the most effective contact poisons. Allegedly, it was used on a saddle in an assassination attempt on Good Queen Bess.'

'Yardley's wife said he'd been sick,' Woods commented, 'and I saw him scratchin' himself and divin' in and out of the bushes in the graveyard.'

'Oh, the diarrhoea and vomiting would only be part of it,' Sir Richard said gleefully. 'His limbs would have been numb and tingling. There'd be excruciating chest pain and palpitations and – as I determined at the autopsy – eventually he died from heart failure. Those missing pantaloons have a lot to answer for. Where are they, by the way?'

'They'd been taken by the time the corpse was found.'

'Stolen?'

'Probably.'

'A contact poison of this nature is the ideal way to kill a man with his skin condition,' Sir Richard surmised.

Lavender found himself shivering as he stared down at the corpse. 'Except he wasn't the intended victim, was he?'

'No, he weren't,' Woods agreed. 'This wheedlin' alchemist were tryin' to kill Baron Poppleton. Those were *his* kickseys.'

'Well, from what I saw of the baron's young, smooth and flawless skin the other day,' Sir Richard said, 'this attempt at murder was bound to fail. Aconitine won't work unless it gets into the bloodstream and the gut.'

'Then this weren't the poison that felled the baron for two days when he ended up in here?' Woods asked.

'No, Woods,' Sir Richard replied, 'that poison still remains a mystery – and we need to find it.'

Lavender's mind was whirling. Up until this point he'd still harboured a tiny niggling doubt about Sir Richard's wild theory. But not anymore.

'I need to get the chronology of these murder attempts into order. How long do you think the poison had been in the breeches, Sir Richard?'

The surgeon shrugged. 'It might linger for days, until the clothing was laundered.'

'I need to find out how long Poppleton had been wearing these pantaloons since they were last laundered. It looks like this was the first attempt on his life. When he had no adverse reaction to the aconitine, the killer tried again with a different concoction. That young man is in serious danger.'

'And so's half of London,' Woods said. 'Them kickseys are deadly to anyone with a cut on their hand. They're still out there, roamin' the city. It's like the bleedin' things have a life of their own.'

Chapter Sixteen

Woods found Constable Barnaby and asked him to lead him to the place where Garbutt's body had been found.

Barnaby was a handsome, ambitious young officer with a side parting in his thick dark hair and a long fringe. He and Woods had often worked together in the past and the lad could be cheeky at times, but it gave Woods a fatherly pride to see how he'd developed over the years under his tutelage.

They rode down Holborn High Street and dismounted next to a narrow alley between a greengrocer's and an ironmonger's. As they tied their horses to a post, Woods casually mentioned his advancement to principal officer. The young lad gave him a sly smile and congratulated him.

Woods puffed up with pride. 'Thank you, son. As I've allus said, good things come to those with patience. You'll be a principal officer one day yourself, if you play yer cards right.'

'Maybe.'

'*Maybe?*' Woods asked in surprise. 'Well, you've changed yer tune. I thought you had ambition?'

But Barnaby just smiled and turned down the passageway. Barely four feet wide, the alley was strewn with rotting vegetables and made narrower by the damaged boxes and rubbish stacked on the wall next to the grocer's. Woods wrinkled his nose at the smell of rat urine and mouldy cabbage. It was a miserable place to meet your death.

Barnaby led Woods around a sharp bend, stopped, and pointed to a dark stain on the cobbles. 'That's where the greengrocer found Garbutt about ten yesterday mornin'. He brought out more rubbish to add to this pile and had quite a shock. I weren't able to identify the poor fella until much later – one of the shopkeepers on the street recognised him.'

'Were he robbed?'

'No, he still had his pocket watch and nearly five shillings about his person.'

'Were he killed here?'

Barnaby nodded. 'There were a lot of blood. I've had a good look around and their ain't no blood splatter or trails elsewhere.'

'You allus had sharp eyes, lad.'

'I think Garbutt were grabbed on the main street, bundled down here and knifed. But he put up a fight. There were a defensive wound on his hands where he'd tried to hold back the blade.'

Woods tried not to imagine the terror Garbutt must have experienced in his last moments and the excruciating pain as he grabbed the knife in self-defence with his bare hands.

He kicked a couple of wrinkled old potatoes out of the way and scanned the filthy cobbles. 'Did you find anythin' else?'

Barnaby's fringe swayed as he nodded. He reached into his coat pocket. 'I found this, sir. But I don't know what it is.'

He held up a small brown stick, about three inches long and crudely carved. It had a collection of brown nutshells attached to one end with fragile leather thongs. It rattled gently when he passed it across.

Woods frowned. 'Gawd's teeth. It looks like a toy belongin' to some little nipper. What the devil is this doin' down here?'

'It looks pagan to me,' Barnaby said. 'Can you see the snake?'

Woods peered closer at the carving and cursed the gloom of the alley. Barnaby was right; the crude outline of a snake with one eye and a forked tongue wound its way round the body of the gnarled stick. It looked like someone had put a dot of red paint into the reptile's eye and more on the end of its tail.

Sighing, he pocketed the thing. Ragged, barefoot children haunted this poor neighbourhood. Many begged for pennies in the shop doorways, accompanied by their younger siblings. This peculiar toy might have been dropped by any one of them.

But he knew better than to overlook anything in a murder inquiry; he'd show it to Lavender later.

They strode back to the main street and Woods took a deep breath, inhaling the more familiar – and far pleasanter – smell of coal smoke and their horses.

'I started knockin' at doors yesterday,' Barnaby told him. 'I asked if anyone had seen anything suspicious two nights ago. But once dusk fell, the shop owners had shut up and scurried off home for their suppers.'

Woods glanced up and down the street. It was lined with shops. At night, it would have been deserted. But several windows in the upper storeys had drapes and a couple had potted plants. He pointed them out to Barnaby. 'It looks like some of those rooms on the upper floors might be inhabited. Give them a knock, will you, son?'

The constable nodded. 'I'll make further inquiries.'

'And Constable, what's happened to your ambition? You've got talent, you know. I know you've allus worshipped the ground Lavender walks on. So, what's changed your mind?'

'Oh, I still want to be a principal officer like Lavender – I just don't want to be as ancient as you when I get my tipstaff, that's all.'

Woods reached out to give the young man a playful cuff round the ear, which he nimbly dodged. They parted, laughing.

Woods' next call should have been at the Soho home of Garbutt's bereaved daughters, but he remembered the bailiffs from the previous day and scowled. It wasn't right those grieving gals should be pestered by debt collectors. He knew the simplest way to make the estate manager, Edwin, call off his thugs was to lie and say Garbutt had been murdered at home and the house was the crime scene.

Today, Edwin wore an embroidered silver waistcoat beneath his peacock-blue coat, and Woods was pleased to discover the silver buttons didn't have the same blinding effect on his eyes as they had yesterday.

The fat man seemed genuinely shocked by the news of Garbutt's murder. He pulled out a lawn handkerchief and dabbed at the beads of sweat that had formed on his forehead. 'Dear me! This is horrible! Murdered in cold blood in his own drawing room? Who would do such a terrible thing to the poor man, Detective?'

'That's what I plan to find out. I've a notion it were someone he's offended with his libels.'

Edwin's forehead bubbled again with sweat. 'Good grief! Surely you don't suspect Sir Bernard Davies?'

'Why not? He'll need to explain where he were two nights ago along with the rest.'

'Surely you don't plan to ask Sir Bernard for an alibi!'

'No, I thought you could do that.'

Edwin spluttered into his handkerchief.

'And while you're at it,' Woods continued, 'you can ask them rogues you employ as bailiffs about their whereabouts the night before last. It wouldn't be the first time bailiffs have gone too far in the execution of their job and topped a fella they was tryin' to put the frighteners on.' He turned to leave. 'And talkin' about them coves, keep 'em away from Garbutt's house on Soho Square. It's a crime scene now, and me and the constables ain't finished with it yet. I don't want your fellas stompin' all over the evidence with their muddy boots.'

Edwin just nodded his assent and Woods left the estate office, grinning.

Figuring that Garbutt was also in debt to his banker, Woods decided to pull the same trick on Alfred Gotobed. All these creditors would descend on Garbutt's house and daughters like a plague of rats now the man was dead. They'd tear their home to pieces looking for juicy morsels of value to take away to offset their debts. But if a little white lie gave those poor gals a couple of days' peace, it was worth it. If the women had any sense, they'd pack up their valuables and hide them.

Gotobed's sharp eyes narrowed when Woods was shown into his luxurious office, and he pushed his round spectacles further up his thin nose in annoyance. 'I thought I told you I can't help you in your inquiries, Detective. I've never heard of a man called Garbutt.'

Woods threw himself down in the chair and tossed his hat on the desk, then crossed his arms, rested them on the banker's desk and leaned across until he was inches away from the man's face. He had the urge to rile the wheedling liar.

'Aye, well, that were before I found out it *were* Garbutt who wrote that libellous pamphlet about *you.*'

Startled, the banker shuffled back in his chair. 'Are you absolutely sure? I don't recall...'

'Then you need to think harder. I've got evidence it were Richard Garbutt. Judgin' from the cove's complaint that you're a *usurer worse than Shylock* and *a defaulter of promises*, I think you've tipped the fella a big sum at a high rate and now called it in.'

Gotobed's eyes flared with anger. 'I take exception to the use of the word *usurer*, Detective. My business is conducted strictly within the law.'

'Is that a confession, Mr Gotobed?'

'A confession?'

'Yes. Richard Garbutt is now dead – I were wonderin' if you'd *taken exception* to him callin' you a usurer?'

'Dead?' Barely a muscle twitched in the banker's face.

'Yes, he were brutally murdered. I'm speakin' to everyone he upset with his libels about their movements two nights ago. I need to know where you was two nights ago.'

Gotobed gave a short and humourless laugh. 'This is ridiculous. But if this is what it takes to get you to leave, you can know I went straight home from the bank that evening – and enjoyed supper with my wife. I also played with my grandchildren. Both my coach driver and my family will bear witness to my statement.'

'This coach driver – that'll be Ulrich Monmouth, will it? The convicted horse thief who were transported to New South Wales on a seven-year ticket.'

Gotobed drew in a sharp breath. 'You know of Monmouth?'

'Aye, I were one of the ones who sent him bayside. Where were *he* on the night of Garbutt's murder?'

Gotobed pushed himself up taller against the back of his chair. 'I've had enough of this. Get out of my office – now!'

Woods ignored him. 'Monmouth's a nasty piece of work and violent with it. For the right money, he'd think nothin' of slittin' a man's throat.'

The banker's neck flushed with anger and he raised his voice. 'Have you never heard of rehabilitation? Or giving a man a second chance?'

Woods grinned. 'No, I ain't, what's that about?'

'Monmouth returned from Botany Bay a changed man. He found Christ in the boiling red desert of that godforsaken country and a good woman to share his life. He lives quietly – and soberly – with his family and I trust him implicitly with my horses!'

Woods snorted and picked up his hat. The idea of Gotobed as a philanthropic type didn't fit his picture of the man any more than the notion that Monmouth had returned from the other side of the world a reformed character. 'Monmouth were allus good with horseflesh. That made filchin' 'em easier.'

'I resent your vulgar insinuations about one of my decent hardworking servants!'

'Maybe so, but I still need to know where he were on the night of Garbutt's murder. You've got a motive to see Garbutt dead and it's a hardworkin' servant's duty to keep the likes of you happy.'

'This is outrageous!'

'And one final thing,' Woods added as he stood up to leave, 'don't send the bailiffs round to Garbutt's house to recoup your loan. That's a crime scene, I don't want no one in there disturbin' the evidence.'

Gotobed's forehead creased. 'But he wasn't murdered at home... what? He was? Oh, I see.'

Woods stared at the banker and Gotobed stared back. The speed with which the banker had corrected himself was impressive but they both knew what he'd said.

Woods put on his hat and bade Gotobed farewell. As he walked out into the chilly street, the same question repeated itself over and over in his mind: *Were it a slip of the tongue?*

Chapter Seventeen

When he left Guy's Hospital, Lavender hurried to Bedford Street to warn Baron Poppleton. But neither the baron nor his sister was at home and the footman, Feathers, had no notion where they were or how long it would be before the young master and mistress returned.

Sighing with frustration, Lavender ripped off a sheet of paper from his pad and scribbled out a note. He didn't mention the poisoned pantaloons. Anyone might read this note and if the would-be murderer was in that house, he didn't want to alert them to the fact he knew about their modus operandi.

He kept it simple, but his tone was urgent. He told Poppleton he'd uncovered disturbing new evidence and begged the baron to contact him via Bow Street immediately.

The need to return to Beverley House and pursue his inquiry into the stolen jewellery pressed on his mind but he ignored it and asked the footman for directions to the home of Mrs Farrow, Poppleton's aunt.

Overlooking the graveyard of St John's parish church in Wapping, Mrs Farrow's home was only two streets away from the bustling and noisy Port of London. Her house had the same flat Georgian front as her wealthy sister's house, but it was on a far smaller scale and in a far less salubrious area. The church and two cobbled streets were all that separated the Farrow house from the overcrowded squalor and disease of the ugly, cramped tenements that blocked out the sun and housed the families of the thousands of dockworkers and sailors.

He hesitated for a moment at the front door, working out how he would conduct this interview. He decided to play his cards close to his chest and not mention the poisons.

History had proved that poison was the preferred murder weapon of women – and there were two of them in this house. Two women who seemed to have a fractious relationship with Humphrey and Lottie Poppleton. It might be nothing, of course. Many families had tense relationships, but he needed to find out what access, if any, Mrs Farrow and her daughter had to Poppleton and his ruddy pantaloons.

A brass plate beside the front door read *Dr H. Farrow, Physician and Surgeon.* As he rang the bell, he wondered if the doctor was still alive; both the Farrow women wore mourning gowns when he first saw them.

A young maid in a mob cap and fraying apron let Lavender into the house. He found himself in a narrow, half-panelled hallway. On his left he caught a quick glimpse of an oak-panelled study, which he assumed was – or had been – the doctor's examination room. He was ushered into the front parlour on the right, which had an excellent view of the cemetery through its bow window.

The maid went to fetch her mistress and left him alone.

The fireplace with its mirrored overmantel dominated the room. The hearth was lined with blue and white Delft tiles depicting windmills and tiny Dutch men. Bookcases filled the alcoves beside the fire, and the leather-bound tomes shared their space with a curious array of nautical ornaments and navigational tools including a mounted black telescope, a brass sextant and an ancient astrolabe.

A quick glance at the spines of the books revealed they were about ships, navigation and medicine. Doctor Farrow had obviously been a ship's surgeon at some time.

But this masculine environment had been feminised with soft cushions and rugs, pale cream drapes and a bunch of daffodils in the bay window. It had a cosy feel to it.

The door opened again, and Mrs Farrow entered in a nervous flurry of black bombazine, with a white lacy cap above her grey curls. 'Detective! This is a surprise!'

Lavender gave what he hoped was a warm smile. Woods was far better than he at putting anxious women at ease. He felt a pang of regret at his absence. 'It's kind of you to find time for me, Mrs Farrow. Please don't be alarmed. I come to seek your assistance.'

She sank on to the sofa and waved her hand at the chair opposite. 'How can I possibly assist *you*?'

Lavender sat down, sighed heavily and launched into his lies. 'It's about your nephew, Baron Poppleton. I haven't been able to get an audience with the young man, and I'm concerned for his well-being after the events of Saturday.'

Mrs Farrow's hands fluttered nervously. 'I understood from my niece that his recent misadventure was no more than a silly scrape due to his excessive drinking.'

'There's more to it than that, I'm afraid.'

'I'm pleased you're concerned, Detective, but I don't see how I can help. I don't have a son of my own and know nothing about the drinking habits of young men. The good doctor and I – my late husband – were only blessed with a daughter, our dearest Diana.'

'There's been another disturbing development following Sir Humphrey's adventure. It's probably just a coincidence and nothing to worry about… but I felt I needed to speak to a member of his family. When I was at Lady Barlborough's the other day, I overheard some of your conversation with your niece, and I gained the impression you're a caring woman, a good Christian and a devoted aunt.'

Her pallid lined cheeks flushed at the compliment. 'Of course! How can I help?'

'Do you remember that when Sir Humphrey was found unconscious, his pantaloons had been stolen?'

'Yes, a most unfortunate occurrence – and most unseemly! I understand he runs with quite a wild crowd, and I do worry for my dear sister that he'll bring disgrace down on the family.'

'Well, we found the pantaloons yesterday, and the thief – but this man is dead, ma'am, in mysterious circumstances.'

Her hand fluttered to cover her mouth as she gasped in shock. 'How awful! Oh, my goodness! You don't think Humphrey had anything to do with his death, do you?'

'No, he isn't a suspect. But I'm concerned about his safety because of his proximity to this dead thief.'

'Of course.'

'And as I've been unable to speak with Sir Humphrey, I immediately thought of his loving aunt...'

'Naturally. I will tell you what you need to know, Detective.' She was relaxed now, her hands folded neatly in her lap.

Lavender pulled out his notebook. 'I knew I could rely on you, Ma'am. Can you tell me exactly how you're related to Sir Humphrey?'

'Of course. Humphrey and Lottie are the children of my sister, Clarissa, and her husband, Baron Poppleton of Netheredge in Cambridgeshire. Clarissa died when they were small children.'

'That must have been sad for you, Mrs Farrow.'

'Yes, it was – although we weren't close.' Her thin lips tightened with disapproval. 'I'm afraid to tell you both of my sisters distanced themselves from me after my marriage to Doctor Farrow. Ours was a love match, but because they had both snared men with titles, they rather looked down on me and the good doctor.'

'That surprises me. I've heard great things about Doctor Farrow. He seems to have earned a lot of professional respect. Wasn't he a ship's surgeon at one time?'

Her lined face erupted with smiles of delight. 'Yes! He sailed with Captain James Cook on his second voyage to the southern hemisphere in 1772. How did you hear about him?'

'I've good contacts with the surgeons at Guy's Hospital, where your late husband is regarded as a great doctor and an astute and compassionate man.' *Well, it was only half a lie...*

Mrs Farrow beamed and named the long list of virtues of her late husband and told him several anecdotes about the humanity Doctor Farrow showed towards the sick and dying savages he encountered on his voyages.

Lavender let her talk for a while, then brought the conversation back to Baron Poppleton. 'You were telling me about the childhood of Sir Humphrey and his sister?'

'Oh, yes.' Her forehead creased into a frown. 'Well, their father turned out to be a drunkard and a gambler. Heaven knows how Clarissa ever thought she'd made a better match than me! The good doctor and I were happy for thirty years. I don't understand the ins and outs of it, Detective, but my husband told me Poppleton lost their estate through foolish speculation in stocks and shares. Anyway, after he'd died—'

'Excuse my interruption, but how did the late Baron Poppleton die?'

A flicker of unease passed across her face and she lowered her voice. 'It's rather a scandal, Detective – so distressing – and such a shock for his children. It was by his own hand.'

'I see. I'm sorry I asked. Was this when Sir Humphrey was at Cambridge University, at Magdalene College?'

'No, it was afterwards. The baron had already pulled poor Humphrey out of university because he couldn't afford to keep him there and tragically poor Humphrey was at home when... it was Humphrey who found his father. He'd hanged himself.' Her voice trailed away with sadness.

Lavender grimaced. 'What happened to your niece and nephew after that?'

'Netheredge had to be sold and they were penniless. I believe at one point Humphrey got a job.'

'He got a job?' Lavender tried to imagine that dissolute, drunken young man in honest employment – and failed. However, on the other hand. he couldn't reconcile the cool and confident Poppleton with the traumatised youngster who'd stumbled across his suicidal father's corpse either. Poppleton was an enigma; a difficult man to read.

'Yes, he was a gentleman's gentleman.'

'A valet?'

'I believe so. The dear Doctor Farrow never had time for such fripperies as a manservant, of course.'

And he wouldn't have been able to afford one, Lavender thought. The social disparity between the lives of the three sisters was obvious. 'What did Miss Poppleton do during this period? Where did she live?'

She blushed. 'I don't know. I'm not sure of any of the details about that time. My family and I weren't close to the Poppletons. The baron had been most rude to my beloved husband, and relations were strained.'

'And what about your other sister, Lady Barlborough? Was she concerned about her impoverished niece and nephew?'

Mrs Farrow laughed. 'Verity? Oh goodness me – no! Verity had made the best marriage in the family – even if Lord Barlborough was a feckless libertine!'

'Wasn't he was the younger son of the Earl of Barlborough?'

'Yes, that's right. But Verity had no time for myself, Doctor Farrow and my darling Diana – and even less for the Poppletons after the disgrace of his bankruptcy and death.'

'But aren't you her only family? I understand Lady Barlborough has no children of her own.' This was a shot in the dark on Lavender's part, but Viscount Cottingham had already indicated that Lady Barlborough had made Humphrey Poppleton her heir.

'No, she doesn't have children. They were never blessed. After Doctor Farrow passed away, she'd condescend to send me a little pin money to help me out with the housekeeping – as was her duty as a good Christian – but my sister Barlborough is the proudest of my sisters.'

'Then how did Sir Humphrey and his sister end up living with her?'

'Well, that is the mystery, Detective. They turned up on her doorstep about a year ago and wheedled their way into her house. Since then, Verity has been distant with me.'

Lavender frowned, his pencil paused over his notebook. *Was this family dispute sufficient motivation for attempted murder?* 'I understand Lady Barlborough is a recluse, and ill.'

'Yes, she has a debilitating disease and hardly sees anyone now – including myself and Diana. And after everything myself and the late Doctor Farrow have done for her too! On top of this slight, she's put Humphrey in charge of her affairs and my allowance has been stopped.'

Lavender paused. Sick and rich old ladies were a magnet for duplicitous relatives – especially when there was a large inheritance at stake.

An unpleasant thought jumped unbidden into his mind. *Is Lady Barlborough safe in the care of her nephew and niece?* 'That must be distressing for you,' he said cautiously. 'Can you tell me when you last saw your sister?'

But before Mrs Farrow replied, the door opened again and her mousey-haired daughter entered the room.

Lavender rose to his feet.

'Diana, darling, do you remember Detective Lavender from the other day at Aunt Verity's house?'

The young woman's impassive mask slipped when the dull brown eyes behind her thick lenses registered a flicker of surprise.

'I've been helping the detective with his inquiries,' her mother continued proudly. 'There's been a development with Humphrey's pantaloons.'

'I'm sure there has, Mama,' Diana said drily. 'However, I'm not sure how much help you'll have been, considering we're no longer allowed over the threshold of my aunt's house.' She had a thin, barely audible voice that Lavender suspected would be grating after a while.

'Oh, it's not as bad as that,' her mother protested. 'The villain who stole them has been found dead – probably killed by other thieves!'

'I just have one final question, ladies. It relates to the day Sir Humphrey disappeared. Did either of you see him on Saturday? Did you perchance visit Bedford Square?'

Mrs Farrow shook her head. 'No, we had a charity engagement all day at the church across the way. Most of the gentlewomen of Wapping attended. We were very busy.'

'You've been most helpful, thank you.'

'Are we suspected of something, Detective?' Diana asked sweetly.

'No, of course not, Ma'am.'

Lavender packed away his notebook and decided it was time to leave – Mrs Farrow may have been gullible enough to believe his lies, but Diana Farrow was more astute. He assured them his inquiries were just routine, bowed, and left.

It was drizzling when he left the house. The grey sky reflected his mood. He wasn't sure if he'd learned anything useful.

Yes, the late Doctor Farrow might have come across some exotic poisons during his travels around the globe, but there was no reason to suppose Farrow had passed his knowledge on to his wife and daughter. Nevertheless, he needed to check their alibi.

He crossed the cobbled street and headed towards the church. His interview with the vicar of St John's was short but helpful. Yes, both Mrs and Miss Farrow had spent the previous Saturday at the church helping with the charity event. They'd been there all day into the early evening.

Lavender sighed as he mounted his horse and turned towards Beverley House.

His investigation into the attempted murder of Humphrey Poppleton was going nowhere.

Chapter Eighteen

Emily Garbutt let Woods into the shabby hallway of her home. Behind the young woman, her sister was dragging a heavy trunk towards the door. All around them were signs of hasty packing: piles of coats and shawls, hat boxes and a mountain of boots and pattens. Both were red-eyed from crying but appeared to be calmer now.

Woods helped the younger sister with the trunk, and when they'd sat down on the spindly chairs in the drawing room he told them he'd bought them some time with their father's creditors.

Emily waved her thin hand towards the battered trunk in the crumbling hallway. 'We have an aunt who lives in Cheapside and plan to stay with her until after Father's funeral. We're not running away from our responsibilities, Detective, but we need some time and space to grieve. We can't face those horrible men who came yesterday...' Her voice trailed away.

Woods nodded and said softly, 'You do right, Treacle. And your father's debts aren't your responsibility – even though those bum-bailiffs will tell you different. Please accept my sympathies and know that I'm doin' everythin' I can to investigate your da's murder.'

Jane's thin shoulders heaved beneath her dowdy dress, and she burst into tears.

Emily put an arm around her. 'Thank you, Detective.'

'If you let me know your aunt's address, I'll let you know when I've caught the villain.'

Emily nodded.

'In the meantime, I need to ask you some more questions. Now, I know yer da ruffled a few feathers with his libels and court cases and such like, and he owed a lot of money to some rough people.'

'But that's surely not a motive for murder, is it, Detective?' Emily protested. 'I understand most creditors want you to pay off your debts.'

Woods nodded. 'That's true, Treacle, and most folks are killed by someone they know. Murder is usually personal in nature. Is there anyone who sought revenge on your da, for instance? Anyone with a resentment or a strong hatred of your father?'

Both women thought for a while, then shook their heads. Woods was pleased to see Jane's tears had dried up again. 'Would it have been a footpad – a robbery?' she asked.

'He weren't robbed, Treacle. What about family feuds – nasty relatives?'

'We have no family apart from our aunt in Cheapside.'

'Has your da ever received any threatenin' letters?'

'Not that he mentioned. We know he'd upset a lot of people,' Jane admitted.

'And neither of you know where he was goin' and who he planned to see the night he went missin'?'

Again, they shook their heads. 'He went out about half past eight.'

'Did you notice anyone hangin' around outside the house that evenin'?'

'No. Father was often troubled by his worries and went out for a long walk to clear his head,' Emily said. 'The enormity of his cases in the court of chancery weighed on his mind. He was much upset by the devious nature of lawyers.'

I'll bet he were, Woods thought. 'Apart from his arguments with his banker, his printer and your landlord, is there anyone else he's crossed recently?'

'He had a case due up in court next week against our butcher. Father had refused to pay him because he'd sent us bad meat,' Jane said.

'Then there was his case against Magistrate Conant for damages against his person during his arrest a few years ago,' her sister added. 'He hoped to receive a favourable judgement. He was badly injured during the arrest.'

'I know all about that, and I've already found out Magistrate Conant has an alibi for the night of your father's murder.'

'I'm sure he has!' Emily snapped.

'It's a genuine alibi, sweetheart. But give me the address of your butcher and I'll check him out.' *Is an argument about bad meat worth killing a man for?* he wondered.

With the women's permission, Woods spent some time going through Garbutt's papers in his dusty and miserable study. All the good furniture, the books, curtains and the chandelier had been sold or pawned. Garbutt had worked on a wonky table with a tallow candle in a bare room. Woods found a huge stack of bills and demands for money, but there were no threatening letters.

Woods left the grieving women shortly afterwards and shook his head at the sadness of their plight and the foolishness of their father.

What was it all for? he wondered. This business of suing folks in a law court? Was fighting in chancery and libelling folks worth dying for if it left your gals homeless, penniless and hounded by creditors?

Woods had a sudden thought that he needed to talk to Betsy. For the past twenty-five years he'd given nearly every penny he'd earned to his wife – and he'd no idea what she'd done with it. When he'd received his shoulder injury and was unable to work, she'd kept them warm and fed from her *savings*. She often mentioned her *savings* in a mysterious tone. He had no idea how much money she had stashed away – or where it was. But his family certainly didn't struggle for food or coal during the time he was unable to work.

But did Betsy have enough saved to look after herself and his little gals if anything bad happened to him? The boys were working now and could fend for themselves. But what about Rachel, Tabby and Betsy herself?

Woods' mood was black when he strode into Harrison's noisy print shop, and he hoped the bad-tempered fella wouldn't give him any trouble – because Woods wasn't in the mood for it.

But Harrison wasn't there.

A stooped, balding and bespectacled man with ink-stained fingers met him at the front desk. Woods recognised him as the poor fella Harrison had been yelling at on his first visit.

The man informed him – with barely disguised glee – that Harrison was already below the hatches. ''E were out drinkin' with 'is pals two nights ago and got maudlin drunk. Then 'e started fightin'. When the constables arrived 'e floored one of 'em and they threw 'im into the clink. 'E were up before the beak yesterday, and 'as been detained at His Majesty's pleasure in Cold Bath Fields prison fer a week.'

Woods' heart sank. 'Two nights ago?'

'Aye.'

This was a disappointment – he'd have wagered a shilling the bad-tempered printer was behind the crime.

But if Harrison had been locked up by the constables on the night of Garbutt's murder, he had the perfect alibi.

Still, he had to make sure. Harrison might have murdered Garbutt earlier in the evening. He took the name of the tavern where Harrison drank and set off to check out this unexpected alibi. He also made a mental note to track down and congratulate the constables who'd managed to overpower the gigantic fella and bundle him into the cells.

An hour later, he walked out of Cold Bath Fields prison on to the busy streets of Clerkenwell, shaking his head in frustration. The huge metal doors clanged shut behind him.

Harrison had a perfect alibi. When he left work, the printer had headed straight to the Golden Anchor and joined in a rowdy and bad-tempered dice game. By eight o'clock, accusations of cheating were flying around the tavern along with the tables and stools.

By half past the hour, when Richard Garbutt left his family home for the last time, the printer Harrison was sleeping off the drink in a cell.

Chapter Nineteen

To Lavender's relief, both the Earl of Beverley and Viscount Cottingham were at home and neither father nor son appeared to be aware of that morning's article in *The Times*.

He was taken to see the two men in the gold and cream drawing room, and the tension between them was palpable. Once more, the peer was pacing backwards and forwards across the Turkish rug in front of the ornate fireplace, while the young viscount sat slumped in a chair. The young man looked like he wanted the ground to open up and swallow him whole.

'I've some interesting new information,' Lavender told them. 'I need to ask you both more questions.'

'What new information?' The earl threw himself down into the chair opposite his son.

'Apparently, earlier this year a private museum in Mayfair was robbed by a young couple. The curator managed to hear them whispering and the man called the woman *Caro*, which is the name of the woman who spent the evening here, sitting on Sir Humphrey's knee.'

The viscount sat upright. 'Was it the same woman?'

'Possibly. Yes.'

'Was she a redhead?' Beverley asked. He turned to his son. 'You said the girl who was with Poppers was a redhead.'

'No,' Lavender admitted. 'There's some confusion here; the curator claims the woman who robbed the museum was a blonde. But if this thief is a former actress, she'll be adept at disguising her appearance. The red hair may have been a wig.'

'Did it look like a wig?' Beverley asked his son.

Cottingham looked confused. 'I don't know…'

The earl scowled. 'You don't seem to know much, Frank.'

The viscount put his hand to his head. 'It's so damned difficult to remember when you're in your cups…'

Lavender felt the tension in the room. The earl's attitude towards his son had hardened over the past two days.

The earl grunted. 'What other questions do you have for this drunken saphead, Lavender?'

'It's not so much of a question as an observation. I've struggled to get any of your friends to admit they knew these women before they latched on to you. All of you claim someone else introduced them to the group. Have you anything to say about that?'

Cottingham looked surprised. 'I was damned sure it was Jonty!'

Lavender shook his head. 'Jonty thought it was Sir Harry. Sir Harry thought it was Baron Poppleton – and he thought it was you.'

'Good God!' sighed the earl. 'They're going round in circles. They're as bad as each other.'

'There's another explanation,' Lavender told him. 'It might be that the viscount and his friends were deliberately targeted by those women, who came up to them in the manner of old acquaintances. Considering their drunken state, it wouldn't have been hard to persuade your son and his friends there was a previous acquaintance, and worm their way into their company for the rest of the evening.'

'But why would they do that?' the viscount asked.

Lavender turned to Cottingham. 'Whose suggestion was it to come back to Beverley House after your supper?'

'It was the woman, Lou. She pestered me to show her my home – claimed she wanted to see *'ow the other 'alf lived*. She was most insistent.'

The earl put his head in his hands. 'The boys were the victim of a sting, weren't they?'

'It looks like it. I don't think this was an opportunistic theft; I think the whole thing was carefully planned. We already know from the museum curator there's an accomplished female jewel thief operating in the capital called *Caro*. I suspect she came here with her pals intending to steal whatever they could lay their hands on. Maybe they'd been watching your son and his friends for a while and knew how susceptible they were when they were drunk.'

'Oh, Father, I'm so sorry!'

'This brings me to my next point,' Lavender said. 'It's a bit of a hunch, but I wonder if they knew the countess's valuable jewels were in the house. And if so, how? Are they normally kept here?'

'Good God, no,' replied the earl. 'We usually store them in the vault at our bank. They were only here by accident. The countess wore them to Lady Jersey's ball the night before we left for our country estate. There wasn't time to send them back to the bank the next morning and we were rushed when we left because we were worried about the bad weather and the roads.' His voice rose with anger as he turned his head towards the viscount. 'But I did ask my wretched son to tell the butler to return them to the bank vault.'

'I forgot...' the young man wailed. 'Look, I'm so sorry, Father. You know I am.'

Lavender frowned. 'How long were they in the strongbox before the theft?'

'About a week.'

'Who else knew they were still here on the premises? Which of the servants?'

'My wife's maid may have known,' Beverley said. 'But she accompanied us on our trip. What the devil do you think happened here, Lavender?'

'I need to talk to your servants. I'm sorry to suggest this, but it's possible these young women knew these valuable items were still in your house – and wouldn't be missed until your later return. I think someone may have told them.'

The earl rounded on his son. 'You didn't tell anyone, did you, Frank?'

The viscount looked miserable and shrugged his shoulders again. 'I don't think so...'

The earl's face darkened with rage. 'If you ever, EVER, get as drunk as that again, I'll...'

Lavender interrupted them hastily. 'And my last question: where's your bank? I need to check their procedures there. There's always a chance one of their staff may have told someone the jewels were still at Beverley House.'

'It's Messrs Nightly and Gotobed's Bank on the High Street in Southwark,' the earl told him. 'It's a newish venture – but they offer secure storage at a surprisingly low rate.'

Well, well, Lavender thought, *another wretched coincidence.*

Lavender spent the next few hours interviewing the servants at Beverley House. It was a frustrating and futile exercise. None of the earl's bewildered staff knew anything about the countess's jewels being in the strongbox and the butler confirmed the young master had never asked him to return them to the bank. No one had seen any strangers loitering in the vicinity of Beverley House and everyone, except the cook, denied telling anyone that the earl and countess had gone away to their country estate.

The cook had a round, ruddy face with scared, blinking eyes. 'I 'ave to tell the butcher and the grocer's that I'll be needin' less food in my orders fer a week,' she explained. 'I don't remember particularly sayin' "they've gone away" but they'll know what I mean when I tell 'em I need less.'

Lavender sighed and closed his notebook. This damned case was hopeless.

Before visiting the bank, he decided to take his bad temper out on that bloody newspaper. It was time to take a tougher stance with those rogues.

He strode angrily into the crowded hallway of *The Times* offices, whipped out his tipstaff and held it aloft. 'Detective Stephen Lavender from Bow Street.' The crowd of people queuing by the desk moved aside and he found himself face to face with a startled bearded clerk in an ink-stained apron.

'I've urgent business with your editor, Stoddard. I demand to see either him or your owner, John Walter, immediately.'

'But…'

'No buts. Tell me where they are *now* – or I'll have you clapped in irons for impeding the course of justice.'

The clerk pointed a shaky finger towards a narrow, twisting staircase at the rear of the hallway. Lavender took the steps two at a time and found himself on a dark oak-panelled landing, faced with several half-open doors. Through one of them he saw a long, smoky room, full of men huddled over desks piled high with paper and scattered with ink bottles and quills.

He strode towards them and almost bumped into Vincent Dowling, who appeared out of nowhere and blocked his entrance.

'Detective Lavender!' Dowling said loudly. 'What a pleasant surprise! How goes your investigation into the stolen Beverley diamonds?' His pockmarked face broke into a welcoming smile.

'Let me past, Dowling. I need to see your bloody editor.'

'Of course, Detective Lavender!'

Why was the damned man shouting? Behind him, every reporter in the room had turned to watch this scene.

'Just give me a minute and I'll see if Mr Stoddard is available to see you, *Detective Lavender*.'

Lavender heard the sound of a chair being hastily shoved back and a door opening.

He forced Dowling aside and strode into the room just in time to see a far door closing behind the booted heels of a slight – and very fast – young man.

Dowling protested at his rough treatment and the other men in the room rose to their feet in alarm. An elderly well-dressed man, with white hair and a silver pocket watch chain swinging from his waistcoat, walked towards them, frowning.

Lavender ignored them all and flung open the door. It led to another flight of twisting, uneven stairs. This old building was a rabbit warren.

'Don't think you can escape from me!' he yelled.

Below him, out of sight, another door slammed shut.

'What are you doing, Lavender?' demanded the man in the waistcoat. 'What do you want? I'm Stoddard. I heard you shouting for me.'

Lavender spun round on the editor. 'Who the devil was that? Who's just left by this staircase?'

Silence fell.

Dowling stepped forward and patted Lavender on the arm. 'Come now, Lavender, old chap. That was no one, just one of the printers come to ask a question about the typesetting. What's upset you?'

'Oh, stop lying, Dowling,' Lavender snapped. 'That wasn't a printer. It was the reporter who's been writing these scurrilous and incorrect articles about me for the last few weeks.'

'I don't know what you mean. As I told you two days ago, I'm a court reporter these days...'

'Rubbish! You know exactly what's going on. You stopped me at the door today, and announced me loudly so he had chance to escape. You also stopped me entering the building two days ago and told me a load of lies about how your editor was out of town. You're in this subterfuge up to your neck.'

'Now, now, Lavender,' Stoddard said calmly. 'I'm sure Dowling had his reasons.'

Lavender pointed at the door. 'Who is his source at Bow Street? Who's feeding your reporter information about our investigations?'

'As you know, Detective,' Stoddard said quietly, 'we always protect our sources at *The Times*.'

'Ha! Well, you won't protect him from me! One more bloody story about *me* and my cases in your paper rag, and I'll arrest the lot of you for a breach of *my* privacy. Do I make myself clear?'

Most of the silent men in the newsroom nodded. Some of them had turned pale, but the corners of Dowling's mouth twitched. 'Is that a genuine felony, Lavender? I just wonder because I've never heard it raised as a crime in the Old Bailey...'

Lavender glared at him. 'Publish my name again and you'll find out.'

The smile vanished.

Lavender turned on the heel of his boots and stormed back out of the room the same way he'd arrived. The news reporters scattered before him.

It won't do any good, Lavender thought miserably as he mounted his horse and set off towards Southwark. *I can yell and threaten them but those buggers will keep on printing their drivel.*

Alfred Gotobed's sharp eyes narrowed when Lavender was shown into his luxurious office and he scowled. 'A second visit from a Bow Street runner in the same day? I'm honoured, I'm sure.'

Lavender's eyebrow twitched at the sarcasm in his tone.

'As I've already told Detective Woods...'

'This is nothing to do with the murder case Detective Woods is investigating. I'm Detective Stephen Lavender and I'm investigating the theft of a valuable necklace and brooch owned by the Countess of Beverley – items usually stored in your vaults.'

Gotobed put down his quill and straightened up in his chair. 'Ah, yes. The Beverley diamonds. The earl is a valued customer.'

Lavender didn't wait to be asked to sit down. He lowered himself into the chair opposite and leaned forward. Gotobed sat back, alarmed.

The sides of Lavender's mouth twitched in amusement. He didn't know what Woods had done to the man earlier, but the banker was nervous.

'You're aware of the robbery at Beverley House?'

Gotobed pushed his round spectacles up his thin nose. 'Yes. Most unfortunate. I read about it in *The Times*.'

'Yes, it's unfortunate – and wouldn't have happened if the jewels had been returned to your bank for safe storage.'

'Quite. How can I help you, Detective?'

'I've a theory that someone knew they'd been left at Beverley House – and that this information was passed on to an unscrupulous person – or persons.'

'I trust you don't think any of my employees would be that indiscreet, Detective?' Gotobed's grey eyebrows rose in annoyance.

'I would like you to humour me, Mr Gotobed. There are questions I need to ask. For a start, which of your staff deals with your valuable deposits and the security boxes in your vaults?'

'Are we not trusted? Are my employees under suspicion?'

'It is more a process of elimination. There are a lot of people in London who might have known the whereabouts of the diamonds last Friday evening. I would like to find out if anyone here knew the jewels hadn't been returned.'

Gotobed hesitated for just a fraction of a second and Lavender saw something unpleasant simmering behind his colourless eyes. He reached out and rang a silver bell on his desk.

A stooped, nervous and balding clerk entered the room. 'Yes, sir?'

'This is Mr Lawrence Wiles, my head clerk,' Gotobed said with an airy wave of his hand. 'He'll show you our ledger, where we register the movement of items to and from our vaults, explain our procedures and answer your questions. Good day to you, Detective.' He picked up his quill again and returned to study the black ledger open on his desk.

Lavender knew he'd been summarily dismissed, but at least he'd got what he came here for. He nodded towards Gotobed's bowed head, thanked him, and followed the nervous clerk into the next room.

Wiles was no help whatsoever. He was able to show Lavender a record of the date and time the earl's steward had arrived at the bank with two liveried footmen to retrieve the jewels, but claimed to be unaware that they hadn't been returned. In fact, the company didn't make a habit of questioning their wealthy clients about such matters. They just assumed their customers would return their items when they were ready.

Lavender sighed heavily as he walked out of the bank into the failing light of the dusk. The lamplighter was already on his rounds down the street. Another wasted trip. The bank's employees wouldn't have known for sure that the jewels were still on the premises; Lady Beverley may have taken them away with her to their country estate. It was unlikely anyone connected with the bank was involved in the robbery.

As he was in Southwark, Lavender decided to call on Woods to cheer himself up.

Chapter Twenty

When Woods left Cold Bath Fields prison, his thoughts returned to his other case: the body snatcher's mysterious death. He decided to visit his second murder scene of the day and explore the spot beside the river where the nightwatchmen had found Yardley's body. *Who knows? They may have missed something.*

While he was at it, he'd pop round to see the resurrection man's widow and find out if their boy, Georgie, had come home yet. That lad was a valuable witness.

Oblivious to the stench of the Thames and the damage to his boots, Woods clambered down the barnacle-encrusted wooden pilings on to the strip of deserted mud that wound like a stained brown ribbon beneath the wharf of the timber yard. The tidal river had pulled back but a quick glance at the detritus cast along the shore reassured Woods that even at high tide the river didn't rise this far.

It was a desolate spot to die – especially at night – but a good hiding place.

Had Yardley brought his son here to hide from those coves who were chasing them?

The only thing he knew for sure was that it was here the aconitine poisoning had overpowered Yardley's organs. Was his lad still with him when he breathed his last? That wheedling sawbones had said it was a terrible death. It must have been hard for the nipper to watch his da die in such agony.

Woods walked, or rather slithered, up and down the mud bank, looking for a clue that the watchmen had missed. But there was nothing to see except a few seabirds scavenging for shellfish. It was quiet down here. The noise of the city was muffled, and the only sounds came from the creaking timbers above his head and the heavy slap of the water against the pilings.

He gave up searching, and clambered back up on to the wharf.

A filthy, barefoot young boy had arrived while he'd been down on the mud strip. The lad had walked to the end of the jetty and was staring at the river taxis criss-crossing the Thames. His back was towards Woods and his shoulders were slumped with misery.

Woods approached the boy cautiously. If it was Georgie Yardley, he didn't want to frighten him.

A board creaked beneath his boot. The boy spun round and screamed. He tried to bolt – but Woods caught his coat collar and hauled the lad into his arms.

'Gerroff me! Let me go!'

For a malnourished child, Georgie fought like a little demon. For one awful minute Woods thought they'd both end up in the river, locked in a tight embrace. 'Calm down, son. You're Georgie Yardley, aren't you? I'm Detective Woods – I'm investigatin' what happened to your da. I'm not goin' to hurt you.'

'NOOO!' yelled the terrified boy. 'They'll skin me!'

'No one's goin' to skin you, lad. I'll keep you safe. I'll look after you, your ma and your little brothers and sisters too.'

At the mention of his family, Georgie stopped fighting and burst into tears. Woods relaxed his tight hold and pulled the sobbing child into his chest for a comforting hug.

Eventually, the boy's sobs shuddered to a halt. He pulled away and wiped his tear- and snot-streaked face with the sleeve of his ragged coat. Beneath the dirt, he had a pale round face, dusted with freckles, and the largest, saddest and most exhausted brown eyes Woods had ever seen on a child.

'The river's taken me da. He's dead.'

Woods hesitated. The poor lad obviously knew what had happened to his father but hadn't been here when the watchmen had found Yardley's body and removed it.

'Are you hungry? Do you want somethin' to eat?'

The child nodded and Woods led him off the jetty towards his tethered chestnut horse. Georgie's shoulders were slumped with grief, exhaustion and hunger. That wouldn't stop him running off once they reached the street, of course. But Woods knew a good way to keep the lad close.

'This is Samson,' he said. 'He's the biggest and strongest hoss in the Bow Street stable and as gentle as a kitten.'

The boy hesitated beside the large animal and squealed when Woods picked him up and plonked him in the saddle. He grabbed two handfuls of the horse's mane to steady himself.

'Ever ridden a hoss before?' Woods asked, as he gathered up the reins to lead the animal.

Georgie just shook his head, but some colour had returned to his pallid cheeks and a spark to his eyes.

'When did you last have a bowl of broth?'

Georgie's eyes widened. 'Meat?'

Woods grinned and tugged on the reins. 'Come on, Samson. Let's take this lad for a meat feast.'

Woods sat patiently in the quiet dockside tavern while the lad sitting beside him devoured his second bowl of beef broth. Always a man who enjoyed his food, Woods was impressed with the child's appetite, but a bit concerned at the speed with which he ate. He'd ordered a large platter of fresh warm bread with a pat of golden butter and Georgie was adept at stuffing the bread into his mouth with his left hand and using his right to spoon in the broth. Woods hoped he wouldn't cast it back up again.

Eventually, Georgie slowed down, belched loudly and wiped away the dribbles from his chin with his ragged coat sleeve.

Sensing his moment, Woods smiled. 'Now, Georgie. You know why I'm helpin' you and your ma. I know it's upsettin' but I need you to tell me what happened to your da. I already know you were out with your da two nights ago... takin' a walk in the moonlight... and you were chased by two fellas.'

Suspicion clouded the lad's eyes. He pointed a grubby finger at the bandage on Woods' head. 'What 'appened to your noggin?'

Woods hesitated and thought quickly. Georgie may have seen those two coves knock him unconscious, but if he admitted he'd seen him and Yardley body snatching, the lad would clam up.

'I were also takin' a walk in the moonlight – lookin' for my lost dog.'

'You 'ave a dog as well as a hoss?'

Woods nodded. 'Do you like dogs, Georgie?'

'Aye, we 'ad one once. We was special mates. 'E were little and cute and ate scraps, but Ma said we couldn't afford the food. She took 'im away.'

Woods patted his hand. 'That's sad. So, that's how I know those coves chased you and your da – because I were lookin' for my dog.'

'Did you find it?'

'Yes. Now, what happened to you and your da? Did they catch you?'

Georgie shook his head and he frowned. 'We ran too fast fer 'em. Da weren't well that night but 'e took me to the riverbank. Said we might 'ide down there. We 'id in the dark behind the pilin's. We was sure we'd thrown 'em off and was safe. Then...' His voice trailed away and his large eyes filled with tears again.

'Then what?' Woods prompted gently.

'Then Da were taken real bad. Something were wrong with 'is guts and 'e started sweatin' like 'e had the fever. 'E fell on the mud clutchin' 'is belly and screamed. I didn't know what to do to 'elp 'im.'

'It must have been hard for you, son.'

Georgie nodded sadly. 'But that weren't the worst of it. 'Is screams brought them coves back. We 'eard them shoutin' on the wharf and they climbed down to the mud.' He glanced nervously at Woods, his eyes clouded with guilt and grief. 'I were so scared I ran off and 'id behind a pilin' at the end of the jetty.'

'You did right, son. If you hadn't, they would have hurt you.'

The child's bottom lip quivered. 'But I left 'im on 'is own to die!'

Woods patted his hand again. 'You didn't know he would die. What happened next?'

'I weren't far away, and I 'eared them yelling' at da. But 'e were just lyin' on the ground, writhin' around, groanin' and moanin'.'

'What did they want?'

'They said 'e 'ad sommat of theirs. That Da was to 'and it over. They was yellin' at 'im real bad. One of 'em kicked 'im.'

'Do you know what it was? This thing they wanted?'

Georgie lowered his head mournfully. 'Then Da went quiet. I think that were when 'e croaked.' His young voice cracked with emotion and Woods squeezed his hand.

Woods' thoughts returned to the stolen pantaloons. 'Did they take anythin' from him?'

Again, the boy shook his head. 'I couldn't see much. They went quiet, like they was shocked. They squatted down beside 'im, and I 'eard one of them say *The bastard's dead.* They searched through 'is pockets.'

'I know this is an odd question, son, but did they remove his kickseys?'

Confusion flickered across those watery brown eyes. 'No. They just went through 'is pockets.'

'Did they find what they was lookin' for?'

'No.' His lip quivered again. 'They stood up and one of them said *The boy must 'ave it.* The other one said *I'll skin the little bastard alive when we catch 'im.*'

The tears fell again. The young lad was terrified. Woods sighed, gave him a hug and weighed up his options. He'd hoped to take Georgie back to his mother but until those coves were under the hatches he was in grave danger.

'Just a few more questions, Georgie, and then I'll take you somewhere safe. Did you recognise either of those coves?'

'No.'

'Do you think you'd recognise them again, if you saw them?'

'No – but I did see somethin'.'

'What?'

'One of 'em 'ad a metal tooth. I saw it gleamin' in the moonlight when 'e were yellin' at me Da.'

'That's good, very helpful. Well done .' *The lad did better than me*, he thought. *I didn't get chance to catch a proper glimpse of the bastards before they bashed me on my noggin.* 'What did you do after they left?'

'I stayed where I were for ages... Da were quiet, just lyin' there... when I felt brave enough, I went over and sat wi' 'im for a bit. But I couldn't do anythin' for 'im, or move 'im. I knew Ma don't 'ave the money for a burial so I thought it might be best if I just left 'im there and let the river tek 'im...'

Woods grimaced. No little nipper should have to face this and make those kinds of decisions.

Georgie turned his large sorrowful eyes towards Woods. 'Then I went away and 'id. I knew I couldn't go 'ome cos those coves would find me and skin me. Did I do right, Mister? I came back today to see if the Father Thames 'ad tekken Da.'

Woods gave him another hug. 'How d'you like a nice large slice of apple pie to finish off yer meal?'

'With custard?'

'Of course!' Woods pushed back his chair and tossed a few coins on to the table. 'Come on, son. I'm takin' you somewhere safe. At my house we've got rich food, a warm bed and plenty of meat and custard – although not on the same plate.'

Georgie leapt to his feet, delighted.

'Just don't tell Mrs Woods we've already had supper,' he warned the boy. 'Or she might not give us any pie.'

That's sorted, he thought with a sense of satisfaction. *Now, where the devil would he find a dog?*

When he walked into the kitchen at Oak Road with a filthy boy who was clutching a matted and even filthier dog, Betsy's face was surprisingly calm. After twenty years of marriage and four children, there probably wasn't much that could surprise her. But she was clutching her metal ladle so hard her knuckles had turned white.

Rachel and Tabitha were sitting at the table and stared at Georgie and the dog with undisguised curiosity. The dog was a pathetic specimen with a ragged left ear, scratches down his nose and a sticky, weeping eye. 'Ain't that the stray mutt that's been hauntin' the street?' Rachel began.

'Our dog got out again,' Woods said loudly, with a warning glance at his wife and daughter. 'This is Georgie, everyone. Georgie, this is my good lady, Mrs Woods. These are my daughters, Rachel and Tabitha.'

'Evenin', missus,' Georgie said quietly. He squeezed the wriggling terrier tighter for comfort and glanced shyly at the two girls. 'What's yer dog called?' he asked.

'Alfie,' said Rachel.

'Bobbin,' said little Tabitha.

Bobbin?

'That's right,' Woods said quickly, 'his full name is Alfie Bobbin. You can call him either.'

'What's goin' on, Ned?' Betsy asked.

His chest swelled up with pride. 'I've been advanced to principal officer, Betsy!'

Her brown eyes widened beneath her greying brows and a smile reached her lips. 'That's good news.'

'Aye well, it's overdue of course...'

'Long overdue.'

'But all things come to those who wait. And now I'm investigatin' my first murder case.'

Her smile broadened. 'Well done.'

'It's my Da that was killed,' Georgie volunteered.

Betsy blinked and compassion swept over the soft, lined skin of her face. But she wasn't a woman easily distracted. She turned back to her husband. 'So has that wheedlin' magistrate given you a tipstaff?'

'No, not yet.'

'And have you got an increase in your wages?'

'No, not yet.'

'But they've given you a dirty boy to bring home and an even scruffier dog?'

'I'll explain everythin' later, sweetheart,' he said hastily, 'when we've had our celebrations. I thought maybe apple pie for puddin' as a treat? Georgie needs to stay with us for a while.'

'Aye, well, he'll need to bathe first before he sits down to eat at my table. Rachel, go drag the bath out into the scullery, please. I'll put on a pan of water. Dan and Eddie will be home soon, they can supervise his bath.' Betsy reached up to the shelf for the large copper pan they used for warming bath water.

'I ain't 'avin' no bath!' Georgie yelled in alarm. He turned on Woods. 'You said nowt about a bloomin' bath!'

'Oh, stop being such a baby,' Rachel said, rising from her seat to do her mother's bidding. 'It won't hurt you. I bathe all the time. It makes you smell nice – less like a river rat.'

Georgie stared at her aghast, but when it came to dealing with the opposite sex, Rachel was her mother's daughter and brooked no nonsense. Georgie seemed to sense this, and his shoulders drooped in defeat. The two of them were about the same age, Woods realised, but Rachel was tall and well nourished while Georgie was thin and gaunt with malnutrition.

'Come and help me lift the bath,' she instructed him.

Mournfully, Georgie followed her into the scullery, still clutching his borrowed dog.

'Good,' Woods said. 'That'll give me chance to tell you what's happened today.'

Betsy glanced over her shoulder, her mouth twitching with amusement. 'I can't wait to hear all about it, Ned Woods – especially the bit where we get to adopt a mangy, flea-ridden stray.'

Chapter Twenty-One

Lavender let himself into the Woods' kitchen via the back door. Betsy was hovering over the range cooking supper, while Ned was leaning back in his chair at the kitchen table looking rather pleased with himself. Dan squatted over some newspaper in the corner, vigorously cleaning his boots, and the two girls were sitting at the table, Rachel with a book and Tabitha with her doll.

Meanwhile, judging from the splashing, the canine yapping and the high-pitched squeals of a child in distress, Eddie was murdering a boy and a dog in the tin bath in the scullery.

Lavender ignored the noise and sank down into a chair next to Woods. Betsy pushed a tankard of ale in front of him. He thanked her gratefully.

'Evenin', sir,' Woods said. 'How's your case goin'?'

'It's a disaster, Ned.' He gave Woods a brief résumé of his miserable day.

'It's a shame you didn't turn up anythin' about Alfred Gotobed,' Woods said. 'I don't like the cove. Gentry or not, he's a wheedlin' rascal. He gave me a rigmarole story about Ulrich Monmouth turnin' over a new leaf, which is codswallop,' Woods continued. 'Leopards don't change their spots.'

Lavender shook his head. 'I've dismissed him and his staff from my inquiries. What about your own investigation into Garbutt's murder?'

'Softly, softly,' Woods said smugly. 'But I'm makin' progress of sorts with the mystery of our poisoned baron.' He told Lavender his news.

'So, I've brought young Georgie home for a while,' he finished. 'I've sent a note round to tell his mother he's safe – but I ain't told her where he is.'

'That's a good precaution.'

'Our Eddie's givin' him a good scrub while we speak – and that bloomin' dog,' said Betsy. She glared at her second son. 'Our Dan were supposed to be helpin' him – but he's an urgent need to clean his new boots before he goes out. Although why new boots need cleaning is beyond me!'

Dan smirked down at his footwear and gave it another vigorous brush. 'Smartness is important, Ma. You never know who will see your boots. And I always like to show a clean pair of heels.'

'Are you goin' out with Eddie tonight?' Woods asked hopefully.

Dan shook his head.

'I think our Dan is seein' a gal,' Rachel suggested, grinning.

Dan just raised his eyebrows and grinned back.

'I wonder what those coves were after?' Lavender said, his mind still on the case. 'What had Yardley stolen from them?'

'Well, it weren't them damned kickseys. Yardley were still wearin' 'em when they left, accordin' to the boy.'

'Then who took them?'

Woods tapped his nose and winked. 'I've got a notion about that. My old conk smells somethin' fishy.'

'It'll be that stinky urchin you brought home, Da,' Rachel said.

Woods ignored his daughter. 'I'll follow up this hunch tomorrow, sir, and let you know.'

'Well, you seem to have had a more successful day than me, Detective Woods,' Lavender said with a pang of jealousy. 'My leads go round in circles. And you don't need to call me *sir* any more, Ned. We're equals now.'

'Ah, but old habits die hard with me. Changin' folks' names confuses my old noggin.'

Lavender smiled.

Woods pulled the strange rattle out of his pocket and handed it to Lavender. 'What do you think of this? I found it near to where Garbutt were murdered. I figured it were a child's toy. It might be somethin' – it might be nothin'…'

Lavender examined the item and frowned. 'It might be a primitive sort of musical instrument, I suppose.'

'It's a nasty heathen-lookin' thing, whatever it is, with that vicious snake,' Betsy said sharply. 'Put it away, Stephen, before it gives the girls nightmares.'

'Take it to show that museum curator, Mr Benson,' Lavender suggested. 'He might have a better idea about its origins.'

Woods pocketed the tiny rattle. 'Where did he say he worked?'

'At the Attlee Exhibition of Historical Artefacts in Mayfair.'

'There's something else I noticed when I walked out of the bank,' Lavender said. 'Baron Poppleton told me that just before he lost consciousness on the night he ended up in the morgue at Guy's Hospital, he found himself in a damp street with broken cobbles and water dripping down the walls.'

Woods shrugged. 'That describes half the back alleys in Southwark.'

'Yes, but he also said there was an old bench next to railings and a church graveyard. I noticed it matches the description of the road that turns off the High Street and leads to St George's church.'

Woods scratched the stubble on his chin. 'That's a stone's throw away from Gotobed's bank. D'you think there's a connection between Gotobed and that drunken wastrel of a baron?'

Lavender shrugged and drained his tankard of ale. 'It wouldn't surprise me if he was a customer – although the bank wouldn't have been open at that time of night.'

Woods laughed. 'Who knows? From what I saw round the back of the bank the other night, they keep some funny openin' hours.'

Lavender reconsidered his suspicions about Gotobed, then dismissed them. Yes, Gotobed seemed to be popping up everywhere. He had a connection to the murdered Garbutt – and the robbery at Beverley House. But they were clutching at straws.

Lavender pushed back his chair to leave. 'This week has just been one unexplained coincidence after another. Thank you for the ale, Betsy. I'll see you tomorrow, Ned.'

Ned winked at him. 'Meet me in the hallway of Bow Street at eight o'clock – I might have a surprise for you about those darned kickseys.'

Darkness had fallen when Lavender walked outside, and there was a chill in the air that threatened to bring with it a late frost. Lavender pulled up the collar of his coat before he mounted his horse and rode back to the stables at Bow Street. As he crossed London Bridge, a full moon arched above him. A myriad stars glittered in the clear black-velvet sky.

At Bow Street, he asked the night clerk on duty if a message had been left for him from Baron Poppleton. None had.

Shaking his head with disappointment, he strode off through the dark streets towards his home in Westcastle Square in the quieter residential area of Marylebone. This was a route he took every day, and he enjoyed the empty streets at this time of night. Apart from the occasional pool of light thrown out on to the street by the flickering candles of a room where the owner had forgotten to draw the curtains, the gaps between the streetlights were dark and full of shadows. But it was a peaceful walk for a man with a troubled mind.

The wind rustled through the branches of the trees in the small park at the centre of the square. He also heard the distant rumble of traffic on Bloomsbury Street, the barking of a dog – and the quiet clipping of heeled boots behind him.

His gloved fingers curled around the handle of the loaded pistol in his coat pocket. He slowed to a pause beside a gap in the iron railings where a short, steep flight of stone steps led down to the basement kitchen of one of the houses.

Then he spun round and saw the heavily cloaked figure twenty yards behind him – and the cold metal of the raised pistol barrel glinting in the moonlight. There was a flash of blue gunpowder.

Instinctively, he threw himself sideways down the steps. The retort of the pistol bounced and echoed off the walls of the houses enclosing the square.

He landed hard on his right hip, bit back the pain and scrambled to his feet with his own pistol in his hand.

But his assailant was fleeing – had fled – back into the gloom of the quiet street.

He started to give chase – but the movement sent a jarring pain down his leg. He limped out into the middle of the street.

It was too late. The would-be assassin had vanished into the night, and he'd had only a fleeting glimpse of a slight figure enveloped in a cloak – or was it a caped greatcoat?

Confused, he hesitated. There was something not right.

And then it came to him.

The light clipping footsteps had been those of shoes with heels, not the flat heavy boots of a man.

His would-be assassin was a woman.

Of course it was. That bloody newspaper had announced to the world he was investigating the Beverley House robbery organised by a group of scheming actresses – and now one of them had decided to kill him.

Chapter Twenty-Two

'Why are you limping?' Magdalena's beautiful dark eyes gleamed with concern when he stumbled into their dining room.

He sank wearily into his chair at the head of the table and reached for the joint of meat and the carving knife. 'It's nothing. I dismounted awkwardly from my horse tonight, that's all. It'll pass.'

Magdalena picked up the serving spoons, placed some vegetables on his plate and raised one finely arched eyebrow. 'Are you sure I don't need to patch you up again?'

After five years of marriage to a Bow Street officer, she was accustomed to the physical and dangerous nature of his job. But he didn't want to distress her with the news that someone had just taken a shot at him.

'No. I've had a foul day, though. To be honest, Magdalena, sometimes I'd just like to walk away from and live quietly with you and the children on your estates in Spain.'

'Ha!' she laughed. 'And you would be bored out of your head in five minutes. As much as I love my native country, Stephen, there's hardly any mystery to be found in the countryside of the Asturias. Now tell me what's happened to put you in such a bad mood and such daft notions in your head.'

Twenty minutes later, he was feeling much happier and the throbbing in his hip had subsided. This had been helped by the anaesthetic quality of the Madeira they'd enjoyed with their evening meal and the fact that Mrs Hobart, their housekeeper, had made his favourite syllabub for dessert.

But the biggest reason he felt more relaxed was Magdalena. She'd listened patiently while he moaned, and her intelligent questions and quiet observations had soothed his fractious mind.

But he was surprised when she suggested he give Magistrate Conant another chance to prove his worth. 'It can't be easy for him stepping into the shoes of an experienced and respected man like James Read. He's probably a good court magistrate, but Marlborough Street is tiny compared to the operation at Bow Street. He has a far bigger range of responsibilities now and the work of principal officers is new to him. He's still finding his boots.'

Lavender smiled. 'The expression is feet – he's still finding his feet.'

'Ah, you English!' she exclaimed. 'With your silly language full of feet and boots and shoes!'

'You were right with the first expression,' he conceded, laughing. 'About how Conant has stepped into the gargantuan shoes of James Read, one of the best magistrates Bow Street has ever known. Those were big boots to fill.'

Magdalena rolled her eyes. 'You're being very silly now. By the way, who has left?'

'*Left?*'

'Yes, which one of the other five principal officers has left Bow Street?' Suddenly she clapped her hand over her mouth in horror. '*Dios mío!* Don't tell me one of your colleagues is dead?'

'No. No one has died. Why do you think that?'

'It is something you told me years ago. The Home Department will only pay for six principal officers for Bow Street. Now Ned has been promoted, I assumed someone had left.'

Lavender's frown returned. She was right; he'd forgotten about that. Conant couldn't appoint a new detective unless there was a vacancy. *Did Conant understand this?* He shook his head and decided to worry about it tomorrow.

Magdalena had already changed the subject. 'I feel for the Earl and Countess of Beverley and the distress their son has caused them. It is sad when your children don't treat your home and possessions with the respect they deserve.'

'Are you worried about Sebastián when he grows up?'

'I'm worried about *all* of them!' she laughed. 'Heaven knows what Jack will get up to when he's twenty-one! And our darling Alice? Everyone says rearing girls is harder than rearing boys. Although when boys make a mistake, it can be very serious. Did I ever tell you the story about the time Eddie Woods brought a friend home to stay the night with Ned and Betsy?'

'No.' He sat back in his chair, his wine glass in his hand, and looked at his gorgeous wife with renewed affection. Magdalena was plumper now than when they'd first met. She hated her more matronly figure, but he liked it. Naturally curvaceous, she carried the extra weight easily.

What more could a man want? he thought. Two beautiful children asleep upstairs in the nursery, a stepson he loved away at school and a beautiful woman to sit with by the fireside every evening.

What had he done to deserve such happiness over the last five years and to attract such a gorgeous woman? His mother and sisters had always told him he was attractive when he smiled. But he knew he didn't do that often enough; he was too serious by nature. He was tall and slim, but not muscular enough, like Woods, to ever be described as a "fine figure of a man". And his eyes were the same muddy brown as those of the majority of the British population. Secretive, slightly hooded eyes. Eyes that spent most of their time hiding his emotions and his reaction to the chaos in the world around him.

'Eddie forgot to tell his parents his friend was un sonámbulo.' Magdalena's gentle voice disturbed his reverie. 'How do you say this in English?'

'A sleepwalker?'

'Yes. That is it. A sleepwalker. In the early hours, Betsy climbed out of bed to use the chamber pot. She hitched up her nightdress and was squatting over the pot when she saw this strange young man standing in the bedroom doorway, staring at her with eyes of glass.'

171

Lavender laughed and choked on his Madeira. 'Did she scream?'

'Oh, yes! Ned woke up and thought they were being murdered in their sleep. He was so shocked he fell out of bed with a crash. The noise woke up the children and brought the neighbours running round from next door.'

They were both still laughing when the dining room door opened and Magdalena's Spanish maid, Teresa, entered the room.

'There is visitors,' she announced. 'Miss April Clare and a market.'

'A market?' Lavender blinked and braced himself for the arrival of half of Covent Garden's florists and fruiterers.

Despite Magdalena's best efforts, Teresa's grasp of English was still eccentric, and her linguistic skills had been hampered rather than aided by her friendship with the lovelorn young cabbie Mr Alfie Tummins, who spoke in the vernacular. However, he wouldn't put it past April to travel with some colourful friends.

'Yes, the market is a swell nib – but his carriage is stopped outside the house where Mr Alfie Tummins stops. It is in the way.'

'I'm sure his carriage won't be there long, Teresa,' Magdalena said hastily.

Satisfied her beau wouldn't be inconvenienced, Teresa harrumphed and moved aside to allow their guests to enter.

April Clare swept into the room in a billowing emerald silk evening gown and an equally billowing cloud of delicious violet perfume. She wore an expensive sable pelisse with a matching fur trim on her velvet bonnet.

The Lavenders rose to greet her, and the two women embraced. 'April! How wonderful to see you again,' Magdalena said. 'You look radiant!'

'You are too kind, Magdalena. I'm sure I look dreadful. I've done two performances today and I'm wilting like a dead flower.'

'No, you look lovely. Would you like something to eat? A glass of Madeira, perhaps?'

172

'No, thank you – we're just on our way to dine.' She turned around to introduce the powerfully built man standing smiling in the doorway. 'Stephen, Magdalena, may I present the Marquess of Kirby.'

Lavender bowed and Magdalena bobbed a graceful curtsy.

'We're honoured by your presence, Your Lordship,' Lavender said.

The marquess acknowledged this with a slight nod of his head. 'I've heard good things about you, Lavender.'

One of the Lord Treasurers of the government and a member of the Privy Council, Kirby had broad shoulders and thighs that were far too muscular to appear to advantage in the prevailing fashion of skin-tight pantaloons. He wore top boots and breeches, and a black coat buttoned high across his broad chest. Along with the streaks of silver in his dark hair, his attire gave the impression of maturity, strength and reliability rather than fashion. He was about twenty years older than the bejewelled and shimmering actress on his arm. But when April's beautiful dark eyes rested on him, they became luminous with affection.

'Please don't believe everything you read in the newspapers,' Lavender replied.

Kirby laughed. 'I don't. But April has told me how you helped her family a few years ago.'

'It was my pleasure, sir.'

'And now it's my turn to help you, Stephen!' April said in delight. 'I've news about two of your villainous actresses!' She opened the clasp on her pearl-studded oyster satin reticule and sank gracefully into one of the chairs at their table.

The marquess also took a seat, and April drew a sheet of paper out of the reticule. She slid it across the table towards Lavender. 'The main details are on there, but I didn't have time to write it all down.'

'Please just take your time and tell me what you know,' Lavender said. He tried not to show his excitement, but Lavender desperately hoped this might be the break his case needed.

'After you asked for my help, I talked to one of my colleagues at the theatre for information about those jilts who robbed the Beverleys. William Broadhurst worked at the Drury Lane Theatre, and he remembered an actress called Annie Southerby who had a scar from a repaired harelip.'

Lavender nodded. He'd met Broadhurst and knew he was a sensible and intelligent man.

'I suppose the scar made her stand out,' April continued. 'She worked briefly in minor roles. She'd come up to London from the countryside – like so many starstruck actresses. She wasn't particularly talented and had to supplement the casual work she gained at Drury Lane by other means.' April paused and gave Magdalena a nervous glance.

'Please go on,' Lavender said. 'Magdalena doesn't shock easily.'

'Well, she was a tremendous flirt with the men – what we know in the profession as a *ladybird*. She had a string of male admirers and protectors who gave her money.'

Lavender nodded. He knew *ladybird* was a term for a woman of light morals who drifted in and out of prostitution. 'Where is she now?'

'That's the problem, Stephen. She hasn't been seen in London for some years, so I don't understand how she turned up at Beverley House on the night of the robbery. William believes she gave up acting to settle down with a squire from the provinces, as his mistress.'

'Does this squire have a name – or a parish?'

'I don't know his name, but he was the squire of Annie's home town, St Ives in Cambridgeshire.'

'Cambridgeshire? Not St Ives in Cornwall?'

'No. Definitely the town in Cambridgeshire. According to Annie, the man had known her all her life and was besotted with her. He'd paid for the operation to repair her lip. Once she left St Ives to come to London, he followed her and pestered her to return home with him.'

'Was she his mistress before she came to London?' Magdalena asked.

'Probably. I know this is not much help, but someone there might be able to help you find her.'

'Hopefully,' Lavender said. 'I know Cambridge well. What about the other actresses? Did Broadhurst remember any of them? I've been led to believe the four women were good friends.'

'He wasn't sure, but he knew Annie had a gaggle of girlfriends like herself – and he's convinced one of them was a blonde called Caro.'

Blonde? 'That's helpful,' Lavender said. That was two witnesses now who claimed the damned woman was a blonde. She must have worn a wig on the night of the robbery.

'Yes, she was the ringleader of their group. He's not seen or heard of this Caro for years either. He believes her life may have taken the same turn as Annie's. Why do you frown, Stephen?'

'Because according to the young men they duped, Caro was the quietest of the actresses and left early before the theft was committed.'

'Oh, for heaven's sake, Stephen – she's an actress!' April exclaimed, laughing. 'If any of us decide we want to melt into the background, we can do it easily!'

'What else did Broadhurst tell you about her?'

'Ah, this Caro speaks like a pat of butter wouldn't melt in her mouth, but she ran with a nasty crowd of undesirables from Shoreditch. She was a talented actress – but she ruined her career when she was arrested and convicted of stealing from one of her many drunken gentlemen admirers.'

'What happened to her after that?'

'She spent some time in the Bridewell house of correction for thieving. The theatre wouldn't take her back. She seems to have disappeared now. I don't know if the staff at the goal will be able to help you track her down?'

'Not without her full name, unfortunately. But I think the information you've given me about Annie Southerby will be *very* helpful. I'll take a trip to Cambridge tomorrow.'

April looked delighted. 'You really think I've helped?'

'Miss Clare, this is the best news I've had about this damned case in the past few days.'

'Excellent! I can enjoy my supper with a clear conscience now I've repaid my debt to you! This is just as well, because I'm starving. I've barely had a bite to eat all day!'

Chapter Twenty-Three

Thursday 14th April, 1814

It was still dark and a bit chilly when Woods rose before 5 o'clock.

Yawning, he dressed and raided Betsy's pantry for a slice of pie for breakfast. He let Alfie Bobbin out into the street to do his business, then checked the five sleeping children before he left.

Georgie Yardley was still there, curled up beneath his blankets in the boys' room. Clean and well fed, the little nipper was swamped in one of Dan's nightshirts and he looked like he was enjoying the best night's sleep he'd had for years. Woods had half expected the lad to run off in the night with the family's spoons. Mind you, he'd heard Betsy banging around the kitchen before she went to bed, and suspected she'd already locked away anything of value.

Woods pulled his oldest pair of gloves out of the drawer and checked them for holes. There were none. Grunting with satisfaction, he pulled them on and walked out into the cold, dark street. He'd a strong suspicion he'd get his hands on those poisoned kickseys before dawn, and if he had to burn his gloves afterwards, he was damned if he'd toss his best pair on to the fire.

To his relief, he found the elderly watchman, Adams, easily. Night after night these men patrolled the crime-ridden streets of the capital, often in the foulest weather. But this morning, Adams was huddled over his smoking brazier, shivering with cold.

'Good mornin', Adams,' Woods said gently.

The fellow raised his tired eyes in surprise and peered at Woods from beneath the wide brim of his shabby hat. 'I didn't expect to see you again so soon, constable.'

'I'm a detective now and I need your help again.' Woods scrutinised the watchman's thin coat and threadbare trousers and knew he'd been right in his suspicions. His old nose hadn't let him down. *How much do these old fellows get paid for this thankless job?* he wondered.

'What now?'

'I need to know where you pawned them fancy kickseys you took from that dead body snatcher. They're evidence and I need 'em back.'

Adams shuffled uncomfortably, coughed and stroked his whiskers with his filthy hand – he wasn't wearing gloves, Woods noted.

'I don't know what you mean, officer.'

'I've got a witness who says the resurrection man were still wearing them flash kickseys when he croaked it. You was the next fella to see him and you raised the alarm. So don't mess me about: where are they?'

Adams scowled and glanced away.

'You're not in any trouble, fella,' Woods continued. 'In fact, I'm doin' you a good turn here. There's somethin' you don't know about them damned kickseys – they're dangerous.'

'Eh?'

'Where are they?'

'I took 'em to Barty Wilton's shop,' Adams snapped. 'The cheatin' bastard only gave me two bob for 'em.'

Woods snorted. *Bartholomew Wilton.* He should have known. The man was one of the most notorious fences of stolen goods in London. 'Thank you,' he said, turning.

'What were that thing you were goin' to tell me about them kickseys?' Adams called after him.

'They was poisoned. Swill your hands under the pump before you touch anythin' else – or you'll regret it.'

He didn't bother to look back and see the effect of his words on the shocked old man.

It was still dark and raining when Woods trudged across the bridge towards Wilton's pawn shop on Drury Lane. But the city had begun to stir. Shopkeepers scurried towards their premises and the roads were filled with a steady stream of brewers' drays, coal wagons and carts bringing in the fruit and vegetables for Covent Garden's market.

He turned down a dank alley beside one of London's most notorious flesh shops. As it was the only building lit in the street, Woods guessed that business was still brisk in there, despite the early hour.

The upper storeys of the alley leaned perilously close to each other and virtually blocked out the faint pink light of dawn. His boots slithered on the discarded slops thrown out of the upper windows and his broad nose wrinkled in disgust at the stench.

Wilton's place was situated in the basement of one of the tenement buildings. There was no shop window displaying his wares. Only the three weathered red globes dangling from a rotten wooden sign marked it out as a pawn shop.

The entire building was still in darkness, so he hammered on the door, dislodging flakes of the peeling paint with his fist. Eventually, a sash window on one of the floors above was shoved upwards and the thin, nervous face of a wizened old man with wire spectacles appeared, still wearing his night cap. He scowled. 'Constable Woods,' he said, 'what do you want at this ungodly hour?'

'I'm Detective Woods now, Barty. Come down. I need to ask you about somethin'.'

Five minutes later, the bolts were shot back on the door and Woods recoiled at the strong stench of damp walls, dirty clothing and mouldy upholstery that wafted out of the pawnbroker's. The damned shop smelled worse than the dirty alley.

Wilton had thrown a threadbare burgundy velvet jacket over his nightshirt and held a smoking brass oil lamp in his hand. The old man was shorter and more stooped than Woods remembered.

Wilton led the way through the jumble of battered furniture, rolls of carpet and piles of unwanted tradesmen's tools towards the counter at the back of the shop. It was a depressing place, stacked to the ceiling with the detritus of people's lives. Once-precious items had been bartered in desperation for a few coins. He saw two clothes rails against a wall but there were no light-coloured pantaloons squashed among the garments on the wooden hangers.

An elderly grey-haired woman stood behind the counter, calmly folding clothes. She was still in her nightgown and cap but had thrown a woollen shawl over her shoulders.

'Good morning, Missus,' Woods said, touching his hat in respect. 'Do I have the pleasure of addressin' Mrs Wilton?"

'You do,' she replied.

Woods grinned. 'My goodness, Barty! All these years I've known you – and I never knew you was married!'

'I've seven children and eighteen grandchildren as well,' Wilton snapped.

'You've been a busy man, Barty.'

'What of it? Havin' a family ain't a crime.' Barty wore a pair of fraying fingerless woollen gloves. His bare and filthy fingers fiddled nervously with the buttons on his jacket. Mrs Wilton wasn't wearing any gloves either as she folded and unfolded the garments and checked the pockets for loose change.

'No, it ain't,' Woods agreed pleasantly. 'But fencin' stolen goods is.'

'I ain't done nuffin' wrong,' Wilton protested.

'Of course you haven't,' Woods replied, smiling. 'You wasn't to know them nankeen pantaloons brought in by Adams the watchman were filched from a dead man.'

'I still don't know what yer talkin' about.'

'Oh, I think you do.' Woods glanced around at the mountains of filthy jumble littering the shop and sighed. If Wilton wouldn't co-operate, it would take him hours to search through this lot for the damned kickseys. It was time to either threaten Wilton with another spell in Newgate – or play his trump card.

He decided on the trump card. 'You weren't to know them pantaloons was poisoned.'

'Poisoned!'

'Aye, with wolfsbane. Have you heard of it? It's sometimes called monkshood.'

The Wiltons turned pale; they'd heard of the poison.

'It's nasty stuff,' he continued. 'It killed the last fella who wore them kickseys – and it won't do your little nippers any good if they come in the shop and touch it.'

Mentioning their grandchildren was a good strategy. There was a sudden flurry of activity as both Wiltons hurried to a huge mound of used clothing piled on the floor and hurled items across the shop. Suddenly, they both stopped and drew back.

'They're there,' said Barty. 'I ain't touchin' them no more.'

Baron Poppleton's creased and stained pantaloons lay in a crumpled heap on the top of the pile.

'They cost me five bob,' Wilton moaned.

'Aye, they did,' his wife said. 'You'll 'ave to give us back the chinks.'

'I tell you what, Barty, I won't charge you for removin' these poisoned kickseys and makin' your shop safe for your family to visit.'

The Wiltons fell silent.

Carefully, Woods picked up the pantaloons and carried them to the counter, grateful for the protection of his gloves.

'Fetch your lamp closer, Barty. And Mrs Wilton? I'd like some brown paper and string, if you don't mind.'

His plan was to wrap up the toxic garment and take it to Sir Richard. Then he remembered what young Georgie had said about those two vicious coves who wanted something from the dying Yardley.

Gingerly, he patted down the pantaloons and, holding them at arm's length, turned them inside out. He'd no idea how much of that damned poison was still left inside them but he didn't want to send up a cloud of dust and inhale the ruddy stuff.

He saw no evidence of powdered poison but there was something sewn into the crotch that made his eyes widen – a small, discreet and padded pocket. That was a swell place to hide something. Even London's notorious pickpockets didn't tend to stick their thievin' paws down the front of a man's kickseys and fiddle with his nutmegs.

He turned to Mrs Wilton, who'd returned with the brown paper and string. 'What did you find in this pocket?'

Her pale watery eyes blinked. 'Nuffin'.'

'Now, don't try that flummery on me, missus. You've been stood here since I walked in, foldin' clothes and checkin' their pockets. Whatever it was you've found will also be poisoned and deadly. If you and your husband sell it, you'll be committin' wilful murder and I'll have to put you both under the hatches.'

The Wiltons scowled and looked at each other. Then Barty walked behind the counter and used a small brass key to open a drawer.

'It's there,' he said, stepping away. 'That brooch.'

Woods moved forward and his mouth fell open. 'Gawd's teeth!' Among a pile of broken jewellery, silver snuff boxes and scattered beads lay an exquisite pearl and diamond brooch. Constructed in the shape of a flower, it glimmered like starlight in the weak lamplight. He recognised it immediately.

'We'd no idea it were there, in those kickseys,' Barty said.

'Aye, it were a surprise,' his wife confirmed.

'It's a surprise to me too,' Woods murmured. *What the devil was the dead body snatcher doing with the Countess of Beverley's stolen brooch? Was this what those coves wanted from him?*

Scooping the jewel out of the drawer, he wrapped it up in brown paper. In a separate parcel, he wrapped up the pantaloons.

With the brooch safe in his pocket and the pantaloons under his arm, he turned back to the Wiltons.

'Scrub your hands and clean your counter.' Woods pointed to the pile of clothing on the floor where they'd found the pantaloons. 'And burn all of those.'

'All of 'em?' Barty squeaked.

'Yes, all of 'em.'

Chapter Twenty-Four

Extract from *The Times*

THE MYSTERY OF THE CURSED TROUSERS!

Further to this week's startling news that Baron P imbibed too much of the demon drink, was taken for dead and carried by a well-wisher to Guy's Hospital, this correspondent has uncovered a new and dramatic twist to this sorry tale. When the baron was discovered prostrate and unconscious, his valuable nankeen pantaloons had been stolen. The thief has since been found deceased in the most mysterious of circumstances!

Surely there never was such an unlucky garment in the history of men's apparel? Sadly, these accursed trousers are still at large and roaming the city. May the thieves of London beware!

However, the matter has been passed into the hands of Bow Street's newest detective, Edward Woods, an able and competent officer who has worked frequently with the esteemed Lavender. This correspondent has no doubt the mystery will be quickly resolved!

Lavender swore and tossed the newspaper to Magdalena, who was sitting on the other side of the kitchen table, feeding baby Jack. 'The bastards!'

Magdalena drew it towards her and read the offending article. The corners of her mouth twitched with amusement. 'Well, at least they aren't reporting *your* cases now.'

'When I asked them to leave me alone, I didn't expect them to turn on Ned!'

Lavender pushed his plate of ham and eggs to one side. He'd lost his appetite. 'But how?' he asked. 'How do they know about this? We've not told anyone at Bow Street about this investigation into the attacks on Baron Poppleton or about Yardley's death. Conant told me to drop the case. The only people who know about these damned pantaloons are Sir Richard and his assistant, Doctor Kingsley.'

'It must be one of them,' Magdalena said softly as she removed her sleepy son from her breast. 'This would fit in with the article earlier in the week that exonerated Sir Richard and mentioned that new invention, the stethoscope.'

Lavender frowned. Magdalena had a point. Sir Richard had appeared genuinely surprised and denied any knowledge of the first article, and Lavender trusted him. But what about Kingsley?

Sir Richard once told him Kingsley was a dedicated young doctor from a poor background, whose family had struggled to pay for his education. In a rare moment of charity, the surgeon had agreed to pay Kingsley to act as his assistant and deal with the less savoury aspects of the job – which, presumably, included procuring a regular supply of cadavers for dissection. Had Kingsley sold stories to *The Times* to augment his meagre income? But how did this account for the first story this week about his dramatic river chase after that cove Hodge? Kingsley wouldn't have known about that.

Oh good God. Surely there weren't *two* informants? One at Bow Street – and Kingsley at Guy's Hospital?

'Well, at least this *correspondent* didn't mention the aconitine and tip off your poisoner,' Magdalena said. 'That's something to be grateful for, I suppose?'

Still seething, Lavender pulled back the newspaper and glared at it. *There was something about the wording that seemed familiar...*

He ripped the article out of the newspaper and pushed it into his waistcoat pocket. He'd think more about it later.

'I'm going to Cambridge today, and won't be home until late. I'll take my shaving things in case I need to lodge at an inn.'

He leaned down, kissed his beautiful wife and sleepy, milky son and left for work.

Ned was standing on the steps of Bow Street talking in a low voice to another principal officer, John Vickery, when Lavender arrived.

Vickery looked worried and exhausted. As tall and burly as Ned, he was unshaven, and his boots and greatcoat were splattered with mud.

'Mornin', sir,' Ned said. 'You'll never guess what cork-brained scheme our magistrate has come up with now.'

'What's happened?'

'He's decided only *one* of us is to accompany the coinage from the Royal Mint to Birmingham,' Vickery said wearily.

'But we've always sent two officers to guard it on the journey!' Lavender exclaimed. Anything else is reckless and irresponsible.'

Vickery shook his head sadly. 'Aye. There'll be plenty of toby men delighted to learn about this.'

'Conant's sendin' the other officer out to drum up business, like he did with me the other day,' Woods said. 'It's Vickery's turn to make a cake of himself today.'

Lavender sighed with frustration. Magdalena was right. Conant was desperate to make a name for himself. But at what cost? Reducing the security and protection of the country's coinage was foolhardy – and downright dangerous for the officers involved in its transport. Conant simply didn't understand the role he'd inherited.

'Have you seen him today?' Lavender asked.

Vickery nodded. 'I've just been upstairs for my instructions. 'He's furious with you two because of the article about Woods in *The Times*.'

Ned grinned. 'Fame at last.'

185

Lavender grimaced. No doubt part of the magistrate's fury was because *The Times* had revealed that he and Ned were still investigating the Poppleton case. But was he also mad because the newspaper had forced his hand and revealed Ned's promotion? Was Magdalena right? Was Conant lying when he'd promised to promote Ned?

He rolled his eyes and shrugged. 'Conant's brought it on himself,' he told the other men. 'I warned him not to flirt with news reporters and editors and turn a blind eye to their antics.'

'Either way, I'd keep away until he's calmed down,' Vickery suggested. 'Anyway, I'm off to pimp the services of Bow Street to a shopkeeper who was robbed. I'll see you both later.'

'Take care,' Lavender said.

Woods handed Lavender a letter. 'This summons has just arrived from Lady Barlborough to call on her at our earliest convenience.'

'At last!' Lavender said. 'Poppleton must have seen sense and granted my request for another interview.'

Woods chuckled. 'Actually, it's addressed to *Detective Woods*. I reckon her ladyship has also seen the report about the baron's cursed duds.'

'We'll both go,' Lavender said. 'I have some time before I need to catch my coach to Cambridge. Did you find those pantaloons?'

'Oh, yes. And I got more than I were expectin'.' Woods pulled a package out of his pocket. 'You might want to see this little sparkler before we see Poppleton.' He opened the brown paper and laid the Countess of Beverley's diamond and pearl brooch on the counter. 'I tracked down the baron's kickseys to Barty Wilton's pawn shop and this were in a secret pocket sewn into them. I reckon it belongs to your countess.'

Lavender gasped and held up the brooch to the weak morning light. It glimmered beautifully. 'It is hers! My God! Well done, Ned! But how the devil did Yardley get his hands on this?'

'I can't unravel this tangle. The likes of Yardley won't get within half a mile of a place like Beverley House. But I reckon this were what them coves were after when they was chasin' him. They knew he had it. Anyway, I took this sparkler and them kickseys to that wheedlin' sawbones.'

'You've already seen Sir Richard?'

'Aye. He asked me to tell you he and Kingsley are now investigatin' the poisons of the West Indies. He cleaned up this jewel so that it's safe to give back to her ladyship.'

Lavender frowned thoughtfully. 'I don't think Yardley knew he was carrying it.'

'How do you work that out, sir?'

'A man doesn't go out body snatching if he's got something this valuable in his pocket. He heads straight to the nearest fence and lives on the proceeds for a few months. Did Sir Richard say anything about the secret pocket?'

Woods rubbed his stubble. 'He reckoned it looked like it were sewn and padded by a good tailor.'

Lavender nodded. 'Yardley probably didn't know what he was carrying around with him. He would have also been quickly distracted by the effect of the aconitine on his guts, when it seeped through his blistered skin. I think Baron Poppleton had that pocket sewn into his pantaloons – and that he's our jewel thief.'

'Gawd's teeth! D'you think he were workin' with that thievin' gang of actresses?'

'Well, he was present at Beverley House on the night it was stolen – and the curator told us the woman Caro was accompanied by a "fair" young man when they robbed his museum. They might be in this together.'

'Where's the rest of the haul? Where's the necklace?'

'I don't know – yet.'

'This case is bafflin' my old noddle.'

'Mine too. But the missing parts of this jigsaw are slowly coming together.'

187

'I thought the baron were a victim of attempted murder – not a ruddy thief.'

'He may be both,' Lavender said.

Woods laughed. 'Heaven and hell! An educated young nob like him – a peer, for heaven's sake – fleecin' his friend's mothers of their sparklers?'

Lavender was thinking aloud now. 'He may be a peer – but he's an impoverished one. He's dependent on a crotchety old lady for his income. And there's a lot I don't know about his history – a lot of gaps. He wouldn't be the first nobleman to turn to crime.'

'So do we arrest him when we get to Bedford Street?'

Lavender shook his head. 'This brooch was found in Yardley's possession and the baron's reputation is stainless. We need more information before we show our hand.'

Woods nodded his wise old head. 'Aye. I can see it makes more sense if a known felon like our resurrection man were in league with these jewel thieves rather than a nob like Poppleton.'

'Exactly. This brooch was removed from a garment worn by Yardley. Poppleton's lawyer will simply argue the jewel was stolen by our body snatcher and is nothing to do with the baron. I'll be able to make more sense of this peculiar mystery after my trip to Cambridgeshire today.'

'Cambridgeshire? Ain't that where the baron hails from?'

'Yes, it is. Yet another strange coincidence, don't you think? I've had a lead about one of those thieving actresses and intend to track her down and find out more about the robbery. By the way, did Sir Richard give you any more information about the death of Richard Garbutt?'

Woods nodded. 'He confirmed the fella had his throat cut. But told me he put up a fight and has human skin behind his nails. The sawbones also said his killer may have a nasty facial scar.'

'That's something at least.' Lavender gave the jewel back to Ned. 'You return it to the Earl of Beverley after we've visited Lady Barlborough. You found it; you take the credit. But just tell him it turned up at an honest pawnbroker, who saw his advertisement and is interested in the reward.'

Woods laughed. '*Honest?* This is Barty Wilton we're talkin' about!'

'At the moment, we need to quietly gather evidence and play our cards close to our chest, Ned. Very close to our chest. There are aspects of all three of our investigations that I don't fully understand and there seems to be a strange link between them. Until we get more evidence, we need to keep everything to ourselves and not act.'

Woods jerked his thumb up towards the magistrate's office. 'Do you want us to keep him in the dark as well?'

Lavender nodded. 'Until I know more, yes. Once we know how these mysteries are connected, we'll present the whole picture to Conant. But for now, we need to quietly work – together.'

Woods grinned. 'Just like old times, eh, sir?'

Lavender smiled. 'In fact, this might work to our advantage, Ned…'

Chapter Twenty-Five

The two detectives collected their horses from the stables and rode to Bedford Street.

After one of the coldest winters in living memory, spring had a tenuous grasp on England this year. The good weather enjoyed for the past few days had vanished. The temperature had plummeted, and the sky was overcast. The gloom outside seemed to have invaded the dismal and shabby hallway of Lady Barlborough's house; it was more depressing than before and as cold as a mausoleum.

The footman, Feathers, led the two men upstairs to her ladyship's private sitting room. As they followed him, Lavender noticed the stains on the servant's uniform and the missing button.

Above their heads, the crystal chandelier was lacklustre and dull. There were also layers of dust on the ornate carved balustrade. The carpet was filthy and one of the faded damask curtains was only half drawn back across the grimy landing window, as if the effort of pulling it back had been too much for some indifferent housemaid. He wondered how often – if ever – the sick old lady came downstairs and if she was aware of the neglect and creeping decay in her home.

Lady Barlborough's sitting room was cleaner and more cheerful than the rest of the house. Here, the dark oak panelling and heavy Jacobean furniture had been polished until it gleamed, and the windows were clean. And it was warmer. A small fire flickered in the hearth, beside which Sir Humphrey sprawled nonchalantly in a chair, half dressed in an open shirt and breeches, with unbrushed hair and dark circles beneath his eyes. He glanced at the detectives with indifference when they were announced by Feathers and remained silent.

The room was littered with evidence of an invalid. On the other side of the fireplace stood a tall Chinese silk screen and beside it was an empty wicker bath chair. There was also a small table, covered with bottles of medicine and pill boxes.

But there was no sign of Lady Barlborough. A second – partially open – door led off from this sitting room into a darker bedchamber. *Maybe she was in there?*

Suddenly, a hoarse, disembodied female voice snapped at them from behind the screen, making both officers jump.

'Don't bother to sit down. You won't be staying long. I don't like police constables on the premises; it sullies the atmosphere of my home.'

Lavender frowned as he cleared his throat, and he felt Woods tense beside him. 'Good morning, Lady Barlborough. We understand you wanted to see us. How may we assist you?'

'I understand you and that muttonheaded surgeon want to solve this mystery surrounding my nephew's illness. He says he doesn't want your help – but judging by the article in *The Times* newspaper this morning, the pair of you are like dogs with a bone and won't give up. I called you here to let you know we don't want your help – and you won't be paid for your services. This is a shoddy way to attract business.'

'We're not interested in your money,' Lavender replied sharply. 'We're concerned about the safety of your nephew – and others in your household – including yourself. Sir Richard Allison, the eminent surgeon at Guy's, believes Sir Humphrey was poisoned on the night he collapsed and was taken to the hospital.'

'Poppycock,' said the disembodied voice from behind the screen. 'That man is a charlatan.'

'We want to find the source of the poison,' Lavender continued. 'Sir Richard is convinced this wasn't the first time an attempt had been made on the baron's life – and when it comes to matters of science and medicine, Sir Richard is rarely wrong – and yesterday he was vindicated. The poison known as wolfsbane was also discovered in Sir Humphrey's pantaloons when they were retrieved. The man who stole them died after absorbing the wolfsbane into his blood through the open sores on his legs.'

'Good God!' Sir Humphrey sat up in his chair and, for the first time, Lavender saw genuine alarm in his face. *'Wolfsbane?* How the devil did it get into my pantaloons?'

'That's what we need to find out.'

'Why wasn't I affected?'

'Your smooth and healthy skin saved your life. The dead man had open sores on his leg through which the poison penetrated his body. But we believe *you* were the intended victim. We think this was the first attempt to poison you. When the aconitine – the wolfsbane – failed to take effect, we think the murderer tried again with another poison last Saturday night.'

'Calm down, Humphrey,' Lady Barlborough said. 'This is the ranting of that deluded surgeon. He is trying to make his name and extract payment from us.'

'The wolfsbane is a fact,' Lavender retorted. 'And your nephew's garment was laced with it.'

'We need to track this poison back to the murderin' cove who peppered your pantaloons,' Woods said.

'If you don't believe us,' Lavender suggested, 'send your own physician to Guy's Hospital to verify this evidence independently.'

The woman fell silent.

Poppleton ran his fingers through his thick blond hair and groaned. 'This is serious, isn't it, Lavender? Some cove wants to turn me into a dustman.'

Self-preservation had kicked in. Poppleton had stopped glancing at the mysterious woman behind the screen now; his attention was fixed on Lavender and Woods. If Lavender didn't suspect him of being a liar and a thief, he might have felt sorry for him.

'Oh, for heaven's sake, Humphrey!' snapped the woman. 'This is nonsense. It will be someone at the laundry who has done this. Some lunatic wants to kill one of his – or her – customers out of spite.'

'But those pantaloons were brand new,' the baron protested. 'They'd never been laundered!'

'In that case, I need to speak to your tailor and your valet,' Lavender said.

'I don't have one – a valet, that is. My tailor is Greenly on Burton Road. I ordered them two weeks ago. They were delivered last Wednesday.'

'Who's touched them since they arrived?'

Feathers brought the parcel up to my room – they were still wrapped at this point.'

'Did the wrapping look like it had been tampered with?'

'No.'

'What happened next?'

'I tried them on to check the fit and hung them in the closet in my dressing room. The next time I saw them was Friday evening when I put them on to go to the theatre with Cottingham and the others.'

Friday? So, Poppleton wore them on the night of the jewellery theft? The earl and viscount had avoided the topic of sexual intimacy between the young men and the actresses, or explained the sleeping arrangements of that night, but it was possible that someone at Beverley House had laced the pantaloons with poison once the baron was asleep. He'd try to get Poppleton alone, away from his aunt, and discretely ask him what happened and who had access to his bed chamber.

'Did you ask any of the servants to press them for you before you wore them?'

'No.'

'Do your closet and dressing room have locks on the doors?'

'No.'

Lavender sighed. 'Then anyone could have gone in there while you were out and sprinkled them with poison. We will investigate your tailor along with your servants.'

'Oh, good grief,' Lady Barlborough snapped. 'Surely you don't suspect my servants. Most of them have been with me for years.'

'I suspect everyone in the house except yourself and Sir Humphrey's sister,' Lavender replied. 'Fortunately, at the moment, the only people who know we've discovered the wolfsbane are yourselves.'

'You will be discreet in your inquiries?'

194

'Very. The last thing we need is for the poisoner to take flight – but you must be careful about what you eat and drink – especially you, Sir Humphrey. It seems to me everyone in this household had the opportunity to commit this crime, and we must concentrate on who had the greatest motive. I've asked you this before, Sir Humphrey, but I ask again. I need to know of anyone whom you've wronged or offended. *Anyone* who might hold a grudge against you?'

'There's no one!'

'Please think, sir.'

'My nephew is a charming young man,' Lady Barlborough said. 'It's hard to imagine anyone hates him that much.'

Poppleton threw his aunt a look of gratitude. 'It must be a misunderstanding. Maybe they *think* I've offended them in some way.'

'Like how?' Woods asked.

'Well, there's the parlour maid, for a start. Occasionally, I flirt with her.'

'Humphrey!'

'It's harmless fun, Aunt. But she has a sweetheart – maybe he's the jealous type? And I'm always teasing Effy, my aunt's maid... about that hairy mole on her chin...' His voice trailed away.

Lady Barlborough snorted. 'Effy wouldn't try to poison you, Humphrey. She adores me and knows how good you and Lottie are for me and my health.'

'What about money?' Lavender asked. 'Are you in debt to anyone? Has there been a misunderstanding about a card game, perhaps? A wager gone wrong?'

'Absolutely not,' the baron snapped. 'I manage my financial affairs well – and no one has ever accused me of cheating at cards.'

'Which is just as well,' Lady Barlborough said, 'because Sir Humphrey also manages my affairs. I have absolute trust in him. If you suspect a financial motive, Lavender, you may as well suspect my irritating sister and her unpleasant daughter, Diana.'

'How so?' Lavender asked cautiously.

'I've recently changed my will. Until a year ago, I saw very little of Sir Humphrey and Lottie. I'd reluctantly decided to leave my estate to my dreadful sister. I had no choice at that point. However, now I have a male heir in the house, naturally I plan to leave everything to Sir Humphrey. Men are so much better at handling money – and my sister is a wet goose. He will dispense a suitable allowance to his female relatives.'

'*Naturally*,' Lavender said drily. Did she know, he wondered, that Poppleton had already stopped the allowance she'd arranged for her sister? 'And what would happen to your estate if Sir Humphrey were to die?'

'It would revert back into my sister's control.'

'Do Mrs Farrow and her daughter know about this change to your will?'

'Of course not. I don't discuss my affairs with them.'

'Diana may know,' Poppleton said. ''She's always in the kitchen talking to the servants. One of them might have been eavesdropping and mentioned the lawyer had been here.'

'Miss Farrow? Really?' Lavender asked. He decided Poppleton and his aunt would be more forthcoming if he played along with their snobbishness. 'That's surprising behaviour for a woman of her class.'

Lady Barlborough's rasping voice became brittle and harsh again. 'Yes, she's a strange girl – a great disappointment to us all.'

'How so?' Lavender asked.

'Miss Farrow has no social graces whatsoever and is gauche and uncomfortable in polite society. Her chances of making a good marriage are remote. She was devoted to her bookish father and still mourns him. He spoilt her and let her follow unladylike pursuits. I believe at one point she assisted him in his medical practice.'

'Shockin',' Woods murmured.

'I've a horrible suspicion that behind those dreadful spectacles of hers, she's a blue stocking.'

Lavender imagined the woman shuddering behind her screen.

'We also think she's a thief,' Sir Humphrey said. 'Things have disappeared – valuable items – on the days of her visits.'

'*Really?*' Lavender exclaimed, in mock surprise. *More thefts?*

'We've stopped Diana coming to the house,' Lady Barlborough added. 'It was the only way to stop the petty theft.'

Lavender paused thoughtfully. If Sir Humphrey had been pawning his aunt's valuables and had blamed his cousin, Diana Farrow had a motive to murder him. And if she knew the will had been changed in his favour, then she had an even bigger one. *But Diana Farrow had been at the Wapping church with her mother on the day Sir Humphrey collapsed...*

'Oh, and by the way, Lavender, where are my pantaloons?'

Here it comes, Lavender thought. This arrogant young popinjay is confident we haven't discovered the stolen brooch; he wants it back.

'They cost me six guineas,' the baron continued. 'I'd like to retrieve them.'

'Good heavens, Humphrey,' his aunt exclaimed, 'they've been poisoned!'

'I'm sure once they're laundered, they'll be safe.'

Lavender thought of the two thugs who'd chased Yardley and hesitated before he replied. The last thing he wanted to do was send those coves to Sir Richard and Doctor Kingsley.

'Those pantaloons are evidence in the murder of Yardley, the man who was poisoned. We're keeping them in the evidence room at Bow Street.'

Woods tensed beside him at the lie. But long experience of working together meant he knew not to let his surprise show on his face.

'We'll investigate Miss Farrow's movements over the last few days as well,' Lavender continued. 'I hope to have some answers for you soon. Now, do we have permission to proceed with this investigation?'

There was a short silence, then the woman behind the screen expelled a rasping sigh of frustration. 'This is an unpleasant business but very well, Lavender – if it makes Humphrey feel safer, then yes, you can. My niece, Miss Lottie Poppleton, manages the household. She can tell you about the servants. And you can tell your magistrate I'll pay for your services.'

'Thank you, Ma'am.'

'Yes, thank you, Aunt Verity.' Poppleton leaned over and took her hands in his out of gratitude. As he did so, he gently pulled them towards him and, for the first time, part of Lady Barlborough became visible.

She wore fingerless lacy gloves. Her fingers and thumbs were pitted with dozens of pus-filled red sores. It was a quick glance, but enough. Lavender gasped with surprise when he suddenly realised the nature of the debilitating condition that made her hide behind a screen and avoid contact with everyone except her nearest and dearest.

Poppleton saw him staring. He dropped his aunt's hands and scowled.

Suddenly, the door to the bedchamber flew wide open and Lottie Poppleton floated into the room in a pretty high-waisted gown of peach cotton trimmed with gold ribbon at the neck. 'I've come to give you your medicine, Aunt,' she said sweetly.

'Good grief, is it that time already?' Lady Barlborough asked. 'Where's Effy?'

Had the girl been listening in the other room? Lavender wondered.

Two tendrils of Lottie's beautiful blonde hair fell down the side of her heart-shaped face in symmetrical curls, but the rest was gently pulled up from her slender neck and tied in a loose swirl on the top of her head. She carried a silver spoon in her hand and picked up a bottle of medicine from the small table.

'I don't know where she is,' the young woman replied, 'so I thought I'd do it. Deary me, Humphrey! You've let Aunt's fire go out!'

Smiling at the admonishment, her brother rose to his feet and picked up the poker.

'You may wait for my niece downstairs,' Lady Barlborough said. 'She'll be with you soon, once I've explained this extraordinary situation to her.'

Lavender bowed and walked out of the room with Woods.

Chapter Twenty-Six

'Well, that's a turn-up for the books,' Woods whispered while they walked down the chilly, deserted staircase. 'It's another one of those ruddy coincidences.'

'What is?' Lavender asked.

'That young lass – she's Poppleton's sister, ain't she?'

'Yes.'

'Well, I saw her and her maid the first time I went into Gotobed's bank. I couldn't miss her – she were the prettiest gal in there. She were wearin' a purple gown.'

Lavender paused on the stairs and cast his mind back to the first time he'd visited this house. Lottie and her maid had returned while he was waiting – and yes, she was wearing a lilac silk gown beneath her dark green velvet spencer jacket.

Mrs Farrow had chided her for running an errand and leaving her sick brother alone with the servants. Maybe her aunt had a point. *What was so important about visiting the bank while her brother was so ill?*

Lavender sighed and resumed his descent of the stairs. These damned coincidences kept cropping up – especially concerning Gotobed's bank. Gotobed kept the Beverley jewels in his vault. Sir Humphrey had been in its vicinity on the night he passed out and now his sister appeared to be a customer at the same bank. Ned had had his suspicions about Gotobed and Ulrich Monmouth all along – and the hunches of his experienced colleague were often proved right. When his old nose smelled a rat, it usually had whiskers and a very long tail.

'Ned, I need to leave to get the coach for Cambridge.'

'I can manage here, sir. I'll search the house for poisons, talk to Miss Poppleton about the servants and check out his tailor. But why did you tell the baron those kickseys were at Bow Street? Sir Richard still has them at Guy's Hospital.'

Lavender stopped and glanced around the deserted hallway to check no one was listening. He lowered his voice. 'I told that lie because I suspect either Poppleton or those two coves who attacked Yardley may try again to get them back. No one knows we've found the brooch. Poppleton thinks it's still hidden in the pocket. I don't want Sir Richard and Kingsley in danger.'

Woods laughed. 'What? You think they'd try to steal them ruddy kickseys back from under their nose?'

Lavender shrugged. 'I don't know how desperate they are. And Poppleton's arrogance and self-confidence are shocking.'

Woods stroked his stubble thoughtfully. 'In that case, I think I'd better warn the fellas at Bow Street there might be trouble. Do you also want me to look into Mrs Farrow's movements on the day Poppleton was collapsed?'

'I've already done that, Ned. She and her mother were at a charity event last Saturday. Neither of them were here. But you can ask Poppleton if he removed his pantaloons last Friday while he stayed at Beverley House and if he thinks anyone there touched them.'

Woods grinned. 'That'll rattle him – I'll enjoy that.'

'Oh, and there's another thing, Ned – take Constable Barnaby with you, wherever you go, especially at night. Some woman took a shot at me last night.'

'What!'

'She missed – but this damned case is getting dangerous. Keep Barnaby close and make sure you're both armed.'

Woods' brown eyes stared at him in concern out of his great moon of a face. 'I think you need to be careful too, sir.'

'Oh, I'll be safe enough in Cambridge.'

Woods grinned. 'Your old stompin' ground. The place of your misspent youth.'

'I wasn't there long enough to misspend anything – never mind my youth.'

Woods glanced back up the stairs. 'What do you think is wrong with the old lady?'

'It's the pox,' Lavender said quietly.

'Gawd's teeth! Smallpox?'

'No, the other one. The French disease. From what I saw on her hands, she's in the later stages of syphilis.'

Woods grimaced in disgust. 'Will she run mad?'

'Possibly. But I understand there can be long periods of lucidity before the disease attacks the brain.'

'What about her face? Her nose?'

'I think that's why she hides behind the screen.'

'I thought it were just harlots and whores who caught the pox – not aristocratic women.'

'She'll have caught it from Lord Barlborough. Mrs Farrow told me her brother-in-law was a libertine.'

Sadness swept over Woods' face. 'It'll explain why she don't have no young nippers of her own.'

Lavender nodded. 'Yes, it will have ruined her life – and her hopes for the future. Her loneliness, fear and misery over the last few years will have been dreadful. She knows she's facing a wretched death.'

'No wonder she's such a bad-tempered old tabby.'

'And no wonder she decided to take in her niece and nephew when they threw themselves on her mercy,' Lavender concluded. 'Mrs Farrow also told me Lady Barlborough had made the best marriage in the family – I think she was wrong. I don't think Mrs Farrow understands half of what's happening in this house.'

Lavender left to catch his coach and Woods waited in the hallway for Lottie Poppleton.

But the baron was the first person to come down the stairs.

'Excuse me, sir – now we're alone, I need to ask you a question on the quiet. Did any of them thievin' actresses get near to your pantaloons last Friday at Beverley House?

Poppleton looked horrified. 'They most certainly did not!'

'Only it's crossed my mind that they had the opportunity to pepper them with poison.'

'That's a ridiculous notion!' Poppleton hurried away to the study at the back of the house, leaving Woods chuckling.

When Lottie Poppleton appeared, she looked pale and upset. 'I can't believe it, Detective!' she said quietly. 'Who would want to hurt dear Humphrey?' She pulled a shawl around her shoulders against the chill when she descended the stairs.

'Don't you worry, Treacle. We'll soon find this felon and get him – or her – under the hatches.'

'Her?' she exclaimed. 'Do you think a woman is behind this?'

'Poison is often a female's murder weapon of choice.'

'An *unnatural* female, Detective! Surely?' She sighed and pulled herself up straighter. 'Let's get on with this unpleasant business. What do you need from me? Where on earth does one begin in a dreadful situation like this?'

'Is there a room where we can talk privately, Ma'am?'

She led him into a gloomy antechamber off the hallway and closed the door behind them. Woods' eyes swept over the peeling wallpaper, the thick dust and the uncomfortable furniture, and he decided to remain standing. He pulled out his notebook and pencil. 'There's three things I need, miss. I want to see where you keep the household poisons – and to search the servants' quarters. You and your brother need to search your own rooms, too.'

'Why?'

'The poisoner might have hidden the bottle anywhere – they're unlikely to keep this damnin' evidence. The bottle may have been thrown away a long time ago. But as yet, the poisoner doesn't know we've discovered the wolfsbane in your brother's kickseys, so it might still be here.'

'I see.'

'I also need a list of the servants' names and everything you know about them.'

'Oh, good grief. Did my brother tell you we've only lived here for a year? Some of the servants have been here far longer than us.'

'Just tell me what you know about them.'

'There's only four of them. Cook – Mrs Jones – has been here since Lord Barlborough was alive last century. She's a slovenly creature and her kitchen is chaotic.'

'The cook is often the first person to investigate when there's poison about.'

'But she seems genuinely fond of my brother,' Lottie protested. 'She often makes his favourite food.'

Woods nodded sympathetically. He knew that was a sign of genuine affection.

'Our footman, Feathers, has also been a servant here since the time of Lord Barlborough.'

'How does he get along with your brother?'

'They seem quite chummy – but they're the only two men in a house full of women, so I suspect this draws them together. Feathers had a military background before he became a footman. Humphrey regularly sends him out to place bets and run errands for him.'

'He trusts him?'

'I'd say so, yes. The housemaid, Hetty Green, is about twenty-two and can be a bad-tempered, rude and quite snooty madam. She sometimes acts as a lady's maid for myself and my aunt. She was employed a few months before we arrived and is engaged to be married. She rarely smiles and I think she can't wait to get married and leave us, but I don't think she has any cause to hate Humphrey.'

'He admits he flirts with her.'

She shrugged her shoulders beneath her shawl and smiled. 'Humphrey flirts with any woman under thirty.'

'Including his aunt's nurse, Effy?'

'He tries, but Effy is a taciturn, unfriendly woman. She's a good nurse but keeps herself to herself.'

'How long has she been here?'

'Only about two months. I'm afraid my aunt can be a difficult patient at times. Her illness comes and goes in severity, and she has had a lot of nurses. I'm surprised Effy has stayed so long.'

Woods asked her for their full names, wrote them down, then snapped his notebook shut. 'Right. Please take me up to their rooms.'

He followed her through a scuffed door at the rear of the hall, which led to the kitchens, the servants' staircase and the rear entrance to the house. It was a long, dirty corridor flagged with stone.

Two women were standing by the back door, talking; the tallest wore a pristine nurse's uniform, the other a cloak and bonnet. The cloaked gal blinked in surprise through her wire spectacles when they approached. She was a plain little thing and her companion, the nurse, wasn't much of a looker either. A skinny long meg with a horny nugget on the side of her huge conk.

'Diana!' Lottie snapped. 'I thought we'd made it quite clear you were no longer welcome here!'

So, this were the thievin' cousin, were it? Woods eyed Diana Farrow curiously and tried to get a glimpse of her hosiery – but to no avail. He wasn't sure what a 'blue stocking' was, but it must be something shocking.

'Oh, don't take on so, Lottie,' the young woman replied in her quiet, high-pitched voice. 'I've called in to bring you a jar of raspberry jam from last year's harvest. My mother found it in her pantry and thought you'd appreciate it.' She held out a glass jar of red jam.

'We don't require any of your mother's jam. And Effy, my aunt needs your assistance to go for her nap. Where were you when it was time for her medicine?'

Shock flitted over the nurse's face. 'Lor! I clean forgot the time. I'm sorry, Miss Lottie, I'll go up straight away. Goodbye, Miss Farrow.'

She hurried past them towards the main part of the house, clutching the jam. As she passed Woods, he reached out and took it from her. 'I'll have this, if you don't mind.'

The nurse stopped in shock. 'Who are you?'

'I'm Detective Ned Woods from Bow Street. I'm investigatin' the theft of Sir Humphrey's pantaloons. This might be evidence.'

'Evidence? Of a trouser theft?'

He winked. 'It takes all forms, Treacle.'

The woman opened her mouth to protest but thought better of it and left.

Meanwhile, Diana Farrow shrugged, turned, and reached for the door handle.

Lottie watched her leave without saying a word, then she sighed. 'My aunt's servants are an outspoken, truculent bunch at times. They've had far too much freedom while she's been ill. And Diana sets a bad example – she's too intimate with all of them. Feathers and Cook have known her since she was a child, of course.'

'It must be hard for you,' Woods said gently.

'Will you check the jam for poison?'

'Yes, ma'am. I'll give it to Sir Richard, the surgeon at Guy's Hospital.'

She led him to a store cupboard at the end of the corridor and pointed to the jars and packets on the top shelf. 'These are our rat poisons. But I'm afraid I know nothing about them.'

There was a box of white powdered arsenic and a bottle of prussic acid. Both had been opened and used, but Lottie was unable to tell him how recently.

Woods made a note for Sir Richard, but he knew the pompous sawbones would dismiss both these deadly – but common – poisons – as irrelevant to their investigation.

They went up the stairs to the servants' quarters. These poky rooms were even colder than the rest of the miserable old house, they were sparsely furnished, and the servants had few possessions for him to rifle through.

As they left the attics, Woods noticed a linen cupboard with a warped door set at waist height in the wood panelling. He was just about to investigate it when the housemaid, Hetty, clattered up the narrow wooden stairs.

'You'll have to come quick, Miss – your aunt has had a bad turn and needs you.' She gave Woods a scathing glance. 'I think it's the upset. Sir Humphrey has sent Feathers for the doctor.'

'I'll come now. Have you finished, Detective?'

'Yes, Ma'am. You go; I'll see myself out.'

Once the two women had disappeared down the stairs and silence had descended on the top landing, Woods jerked open the cupboard door. It was full of old sheets, pillowcases and towels for the use of the servants, but right at the bottom he felt something solid and metal.

It was a flintlock pistol with an engraved silver barrel and decorated walnut handle. Beside it was a box of round pistol shot and a pouch of gunpowder.

'Heaven and hell!' he murmured, frowning. 'I weren't expectin' this.' He snapped open the barrel and saw it was loaded and primed.

There was no way to tell who owned this weapon. His first thought was that Feathers had put it there, to grab for protection if the house was ever invaded or burgled. Men who left the army often brought home pistols. But someone had taken a shot at sir the night before. Maybe it wasn't one of those thieving actresses who'd tried to kill him. Maybe it was the poisoner.

And if the poisoner got desperate, what was to stop him – or her – shootin' Sir Humphrey?

Lavender had told him to play his cards close to his chest and just gather evidence, but he wasn't comfortable leaving a loaded pistol lying around.

He removed the deadly ball and pocketed it, along with the box containing the rest of the shot.

He replaced the pistol, closed the cupboard door and made his way downstairs.

Chapter Twenty-Seven

Lavender had plenty of time to think about these latest revelations surrounding Sir Humphrey while his coach rattled towards Cambridge. But he found it easier if he combined the chronology of the past few months with what he knew about Poppleton's accomplice, the mysterious actress and convicted thief known as *Caro.*

Last winter, Caro and a fair-haired young man had robbed the Attlee museum in Mayfair of a valuable Egyptian artefact known as a wesekh. If Sir Humphrey was this young man, perhaps Joseph Benson, the curator, would be able to identify him?

To dispose of such a highly unusual and valuable item as this broad collar, Poppleton and Caro would need to be part of a sophisticated gang of crooks, fences and corrupt jewellers who had links on the Continent. It would take skill to remove the carnelians and the turquoises and melt down the gold. And this was his first unanswered question: how on earth did an educated and aristocratic young man like Poppleton become embroiled in a criminal gang?

Last Friday, both Caro and Sir Humphrey were present at Beverley House when the jewels were stolen in a well-organised sting.

How they knew that the jewels were still in the house was a mystery, but he had a strong suspicion it was something to do with Viscount Cottingham. In fact, he'd wager a sovereign it was that silly young man who'd let the cat out of the bag while he was drunk. Cottingham had been asked by his father to tell the steward to return the jewels to the bank. But he forgot and may have casually mentioned this to his friend Poppers.

Everything became so much clearer now Lavender knew of Poppleton's involvement in the crime. For the first time, he was enjoying this case. He'd got the bit between his teeth and felt excited. The weariness that had dogged him since his father's death had lifted.

The baron and Caro had arranged the sting between them, and she'd roped in her friends to help. When the drunken young men left the theatre, they were approached by the actresses, who claimed an old acquaintance. Poppleton had probably already told them the names of the young men and various other personal details that gave credence to their claim of a prior acquaintance.

Interestingly, Poppleton and Caro seemed to have kept their heads down during the actual robbery. It was the thin pale blonde actress called 'Lou' who'd bewitched the viscount and pestered him to take them back to Beverley House. It was Lou who asked about the jewels in the portrait, and persuaded Cottingham to get them out of the strongbox.

Sometime during the night, Lou had returned to the earl's bedchamber and removed the valuables. Was Caro her accomplice? Or was it Poppleton? Caro had left Beverley House early, but she may have still been there when the theft took place.

The baron was wearing his new pantaloons and obviously slipped the brooch in the secret pocket to get it out of the house. But where was the damned necklace? Presumably one of the women had hidden it about her person and carried it out. But it seemed odd that the baron still had the brooch the next night when he set off to join his chums at the dog fight in Southwark.

Was it his intention to hand it over to his fence before he met up with the others? An intention unexpectedly thwarted when he mysteriously collapsed in that alleyway?

Obviously, those two coves who'd chased Yardley and attacked Ned suspected the resurrection man had the brooch in his possession – but they didn't seem to know about the baron's secret pocket in his pantaloons. If they were part of Poppleton's villainous network and he'd sent them to recover the brooch, why hadn't he told them about the secret pocket?

And who the devil had tried to poison the man? And why?

There was no honour among thieves, but when they had disagreements they tended to grab a blade and slit each other's throats rather than resort to poison.

Lavender sighed and glanced out of the window. There were still too many unanswered questions and gaping holes in this case to make sense of it all. But he was hopeful that by the end of the day he'd have some more answers.

The rain drummed on the roof of the coach and the condensation and rivulets of water that ran down the glass made it difficult to see outside. Not that there was much to see, if he remembered rightly.

They were hurtling along straight roads through the flat black earth of the watery fens. Occasionally, the gradient increased, and they'd find themselves dashing through a village that clung to the security of the high ground. Sometimes he'd glimpse the low roof of an isolated farm that looked half submerged in the peat. The landscape would be saturated after such a wet winter and spring, the ground waterlogged.

He'd first taken this trip as an excited eighteen-year-old student on his way to read law at King's College. The cleverest boy at St Saviour's Grammar School, he'd earned a place as a sizar at King's. He was one of two undergraduates who were given a free education in exchange for performing menial duties for the master. This wasn't as onerous as it sounded because their master turned out to be a kindly man with few needs.

Lavender quickly made friends with the other sizar, a philosophy student called Simon Durham. It wasn't easy for either him or Durham to be surrounded by hundreds of extremely wealthy and titled young men who often bullied and patronised them because of their charitable status.

But it wasn't the stigma of his genteel poverty that made Lavender leave at the end of the first year. It was the boredom – and the prospect of a future without mystery. He didn't want to fight crime in a courtroom. He wanted to do it on the streets of the capital, like his father.

John Lavender had been a taciturn man, devoted to his wife and family – and his job as a Bow Street constable. Lavender couldn't remember how old he was when he first realised that every evening after his mother had put them to bed, his father would sit down by the fire with his pipe and tell his wife about his day and how his investigations progressed.

It was better than a bedtime story. Night after night, he sneaked downstairs and listened at the parlour door. He loved hearing about the arrests the best. He felt a surge of personal pride every time his father clapped the iron handcuffs on another felon.

Was my undemonstrative father ever proud of me? he wondered. The snake of grief uncurled in his stomach again as he realised it was too late to ask.

When he'd returned home after his first year at Cambridge and announced he wanted to become a Bow Street officer, his father had just nodded. 'Aye, I thought you'd be back. I'll take you there tomorrow. Ned Woods will take care of you – he'll show you the ropes and see you all right.'

Lavender had never regretted his decision but he'd no notion how his father had felt. Not every man wanted his son to follow in his footsteps and fighting crime in the seedy underbelly of the capital was both dangerous and dirty. Would his father have preferred him to continue with his legal studies, he wondered, and spend his days in the safety of a dusty lawyer's office?

His mind drifted back to his old friend Simon Durham. They'd kept in touch after Lavender left Cambridge but he hadn't seen Durham for fifteen years. His friend had done well in academia and had become a senior fellow at Magdalene College.

Lavender remembered with a jolt that this was the college attended by Poppleton, Cottingham and their chums. Would Durham remember those young men? He resolved to call into Magdalene on his way back and find out.

The rain stopped and the spring sun came out to welcome them when they drove through the Leys, that stretch of unenclosed fields and marshy waste that bordered Cambridge on the south. The verges of the road were lined with the blue and gold of scillas and daffodils. Ahead, he caught a glimpse of the gleaming spires and pinnacles of the colleges. Above them all was the soaring tower of King's College Chapel. And in its shadow clustered the lesser buildings and smoking chimneys of the townsfolk.

The carriage came to a gentle halt in front of an inn with stables behind it on Trumpington Street. The coachman shouted 'House, there!' and the landlord and the tapster both came out in a bustle of welcome.

Lavender climbed down and stretched out his back and limbs. Apart from the usual smell of coal fires and horse manure, the air in Cambridge was fresher. It was good to get out of the smoke and smog of London for a while.

The streets were meaner than he remembered; the houses small and ugly, huddled in on themselves as though for protection. The citizens scurried about with surly faces. And much to his surprise, there wasn't a single black-gowned undergraduate in sight.

He turned towards the ostler. 'Where are the students?'

'Gone 'ome, sir. It's the fever.'

'Fever?'

'Aye, there's nine or ten dead. They've shut them colleges.'

'And the masters?' Lavender asked in surprise. 'Have they also left the city?'

The man shrugged. 'Some 'ave.'

Lavender enquired about the next coach to St Ives and was told it would be another two hours before it arrived. Sighing, he hired a horse to complete the rest of his journey. *Why was it always two steps forward, one step back with this damned case?*

But the stables gave him a decent mount and by the time he'd left the bustle of Cambridge he felt happier. The sun was pleasantly warm on the back of his neck and the rich loamy smell of the fens washed over him.

His route took him down a network of lanes edged with buttercups still glistening with rainwater. Occasionally, there'd be a break in the straggling hedges, and he saw fields of absurd lambs gambolling around in circles on spindly legs. He rode through a copse of limes and chestnuts, their wet leaves blindingly fresh with the green of early spring.

These were the last trees he saw for miles as the road stretched over the flat watery terrain beneath an immense ice-blue sky. Everywhere he looked there was water glistening around him. The landscape was dissected with dykes and sour-smelling ditches. Apart from one private carriage and a drover with a herd of plump cattle, he saw no other life except the waterfowl.

Eventually, the church tower and chimneys of St Ives appeared on the horizon. At this point the road forked and Lavender stopped at the battered old road sign in surprise. One wooden sign pointed to St Ives; the other to Netheredge.

Well, well. Who would have expected this? he thought, and smiled to himself.

St Ives was a medieval market town with old wooden houses clustered around the banks of the Great Ouse river. The vast number of taverns in the broad central street suggested that on market day this town was bustling, boisterous and bawdy. But today it was quiet, with only a handful of shoppers and a few wisps of straw drifting in the breeze over the cobbles.

Most of the activity in the town was down on the banks of the sluggish grey river. A six-arch stone bridge with a medieval chapel at its centre traversed the oily water. In its shadow on both banks, stevedores scurried around like ants loading and unloading their goods off the barges.

Lavender chose a tavern called The Dolphin and asked the ostler to feed and rub down his horse.

The landlord, a gruff, whiskery fellow in a stained apron, was surprised and a bit wary of the sudden appearance of a Bow Street runner in his smoky and gloomy tavern, but he quickly dispatched his potboy to fetch the local constable. Lavender used the wait to enjoy a tankard of ale and a large slice of meat and potato pie.

Constable Starmer was about thirty, red-haired and freckled, and had sharp, intelligent eyes. He was also flushed and out of breath. Lavender suspected he'd been running, and liked the man on sight. Rural constables could be lazy and incompetent. His first impression of Starmer was that he was neither. He wore an open-necked shirt and a dirty necktie tied in a knot.

'I'm looking for a woman called Annie Southerby.'

'Aye, I knows her. She went to the dame school with my sister. My sister keeps 'ouse for me.'

'Can you describe her?'

Confusion flickered across Starmer's face for a second. 'My sister? No, yer meant Annie, didn't yer? Well, she's dark-haired and a buxom wench – not my sort. But others seem to think 'er pleasin' to the eye.' He touched his upper lip. 'She has a scar 'ere.'

Lavender nodded, satisfied. 'It's the same woman. Whereabouts does she live?'

'In a cottage on the edge of town – near Stock's estate.'

'How does she pay her rent? Does she work?'

Starmer's neck flushed above his necktie. 'I'm guessin' you already knows the answer to that question, Detective. No, she don't work. She's got a couple of young lads – and their da pays for their upkeep.'

'She has children?'

'Aye, a baby and a lad of about three. Not that she's much of a ma to them lads. Accordin' to my sister, she's forever leavin' 'em wi' her neighbour to swan off.'

Lavender smiled. He had a funny feeling that, between them, Starmer and his sister knew the business of all the residents of St Ives. 'Who's their father?'

'It's Master Stocks – the owner of the estate. 'E set her up in that cottage a few years back.'

'Is he your squire?'

Starmer grinned. He had a pleasant smile but was missing a couple of teeth. 'Stocks likes to think 'e is. 'E's the richest landowner 'ereabouts since the Poppletons sold up and left. But 'e's just a nabob who struck it lucky out in India.'

Lavender's ears pricked up. 'Does Annie Southerby know the Poppletons?'

Starmer frowned. 'I don't think so. Sir Humphrey were a bit of a lad and sometimes came into town to drink wi' his chums, but I ain't 'eard of no scandal with the local women. Look, what's this about, Detective? What's Annie done?'

'We think she was involved in a burglary in London last Friday night.'

Starmer's ginger eyebrows rose in surprise, and he let out a low whistle. 'That ain't like 'er. She's a silly jilt and a bit lonely because most of the women 'ereabouts shun 'er – but she ain't ever been in any trouble.'

'Does she have any friends?'

'Most of the women in this town are respectable, Detective, and Annie ain't no better than a whore, so I'd say not. But I do remember she went to Lunnen once and went on the stage. But she came back to Stocks. Perhaps she had a friend or two in Lunnen?'

Lavender nodded, satisfied. It was the same woman April Clare had described. 'Do you happen to know if she left town last week to travel to London?'

Starmer shook his head.

Lavender finished his ale and stood up. 'I think it's time you took me to meet her. Let's hope her neighbour will take the children again tonight, because I think she'll be spending some time in your gaol.'

Chapter Twenty-Eight

It didn't take Woods long to decide that Master Atkins, the manager of the tailors, had nothing to do with the poison in the kickseys.

The tailor's thin nostrils flared at the suggestion. He waved his elegant hands around his workroom, where half a dozen men sat hunched over half-finished velvet coats and silk waistcoats. Most of these snips had needles or scissors in their hands, tape measures hung round their necks, and were squinting at their close work through spectacles in the poor light.

'We're a high-class establishment, Detective, with a dozen members of the nobility among our clients. I oversaw the construction of the baron's pantaloons myself – quite a nice piece of nankeen, if I remember. And no, we don't keep vermin poison on these premises. Establishments such as ours do NOT have a problem with vermin.'

Woods could barely hide his grin. 'Of course you don't, sir. But one final question – do you remember the little pocket the baron had sewn inside his kickseys?'

'Of course I do. It was an intricate operation – which is why I oversaw the construction of the garment myself.'

'Did Sir Humphrey say why he wanted that secret pocket?'

'No – and I never asked him.'

Woods left, smiling. They were narrowing it down. The mysterious poisoner had tampered with the baron's pantaloons while they were in the house on Bedford Street; it was a member of Lady Barlborough's household.

He remounted his horse, glanced down the street and realised he was on the edge of Mayfair. This seemed like as good a time as any to take that peculiar rattle to the museum curator. Besides which, his pockets had become rather bulky, what with the rattle, the jar of jam and the countess's diamond brooch. If the rattle turned out to be unrelated to Yardley's murder, he'd discard it.

Apart from a strong dislike of trees and open rural spaces, very little agitated Woods; he wasn't a superstitious man. But the moment he entered the Attlee Exhibition of Historical Artefacts, the hairs on the back of his neck began to bristle. The sour, musty smell of dust, ancient stone and timbers and dead fossilised remains was enough to turn anyone's stomach.

A porter at the door directed him to Mr Benson's office and he found himself squeezing through narrow aisles between glass display cases. They were crammed with ancient artefacts, old bones and broken pottery. Everything was labelled in tiny handwriting – much of it in Latin – on yellowing cards. On the walls was a vast array of stuffed birds and animal heads, mounted on wooden plaques. Many of the birds looked too big and exotic to be British and all of their feathers drooped.

Not much worth stealing in here, Woods thought. But then again, Benson had said the most valuable items of the collection were upstairs and only accessible at a private viewing.

Woods knocked, and entered the office. The silver head of Joseph Benson was bent over a pile of blackened amulets on his cluttered desk. Woods explained his business and pulled the rattle out of his pocket. The nutshells on the carved stick rattled when he passed it across. Benson took off his spectacles and wiped them clean with his handkerchief. 'Interesting, very interesting…' he murmured. 'The snake carving is crude, of course, but it's still an item of interest.'

'What it is?'

'Well, it belonged to an indigenous person – probably from one of our colonies. I think it might be a musical instrument for a tribal ritual.'

'Which colony?' Woods asked. 'We've got dozens.'

Benson scratched his chin and stared hard at the snake. 'The snake motif is common across the hotter climates of the globe. There's only one way to tell, and that is to identify the nuts and the wood. Fortunately, we've a natural history department. Come with me.'

He led the way out of the room and down a dingy back corridor into a large storeroom filled with shelves and drawers. He threw open the wooden shutters on the high windows and opened the wide shallow drawers, examining each of their contents in turn.

Woods peered over his shoulder at the dull dried-up contents. Occasionally, there was a pressed flower or an old root but mostly the drawers seemed to contain small compartments of wizened fruits, nuts and bark. They all looked the same to him. 'Did Lord Attlee bring them home with him from his travels?'

Benson's thin lips smiled. 'No, not all of them. Once Lady Attlee opened this establishment, many other members of the nobility donated treasures from their own Grand Tours.'

Treasures wasn't the word Woods would have chosen. Betsy wouldn't have any of these things in her house. Woods suspected the other nobs had just jumped at the chance to offload a hoard of musty remains on to the Attlees.

Suddenly, Benson stood up with a tray of brown objects in his hand. 'Here we are.' He placed the tray on the top of the drawers and picked up the card that accompanied it. '*Macadamia integrifolia*. These are the shells of the macadamia nut. The *Macadamia integrifolia* is a small tree native to New South Wales.'

'Botany Bay?'

'Yes, *Terra Australis*. We've introduced some of these seeds into Hawaii for commercial development, I believe, but the macadamia nut is indigenous to New South Wales.'

Hardly able to speak with excitement, Woods thanked him and left.

Woods headed straight for the nearest tavern, ordered a tankard of ale and some lamb cutlets, then sank down on to a stool at a table in a quiet corner and tried to make sense of it. His old noggin ached with the effort.

Botany Bay. Ulrich Monmouth. Alfred Gotobed. Richard Garbutt.

He knew his evidence was circumstantial but every sinew in his body – and his old nose – told him it was the ex-convict Ulrich Monmouth who'd dropped the rattle in the alleyway next to Garbutt's dead body. Monmouth murdered Richard Garbutt on Gotobed's orders, after the foolish man had slandered the banker.

The only thing that stopped him arresting the cove right now was Lavender's reluctance to believe Gotobed was behind this revenge killing – and sir was rarely wrong. But surely there wasn't any other explanation?

Yes, Gotobed was a gentleman – but so was Baron Poppleton. And that damned banker's name had turned up all over the place.

Woods' old noggin ached with the mystery of it. He ordered a second plate of lamb cutlets to distract himself. It worked. By the time he'd devoured this second helping, he felt better. He belched with satisfaction, wiped his greasy mouth on his coat sleeve and stood up to leave.

Lavender would have to unravel this tangle when he returned. In the meantime, he'd collect more evidence. They'd need more than a child's rattle from Botany Bay for a British jury to convict Ulrich Monmouth of Garbutt's murder.

The first thing to do was check with Constable Barnaby and see if his own inquiries had turned up any new evidence. But when he left the tavern and swung himself up into the saddle of his horse, another strange thought slapped Woods in the face, along with the cold wind.

This was the second time Botany Bay had cropped up this week.

What was it Lavender had told him about the Farrow family?

Doctor Farrow had travelled with Captain Cook on his second voyage to New South Wales.

Now what would be the odds of that? he wondered. A fella might go months without thinkin' about that stinkin' penal colony. Why! He reckoned half of London never gave it a second thought. It was another one of those damned coincidences.

His nose wrinkled and twitched as it scented something important. Lavender had dismissed both the Farrow women of involvement in the baron's poisoning... but as far as he knew, Sir Richard and Kingsley hadn't investigated the poisons of that new continent.

It was worth a try.

He crossed the river and called at Guy's Hospital.

Sir Richard and Kingsley looked up in surprise when he put his head around the office door for the second time that day. Both men were sitting in their shirt sleeves, poring over huge books. Both looked fed up and tired.

Woods placed the jam jar on the cluttered desk. 'I've brought you some jam from Sir Humphrey's house in Bedford Street.'

'That's kind,' Sir Richard drawled sarcastically. 'We'll have it on some toasted crumpets later.'

'I'd test it for poison first,' Woods advised.

'Fetch the rats, Kingsley.'

'And there's summat else... it might be nothin'... it's only a hunch...'

'Well, spit it out, man!'

Woods braced himself for their ridicule. 'I think you should investigate the poisons of the South Seas. Around Botany Bay and such like.'

Sir Richard said nothing for a moment and just stared at him. 'Why?'

'Because my old nose tells me there's somethin' fishy going on in those South Seas.'

The corners of the sawbones' mouth curled into a smile and his tired eyes lit up. Woods braced himself for a scathing reply, but Sir Richard slapped his fist down on the desk in delight.

'Of course! Of course! Why didn't I think of it before? What a cork-brain I am – and what a clever man you are, Woods!'

'Do you know what the poison is?' Woods asked hopefully.

But Sir Richard ignored his question and turned to his assistant, who'd already risen to his feet. 'Forget the rats, Kingsley! Find me a copy of *A Voyage towards the South Pole, and Round the World. Performed in his Majesty's Ships the Resolution and Adventure, in the Years 1172, 1773, 1774, and 1775* by Captain James Cook. Go to a bookshop – the public lending library – or call in at my home for my own copy.'

Woods blinked at the length of the title – and Sir Richard's incredible memory. 'It might be somethin' and nothin',' he warned.

The surgeon smiled. 'If there's one thing I've learned about you over the years, Detective Woods, it's that you're as good at your job as I am at mine – and your instincts are worth following.'

Woods grunted in surprise.

'But don't get cocky, Woods. It's the only good thing about you.'

Chapter Twenty-Nine

Annie Southerby was in tears – and protesting her innocence. To Lavender's disappointment, her distress seemed genuine. She was a plump young woman with a fleshy face. Tendrils of lank dark hair fell out of her white cap as she sat sobbing in a faded velvet armchair in front of her empty hearth.

The kitchen in her tiny cottage was filthy and untidy: children's clothes and toys were scattered everywhere, and the sink was piled high with unwashed crockery and saucepans. The woman was an indifferent housekeeper.

Besides the velvet chair, there were a few other signs of luxury in the cottage, as befitted the mistress of a rich man. Through the open door of the back bedroom, Lavender caught sight of an elaborate four-poster bed draped with rose damask curtains, and Annie's dress was made of silk, although far too low-cut for modesty.

'It was only supposed to be a bit of fun!' she wailed. 'I just wanted a night out – a bit of fun.'

She'd crumpled into tears the moment Lavender towered over her in his grimmest mood and accused her of stealing the Beverley jewels. Starmer hastily took her two young sons to the neighbour's cottage while Lavender continued his interrogation.

'I'm not a thief! I didn't steal anything! I don't know anything about a robbery!' She had no accent, he noticed, and her tone was gentle, despite the panic in her eyes.

'If you want me to believe you, you'd better tell me everything.'

Annie made a valiant effort to stop crying, but her body still heaved, and she developed hiccups.

Rolling his eyes, Lavender found a cleanish cup and poured her some water from a jug on the table. Her nose had run. Reluctantly, he handed her his handkerchief.

He'd come across many women in Covent Garden who sold their bodies in order to survive and he always tried not to judge them. But Annie Southerby was clearly a cut above the Covent Garden nuns. Judging by the romantic and Gothic novels scattered about the kitchen, she'd also had some education and was literate.

'Caro wrote to me… two weeks ago,' she said in between the hiccups. 'She invited me to come to London for a night out. I was bored and a bit down. I thought it would be fun to meet up with the girls again. She sent me five shillings for my fare too – and told me I could stay with Lou and Mary.'

Lavender pulled out his notebook and pencil. 'What are their full names and addresses?'

Annie's face crumpled again as she gave up the names of her friends. 'Mary Roper, Lou Jacobs – that's Louisa. They share a room in a lodging house off Covent Garden.'

'The address?'

'Number seven James Street.'

'And your ringleader? The woman known as Caro?'

'Her full name is Carlotta Meyer – her father was a Prussian.'

'Carlotta? Not Caroline?'

'No, she's Carlotta.'

'And where does she live?'

'I don't know.'

'Don't give me that nonsense, girl!'

She looked up at him earnestly. Her red-rimmed brown eyes were wide and unblinking. 'It's true! She's got some fancy fella now – he keeps her in real style. She's gone up in the world, has Caro.'

Lavender laughed scornfully. 'Women who've *gone up in the world* don't go out thieving. Who's her fancy man?'

'I don't know. I've never seen him, and she didn't tell us his name. Lou and Mary don't know either.'

'So why was she out flirting with other men?'

Annie blew her nose again. 'The others told me she was bored and wanted some fun, the same as me. She'd found four fellows who'd buy our supper. The three of us met up with them at a tavern a few doors down from the Sans Pareil Theatre. They were all young lords as well! Proper swells.'

'The other women didn't mention they planned a robbery? Did they try to recruit you to join in? Were you promised a share of the loot?'

'No! I swear on the life of my children – I knew nothing about that.'

Lavender decided he'd get Caro's address from Mary and Lou when he arrested them. 'What happened next?'

'Viscount Cottingham and the others treated us to supper.'

'Had you ever met any of them before?'

She shook her head. 'I'd seen the one they called *Poppers* before, but I've never talked to him. He's the new Baron Poppleton, isn't he? He used to live near here and I've seen him ride through town sometimes – but he'd no idea who I was.'

Or so she thinks, Lavender thought.

'What happened when they took you back to Beverley House?'

'We had a look round – it was a swanky place. Just like a palace. Lou persuaded the viscount to let her wear his mother's diamonds for a bit. She was funny, paraded around like a queen, talking and giving orders in a daft voice. She made everyone laugh. I don't know much about what happened later. The one called Sir Harry got a bit fresh with me – he pulled me on to his knee – and I spent the rest of the night fighting him off.'

'I thought you'd gone there for a bit of *fun*.'

'Not that kind of fun. I just wanted a laugh and a free supper.'

'But you spent the night there.'

'I didn't have a choice. Lou slipped off somewhere with the viscount and she had the key to their lodgings. I just curled up on a sofa, slept off the drink and caught my coach home the next morning. I swear to you, sir, I know nothing about a theft.' Once more, she turned her tearful eyes up towards his face.

Lavender frowned and chewed his pencil. It was possible she was as innocent as she claimed and had simply been dragged along to make up the numbers. But either way, he couldn't let her go free until he'd verified the information she'd provided.

'Tell me what else you know about Carlotta Meyer.'

Everything she'd told him, he'd already learned from April Clare. Carlotta had worked at Drury Lane, used to run with a wild crowd from Shoreditch and was sent to gaol for petty theft. She was blonde and pretty. Lavender sensed Annie was in awe of Caro and jealous of the woman's apparent success in London.

'I was told that on the night of the robbery she was red-headed and had a big nose.'

Annie sighed. 'She'd disguised herself with a wig and false nose. Like I said, she has a lover. Mary and Lou said he can be the jealous type. She didn't want anyone to recognise her when she was on the arm of another man.'

Lavender tapped his pencil on his pad. This didn't ring true; either Annie was lying, or the other women had fed her a load of lies.

If he was right and Poppleton and Caro had worked together before on the robbery at the Attlee Museum, he'd wager Poppleton was her mysterious lover. 'Did you get the impression she was intimate with Baron Poppleton? The one they called Poppers?'

Annie shrugged. 'He was the one who'd arranged for us girls to join up with them. When we walked up to them, he and Caro greeted each other like old friends. She was very quiet that night and left early. Normally, she's so lively and bosses the rest of us about.'

Why? Lavender wondered. *Why merge into the background? Why leave early? And why the disguise?*

The door to the cottage opened and Starmer reappeared. 'Your lads are settled with Mrs Latimer next door,' he said gently. 'She'll keep them as long as necessary.'

Lavender sensed the young constable had a soft spot for Annie. 'That's just as well, because until I've checked out this information you've given me, we have to lock you up.'

Annie burst into hysterical tears again.

'I assume you've a cell somewhere in town, Constable Starmer?'

The young man nodded. 'What's the charge, sir?'

'The theft of property belonging to the Countess of Beverley on Friday last.'

'But I'm innocent!' Annie sobbed.

'You may well be.' Lavender snapped shut his notebook and pocketed it, along with his pencil. 'But I can't leave her free to warn her friends back in London that I'm on their trail. I've more inquiries to conduct here in Cambridgeshire. Just keep her contained, Constable. I'll send you a note if we decide she's innocent. Can you get her back to St Ives yourself?'

Starmer nodded and Lavender bid him farewell and walked out of the cottage, relieved to be out of earshot of the woman's distress.

On his way back to Cambridge, Lavender took the fork in the road that led to Netheredge. He was immediately plunged into a network of lanes confined between high embankments and straggling hedges. His horse stumbled over potholes and ruts. The flatness of country and the clarity of the air made him feel like he was a mere speck, lost in the immensity of the heavens.

He wasn't sure what – if anything – he'd find out at Netheredge. But he was determined to leave no stone unturned. By all accounts, it was several years since Baron Poppleton had sold his estate and hired himself out as a gentleman's valet before he turned up on his wealthy aunt's doorstep.

He passed the entrance to a farm and dogs barked in a ragged chorus, rattling their chains. Beyond the farm he found a pair of high and ornate metal gates that gleamed with fresh paint. A short, well-tended drive led up towards a low manor house of honeyed stone that glistened in the sunlight. There was a wooded glade of ancient oaks and elms on the right of the path and a vast natural lake on the left, where the giant leaves of waterlilies clustered like a ruff around the edge.

Two neat and tidy little girls with ribbons in their hair played with a hoop close to the porticoed entrance of the house, and a gardener stooped to pull up weeds. Poppleton's former home had new owners now. Servants tended to be cagey when it came to talking about their masters – even their former ones. And the new owners would barely know Sir Humphrey.

Inevitably, as his eyes drifted over the grounds of the Poppletons' estate, Lavender's thoughts drifted to the estates belonging to Magdalena and Sebastián in the Asturias – property that he had never seen. Magdalena had fled to England with her son when Bonaparte's French troops invaded Spain. He'd hoped to take them to reclaim their inheritance this year, but her pregnancy and his father's illness and death had made this impossible.

Magdalena was thirty-five years old now. For the first three years of their marriage, there had been no sign of any little Lavenders. This hadn't bothered him; he was quite happy with Magdalena and Sebastián. But Mother Nature had proved herself to be capricious and Alice and Jack had been born in quick succession. He adored his children, but travelling to Spain with two small infants would be virtually impossible.

Fortunately, since the French retreat, they'd managed to employ the services of a Spanish lawyer with passable English, who was now overseeing Magdalena's affairs in Spain. They'd had bad news about her first husband's estate, which had been razed to the ground by the French. The wells had been poisoned and the crops left to rot in the fields, which were now high with weeds. The *casa solariega* and many of the haciendas had been reduced to piles of blackened rubble.

However, the estate she'd inherited from her father was still farmed by their tenants and a family had leased the casa solariega. Income from the estate had begun to trickle through to Magdalena. It was less than the estate previously generated, and Magdalena suspected the lawyer was cheating them. But it paid for Sebastián's school fees, for which they were grateful. With two more young children to feed, clothe and educate and the additional expense of caring for Lavender's elderly mother and his sister over the next few years, they needed all the income they could get. Magdalena had told him last night that his mother and sister had agreed to move in with them.

Lavender's mind returned to his case.

A quarter of a mile away, a handful of roofs and a church tower rose into the pale-blue sky. Perhaps the vicar knew more about the enigmatic young baron? He urged his horse forward.

Netheredge village consisted of a handful of cottages huddled around a dilapidated tavern and a village green with a duck pond, which was more of a large ditch. Its edge was lined with nettles, and it smelt sour. A solitary duck rose with agitated squawking as Lavender rode past. Apart from a large ginger cat sunning itself on the cobbles and a child with large, curious eyes sitting on a doorstep, the place seemed deserted.

Lavender wondered if Netheredge was large enough to have an incumbent vicar. But from the back of the tavern, he heard the chink of hammering, metal on metal, and the faint but unmistakable creak of a watermill wheel. He took heart; if the village had a forge and a mill, more than likely it had its own minister.

The lane took him past another farm with a yard and substantial barns before he reached the church, which stood apart from the village with the gravestones planted around it in the nettles, like crooked teeth.

The church also showed signs of years of neglect. Its buttressed walls were crumbling, the rusty iron gate had come off its hinges and much of the graveyard was overgrown. But one section had been carefully cleared and a new gate leaned against the boundary wall, waiting to be set in place.

Two men stood at the far side of the graveyard, talking. He suspected that the elderly, stooped figure clutching a spade was the sexton. The other wore a cassock.

Lavender tied his horse to the rusty gate, approached the men and introduced himself.

A welcoming smile spread across the round face of the vicar. Reverend Greenaway was in his fifties and had an unruly head of wiry grey hair that he struggled to tame with a comb. 'How can I help you, Detective?'

'I would like some information about the Poppletons – the family that used to live in the manor.'

'Ah, yes,' Greenaway said, shaking his head sadly. 'Such a tragic story. I suppose you'll want to see the late baron's resting place?'

Lavender nodded, and braced himself for the vicar's curiosity about why he was so interested in the Poppletons, but no questions were forthcoming.

'Did you know the Poppleton family lived at Netheredge for over two hundred years?'

'I did not.'

'But the new squire is a caring man,' the vicar continued cheerfully. 'And his lady wife has made a wonderful impression on the community with her kindness. They've already made many improvements in the village.'

'That's good for your parish.'

'Indeed, indeed! Come with me.'

Lavender followed him across the graveyard to an isolated spot. It contained a single, large gravestone beneath a wind-bent yew tree. 'That's the grave of the last Baron Poppleton. The new baron, Sir Humphrey, lives in London now, I believe.'

The gravestone was half obscured by nettles and weeds. Lavender could just make out the words: *Sir Simon Poppleton, Bart, 1749 – 1809.* 'I understood he hanged himself,' Lavender said. 'I'm surprised to see him buried in consecrated ground.'

The vicar grimaced and held out his hands in a gesture of resignation. 'The bishop wasn't pleased about it, but Sir Humphrey insisted. In the end, we took into consideration Sir Simon's recent tragic loss and the effect on his poor tortured mind. We decided it was the Christian thing to do. This is a quiet spot – away from the rest of the graves. It hasn't upset any of my congregation.'

Lavender frowned, puzzled. Mrs Farrow had told him the old baron had hanged himself because of his terrible debts and impending bankruptcy. 'I'm sorry, but what do you mean by "recent loss"?'

"It was his daughter's death that devasted him. Sir Simon killed himself a few days after his daughter drowned. His grief was unbearable. She's buried with him, and her innocence made it easier for the bishop to agree to this grave in consecrated ground.'

'Sir Simon had two daughters?'

'No, only the one. A lovely young girl called Charlotte. It was a terrible tragedy. Miss Lottie – as she was known – drowned in a boating accident in the lake in the parkland of Netheredge Manor.'

Lavender gasped. *Lottie Poppleton was dead? Then who the devil was the woman living at Lady Barlborough's house?*

'What happened?'

'She was in a rowing boat with her brother and her maid when it capsized. Sir Humphrey managed to swim to the safety of the bank, but both girls drowned. Neither of them could swim.'

'Did Sir Humphrey try to save them?'

The vicar shuffled uncomfortably. 'He was too drunk, I'm afraid. His father had just dragged him back from his studies at Cambridge and he'd spent a week stomping about the estate in a drunken rage. At the inquest, he admitted to reckless behaviour. He'd been teasing the girls by rocking the boat.'

'Good lord!'

'The young man was devastated about what had happened. He confided in me at the time. His father blamed him – and Sir Humphrey blamed himself.'

Lavender thought of Poppleton's guileless, smiling face… there was no devastation or remorse there now. *Poppleton should have joined his women friends on the stage*, he decided. He was a better actor than any of them.

'The baron's grief over his daughter – and his disappointment in his son – was too much for him to bear. A few days later, Sir Simon killed himself.'

Lavender crouched down and used his gloved hand to pull away the weeds and nettles at the bottom of the headstone.

Also, Charlotte Marie, his daughter. 1793 – 1809.

He paused thoughtfully – and out of respect. 'What about the maid? Who was she? Was she a local young woman, with a family?'

'She was from Cambridge. Her name was Emma Smith.'

Lavender grimaced. Smith was the most common surname in England.

'She was seventeen,' the vicar continued. He waved towards the area with smaller, less expensive headstones. 'We buried her over there. She had an older sister called Euphemia, who came for the funeral. This sister lived and worked in Cambridge.'

'And Euphemia – was she unmarried? Does she still go by the name Euphemia Smith?'

'I don't know. She may have married. I don't know where she is now. This accident was a terrible tragedy for Euphemia too.'

Except it wasn't a tragic accident, Lavender thought angrily. Poppleton's stupidity had killed two women. It was the sort of act that might incite a grief-stricken sister into an act of revenge.

He straightened up and stared off into the distance at the flat wildness of the fens. It all made sense now. Following Sir Richard's suggestion that he questioned the people on the fringes of the young man's life had paid dividends.

It didn't always work, of course. His interrogation of Mrs Farrow had only revealed what Sir Humphrey had told his London aunts. Mrs Farrow was as much in the dark about Sir Humphrey's past as Lady Barlborough herself.

That's the problem with estranged families who don't keep in touch or see each other for years, he realised. You can keep secrets, tell lies and introduce anyone to your aunt and claim she's your sister.

'What happened to Sir Humphrey after he'd buried his father?'

'I'm afraid I don't know. The manor house was sold to pay the late baron's debts and Sir Humphrey left the village. He hasn't been back since. Perhaps that's not surprising,' he added sadly.

Lavender thanked Reverend Greenaway and strode back to his horse. It was time to track down his old friend Simon Durham in Cambridge.

Chapter Thirty

Constable Barnaby and Principal Officer Vickery were loitering in the grimy hallway of Bow Street when Woods arrived. They were talking to the chief clerk, Oswald Grey. Above their heads, a greasy and smoke-blackened chandelier hung precariously by a fraying rope. It was the last surviving remnant of the more elegant days of the building, when it had been home to Bow Street's founder, Sir Henry Fielding.

The hallway was surprising empty for once. But none of the three men looked pleased about this unexpected lull in the capital's crime. Grey and Vickery were both scowling. Woods wondered what Magistrate Conant had done to upset them now.

But Barnaby's young face lit up at the sight of him. 'I've got interestin' news for you, sir. I've found a witness – a woman – who lives in one of them rooms above Holborn High Street. She were lookin' out of her window and saw two coves draggin' another fella down the alleyway where Garbutt were murdered.'

'Good lad – I knew I could rely on you. Did she describe them?'

Barnaby grimaced. 'Not really. She said they had their hats pulled low, it were dark and she were lookin' down at them. But she did think one of them had a bad limp.'

Satisfaction surged through Woods and his broad face broke into a wide grin that revealed a few blackened teeth. 'A limp, eh?'

'Yes. Is that helpful?'

'Very. This woman didn't mention if the other one had a gold tooth glintin' in the moonlight, did she?'

'No. She said they had scarves over the lower parts of their faces.'

'Do you think you know your murderer, Ned?' Vickery asked.

Woods chuckled. 'Oh, I've a strong notion of him now.'

'That's fast work, Ned. Advancing you is the one good thing Conant has done since he arrived.'

Oswald Grey cleared his throat and said sadly, 'Actually, Detective Woods – I'm sorry to be the bearer of bad news – but there might be a problem with your promotion.'

Woods braced himself and the other two men fell silent. 'How so?'

Grey was the backbone of their operation at Bow Street; he knew everything that went on and was privy to all the politicking.

'Magistrate Conant believed John Townsend was to be taken into the private employment of the Prince Regent. But Prinny's changed his mind.'

Vickery laughed unpleasantly. 'I guess the prince decided he didn't want the expense of a private bodyguard and still wants us to foot the bill for the cost.'

'Something like that,' Grey replied. 'I'm sorry, Woods. But there's no opening for another principal officer at this time.'

'That's bad, that is,' Vickery growled in disgust.

Woods bit back his disappointment and the curse that sprang to his lips. Vickery was right. Conant was a snake in the grass to treat a fella this way. Dangling advancement in front of a fella's eyes and whipping it away.

Then he remembered Lavender's cryptic comment earlier that morning about a plan that might work to their advantage... and hope surged in his breast. 'Lavender will sort out this tangle when he returns.'

'Returns?' Grey asked sharply. 'Where's he gone?'

'He's following up a lead in Cambridge.'

'Cambridge! He went off to Cambridge without permission?'

Woods snorted. 'Sir don't need the magistrate's permission for anythin'. He knows how to catch felons better than the rest of us put together.'

'That's true, Mr Grey,' Barnaby said. 'Let's be honest here, lads, Lavender's run the policin' side of things here for years – along with some help from you, Mr Grey, of course. Magistrate Read were happy to let the two of you get on with it while he dealt with the felons in court.'

'It's a shame Lavender ain't put in charge,' Vickery said grimly. 'This place is going to rack and ruin. Don't you agree, Mr Grey? I know you and your clerks are having a hard time under Conant.'

The chief clerk looked flustered by this challenge to his loyalty. 'I can't comment on that.'

'Lavender is *the chief of constables*,' Barnaby added, grinning. 'Well, that's what it says in the newspapers – and Woods should be the *assistant* chief constable.'

Grey pulled his thin shoulders up straighter. 'Well, Magistrate Conant is in charge now and he's most insistent that all deployment of our officers is authorised by *him*. And I warn you now, Woods, he's in a foul temper with you and Lavender about the article in *The Times* this morning. He's in court today – but he isn't tomorrow, and I wouldn't like to be in your boots when he tracks you both down. In fact, if I were you, I'd pop over to the courthouse right now and see if he has five minutes to speak to you.'

Woods chuckled at the thought. 'It'd be rude to disturb him.' He turned to Barnaby. 'You're with me for the rest of the day – Lavender's orders,' he added with a wink.

The young officer grinned in delight. 'Yes, sir!'

Grey opened his mouth to protest, but Woods turned to him quickly. 'There's somethin' else, Mr Grey. You might get a couple of unwanted visitors here tonight lookin' for them stolen kickseys that belong to Baron Poppleton.'

Grey's voice rose an octave. 'Here? But we don't have them here! And what sort of unwanted visitor are you talking about?'

'Undesirables. Lavender has told an undesirable we're storin' them kickseys here in the evidence room.'

'But we don't have an evidence room!'

'Has Lavender laid a trap?' Vickery asked sharply, his curiosity piqued.

'Maybe. There's some nasty coves out there who are keen to get their filthy paws on them kickseys.'

'He did right – to lure them here.'

'But what will my clerks do if they turn up?' Grey asked, in alarm. 'Young Simpson is on duty tonight. My clerks aren't armed like you officers – and they wouldn't know how to fire a pistol if they were.'

A slow grin spread across Vickery's face. 'Don't you worry, Mr Grey – I'll be lurkin' in the side office with my pistol primed.'

Woods was relieved. 'You'd do that to help us out, sir?'

'Of course, Ned. I've spent a borin' mornin' trampin' the streets, toutin' for business for this place – like a bloody peddler. It'll be good to do some proper police work for a few hours. And if I catch these coves, at least we won't have far to drag them in irons to the cells.'

'Thank you, Vickery. I'll leave it to you. Barnaby and I may get back here later to help. But right now, we've got evidence to gather and a murderer to catch. Come on, Barnaby.'

The two officers strode towards the door that led to the stables, leaving Vickery to placate the frazzled nerves of the chief clerk.

'Oh, by the way, Ned,' Vickery called out to him. 'Your lad, Eddie, is workin' tonight.'

Woods pulled up short at this unwelcome news. Then he waved his thanks to Vickery and continued towards the door. He knew Eddie was ready for more responsibility; he couldn't wrap him in cotton wool forever.

Eddie was brushing down a horse with a handful of straw when they reached the stables. His brown eyes – Betsy's eyes – lit up with excitement when Woods explained what he wanted him to do. 'Nothin' may happen, but you need to be prepared for trouble. Go to Mr Grey and ask him to issue you a pistol. At least you know how to use one, unlike those bloomin' clerks.'

'Thanks, Da. I won't let you and Uncle Stephen down.'

'I know you won't, son. And remember what I taught you about aimin' to disable 'em rather than kill. And don't forget these pistols have two shots in them.'

Woods and Barnaby hoisted themselves up into their saddles. 'I think we'd better go home for a bite to eat first,' he told Barnaby. 'And you can change out of your uniform into somethin' dark and warm. Meet me in the tavern opposite Gotobed's bank on Southwark High Street just before five o'clock. We'll be stalkin' some nasty coves tonight and they'd spot a constable in uniform at fifty paces.'

'Yes, sir.'

'It's goin' to be a long night. Let's go home and eat.'

Barnaby's grin widened. 'Are you hungry again, Detective Woods?'

'Don't be cheeky, lad.'

Alfie Bobbin was sitting on the front doorstep when Woods arrived home. The little dog looked very white and fluffy after his bath, although his eye was still gungy and cloudy.

'Hello, little fella. Have you been out all day?'

Alfie Bobbin looked up at Woods with a trusting face, put his head on one side and wagged his tail.

Tabitha was in the hallway when he opened the door.

Woods held open his arms. 'Hello, Treacle. Come give your old Da a hug.'

'Alfie Bobbin!' Tabitha squealed in delight. 'Rachel! Georgie! Alfie Bobbin is here!' She picked up the dog and clutched him to her chest.

Suddenly the hallway was full of children, all fussing over the dog.

'Where've you been?' Georgie asked.

'Quickly, Tabby!' Rachel said. 'Take him into the kitchen – he hasn't had any food all day.'

They trooped off with the dog, leaving Woods stunned on the doorstep. He followed them into the kitchen. Tabitha was finally persuaded to release her wriggling captive into a warm spot in front of the range.

Betsy also ignored Woods' arrival. She rushed into the pantry and returned with a saucer of meat. 'I've saved him the choicest morsels from tonight's joint.'

This was too much for Woods. 'Mrs Woods,' he growled, 'your husband is home, and *he* gets the choicest morsels.'

'Heavens above, Ned!' Betsy snapped. 'Please don't be jealous of the poor little mite!'

'And Da,' Rachel scolded, 'next time don't let him out into the street. He runs off. You must let him out into the back yard to do his business.'

Tabitha turned her big brown eyes towards her father and for one horrible moment Woods thought his darling baby was going to burst into tears. 'I've been upset all day, Da. You lost us Alfie Bobbin! I cried and cried.'

Woods sank wearily into a chair, wondering if other men were browbeaten by their womenfolk. He waited for someone to notice him. To his surprise, it was young Georgie who shyly approached him and offered to fetch him a tankard of ale from the pantry.

Betsy nodded in approval as the boy carefully carried the ale to Woods and placed it on the table. 'Well done, Georgie. That's a good lad.'

Alfie Bobbin had already wolfed down his meat and was licking his lips and having a good scratch. Betsy suggested the three children took the dog upstairs. 'I want to talk to your father,' she added.

'How's he been?' Woods asked.

Her reply surprised him. 'Georgie couldn't have been sweeter. He's helped me around the house and never moaned once.'

Sweet? Betsy rarely had a good word to say about young lads. Mind you, their own two had been anything but sweet at that age.

'He should be at school.'

'Yes, of course he should – but he didn't want to leave the house because he said there's bad men out there who want to skin him.'

Woods nodded. 'Ah, yes. I forgot about them coves. But I'll have them under the hatches by tomorrow. I'll be late tonight, Betsy.'

While Betsy served up her husband's meal, he told her about his day, although he didn't mention Oswald Grey's worrying comment about how that damned magistrate had lied to him over his advancement.

She listened and occasionally nodded, but he sensed she was distracted about something. 'What's on your mind, Sweetheart?' he asked when she gave him his plate of roast beef and vegetables.

'Ned, how long did you plan to keep Georgie here?'

'I don't know. But I'm sure the lad will feel safer and happier about goin' back home once I've caught those coves. Then he won't be under your feet...'

'He's not been under my feet. I've enjoyed havin' 'im here.'

Relieved, Woods took another forkful of food. 'Good,' he mumbled with his mouth full.

'But we've a problem. That watchman, Adams, paid me another visit this afternoon with a message for you.'

Woods paused with his fork in mid-air.

'He says that Georgie's mother has run off. She's taken the younger children and disappeared.'

Woods swallowed hard, got food caught in his throat and choked. He reached for his tankard of ale and swilled it down.

'Was there any sign of violence at the house?' he gasped.

'No. Nothing like that. She just packed her bags, grabbed the children and left. One of the neighbours watched her go.'

'Heaven and hell! Has she buried her husband yet?'

'No, she hasn't – she's just left him to rot in the morgue. And she's left Georgie too. No one knows where she's gone. I don't know whether she's the most callous wife and mother I've ever heard of – or the most scared.'

'I were only keepin' him a few days for 'is own safety!'

Woods was stunned – and horrified at the distress this would cause the child. But another darkness, a nasty memory, clawed at his stomach and put him off his food. He pushed his plate away in anguish. It was Betsy who voiced his fear.

'What will happen to Georgie, Ned? Will he have to go to the workhouse?'

Woods stared across the room, distressed. His fists were clenched beneath the table, and beads of sweat erupted on his broad forehead. 'I can't do it, Betsy,' he whispered hoarsely.

She didn't reply. She waited for him to say more.

'It were bad enough when my own Da ran off – and our Alby got into trouble with the law and had to flee. Ma had to go out to work. Folks suggested she went into service as a live-in servant and sent me to the workhouse.'

She stroked his head. 'I know Ned, I know.'

'I were terrified she'd do as they said and just dump me there – on my own. I had bad dreams about it for weeks.'

'But she didn't,' Betsy reminded him.

He swallowed hard. 'No. She worked her fingers to the bone instead. When she got 'ome from the factory, she took in laundry and ruined her eyesight with sewin' by candlelight. She did everythin' she could to keep us together and under the same roof.'

'I know she did, Ned.'

'Do you want him to go to the workhouse, Betsy?'

'Of course, not – you muttonhead!' she snapped. 'I'd never throw any child on to the mercy of the parish! I were just askin' to see how *you* felt. If you like we'll keep him here.'

Relieved, he grinned and pulled his diminutive wife down on to his lap. He held her face gently between his large hands and kissed her on her lips. 'You're the best woman in the world, Mrs Woods. And I'm the luckiest man.'

'Behave yourself,' she scolded. But her voice was soft, and she was laughing. 'Besides which, with your advancement – we'll easily be able to afford to keep him and Alfie Bobbin.'

'Oh, so the mutt is to stay too, is he? Well, I've one condition about all this, Mrs Woods – they can both stay provided you keep the choicest morsels for *me*!'

'Aw, poor Alfie Bobbin!'

He grabbed her again for another kiss. She squealed and tried to beat him off.

'For God's sake, stop it, the pair of you!'

They glanced up, surprised. Dan stood by the door, a look of mock horror on his face. 'You're too old to behave like this in front of your children! Put down my mother, sir!'

'You're hardly a child, son,' Woods said, laughing. 'How long have you been standin' there?'

'I'm a child,' Dan said, lifting his hand to his forehead in a dramatic gesture. 'And I think I'm about to have an attack of the vapours after witnessing this lewd behaviour. Only the *choicest* morsel of meat will revive me.'

'You wait your turn, son,' Woods said, grinning. 'There's a bloody queue for that in this house – and you and I ain't at the front of it.'

Chapter Thirty-One

Memories of Lavender's college days flooded back into his mind when he entered through the tunnel of Magdalene College's principal entrance and paused beside the porter's lodge. Ahead of him lay a quiet grassy courtyard surrounded by gracious buildings, all Gothic and picturesque. The late afternoon sunlight, heavy and golden, illuminated the mullioned windows.

Lavender was relieved when the porter told him Master Durham was still in residence at the college and led the detective towards Durham's rooms. The old porter had an arthritic hip and walked with a peculiar lurching gait.

A pair of fat doves pecked around on the well-tended lawn but the place was eerily deserted. Normally, the courtyard would echo with the sound of tramping feet, laughter and sometimes bursts of drunken shouting, but now the only noise came from the iron-rimmed wheels of carts trundling over the cobbles behind him and the fractious ducks squabbling on the river.

'It's so quiet without the undergraduates,' Lavender said as he followed the limping old man.

'Aye. They were sent 'ome a while back when the fever came,' the porter said. 'We lost quite a few of 'em. Their folks don't mind what japes they get up to while they're 'ere – but they don't like us sending 'em back dead in a wooden surcoat.'

Simon Durham had lost most of his hair and doubled in girth since the last time Lavender saw him, but the senior fellow grinned with pleasure when they met and shook his hand. His hooded brown eyes were the same, though, and still twinkled with boyish mischief. 'Stephen! What a lovely surprise!'

Durham led him into a large but simply furnished drawing room overlooking the sluggish river. A plain grey-haired woman was sewing by the fireside. She smiled and rose to her feet when they entered.

'It's my old friend, Stephen Lavender,' Durham informed her.

'I hope I'm not intruding?' Lavender asked.

'Not at all, not at all! In fact, you're a welcome distraction. This is my wife, Amy.'

Lavender bowed. 'How do you do, Mrs Durham? And may I congratulate you on your bravery in taking on this dusty old classics scholar?'

Both the Durhams laughed.

'Seriously, though, Mrs Durham, I think you made an excellent choice.' He turned to his friend. 'It looks like you've done well in your chosen career, Simon. Do you have children?'

'Yes, a boy and a girl,' Simon said with pride.

'Then our lives continue to mirror each other,' Lavender said, 'although I also have a stepson.'

They swapped family news and chatted about their children for a while, then Mrs Durham announced she would leave the two men in peace. But on her way out of the room she asked if Lavender would like to stay to supper. 'We dine early because of the children,' she added.

Lavender couldn't imagine anything pleasanter – and he might still be able to catch the mail coach back to London. 'That would be delightful. Thank you.'

Durham eased his bulk into one of the fireside chairs and Lavender sat opposite him. The smile dropped from Durham's face. 'You've heard about our outbreak of typhus, I assume?'

'Yes. I'm sorry. It must have been devasting for the families of those who died.'

Durham nodded sadly. 'It was shocking how fast they died – one after the other in rapid succession: very distressing. We lost some wonderful boys – all struck down in their prime. We've sent the undergraduates home for the rest of the academic year. I've been twiddling my thumbs with boredom for weeks. Anyway, how can I help you, Stephen? I assume you're here on official business. I've read a lot about your exploits in the newspapers. It sounds like you've also done well in your chosen career.'

'Please understand that much of what is written in the newspapers is false or exaggerated.'

Simon chuckled. 'It always was. But they call you the *chief of constables* now. Your family must be so proud of you. I remember your parents – and your sisters. I was quite in awe of your large family – especially your youngest sister, Elizabeth. She was the most beautiful girl I'd ever met – until my eyes alighted on the fair Mrs Durham, of course.'

Lavender smiled. Several of his male friends had been smitten with Elizabeth and on occasion, when their attentions had become too ardent, she'd asked him to play the aggressive older brother and warn them off. But he hadn't realised that Durham had also nurtured a calf love for Elizabeth.

'My mother is proud of me but sadly my father died a few months ago,' Lavender told him. 'He rarely expressed an opinion about my life and work. He tended to leave that sort of thing to my mother and sisters. You may remember that my sisters – especially the older ones – were always full of opinions.'

Durham smiled. 'I remember. I'd never met such a crowd of intelligent, confident and quick-witted women! To a naïve and bashful boy of eighteen, they were quite frightening at times – but not Elizabeth. Never the lovely Elizabeth. I'm sorry to hear about your father, Stephen,' he added. 'He was a kind gentleman. You must miss him. And don't worry about his lack of comment on your success. From what I saw, the poor fellow probably couldn't get a word in edgeways!'

Lavender smiled and let his gaze drift out of the window. It had a wonderful view of the quaint stone bridges and the ancient willow trees with their boughs trailing in the river. 'I do miss him...' he confessed. 'The last few months have been hard, very hard. At times I wanted to run away. I planned to abandon London and my job and take Magdalena and the children away to live a simpler life on our estates in Spain.'

Durham's brown eyes filled with compassion. 'That would be a sad loss for British justice,' he said. 'And I think you would have been bored beyond belief within three days. But I do understand those feelings – that need to get away. The death of our parents is one of the hardest things to bear in life. It wasn't until I got away and came here as an undergraduate that I became reconciled with the loss of my own.'

Lavender remembered with a guilty jolt that his friend had lost both of his parents to smallpox. 'I'm sorry, Simon. I'm rather wrapped up in my misery at times.'

Durham smiled. 'It always helps to talk about these things with old friends.'

He was right, Lavender realised. It did.

'And you were there for me when I needed you during my own sadness. If it's any consolation, Stephen, the ancient Greeks believed the worst of grief lasts for a hundred days. You never forget those you've loved, but the grief gets easier to bear after that. I found this to be true when my parents died.'

Lavender did a quick calculation and was surprised to find his one hundred days was almost up. *Were the ancient Greeks right? Is this why I feel more at peace with the loss of my father today?*

'Anyway, what brings you back to your old haunts and friends in Cambridge?'

'I'm investigating a young man called Sir Humphrey Poppleton, who was a student here at Magdalene about five or six years ago.'

Durham's brow creased in confusion. 'I don't think I remember him…'

'He was only here for a year before his father removed him for financial reasons,' Lavender added hastily. 'He was friends with the Viscount Cottingham, Sir Harry Lawson and Lord Jonothan Furnish.'

Durham laughed. 'That crowd?'

'You remember them?'

'Indeed I do. It's all coming back now. They called Poppleton *Poppers*, didn't they? And Sir Jonothan Furnish was *Jonty*.'

'That's right.'

Durham chuckled. 'Everyone of them was a young scamp, and not one of them had an academic bone in his body.'

'That must have been disappointing for you.'

His friend shrugged and smiled. 'I'm resigned to it. A large number of our young men are not here for an education. Cambridge is just somewhere their wealthy fathers dump them for three years while they grow to manhood. But there is always a clutch of brilliant academic diamonds among each new intake. Poppleton was the cleverest of the group – and their natural leader.'

'How so?'

'He was the brains behind their pranks, their drinking games, their drunken boat trips on the river and their outings to the theatre. He was fond of the theatre – and the young actresses – if I remember rightly.'

Lavender's eyebrow rose sardonically. 'He still is. Was he ever in any trouble?'

'Nothing unusual. There was a bit of scandal when they tried to smuggle a gaggle of actresses from the touring theatre company into their rooms one night – but the porter caught them sneaking the girls up the stairs and they were reprimanded. The others seemed a bit lost when Poppers didn't return for his second year. I believe at this point Sir Harry was so bored without him, he immersed himself in his studies. What has Poppers done, Stephen? Why are you investigating him?'

Lavender sat back in the comfort of the chair and told his old friend everything he knew about the robberies at Beverley House and the Attlee Museum.

At the end of his explanation, Durham's face was pale, his expression grim. 'My goodness! When clever young men turn to crime, they really know how to cover their tracks. Who'd have thought he was capable of such felony?'

'What else do you remember about the four of them?'

'Four of them? There were five in that particular gang of friends.'

'Five? Who was the fifth?'

'Young Bert Gotobed, of course. I thought you knew this when you mentioned the Beverley jewels were kept at his father's bank?'

'I didn't,' Lavender stammered. '*Bert Gotobed?* Is he the son of Alfred Gotobed?'

Durham nodded.

'The Gotobed name regularly crops up in this investigation – but I haven't heard anything about a son.'

'Oh, the five of them were inseparable.'

'That's a surprise. From what I remember, the sons of the peers don't often mix with the sons of the rich merchants who study here. I thought the aristocrats tended to stick to their own kind.'

Durham nodded. 'Yes, that's true, and I'd heard rumours Alfred Gotobed wasn't respectable.'

'What sort of rumours?'

'That he was more of a usurer and an illegal moneylender than a banker; that he enforced his repayments brutally. But he seemed to be determined to place himself and his family in the gentry. His son, Bert, was a pleasant, affable chap, much richer in the pocket than the others – thanks to his father's generosity.'

'Did his father give him money to *buy* his friends?'

Durham chuckled. 'Let's just say Bert was generous with his loans. The other four boys were always in debt and rather than risk their father's wrath by begging for more money, they'd turn to Bert. He gave them a low rate of interest. Behind his affable manner, he was quite shrewd. I think he recognised these wealthy young lords might be valuable future customers for the family bank. But he realised he would never be part of their "set" once they left Cambridge.'

'None of them mentioned young Gotobed when I interviewed them.'

'Ah, maybe that's because they don't see him anymore – except in a business capacity. Bert left here and went straight to work in his father's bank in Shoreditch—'

'*Shoreditch?*'

'Yes, Shoreditch. Gotobed has several banks, I understand, and is still expanding his empire. Bert also married young – almost as soon as he left Cambridge – and he already has children. Unlike those other young bucks, Bert Gotobed has responsibilities.'

'How do you know so much about him?'

'I keep in touch with several of my students and Bert is one of them. We correspond occasionally.'

'Do you know what happened to Sir Humphrey after he was withdrawn from Cambridge?'

'Yes, but only because Bert wrote and told me about it. Sir Humphrey was desperate for money when his father died, and the estate was sold. He had family – aunts – but they were estranged. The Gotobeds took pity on him and Old Man Gotobed employed him as a valet. Like I said, Alfred Gotobed had ambition – he wanted Poppers to teach him how to act and dress like a gentleman.'

And what, wondered Lavender, *did the banker, Alfred Gotobed, teach Poppers in exchange?*

Chapter Thirty-Two

Constable Barnaby was waiting for Woods in the tavern, opposite Gotobed's bank. He'd already ordered them both a tankard of ale and was sitting at a table with a good view of the bank building through the dirty window.

Shortly before five o'clock, Gotobed's carriage drew up outside the bank. Ulrich Monmouth climbed down from the driver's seat, and Woods got a good look at his face. A fresh jagged scar snaked down his left cheek.

Woods grunted with satisfaction. 'That's the villain we're followin' tonight.'

'He looks like a bracket-faced cove,' Barnaby murmured.

'He got that scar from the poor fella he murdered the other night.'

Once Alfred Gotobed appeared and boarded his carriage, the two officers left the tavern, mounted their horses, and followed the vehicle at a discreet distance. Monmouth didn't look back as he steered the carriage through the busy London traffic.

To Woods' annoyance, Gotobed went to his club in Mayfair rather than straight home. Monmouth pulled the coach up behind a line of other vehicles at the kerb and spent his time chatting with the other coach drivers, while his employer was inside the building. They couldn't risk being seen while Monmouth was milling about on the pavement, so they rode the horses round the corner, where Barnaby held on to them while Woods returned to the square. He squatted behind a bush in the park in the centre while he kept his peepers fixed on Monmouth.

By the time Gotobed reappeared and climbed inside his carriage, darkness had fallen

'I know it's been borin', lad,' Woods said, as they remounted their horses and followed their quarry back to Shoreditch. 'But it's better for us now the light's fadin'.'

Gotobed's house was in the leafy part of Shoreditch, not far from its ancient church. It was an area of four-storey Queen Anne houses in tree-lined streets, with gardens enclosed behind high brick walls. Despite the rapid development of the city, this part of London was still semi-rural with market gardens and smallholdings scattered between the rows of houses.

Gotobed climbed out of the carriage and disappeared inside his home. Monmouth drove the horses to the stables at the rear of the building.

The two officers reined in about fifty yards away under the shadows of a large oak and waited while Monmouth unharnessed the carriage horses and settled them down for the night. The stables backed on to a large, pitch-black uncultivated field that stank of manure and farmyard slurry. Eventually, Monmouth appeared with a lantern and limped towards one of the mews cottages.

Woods slid down from his saddle. 'Wait here, Barnaby. I want a closer look.'

Moving quietly through the deep shadows of the buildings, Woods was just in time to see Monmouth arrive at the door. He was greeted by a dark-haired, dark-skinned woman with plaited frizzy hair. On her hip she carried a boy of about two years old. She raised her head to kiss Monmouth and, in the light of his lantern, Woods saw her profile. She had the unmistakable heavy brow ridges and broad flat nose of an Aboriginal. Monmouth had brought his woman back from Botany Bay.

Woods grunted with satisfaction again and returned to Barnaby and the horses. 'We'll wait for him to eat his supper and then see where he goes.'

'Does the man never sleep?' Barnaby asked.

'I don't think so. I've a notion he takes a nap during the day while his master is at the bank and spends the night doing his villainous bidding.'

They had another long wait.

When Monmouth reappeared, he went back to the stables, saddled and mounted a horse and trotted off back in the direction of the city. The streets became crowded with carriages and drunken revellers. The increased traffic made it more difficult to keep their quarry in sight and several times Woods was grateful for Barnaby's sharp eyes.

They crossed the river on the London Bridge and headed into Southwark. Monmouth left his horse at a livery stable and when he reappeared in the street, he was accompanied by a man with a gaunt face, hard features – and a gold tooth that glistened in the weak light of the streetlamps.

Woods grinned with surprise and satisfaction. Another ruddy coincidence. He didn't know what it was that connected Monmouth and Gotobed with the cove who'd chased Yardley and little Georgie for the countess's diamond brooch, but he was pleased to see him. He rubbed his loose tooth, wondering if Monmouth had been the other cove in the graveyard the night he himself was attacked. He had the vague sense that tonight he might kill several birds with one stone. And if there weren't any stones or birds handy, someone would get a good hiding for loosening his tooth.

Woods dismounted and gave his reins to Barnaby, along with instructions to take the horses into the same stable. He intended to follow their quarry on foot and told Barnaby to catch up with him when he could. Woods resigned himself to the fact that Barnaby might lose him in the bustle of the narrow streets, but the two coves had barely gone three hundred yards when they approached a butcher in a bloodied apron, who was pulling down the shutters of his shop. Woods assumed the man had stayed open late to sell his meat pies to the dozens of revellers staggering from tavern to tavern.

The butcher scowled and led Monmouth and his chum inside, leaving the shutters half down and enough window for Woods to see inside. The unhappy shopkeeper handed over a bag of coins to the two coves. *What is this?* Woods wondered. *Is Monmouth collectin' loan repayments for his master? Or is it somethin' more sinister?*

Two shops further down, at a tobacconist's, the process was repeated.

Arrogantly confident that their criminality would go unchecked, the coves left the door open this time. Woods wedged himself into the opening of a narrow alley on the opposite side of the road and watched the nervous old shopkeeper count out coins on his wooden counter with shaking fingers. The fella clearly didn't hand over enough of the chinks because Monmouth smacked him around the head and dislodged his hat – and probably an ivory or two in the process.

Woods gave an involuntary growl, rubbed his cheek and felt his own loose tooth once more. Monmouth seemed to enjoy belting fellas around the head. Was it Monmouth who'd thumped him a few nights ago in the graveyard?

Barnaby appeared at his shoulder.

'They're either brutally recoupin' the money paid out in loans – or extortin' money under false pretences,' Woods said quietly. 'They're runnin' some sort of racket. If the shopkeepers don't pay up, they get rough.'

'Do you reckon Gotobed knows about this?'

'Of course he does. This'll be how Gotobed financed his lucrative money-lendin' business and opened his first bank. He and Monmouth are a right pair of filchin' villains; they're robbin' the poor to get the chinks to give lucrative loans to the rich.'

'Shall we arrest them?'

Woods remembered Lavender's words. 'Not yet. Let's make a note of which shopkeepers they're frightenin'. We can always come back and persuade them to serve as witnesses.'

Monmouth and his glittering-toothed accomplice visited five more establishments and a couple of private homes before they settled down in a raucous tavern and started drinking heavily.

Woods and Barnaby squeezed behind a corner table and ordered a tankard of ale, which they sipped while trying to stifle their yawns.

They were there for hours. And Monmouth and his chum were foxed when they finally rose and staggered out of the tavern. They weaved their way drunkenly back towards the livery stable and collected their horses.

Woods was glad to be outside. The chilly breeze refreshed him.

'For heaven's sake,' Barnaby exclaimed, 'it's nearly dawn. Do you think they're goin' home?'

Woods heard the exhaustion in his young constable's voice. He shook his head. 'No, I've a notion they're headin' over to Bow Street to get those kickseys.'

'But they're foxed! And Monmouth will need to be back home soon to drive his banker to work.'

Woods stifled a yawn. 'They've still got time yet – and hard drinkers like those two sober up fast.'

He was right.

Once back over the river, the two coves rode towards Covent Garden. They tied their animals to a railing at the top of Bow Street and strode towards the magistrates' court, pausing at the entrance at the top of the steps.

The police office was well lit with external lanterns and light streamed out of the tall – and wide open – doors. Silhouetted against the doorway, the two men still seemed to be hesitating. Then Monmouth pulled a pistol out of his coat packet and checked it.

Woods' stomach lurched at the thought of Eddie inside that building.

Then Monmouth did something Woods didn't expect. He left his chum at the top of the steps and went inside alone.

Woods had no idea if this second fella was armed or not, but he didn't hesitate. He bounded up behind him, grabbed him with one hand and clamped the other over the cove's mouth to stop him shouting out.

The villain struggled violently in Woods' grip and tried to bite his hand, but Barnaby was beside them in a second with the cold muzzle of his own pistol pressed against the fella's cheek.

'Shout out and I'll blow your bloody head off!' he hissed quietly.

The cove hesitated and went limp. It was long enough for Barnaby to search him and whip the villain's pistol out of his pocket. Woods dragged the fella down the steps and wrestled him to the ground a few yards away from the entrance, twisting his arms behind his back.

Barnaby pulled out his metal handcuffs and clapped them on while Woods gagged the fella with his own scarf. They'd worked quickly and silently and the whole thing had barely taken a minute – but it wasn't quick enough for Woods when his son was in danger.

'Leave him here!' he snapped. 'Let's get Monmouth.'

As they ran up the steps to the entrance, a pistol shot rang out, followed by an enormous crash and the sound of breaking glass. The blue flash of gunpowder lit up the open entrance.

'Gawd's teeth!' Woods hurled himself through the door.

A terrible sight met his eyes. Vickery lay crumpled and bleeding in a pile of broken glass and crystal. Monmouth stood over him with his pistol aimed at his head. Behind the clerk's desk, Oswald Grey stood ashen-faced and shaking like a leaf. *Where the devil was Eddie?*

Woods raised his pistol. 'Drop your pistol, Monmouth. Or I'll shoot you in your good leg!'

'Constable Woods.' Smirking, Monmouth turned towards him.

'It's Detective Woods now – I've had an advancement.'

Monmouth laughed and raised his pistol towards Woods.

Another shot rang out.

Ulrich Monmouth crumpled into a heap on the floor beside Vickery, and Eddie appeared from the shadowed hallway that led to the stables, his pistol still smoking.

It only took Woods a quick glance to reassure himself that his son was unharmed. He dashed over to Vickery, while Barnaby retrieved Monmouth's pistol.

Vickery groaned and raised his bleeding head.

'How bad is your injury?' Woods asked, as he offered a hand and hauled his colleague to his feet.

Vickery rose unsteadily. Broken glass slid off his coat and tinkled to the floor. 'I'm all right, Ned. The bastard caught me by surprise. I had my back to the door. He shot the chandelier above my head and the fallin' glass stunned me.'

'Yes, the cove likes bashin' fellas around the head,' Woods growled.

Monmouth rolled over in the shattered glass, groaned and clutched his bleeding leg. 'You bastards! I need a surgeon – get me a bloody surgeon!'

'Did I do all right, Da?' Eddie asked, nervously.

Woods swallowed back his emotion and said gruffly, 'You've done splendid, son. I'm proud of you.'

Eddie rushed towards Woods, and for a moment it looked like his huge six-foot child was about to throw himself into his arms. But Eddie jerked to a halt as a familiar voice behind Woods screeched with indignation and shock.

'What the devil happened here? Who's shot down our founder's chandelier?'

Magistrate Conant had arrived early to do his administration.

Chapter Thirty-Three

Friday, 15th April, 1814

Lavender enjoyed a delicious supper with the Durhams and their children in Cambridge before catching the mail coach back to London.

As the vehicle hurtled towards the capital, he sat back on the cracked leather seat and enjoyed the physical pleasure of a full stomach and the satisfaction of a job well done.

He hoped Woods had managed to make some progress with his investigation into the murder of Richard Garbutt, because the other two mysteries were now solved. He knew who had stolen the countess's jewellery and who had poisoned Poppleton.

He relished the moment and the sense of peace that came with it – it didn't always work out as well as this. He hadn't felt this happy for months.

There was only one mystery left to solve now – the identity of the informant leaking news from Bow Street to *The Times*. He reached into his coat pocket and pulled out the newspaper cutting. In the dim light of the smoky lantern in the coach, he could just about make out the print:

Surely there never was such an unlucky garment in the history of men's apparel? Sadly, these accursed trousers are still at large and roaming the city…

What the devil was it about the wording of this article that caught his attention this morning?

The truth hit him like a brick. He stopped breathing with shock. *No! Surely not?*

The elderly bearded gentleman sitting opposite put down his newspaper. 'Are you in good health, sir?' he enquired. 'You've gone quite pale.'

Lavender exhaled, and a slow smile spread across his face. 'I'm quite well, thank you. I'm sorry I alarmed you. My thoughts had *roamed* on to something unpleasant. But I've resolved the issue now.'

'That's good news, I'm sure.'

Still smiling, Lavender folded up the clipping and returned it to his coat pocket. He closed his eyes. Despite the jolting of the fast-moving coach, he managed to get some fitful sleep.

By the time the coach reached London, the first pink tinge of dawn had spread across the smoking chimneys and roofs of the city like delicate rosy fingers against the grey gloom. Huge wagons of produce for the market were already rolling into Covent Garden, but apart from the stray dogs, the streets were deserted.

Lavender strolled towards Bow Street, enjoying the dawn chorus of the birds and the relative calm of the sleeping city.

The first thing he saw when he turned into Bow Street was a man clapped in handcuffs lying on the pavement. The corners of his mouth twitched with amusement. The second was Magistrate Conant alighting from his carriage at the entrance to the building.

Suddenly, the gentle peace of the early morning was shattered by the unmistakable crack of a pistol shot.

Lavender broke into a run and bounded up the steps after Conant.

He took in the scene in a swift glance. A man whom he recognised as the horse thief Ulrich Monmouth lay wailing in pain on the floor. Woods was leaning over Vickery, who seemed injured – but alive. Ned, Eddie, Oswald Grey and Barnaby looked tired but unharmed.

But the tiny, elderly magistrate was incandescent with rage. His thin neck and face were bright red beneath his fluffy white hair.

'I ask you again, what the devil has happened here? And why is there a man in handcuffs lying out in the street?'

Lavender smiled. 'Well, it looks to me like your officers have just thwarted a nasty attack on Bow Street. Well done, everyone.'

'Welcome back, sir,' Woods said.

'An attack on Bow Street!' Conant yelled.

Woods gave Vickery his handkerchief to staunch the blood and brushed the broken glass and crystal off his coat.

'I'll live,' Vickery said. 'And well done, Lavender. The trap you laid worked.'

'Trap?' Conant spun round on Lavender. 'You've used *my* magistrates' court to set a trap? And why the devil have you been to Cambridge?'

'I've solved the case of the stolen Beverley diamonds.' Lavender turned to Woods and Vickery. 'Did Monmouth come for the poisoned pantaloons?'

Woods nodded and Conant spluttered with fury. 'Those damned trousers! Didn't I tell you to leave that case alone, Lavender?'

Lavender's smile widened. 'That wasn't possible, sir. It turns out those trousers were the key to solving the Beverley robbery.'

Woods pulled the diamond brooch out of his pocket and held the glittering jewel up for inspection. 'When I tracked down them poisoned kickseys, I found this sewn in the lining. It belongs to the Countess of Beverley.'

If Woods had hoped that the sight of the jewel would please Conant, he was in for a disappointment. The magistrate's face hardened. 'I gather from this that, despite my instructions, you and Lavender have been working together on your investigations.'

'Of course we have, sir,' Lavender said calmly. 'It's what we do best.'

'Lady Barlborough asked us to find out who was trying to kill her nephew,' Woods added. 'She intends to pay us and wants you to send her the bill.'

'Well, that's something, I suppose,' Conant spluttered.

Woods pointed towards Monmouth. 'I've also got evidence he and his chum outside were responsible for Garbutt's murder.'

'You've solved the Garbutt murder?'

'Yes, sir.'

'I appreciate that Ned and I owe you a full explanation,' Lavender said. 'We have a lot to report. Can I suggest we join you upstairs in your office in a few minutes?' He waved his hand at the carnage in the hallway. 'I think we'd better clean up down here first.'

'Aye,' Woods agreed. 'We need to throw Monmouth below the hatches and drag in that cove from the street before the neighbours complain we've left filth lyin' around.'

'You hard-hearted bastards!' Monmouth yelled from the floor. 'I need a bloody surgeon! I'm bleedin' to death!'

'That's a shame,' Woods said. 'But it'll save the hangman a job.'

'Did someone call for a surgeon?' said a familiar voice behind them.

Sir Richard Allison strode into the hallway, the picture of elegance and high fashion. He held out his hand towards the startled magistrate. 'Sir Nathaniel Conant? I'm Sir Richard Allison and I bring good news for Lavender and Woods.' He scanned the destruction in the hallway. 'Good gracious me! What a mess! You've obviously had a busy night. Who shot this chap on the floor?'

'I did,' Eddie said nervously.

His father growled. 'And that bastard ain't a "chap", he's a murderin' cove.'

'Would you please check Detective Vickery's injuries?' Lavender asked.

Sir Richard began to unbutton his smart blue coat. 'Certainly. And I'll remove the pistol shot from your prisoner's leg. We don't want him dying, do we?'

Woods leaned over Monmouth and said with gruff satisfaction, 'You couldn't be in safer or gentler hands than Sir Richard's. It won't hurt a bit.'

Monmouth understood his meaning and whimpered in fear.

Conant shook his head in disbelief and turned towards the staircase. 'I'll see you in my office, when you've finished here.'

When he'd gone, Eddie threw himself into his father's arms, nearly bowling him over. 'I thought he were goin' to kill you, Da!'

'You've done well, son,' Woods said gruffly, gently removing the pistol from the boy's hand.

Sir Richard finished his examination of Vickery's head. 'My goodness, fella, you've been lucky. What an incredibly thick skull you have!'

'It's my best feature,' Vickery replied proudly.

'Still. You'd better go home for a while and sleep. You have concussion and will get a terrible headache.'

Despite his bravado, Vickery nodded gratefully. He sat down on a wooden chair while Eddie ran outside to find him a hackney carriage.

Between them, Lavender, Barnaby and Woods retrieved the manacled man from the pavement and locked him up in the cells.

Sir Richard told them he'd operate on Monmouth's leg on the slab in the morgue at the back of the building. 'Fortunately, I keep a spare set of autopsy knives and other equipment in there.'

'I ain't goin' in a room with no dustmen!' Monmouth screamed. They had some difficulty dragging him out to the stinking and chilly morgue and had to leave Barnaby with Sir Richard to restrain Monmouth while the surgeon operated.

Back in the main building, Woods gave Lavender a full report of his discoveries.

Lavender listened thoughtfully and only interrupted him to ask to see the names of Lady Barlborough's servants. He smiled when Woods recounted the bit about how Barnaby had said Lavender should be chief constable and Woods his assistant. 'What an excellent idea,' he murmured. 'Did you say Conant isn't in court today?'

'Yes sir, he plans to catch up on his administration.'

'Administration be damned,' Lavender snapped. 'It's about time he came out in the streets with us and watched how we work.'

Lavender turned towards Eddie, who'd tagged along after them. 'The horse patrol will arrive back from their night shift soon, Eddie. Meet them at the stables and ask if any of them would like some extra pay. I need about a dozen of them to help us round up a large number of coves.'

'Yes, Uncle Stephen.' Eddie turned and ran out to the stables.

'Conant won't like payin' 'em extra,' Woods warned.

'Oh, I think you can leave Conant to me,' Lavender said as he turned to the staircase.

Magistrate Conant was sitting behind his desk. He looked calmer; the soft wrinkled skin of his face was white again.

Lavender picked up a couple of chairs and arranged them opposite Conant's desk, while the magistrate looked on in surprise. 'That's better,' he said as he sat down.

'This is just like old times, sir,' Woods said with a wink.

Lavender turned to Conant. 'I've a long story to tell you, but you need to know that what Woods and I have discovered will only enhance the reputation of Bow Street – and your own, as our magistrate – especially when I inform *The Times* newspaper about all the arrests we'll make today.'

Conant's eyes widened in surprise. 'You plan to work with the reporters?'

'Yes. I feel I've misjudged them – and underestimated the use they might be to us in future. I would like to volunteer to liaise personally with *The Times* about the work we do here at Bow Street. This way, we can use them to promote our work in a controlled manner that suits us.'

'Gawd's teeth! You're singin' to a different tune!' Woods murmured.

'But I think you should accompany us to these arrests, sir. It will enhance your status if the newspapers report your presence.'

The magistrate rubbed his chin thoughtfully. 'Yes, yes, I can see how that would work et cetera et cetera. I'll come with you.' He reached in his desk for a pile of blank arrest warrants. 'How many warrants will we need?'

'Lots – and a search warrant for Gotobed's bank.'

'Gotobed's bank?'

Lavender calmly and succinctly explained everything they'd discovered over the last few days. 'It is my belief,' he concluded, 'that Alfred Gotobed has masterminded a gang of criminals for several years. That thieving actress, Carlotta Meyer, is reported to have been involved with a bad crowd from Shoreditch, which is where Gotobed lives and opened his first bank. And it's my belief Sir Humphrey Poppleton was enticed into their evil web and a life of crime when he worked for Gotobed as his valet.'

Conant was horrified. 'Are you telling me Alfred Gotobed – a respected London banker – is behind this thievery? The man is a member of my club!'

'There ain't nothin' respectable about him,' Woods said. 'Barnaby and I watched his henchmen terrorisin' shopkeepers and homeowners last night. The man's extortin' money with menaces from folks and is probably runnin' several protection rackets.'

'I also think he runs this gang of female jewel thieves – who've been aided and abetted by Sir Humphrey Poppleton,' Lavender added. 'I expect to find the countess's diamond necklace hidden in Gotobed's bank and evidence of usury and illegal moneylending in his books.'

'On top of this,' Woods added, 'we think he set Monmouth and his chum on Richard Garbutt the other night. Whether the plan were to murder the poor cove – or not – I don't know, but murder were the outcome. Garbutt had drawn too much attention to the banker with those pamphlets that accused him of usury. Gotobed wanted him silenced.'

Before Conant could react, there was a knock on the door and Sir Richard and Barnaby entered. Sir Richard had scrubbed himself well after dealing with the bloody flesh and gore of Monmouth's leg. He was once again a distinguished man of fashion.

Woods gave up his chair for the surgeon and stood behind with Barnaby.

'We are honoured by your visit, Sir Richard,' Conant said. 'It was most fortuitous that you were passing. I'm grateful for your medical assistance – especially for poor Vickery.'

'I was glad to assist,' Sir Richard replied. 'I've sent Vickery home. He's had a nasty concussion. Oh, and I wasn't passing. I came here to tell Detective Woods that thanks to his intuition – and acute sense of smell – I've discovered the poison that I think was used on Baron Poppleton.'

'I were happy to help,' Woods said stiffly. 'Although I don't know where my sense of smell comes into it.'

'Ah, but my good fellow! When you said you smelled something *fishy* – it came to me immediately!'

Conant frowned. 'I was under the impression Baron Poppleton was overcome by strong liquor.'

'Not so. He had been poisoned by a rare – and barely known – substance extracted from a fish from the Tetraodontidae family. Common sailors call it the blowfish, or the pufferfish, due to its defensive habit of blowing itself up into a spherical ball, which often chokes its prey. It is extremely poisonous if ingested – as Captain James Cook discovered when his entire crew caught and ate some of the creatures and became ill on his second voyage around the world in the 1770s.'

'Is that why you sent Kingsley for the captain's book?' Woods asked.

'Yes. The toxin is called tetrodotoxin. It can also induce a catatonic state or torpor in the victims. They often enter a death-like coma. The toxin paralyses the diaphragm muscle, which leaves the victim barely breathing. This is what happened to Poppleton. In his book, Captain Cook reports that in the Indonesian islands and Polynesia, suspected victims of pufferfish poison were laid out next to their coffin until the corpse showed signs of decay, just in case they revived.'

'Good grief!' Conant exclaimed. 'I've never heard of such a thing!'

Sir Richard smiled. 'I fancy very few people in London have. This is why the paper I plan to write and the lecture I will give will be such a revelation!'

'Oh, I think I know someone who is familiar with the lethal effects of tetrodotoxin,' Lavender said grimly.

'So do I,' Woods said. 'It's that damned Monmouth again, isn't it? He were at Botany Bay and has brought a native gal home for his wife, along with that poison!'

'Not necessarily, Ned,' Lavender said, smiling. 'I can think of a better suspect for this attempted murder of Poppleton – in fact, I can think of two.'

'Well, I don't care who it is,' Sir Richard said. 'As long as they still have a sample of the poison! I would like to explore its effect.'

'I hope they do,' Lavender reminded him, 'because we also need it for evidence. I'd like you to come with us, Sir Richard, when we make the arrest. We need you to identify the tetrodotoxin.'

'Yes, of course. I can't wait to write up my paper about this substance and the effect it had on Sir Humphrey! It will stun the medical profession! This is the first known case of tetrodotoxin poisoning in England! Do you think Sir Humphrey would be willing to attend the lectures I plan to give?'

'I doubt that,' Lavender replied, 'because I need an arrest warrant for him too. Sir Humphrey Poppleton will spend many years in Newgate for theft and may face transportation.'

Sir Richard's face creased with frustration. 'I say, that's bad form, Lavender! I need the fellow. Can't you hold off with your arrest for a month or so while I make use of him?'

Lavender smiled. 'I'm afraid not. Woods will go with you to the Farrow household in Wapping to retrieve the poison and arrest the daughter, Diana Farrow. Meanwhile, I will lead the raid on Gotobed's bank.'

Woods frowned. 'I thought you'd dismissed that young gal from your list of suspects on account of her havin' an alibi for the day Poppleton were poisoned?'

'Oh, she wasn't working alone. She provided the poison, and another hand administered it. Miss Farrow helped her father, a former ship's surgeon, with his work and she has access to the specimens he brought back from his voyage with Captain Cook. I suspect we'll find a bottle of this pufferfish poison in his study – along with some aconitine. Diana Farrow has a strong motive for the murder: she would gain a lot of money from her cousin's death.'

'This girl's father might also be useful to me,' Sir Richard said.

Lavender smiled and stood up. 'I'm afraid he died recently. While you and Woods deal with the deadly Diana, I've asked some of the horse patrol to wait downstairs.' He turned towards Conant. 'I've promised them extra pay, to work overtime. I need their help to raid the banks of Alfred Gotobed. I also want two of them to go to James Street and arrest a couple of actresses: Mary Roper and Louisa Jacobs. I'll also need another arrest warrant for a third actress, called Carlotta Meyer.'

Sir Richard laughed. 'My goodness, Lavender! You like to keep everyone on their toes, don't you?'

Conant scowled and looked up from his desk, where he was hastily scribbling out arrest warrants. 'You seem to have taken charge of my office, Lavender.'

'It's all part of working as an effective team,' Lavender said quietly.

'And he is the *chief of constables*, sir,' young Barnaby said with a wink.

Chapter Thirty-Four

The hallway was packed with twelve hard-faced and bleary-eyed powerfully built men. It reeked with the stench of wet horse and male body odour. Most had been up all night, needed a shave and were scowling. A deep, underlying growl – interspersed with the occasional curse or short burst of ribald laughter – emanated from the crowd.

Magistrate Conant watched in a trance while Lavender issued instructions and iron handcuffs were distributed. Several of the officers leaned against the walls priming their pistols, their boots and uniforms splattered with the mud of the outlying roads of the capital where they had spent the night on patrol.

Eddie hovered at the edge of the group. Oswald Grey stood like a sentinel at the clerk's desk.

For the first time that morning, Conant seemed to notice his chief clerk. 'What are you doing here, Grey? I thought Simpson was supposed to be on duty?'

'Mr Grey knew about the trap,' Woods said, 'and I rather fancy that a decent man like him wouldn't put his young clerks in danger. He took Simpson's shift.'

'Well done, Mr Grey,' Lavender said quietly. 'If you've been here all night, I suggest you go home to bed now.'

'I understand you might bring back some accounts ledgers to be deciphered, Lavender,' Grey said. 'I thought I'd stay for a few hours longer to see if I can help.'

'Good man,' Woods said.

Officers were dispatched to arrest the actresses Louisa Jacobs and Mary Roper, and the rest of the group was split into two. Half came with Lavender and Conant to Gotobed's bank in Southwark; the second group was sent to his branch in Shoreditch.

'You come with us, Eddie,' Lavender said. 'You've shown your mettle today and it's time you had some experience of the work of the horse patrol constables.'

When Lavender, Conant and their men burst into his office, Alfred Gotobed was sitting behind his desk with his elderly clerk, Lawrence Wiles, standing beside him.

'*You* again!' Gotobed yelled, rising to his feet. 'I thought I'd got rid of you!'

'She missed,' Lavender replied calmly. 'She's a terrible shot.'

Gotobed reached towards something in his top drawer.

But Lavender was quicker. He aimed his pistol at the banker's head and Gotobed froze.

'Get his pistol, Eddie,' instructed Lavender.

The young lad dashed round to the desk and removed a flintlock pistol from the top drawer. Another officer dragged the cursing banker from behind the desk and clapped him in irons. The terrified clerk pressed himself up against the wall.

'I'm sorry if my presence in your bank upsets you, Mr Gotobed,' Lavender said, 'but this is Magistrate Conant from Bow Street. He has a warrant to search these premises.'

'This is an outrage!' Gotobed yelled. 'How dare you treat me in this way! I'm a gentleman!'

Conant's face flushed with anger. 'You are no gentleman, sir! We are here to recover the stolen diamond necklace belonging to the Countess of Beverley and to examine your ledgers for evidence of usury and extortion.'

'Mr Wiles,' Lavender said to the clerk, 'you will go with our officers and open all your back vaults and security boxes.'

The trembling man gulped. 'All of them?'

'Yes, all of them.'

Eddie was staring down into the open top drawer of the desk. 'Actually, Uncle Stephen,' he said, 'I think there's something here...' He reached into the drawer and drew out a heavy velvet bag that jangled with metal.

He tipped the contents on to the desk. A cascading, glittering waterfall of gold beads, diamonds, carnelians, turquoises and rubies slithered out on to the polished teak.

Magistrate Conant smiled and his deadly, silky voice sent shivers down the spine of the rest of the men in the room. 'Alfred Gotobed, by the power vested in me by His Royal Highness The Prince Regent, in the name and on behalf of His Majesty King George III, I arrest you on suspicion of the theft of the necklace belonging to the Countess of Beverley and an ancient artefact known as a wesekh belonging to Lady Attlee.'

The *whispering assassin* had spoken.

'Go to hell!' Gotobed screamed.

Back at Bow Street, the cells were filling up. Apart from Gotobed and the two actresses, Woods had also returned with Diana Farrow. She cowered in the same cell as the two outraged and screaming actresses.

'They all deny any wrongdoin', sir,' Woods informed Lavender.

'Of course they do.'

'Do you want to interview them now?'

'No, let's pick up the rest first. Where's Sir Richard, by the way?'

'Oh, he found both the wolfsbane and that puffy fish poison in the Farrow house. He's gone back to Guy's Hospital to try them out on a few folks.'

Lavender sighed. 'I hope you're jesting, Ned.' He turned to Magistrate Conant. 'Would you like to accompany us to make the final arrests, sir?'

Conant's eyes gleamed beneath his black eyebrows. 'Absolutely. I haven't had so much excitement for a long time, Detective.'

Lady Barlborough complained bitterly from behind her screen when Lavender, Woods, Magistrate Conant and Constable Barnaby were shown into her sitting room by the footman. 'What is this outrage! Feathers! You know I don't receive uninvited visitors.'

Both Sir Humphrey and Lottie Poppleton were standing close to her and the blazing fire that raged in the hearth. Lottie wore a satin housecoat with large pockets over her muslin dress. Lavender scrutinised the pair of them and noted that despite both being blue-eyed, fair-haired and good looking, there wasn't much of a family resemblance. Their noses and eyebrows were different shapes. Her bone structure was finer, her face oval and his square. Her eyes were also closer together than his.

Lavender was pleased to see the nurse, Effy, was also there. Good. That would make things easier. The room was hot and crowded.

'Please accept our apologies for the intrusion, Lady Barlborough,' Conant said pleasantly, 'but you'll be pleased to know my officers have uncovered the poison used on Baron Poppleton and are aware of the identity of the poisoner.'

The nurse sidled towards the door, but Barnaby cut her off and grabbed her arm.

'Gerroff me!' she squealed.

'What's happening?' demanded the old woman from behind her screen.

'We believe your nurse, Effy – working with your niece, Diana Farrow – tried on two occasions to poison Sir Humphrey.'

'Good God!' Poppleton turned pale with shock.

'Effy?' Lottie stammered. 'I can understand Diana wanting Humphrey dead – but not Effy! Surely?'

'She is not who she seems,' Lavender continued. 'Diana Farrow provided the poisons from her father's collection – and Effy administered them. She's the one who sprinkled the wolfsbane into Sir Humphrey's pantaloons.'

'You damned bitch!' the baron shouted across the room. His handsome faced contorted with anger.

'This is outrageous!' Lady Barlborough said.

Lavender turned to Sir Humphrey. 'When the wolfsbane failed to take effect, she gave you a dose of the little-known poison extracted from the tropical pufferfish. This was why you ended up unconscious and barely breathing. Can you remember any occasion last Saturday when she brought you something to eat or drink?'

The so-called siblings fell silent. Then Lottie threw up her elegant hands in the air as realisation dawned. 'It was the tea, Humphrey! Don't you remember? After we'd eaten and you'd downed that bottle of claret, I ordered Feathers to fetch us a pot of tea. I thought it might sober you up before you went out. But it was Effy who appeared, with two separate cups – she said Feathers was busy. Your cup must have been poisoned – and mine wasn't.'

'I thought it was bitter! But I was too drunk to care.'

'I remember thinking,' Lottie continued, 'that Effy should have brought in the teapot on the tray, but knowing she was just a common nurse, rather than a parlour maid, I let it slide.'

'What have you got to say for yourself, woman?' Sir Humphrey demanded.

But Effy stood limp in Barnaby's grasp, with her head bowed and shoulders slumped.

'Why?' Lady Barlborough demanded. 'Why did Effy want to kill my poor nephew? I can understand that that vixen Diana was after my money – but what had Effy to gain?'

For the first time, Effy spoke. 'It were Miss Farrow – she forced me to do it!'

'Of course she didn't,' Lavender snapped. 'You wanted him dead as much as she did. It was revenge on your part, pure and simple.'

'No! I just planned to shame him – it were Miss Farrow who corrupted me and persuaded me to murder!'

'Shame me?' Poppleton sneered. 'How could *you* do that?'

'Do you recognise this woman, Sir Humphrey?' Lavender asked.

'No. She arrived here a couple of months ago to be my aunt's nurse. I've never seen her before.'

'Do you know her full name?'

Poppleton gave an ugly laugh. 'Why should I? My sister deals with the servants.'

'It's Smith, isn't it?' Lottie asked.

'Her full name is Euphemia Smith,' Lavender said quietly. 'She's from Cambridge and was the sister of Emma Smith, a young maidservant who died in a terrible boating accident at Netheredge – your family estate. An accident for which the stupidity of Sir Humphrey was responsible.'

Lady Barlborough's shrill voice became even more high pitched. 'How dare you! What accident? Why do I not know about this accident?'

'Your nephew has kept things from you, Lady Barlborough – a lot of things.'

'I see you've been investigating my past.' The baron's tone was icy.

Lavender turned to face him. Poppleton stared back, with a dangerous look in his eyes. Lavender's hand hovered over the primed pistol in his pocket.

'This vengeful woman tracked you down to this house,' Lavender continued cautiously. 'She gained employment here, intent on revenge. But then she met a kindred spirit – your cousin Diana – and the two of them decided to join forces to plot your downfall.'

'Oh, well done, Lavender,' Poppleton said sarcastically. 'Thank you for solving the case. But if you don't mind, I'd like you to leave now.'

'Unfortunately, I can't. We also have an arrest warrant for you, Sir Humphrey Poppleton, for the theft of jewels belonging to the Countess of Beverley and Lady Attlee.'

'What? What new nonsense is this?' screamed Lady Barlborough.

'During the years since his father's death and his arrival on your doorstep, Lady Barlborough, Sir Humphrey has worked for a known felon, a man called Gotobed, who operates several criminal gangs in the capital. Your nephew, along with a former actress and con woman known as Carlotta Meyer, robbed the Attlee Museum of a valuable gold artefact and the Countess of Beverley of her jewellery. He's a common thief – and a fraudster.'

'Nonsense!' screamed the old woman.

Lavender smiled. 'I'm afraid I've a witness who can identify him. Besides which, Lady Barlborough, you need to know that you've also been a victim of the lies of this man.'

'How so? What are you talking about?'

'When the maid, Emma Smith, died in that boating accident – she wasn't alone. Sir Humphrey's sister, Charlotte Poppleton, died with her.'

'This is ridiculous! My niece is here!' A pair of bony, quivering arms clad in long black sleeves and fingerless gloves reached out from behind the screen. The hideous sores on her fingers and thin wrists were visible for all to see. 'Come to me, Lottie, my darling!'

But the young woman known as Lottie Poppleton was rooted to the spot, glaring at Lavender with hatred.

'This is not your niece, Lady Barlborough,' Lavender continued. 'Lottie Poppleton died in 1809 – I've seen her grave. This young woman is Carlotta Meyer, Sir Humphrey's thieving accomplice and his lover.'

'What!'

'Your nephew brought his mistress – a common criminal and an actress – into your home to live with him. *Carlotta. Caro. Charlotte. Lottie.* Why! She barely even had to change her name.'

Before anyone could react, Carlotta Meyer reached into the pocket of her house coat and pulled out a pistol. 'I've had enough!'

She waved the weapon at the officers, indicating that she wanted them to step aside from the door. 'I'm leaving. Don't try to stop me or I'll shoot. And you, Lavender – move your bloody hand away from your pocket!'

Lavender hesitated. *Could he whisk out his pistol before she fired?*

Then Woods stepped towards Meyer. 'Now, now, Treacle, you don't want to make things worse than they already are.'

'Ned!' Lavender's heart lurched in his ribcage.

'Theft and fraud are crimes that'll see you sent Bayside,' Woods continued pleasantly as he crossed the carpet. 'But murderin' a police officer is an 'angin' offence.'

She responded by firing the pistol straight into Woods' chest. The trigger clicked and clicked again.

'Argh!' Lavender dashed forward to catch his wounded colleague before he fell.

But Ned had already disarmed the squealing woman, spun her round and clapped her in irons. A wide grin spread across his broad face. 'It's all right, sir. I found this pistol the other day and emptied it. I knew it weren't loaded.'

'The pistol didn't fire, Lavender,' Conant said, smiling.

Lavender's heart pounded in his chest. 'You might have bloody told me, you great muttonhead!'

'Now, now, sir. Don't get testy.'

Chapter Thirty-Five

They bundled Poppleton, Meyer and Effy Smith into a prison wagon to take them back to Bow Street. Lavender told Barnaby to climb up to the box and take the reins.

Lavender, Woods and Conant climbed into Conant's carriage for the return journey. Before they left, Lavender suggested to Feathers that he fetch Mrs Farrow to comfort her distraught sister.

'I thought they hated each other?' Woods said.

Lavender shrugged. 'Who knows? They're all each other has now.'

Lavender and Woods sank back wearily into the comfortable cushions of the coach. Woods couldn't stop yawning. 'Gawd's teeth! It's been a long day and night!' His eyelids drooped but the coach lurched forward and jolted him back awake. A frown creased across his forehead. 'But there's a few things I still don't understand about this case, sir.'

'What are they?' Lavender asked.

'For a start, why were the brooch and the necklace separated? Why didn't Poppleton hand them both over to Gotobed?'

'I suspect our devious baron planned to keep the brooch for himself and not share the profit from it with the other villains in his gang. Everything Poppleton did was about money: from the robberies to charming his elderly aunt and persuading her to let him and his lover move into her home. To be honest, now Lady Barlborough's will has been changed in his favour, I suspect she may have soon met with an early demise at his hands.'

Woods scowled at the thought.

'So, he had the secret pocket in his pantaloons made to keep the brooch out of the sight of nosy servants until he'd had chance to find an independent fence who would pay him for it.'

'But wasn't there always a chance one of them actresses might tell Gotobed he'd withheld it?'

'Yes. And when I first told him about the poisoning and asked if there was anyone who held a grudge against him, he looked alarmed. Obviously, the rest of the gang were on his mind. That was when he decided to mention to his fellow coves that the brooch was in the pantaloons on the night they were stolen from him. Although he didn't tell them about the secret pocket. He hoped he could still retrieve it once the pantaloons were found. Meanwhile, Gotobed and the rest thought Yardley had hidden it somewhere.'

'So, if it hadn't been for Poppleton's greed – and those damned kickseys – would you have connected him with the robbery at Beverley House?'

'No, probably not. But once I'd connected Poppleton to the theft and heard his sister was dead, it was easy to discover the whereabouts of Carlotta Meyer, who's been hiding in plain sight, impersonating his sister.'

Woods grunted and settled back in his seat again.

Lavender stared out of the window at the bustling street and traders behind their colourful stalls on the pavement. The traffic was heavy and the carriage was moving slowly. This would be an ideal time, Lavender realised, to put his suggestions to Conant about some reorganisation at Bow Street. The magistrate was in an excellent mood. *But how to bring up the subject?*

Conant distracted him from his thought. 'I also have a question about the case, Lavender. Effy Smith would have known Meyer was an imposter the minute she joined Lady Barlborough's household. The real Charlotte Poppleton drowned with her own sister. Why didn't Smith expose Meyer's impersonation to her employer?'

Lavender shrugged. 'She probably planned to – that was the shaming she mentioned. But I suspect Diana Farrow had other plans. She wanted Poppleton dead, and she persuaded Effy to keep silent about Meyer until they'd killed Poppleton. Once he was removed from the scene, Smith would have exposed Meyer's fraud. That way, Diana Farrow got rid of both of her troublesome cousins.'

Woods had woken up again. 'Why were Carlotta Meyer so quiet durin' the robbery?' Woods asked. 'Everyone else said she were always the bossy ringleader of the gang.'

'Ah, that's because of Viscount Cottingham, Sir Harry Lawson and Lord Jonothan Furnish. As Lottie Poppleton, she probably mixed socially with those young men. To avoid recognition, she wore a disguise – a red wig and a false nose – and kept quiet. Sir Humphrey made sure the men were drunk when they met the women, to blur their faculties. Meyer and Sir Humphrey didn't want the young men to recognise her. She provided the introduction, she slipped out of Beverley House quickly and left the other actresses to steal the jewels.'

Woods laughed. 'Those young bucks will be embarrassed to find out how she gulled them.' He yawned again.

'You must be exhausted, Woods,' Conant said. 'And you too, Lavender. Unless there's anyone else you want me to arrest today, I suggest the pair of you go home for some sleep.'

'I don't think there's anyone left in London to arrest,' Woods said with a grin.

Conant smiled. 'You've done well, both of you. Especially you, Lavender. I admire how you handled and organised the other officers. I've also been impressed today with the way the pair of you worked together to solve these mysteries et cetera et cetera. You complement each other. I may have been wrong to keep you apart.'

'As that cheeky young scamp Barnaby pointed out,' Woods said, 'Lavender is *the chief of constables*.'

'It's a pity the title isn't official,' Lavender said.

'Are you angling for a promotion, Detective?' Conant asked.

'Well, I have to confess I've enjoyed myself. It's days like today that remind why I stay with Bow Street.'

Conant looked shocked. 'Have you thought about leaving us?'

Lavender nodded. 'As you may know, sir, thanks to my wife's Spanish estates, I'm a man of independent means.'

Woods, who knew the true state of Magdalena's ravaged estates, stiffened at this lie. But he remained silent, and waited to see where Lavender's comments were leading.

'Are you saying that if you were given the honorary title of Chief Constable, you wouldn't expect a rise in pay?'

'No. I'd do it for the love of the job. There are many days when I long for a different challenge,' Lavender continued vaguely. 'I would welcome more days like today, when I spend my time deploying men on different investigations and organising us into teams.'

'But what about your detection work? You are the shrewdest, most successful detective we have at Bow Street – especially when it comes to complicated cases.'

'Oh, I'd need an assistant, of course. If I had an *assistant chief constable*, I would be able to do both – and take on the responsibility of liaising with the newspapers.'

Conant stroked his chin thoughtfully. 'There's some talk at the Home Department about the benefits of pairing up constables – but I suspect this is an idea for the future.'

'Bow Street has always led the way with innovation,' Lavender observed. 'Did you know I sometimes fulfilled this unofficial role of chief constable for Magistrate Read?'

'I didn't.'

'Yes – and Mr Grey helped me to allocate the jobs. The role and responsibilities of the Bow Street constables have grown considerably over the last few years. The city is expanding dramatically and so is the number of crimes we're called upon to solve. Magistrate Read was often overwhelmed with his court duties. He welcomed my help. Do you find your workload in the court overwhelming at times, sir?'

Conant nodded. 'I do.'

'But I suppose your duties will become less onerous now we've seven principal officers,' Lavender continued. 'It's an improvement. I'm sure you'll agree, sir, that Ned has more than justified his promotion to detective.'

Conant shuffled uncomfortably. 'Yes, there's no doubt, Woods, that you've excelled yourself this week. And there will be something extra in your wages for all your hard work et cetera et cetera. However, I'm afraid I was a bit premature with the offer. It turns out I can only employ six principal officers – and John Townsend isn't leaving. There isn't an opening.'

'So I've heard,' Woods said, scowling.

Conant paused and stared over Woods' shoulder. He was making a decision. 'However, I think Lavender's idea is a good one. I can't create additional principal officers against Home Department instructions, but I can make Lavender honorary Chief Constable and you can be his assistant. Naturally, there will be an increase in remuneration for you, Woods. Although I don't know what we'll do about the gap you'll leave in the horse patrol.'

'Oh, I think there's a simple answer to that,' Lavender said. 'Eddie Woods has more than proved himself today. He needs to leave the stables and become a constable in the horse patrol.'

'But the boy is what? Only seventeen?'

Lavender shrugged. 'I wasn't much older when I began working with Woods.'

Woods winked. 'I taught Lavender everythin' he knows.'

Lavender smiled. 'Eddie's been groomed for the role of constable by his father since he was in his cradle – and as we saw today, he's a crack shot.'

'Well, in that case, I think this is an excellent idea – if Assistant Chief Constable Woods agrees, of course? We'll set young master Woods to work with Barnaby. What do you think, Woods? I will increase your pay as promised.'

'Would I still be able to wear my old uniform?'

'Why, yes. Is that what you want?'

Woods nodded, satisfied. 'You see, since I were advanced to Detective, I've torn my old brown coat, lost my favourite hat and had to burn my gloves. In addition to all this expense, the job has forced me to adopt a small boy into our home and a mangy mutt called Alfie Bobbin. It's been a pricey week.'

'That's all very unfortunate,' Magistrate Conant murmured sympathetically.

'Especially the name of the dog,' Lavender said.

'So, to my way of thinkin', it'll be better to be Assistant Chief Constable in my old uniform, rather than a detective. It's less pricey.'

The carriage drew up outside Bow Street. Conant was on his feet first and opened the door. 'Then it's settled,' he called over his shoulder. 'Now go home, the pair of you, and get some rest. You can interview our suspects tomorrow. They're not going anywhere.' He climbed down and scurried up the steps into the building.

His two exhausted officers were slower to get out. They stood for a moment on the bustling pavement, enjoying the refreshing breeze.

'We've done well, haven't we, sir?'

'Yes, Ned. We've done very well.'

'And not only have we got all those coves under the hatches, but now we're in charge, Bow Street will be a better place to work for everyone, won't it?'

'Yes, it will.'

'You handled Conant well – but you should have pushed for a rise in your own wages too.'

'I've got you back by my side,' Lavender said softly. 'That's reward enough.'

Woods gave him a quizzical glance. 'You seem different today, sir. Less tetchy and cross.'

'The trip to Cambridge did me good. It helped me to settle my mind about a few things.'

'Like the loss of your Da?'

Lavender nodded, and Woods reached out to give him an affectionate and hearty thump on his back. 'He'd have been proud of you, sir. Now, how about a tankard of ale to celebrate before we go home?'

Lavender shook his head. 'Not just now. There's still something I have to do.'

Woods' face fell with disappointment.

'But I'll come round this evening with Magdalena and the children, if that's all right? I think we need to meet this Alfie Bobbin.'

Woods grinned, said farewell, and strode off towards Southwark.

Chapter Thirty-Six

The sun had gone behind the clouds by the time Lavender reached Printing House Square. Clumps of straw and litter swirled over the cobbles in the cold breeze. Lavender stood beneath the dark shadows of a gnarled oak tree and pulled up the coat of his collar against the cold.

He had no idea what time Dan Woods finished work for the day, but he suspected it would be soon. Sure enough, about twenty minutes later, the young lad came out of the offices of *The Times*, accompanied by Vincent Dowling.

Dowling. He should have known.

As tall as the older man, Dan's brown eyes were gleaming with excitement as he chatted away. He had a leather satchel slung over his shoulder, and his fingers were black with ink. The pair were so engrossed in their conversation they didn't see Lavender until he stepped out of the shadows of the tree in front of them.

'Good evening, Dowling. Hello, Dan.'

'Uncle Stephen!' Dan's face flickered, half with fear and half with defiance.

Dowling recovered first. 'Ah, good evening, Lavender. Look who I've just stumbled across! I believe this young man is the son of Detective Woods?'

'The game's up now, Dowling. I know what's going on.' He turned towards Dan. 'I need to speak to you. Would you like a cup of chocolate? There's a good coffee house round the corner.'

Dan gave a strangled laugh. 'I'm in trouble, aren't I? If it's still the tradition to give a condemned man a last request, I'd prefer a tankard of ale in a tavern.'

Lavender smiled. 'Like father, like son. Come on then. We'll go to the Black Prince.'

'Be gentle with the lad, Lavender,' Dowling called out when they turned and walked away.

The interior of the Black Prince was almost as black as its name. Poorly lit from its small windows, its uneven wooden floor and the exposed beams of its low ceiling were blackened with age and smoke. But Lavender knew it was quiet at this time of day and served good ale.

According to Dan, it also made excellent meat pies. When the barmaid arrived at their table, Dan ordered two for himself and one for Lavender. *Like father, like son...*

But Lavender didn't mind. He couldn't remember the last time he ate anything.

'The last meal of the condemned man,' Dan joked.

Behind his defiant smile, Lavender saw the nervousness in the boy's eyes. He let Dan sweat for a while and didn't ask his questions until their ale and pies had arrived. 'Well, Dan – your parents think you're a clerk in a shipping company down at the docks.'

Dan paused, his fork halfway to his mouth. 'Yes, that's right.'

'But in truth, you work as a reporter for *The Times* newspaper.'

'A junior reporter,' Dan corrected him, with a mouth full of pie. 'It's like an apprenticeship. If they think I'm good enough in a few months, they'll keep me on.'

'Are you good enough?'

Dan's thick mop of brown curly hair wobbled as he nodded his head. He swallowed his food. 'Mr Stoddard, our editor, is pleased with me.'

'I'm sure he is,' Lavender said drily. 'How did you get the job? Did Dowling recruit you?'

'Yes, how did you know? He met me on the street one day, told me who he was. He said he'd heard I was after a clerical position and asked if I'd ever thought about newspaper reporting. I had. I'd always thought it looked like an exciting job. I still don't know how he knew about all that – or who I was.'

Lavender rolled his eyes at the boy's naivety. 'Would it surprise you to learn that Dowling used to be a spy for the Home Department?'

Eddie's eyes – Betsy's eyes – widened with surprise. 'Really?'

'There's not much Dowling doesn't know about what's happening in this city. He's probably had his eye on you for years. Was it his idea or your own to eavesdrop on your father and myself and use the information we shared in your newspaper?'

Dan squirmed on his stool. 'It was Dowling's.'

Lavender shook his head. 'He's used you, Dan. He and Stoddard wanted news of our investigations at Bow Street.'

'I've tried to be as discreet and complimentary as I could,' the boy said defensively.

'You also made things up – especially earlier this week, when I was reported to have taken part in a dramatic river chase to catch that villain Hodge.'

'Yes, I'm sorry about that, Uncle Stephen. I got carried away. Mr Stoddard wasn't pleased about it either – especially when Magistrate Conant made him print a retraction. He said the truth about your work was exciting enough and I shouldn't invent things – and I was to stick to the facts from now on.'

The boy looked so crestfallen Lavender felt sorry for him. He was nothing more than an excited child – Ned and Betsy's child – feeling his way around the cold and alien adult world of work. But he was also a talented young man.

'I'm glad to hear it won't happen again. I must confess, though, Dan, the next article you wrote about Baron Poppleton and Sir Richard's stethoscope was impressive. I assumed Sir Richard Allison wrote that himself.'

Dan's eyes lit up again. 'I enjoyed researching for it. After I overheard you telling Da about it in the parlour on Rachel's birthday, I went to Guy's Hospital and spoke to several of the young doctors. They told me what had happened to Sir Humphrey, and how they'd used this invention called a stethoscope to listen for signs of life. It's much better reporting cases like this. It's fun to be out and about interviewing people and roaming the streets rather than cooped up in the office all day.'

Roaming the streets. Lavender smiled. 'That article may have saved Sir Richard's reputation and Kingsley's job,' Lavender conceded.

'I also talked to the housemaid at Beverley House and got all those details about those actresses.'

'And – as your father pointed out to me – that article brought forward a new and valuable witness.'

Dan's eyes widened. 'Did it? That's good, isn't it, Uncle Stephen?'

Lavender ignored the appeal in the young man's face.

'Were you ever tempted to mention the poisoning?'

'Good grief, no! I knew that would let your poisoner know you were on to them.'

Lavender hid his smile. There was a streak of the police constable inside Dan after all. 'I suppose your job explains why you're out nearly every night and have abandoned your brother.'

'Yes, poor Eddie. I feel bad about that.'

'Well, I wouldn't worry about Eddie. He's just been promoted to the horse patrol. He won't have much time to spare for you from now on.'

Dan was genuinely delighted for his brother.

'Why didn't you tell your parents the truth about your job?'

'I couldn't. Da hates reporters as much as you.'

Lavender winced. The boy's honesty made him feel guilty. 'You'll have to tell them now, Dan.'

Dan sighed heavily. 'I know. Da will be furious. He'll force me to leave the newspaper – and give me a good hiding.'

'No, he won't,' Lavender said, smiling. 'For a start, you're too big to thrash. Secondly, despite his threats, Ned has *never* given you – or Eddie – a good hiding.'

'He's often threatened to!'

'Threatening, isn't doing. And thirdly, you're now working for me.'

'What?'

Lavender explained the decision he'd come to about Bow Street, the newspapers, and the role he'd volunteered to take. 'So, from now on, I will liaise with you and provide you with the facts we want you to know about our cases. But you need to promise me, Dan, that you won't use your imagination and elaborate on any of the information I give you or exaggerate it. You've come close to compromising both our investigations and our reputation a few times this week.'

'I promise! I promise! Oh, Uncle Stephen, this is incredible news – Mr Stoddard will be so impressed!'

'Well, what are you waiting for? Take out your notepad and I'll give you the first story. We've solved a string of mysteries this week.'

Dan had his satchel open and his paper and ink bottle out in a flash.

Twenty minutes later, as Dan was packing his tools away, a thought seemed to pass through his mind. He gave Lavender a wary sideways glance. 'How did you know it was me? I thought I'd done a good job covering my tracks.'

'For a start, there was your cheeky comment the other day when you were cleaning your boots, about how we never know to whom we might have to show a clean pair of heels. Earlier that day, I'd nearly caught you in your office.'

Dan chuckled. 'I couldn't resist it!'

Lavender pulled the newspaper clipping out of his pocket and spread it out on the table. 'Then there was yesterday's article, where you wrote: *"those accursed trousers are still at large and roaming the city…" Roaming* is one of your father's favourite words. Earlier that day, he'd pointed out to me that the poisoned kickseys *"…are still out there, roamin' the city".* He probably used the same phrase when he told your mother about it. A conversation to which – I've no doubt – you were listening.'

Dan's face lit up in surprise. 'Gawd's teeth! You found me out because of a *verb*!'

Lavender suppressed a yawn and smiled. 'You copy your father's way of speaking. It was also the only thing that made sense. You reported things I'd only discussed with your father. Ned and I have always talked over our cases together and I guess we've become careless. We've never given a thought about the little ears in the same room.'

'You're an amazing detective, Uncle Stephen!'

'I'm also a very tired one. I need to go home now, Dan. And so do you. Make sure you tell your parents the truth tonight.'

'I will! I will!' Dan drained the last of his ale, pushed back his stool and stood up. Then he stopped and smiled down at Lavender.

'You and Da have done well this week, haven't you?'

Lavender smiled, pulled on his hat, and he too stood up. 'Yes, we have – especially your father. You've every right to be proud of him, Dan. Just remember to tell him sometimes. It's the most important thing a man can hear.'

AUTHOR'S NOTES & ACKNOWLEDGEMENTS

I first came across a reference in *The Times* to '*the chief of constables, Stephen Lavender*' in a report into the assassination of the British prime minister Spencer Perceval – which was the subject matter of my fourth novel, *Plague Pits & River Bones*.

During the same research trip to the National Archives in Kew, I also found a small retraction in *The Times,* which admitted they'd wrongly reported a dramatic incident on the River Thames where they claimed Stephen Lavender had leapt from the deck of one boat to another to arrest a suspect.

Journalistic integrity wasn't rigidly enforced by our broadsheets two hundred years ago, and often their style of writing was more akin to what we now expect from tabloids. I've read many articles from this period in *The Times* that dwelt on the sensational and the lurid.

All the British newspapers were fascinated by Lavender and the other Bow Street officers. The provincial newspapers shamelessly plagiarised reports from the London newspapers when copies reached them a day or two later. In fact, when the real Stephen Lavender died, over thirty newspapers in England reported his death and wrote a short obituary.

Anyway, *The Times'* apology about the boat chase on the Thames amused me and I wondered how the real Stephen Lavender felt about being misrepresented. I decided to use this incident in a future novel and explore the age-old theme of the tension that exists between celebrities and the Press.

All the newspaper extracts that appear in this book are fictional, although I've tried to replicate the tone and style of writing used in *The Morning Post*, *The Times* and others.

Cross Bones Cemetery still exists, and it's possible to visit it on an open day if you're ever in that part of London. Its history is as grisly as I've described, and the practice of body snatching for medical dissection was rife in London in the early nineteenth century.

My inspiration for this novel was the opening scene, where Baron Poppleton wakes up on Sir Richard's dissection table. The idea jumped into my head and swirled around gleefully. It made me laugh.

But to keep the baron unconscious for so long, I needed a poison akin to the one the priest gives to Juliet in Shakespeare's play *Romeo and Juliet*. My research soon revealed there was no such substance circulating in Elizabethan England; as Sir Richard says: 'it was a figment of the bard's imagination'.

However, once I learned about the shocking effects of tetrodotoxin, I realised I could use this. The bonus for me was that Captain James Cook is a local hero in the area where I live (his parents are buried in my village churchyard), and it was he who first brought news of this weird substance to England. During Cook's voyages, he came across islanders who, if they suspected their dead relatives had eaten pufferfish, left the bodies next to their graves for a while in case they woke up.

The story of Richard Garbutt and his addiction to chancery court cases and libellous pamphlets and advertisements is an embellished version of the story of a man called Richard Gathorne Butt, who sued both the Lord Chief Justice and the magistrate Sir Nathaniel Conant – among others. He also brought a writ claiming that magistrates didn't have the authority to arrest people. He wasn't murdered – but he did bankrupt himself in the process.

For the purposes of my novel, I also brought forward the invention of the stethoscope by Dr René Laënnec by two years.

When I researched the history of Cambridge University for this novel, I was startled to discover that in 1815 the students were sent home due to a deadly outbreak of typhus fever. This is the only time in its 900-year history – apart from the recent Covid pandemic of 2020 – when this prestigious establishment closed its hallowed halls. I decided to bring this event forward a year.

And talking about Covid, those of you who read book six, *The Willow Marsh Murder*, may have expected this novel to be about Lavender's trip to northern Spain to visit Magdalena's estates.

It was my intention to follow *Willow Marsh* with a mystery set in the Asturias. I wanted to fly out there with an interpreter to research it. But when the pandemic hit, oddly enough, I lost interest in foreign travel. The thought of sitting in a flying tin can, breathing in other people's regurgitated germs, still fills me with unease.

As a result, Lavender and Woods have taken a different journey. I hope you've enjoyed it.

I would like to thank my editorial team, Jenni Davis and Jill Boulton, for their help with this novel and also pay tribute to my wonderful cover designer, Lisa Horton, who never fails to delight me with her imagination and flair.

Finally, to you, the reader, thank you for reading my novel. If you've enjoyed it, please leave a review on Amazon.

Karen Charlton
www.karencharlton.com
5 December 2023
Marske, North Yorkshire

ABOUT THE AUTHOR

Karen Charlton is the best-selling author of The Detective Lavender Mysteries and The York Ladies' Detective Agency Mysteries.

A former English teacher, with two grown-up children and two grandchildren, she lives in North Yorkshire with her two cats and writes full time. She enjoys gardening and dressmaking, a good mystery, and historical dramas on TV.

She's an avid fiction reader herself and loves to hear from her own readers. You can contact her via her website. For the latest news about her fiction, public appearances, and some special offers, sign up for her occasional newsletter on the home page. www.karencharlton.com

ALSO BY KAREN CHARLTON

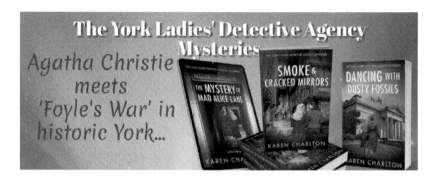

AGATHA CHRISTIE MEETS FOYLE'S WAR

The York Ladies' Detective Agency Mysteries follow the adventures of two bright young women who set up a private detective agency in York during the Second World War.

Best friends since school and passionate fans of the Golden Age detective stories of Agatha Christie and Dorothy L. Sayers, these enterprising young women quickly discover that their clients have more secrets than the people they want them to investigate.

Perplexing mysteries and unsolved murders abound as they pick their way through the blacked-out wartime streets of their historic city.

Recommended for fans of the highly acclaimed TV series *Foyle's War* and for fans of Richard Osman, Alexander McCall Smith and Agatha and Dorothy – those 'Queens of Crime'.

Made in the USA
Columbia, SC
08 April 2024

34117354R00161